A NEXT GENERATION NOVEL

FINALLY Us

J.M. WALKER

IBSN: 978-1-989782-16-3

FAMILY TREE

Angel and Genevieve "Jay" Rodriguez
(Grit, King's Harlots #1/Grim, King's Harlots #3)
Angelica "Gigi"
Ryder
Meadow

Asher and Meeka Donovan
(Stain, King's Harlots #2)
Aiden
Ashton

Coby and Brogan Porter
(Rude, King's Harlots #4/For You, King's Harlots #7)
Zachary "Zach"

Dale and Maxine "Max" Michaels
(Numb, King's Harlots #5)
Piper

Vincent "Stone" and Creena Stone
(Rust, King's Harlots #6)
Luna
Vincent Junior

Greyson and Eve Mercer
(Greyson, Hell's Harlem #1)
Jaron

Tray and Zillah Lister
(Tray, Hell's Harlem #2)
Beatrix "Bee"

John and Beatrix "Trixie" Butcher
(Hell's Harlem Series)
Cyrus
Samson "Sammy"

WARNING: Please be advised that there are scenes in this book that deal with infant loss. If you have triggers, please read with caution.

PROLOGUE

Gigi

I ENJOYED THROWING PARTIES. Planning them. Organizing the food. Decorating. Inviting people. Whether it be at my place or someone else's, I loved it all. I even enjoyed cleaning up after. My sister said that I was a party planner in a previous life and should have made a career out of it. Maybe she was right. But it wasn't my calling. Not in this life anyway.

I danced.

I lived and breathed ballet. At first it was all I could think about. Sliding my feet into those slippers. Standing up on the tips of my toes when it should be humanly impossible and painful as hell. I loved the calluses, the broken skin, and the agony.

When my muscles hurt after a good and long routine, I knew that I had done what my heart set out to do.

But now, so many years later, I loved more than just ballet.

"You are going to be the next best thing that came out of Julliard." My dad beamed. "I'm so proud of you."

That would have probably been the case too if I hadn't blown my knee out. Maybe not the next best thing but definitely good enough to go on tour, have a career, and just do what I loved to do. For a living. Most people couldn't say they enjoyed their jobs. But I did. Or I would have if I'd never fallen and hurt myself. That had been over six months ago. My knee was still tender at times. Especially when the weather was cold, or it rained. But for the most part, it was fine. I was just feeling down on myself and having a pity party for one.

"Gigi?"

My body tingled as Vincent Junior's deep voice came from behind me but I continued walking toward my car.

"Hey, Queenie. What's wrong?"

I hated the sympathy in his voice but what I hated even more was that I craved it just the same. Vince was an addiction I couldn't kick. I wanted him. God, did I ever want him. He was eighteen now and looked like a damn god. He was five years younger than I was and going off to school. But it didn't make this need for him dwindle any less.

An idea came to me. Maybe we could have some fun before he left. It *was* his birthday and all.

"Gigi, talk to me."

My skin tingled the closer he got to me. My body vibrated, anticipation bubbling inside of me over what he would do or say next.

We had been going back and forth for the last year. We were friends, talked constantly, and texted often, but it had never amounted to anything more than that. Our families were close and although he was only eighteen, he had grown up over the summer. We had always just been friends but now my feelings for him had changed. But I didn't want to dwell on my little crush on him and just have fun tonight instead. Even if it was just for a little bit.

I had thrown him a birthday party like I had done for the rest of our friends and wanted it to be a memorable night for him. The parties were usually held at my place but because it was Vince, I decided to hold it at a restaurant instead.

"Gigi."

I looked up then at the rough use of my name.

Vince came toward me, his hands shoved into his pockets. His dark hair was cut short, that strong jaw of his, clenching the longer I didn't say anything to him. His cheekbones were sharp and his lips full. He was half Italian and half Japanese which made him almost exotic looking. He got his mother's almond shaped eyes and his dad's natural tan. While he was beautiful and looked like he walked right off a magazine, it was his dark eyes that held my interest. They pierced into mine, inviting me into the deepest parts of his soul. They held secrets in their murky depths and if I played my cards right, maybe I could find out exactly what those secrets were and how deep they went.

When I reached my car, I went to open the back door when a heavy hand slapped against the top of it.

My body vibrated at feeling Vince this close to me. We had only ever been friends. Just friends. As much as I wanted more, it had felt almost too taboo to take it further with him. He was also one of my best friends' younger brother. Even though I wasn't that much older than him, I couldn't let him use me when he was leaving in only a matter of days to go off to school. He would meet a bunch of girls, go to party after party, and probably meet someone else.

"Hey." His hot breath fanned over my head. "What's going on, Gigi?" he demanded, his voice rough. "You were crying. I don't like seeing you cry unless I'm the one who causes those tears."

My eyes widened. "You want to make me cry?"

He chuckled, brushing his finger down the length of my arm. "Not because I hurt you but because I make you feel so fucking good, you can't help but sob for me."

My mouth fell open.

I turned around, leaned against the side of the car, and stared up at him. "You think you can make me feel good?"

"No." Vince grinned, leaning his other hand on the door, caging me in. "I *know* I can make you feel good."

Was he that experienced? Had he been with other women already? Maybe he read and did research. God, now I was jealous over something that shouldn't be happening between us in the first place, but I couldn't help the way my body reacted to him. I was damn near vibrating out of my skin just to have him touch me and feel his lips on mine.

As much as I didn't want to be used, the darker part of me, the part that would win out, wanted to use him up, spit him out and give him something to remember me by.

Vince reached out, brushing his fingers beneath the gold chain around my neck. It had been a present from him so many years ago. He had saved up enough money after getting his first job and bought me the necklace for my birthday with his own money. It meant everything that he did that for me, and I hadn't taken the necklace off since.

"Why now?" I asked, trying not to focus on the fact he had my necklace in his hand. Or the fact my heart started racing even more now that he was standing so close to me. Or the fact he smelled so damn good. Like spice mixed with a hint of honey. It was sweet, yet toxic, and it messed with my head.

"Why not now?" He took a step closer. "It is my birthday after all."

"I know. I planned your party remember."

He leaned down toward me, his mouth mere inches from mine. Just when I thought he was going to kiss me; he brushed his lips over my ear. "I know and I still haven't received my present from you."

"What present?" I swallowed hard. "The party is your present."

He chuckled, gripping my hip in a rough hold.

I bit back a gasp. His touch burned me through the fabric of my dress. If I was reacting this way to him before anything happened, I couldn't imagine how it would be once we finally took it to the next level.

"Really, Gigi?" In a quick move, he kicked my legs apart.

The gasp broke free that time, my body falling back against the side of the car.

"You see." His hand on my hip moved lower, hitting the hem of my dress and sliding beneath the fabric. "I think you're lying. I happen to know that you do have a present for me. You've been wanting to give it to me for a while now. Maybe you didn't even realize it until now."

"W-What present is that?" I asked him, tilting my head to give him better access to my throat.

A deep rumble left him, the sound vibrating through every inch of me. The back of his hand brushed up my inner thigh, sending a wave of goosebumps in its path. "Your body."

My stomach flipped at what he was suggesting. "Vince."

"Shhh…" He cupped my jaw, turning my head toward the restaurant. The restaurant I had thrown him the party at. That housed our friends and family inside. Where anyone could walk out and see us standing by my car.

My body tingled at the idea of being caught. My core clenched, aching to be filled the longer time wore on where he wasn't inside me. Knowing that at any second someone could see us, sent a thrill throughout every inch of me.

"Hmm…you like the idea of being caught," Vince murmured against the side of my throat. While his hand that was between my legs, curled around my thigh, a low growl left him. The hold he had on me made me feel as if I was owned by him. He brushed a finger of his free hand along my mouth before dipping it between my lips.

The tiny hairs on my skin vibrated. Desire unfurled deep in the pit of my belly. Taking a chance, I licked along his finger, sucking it deeper into my mouth.

A soft groan left him. Much to my surprise, he started thrusting his finger back and forth along my tongue.

My body wept with need for him, my desire for him leaking between my thighs.

While Vince slid his finger along my tongue, his other hand brushed higher up my inner thigh.

Squeezing my eyes shut, I imagined what it would be like to have him inside of me. To feel him moving along the ridges of my body. To push me over the edge and fall right along with me until both of us were writhing and panting for more.

"Vince," I breathed around his finger.

He released me, taking a step back.

I panted, trying to catch my breath.

His dark eyes stared into mine. He was challenging me, daring me to shove him away and go home.

Instead, I slipped into the back seat of the car and waited for him to join me. I no longer cared that he was going off to school. I would give him something to remember me by.

Vince leaned an arm against the hood of the car. "Tell me."

I crooked a finger. "I think you should come here, and I'll show you instead."

A wicked grin spread on his face. "And if I don't?"

I scoffed. "You started this first, remember? I was just going to go home but then you joined me out here and started touching me."

"You complaining, Queenie?"

"Never."

"I came out here because I thought something was wrong." He paused, waiting for me to tell him what my issue had been, but I refused.

Truth was, I was upset that he was leaving but it was too soon for that confession. Instead, I moved to all fours and crawled toward him. Reaching out, I placed a hand on his chest and let it trail down to his waist. The large bulge behind his black dress pants jumped beneath my touch.

"What do you want?"

"The same thing as you." I unbuckled his belt, pushing down the fly to his pants. I brushed a finger along the edge of him, reveling in the way it swelled.

I was half-expecting him to stop me. We were out in the open after all. But this was thrilling. This newfound awareness tingled through every inch of me. I wanted to explore all of those kinky desires I was accused of not having. I had been called a prude for years. But it wasn't true. I just had no one to explore these desires with.

"What are you doing, Gigi?" Vince asked, not because he wanted me to stop but because he wanted me to keep going. He was giving me all the permission I needed to show him what exactly it was I wanted, and more.

I pushed a hand beneath his shirt, my palm coming into contact with his hot skin. His abs jumped beneath my touch. My mouth watered, my tongue tingling with anticipation over what it would be like to taste him.

Vince cupped my cheek, brushing his thumb over my bottom lip. Without waiting for me to do whatever it was that I was going to do, he pushed me back and joined me in the back seat. He shut the door behind him before turning toward me.

We sat there, staring at each other. Neither of us took it to the next step, whatever that step may be.

Getting a sense of bravery, I licked my lips. "I think you should make good on your threat."

"This my birthday present, Gigi?" he asked, his gaze dropping to my mouth.

I grinned, crawled onto his lap, and straddled his waist. "Is that what you want?"

His hands slid up my thighs to my hips. "More than you will ever fucking know."

"Good." Crushing my mouth to his, I took his breath deep into my lungs and made it my own.

Vince groaned, digging his fingers into my hips. With a firm grip on my waist, he moved me back and forth over his lap.

My lips tingled at the bruising kiss. I couldn't believe this was happening. The fact he had just turned eighteen no longer hung between us as he completely devoured my mouth.

His hold on my hips tightened, the skin no doubt bruising beneath his rough touch. The burn inside of me ignited into a raging inferno.

Vince was finally touching me. Holding me. Kissing me.

He released my mouth and trailed his lips along my jaw. "You taste like cinnamon," he murmured against my throat. "You do a shot?"

A husky laugh left me. "No, it was gum."

He smirked. "I like it."

My smile grew.

Although, a shot would have given me courage to go through with this, it wasn't like this was planned. I was doing this on a whim and thankfully, Vince wasn't turning me down. I was a virgin, but I feared telling him that. I wasn't sure why. I didn't know if he was one as well but at this point, I didn't care.

"Tell me what you're doing."

I lifted my head, running my fingers along his square jaw. "I'm going to give you a going away present. This is just sex since you're going off to school."

"This is some going away present." He grabbed the hem of my dress and lifted it up and over my head. My dark curls fell down around my shoulders. He took in the curves of my body, his eyes shining intently into mine and then drifting down, appreciating that I had gained a little weight in the chest since ending my ballet career. He licked his bottom lip, taking in every inch of my figure that I tried hard to maintain even though I wasn't dancing as much as I used to.

His eyes moved back up to my chest that was covered by a lacy white bra. "So pure." He fisted the necklace wrapped around my neck. His thumb and forefinger brushed over the tiny pink ballet slippers pendant.

"I didn't want you to forget me," I whispered, watching his strong fingers move along the pendant.

"Never, Queenie." His dark eyes popped to mine. "I will never forget you." He tugged the chain, pulling me forward until our lips met in the middle once again.

He breathed me in, taking everything I was made of and kept it for himself. He took, he gave, he completely consumed me. For someone so young, he was in complete control.

Maybe he was more experienced than I thought. Not that I wanted to think about who he had experienced anything with.

"Gigi," he murmured against my mouth. "Kiss me, baby. Stop thinking. It's just us here."

"Too bad," I blurted. I coughed, realizing my mistake.

He broke the kiss, staring at me. "You want an audience?"

My cheeks burned. "I want you. That's it." For now, went unsaid. Truth was, I had no idea what my sexual desires were but the possibility of getting caught, was exciting. No. Getting caught and still going, was even better.

"Alright, Gigi." He kissed my jaw, tightening his hold on the necklace. "We'll talk about that later."

Good, because I didn't want to tell him that I wanted to get caught by strangers, friends, or family. I didn't care. I didn't want to tell him that voyeurism excited me, in case it scared him away. So instead, I reached around to my back, unclipped my bra, and tossed it to the seat beside us.

Vince's gaze roamed down the length of me. His eyes burned into me, heating my skin on fire the longer he stared. But instead of commenting like I thought he would, he tugged the chain, pulling me closer and slammed his mouth down hard on mine.

Reaching into his pants, I wrapped a shaky hand around his thick shaft. A whimper left me; my fingers unable to close around him. My body trembled, knowing he would hurt but feel good at the same time.

He cupped the back of my head, fisting my hair and holding me in place as he devoured every inch of my mouth.

Pulling him free from his pants, I rose to my knees and brushed my center over him.

He shivered, sliding his hand down my spine.

Keeping my mouth locked with his, I hooked a finger in the crotch of my panties and pulled the fabric to the side.

"Fuck," he growled against my lips. "Give it to me, baby."

"Condom," I whispered.

"No." He nipped my bottom lip. "I want to feel you."

I shivered. "Oh thank God." I circled against him, the tip of him pushing against my opening. The more I moved, the deeper he went. He stretched me. Owned me. Completely controlled every inch of me. I couldn't breathe the deeper he went.

Trying to pull away, I needed to catch my breath but his hold on the back of my head, tightened. In a quick move, he dropped me onto him. He swallowed my scream, deepening the kiss.

I wasn't able to get used to his size as he lifted his hips, powering into me with so much strength, I broke in a matter of minutes. His name left my lips on a hard cry.

He grunted, holding me against him and kept his fingers wrapped in my necklace. He broke the kiss, staring at me with lust in his dark eyes. He brought the pendant up to his lips, giving it a kiss.

I stared at him with awe.

And then he said the unexpected. Something that I never thought I would hear from him. Or anyone for that matter. I wasn't sure why I was surprised but I was, and I prayed with everything in me that I would hear that single word again. Maybe in time. Maybe when he was done school and came home to me. Little did he know that I would wait for him. I would be there for whenever he was ready.

Vince kissed the corner of my mouth. "*Mine.*"

ONE

Gigi

3 years later

WATCHING THE YOUNG GIRLS move as I instructed gave me a sense of satisfaction, I never got from hardly anything else at all. Although when I was dancing to try and further my own career, I was satisfied from that. Or that was what I told myself on a daily basis anyway. My accident had put a damper on my life. Things had taken an unexpected turn when I fell and felt my knee twist in a way it wasn't supposed to. I knew my career path was over before the doctors told me I could no longer dance. Not how I used to anyway. No more high jumps for this girl. I was finally able to start running again but only if I was careful.

The day I hung up my ballet slippers so to speak, I ended up at a strip club. I couldn't even remember how I got there. Friends of mine wanted to go out but not to our usual place. We found Rouge, I met the owners, told them I could dance and was hired. Not to strip but to teach the actual strippers how to dance. Although men loved it when a woman took off her clothes, they enjoyed the sensuality in the way she could move her body as well. That was where I came in and I loved every second of it. I also got some new friends out of it, so it was a win-win.

My parents had asked me how my career was going, and I told them without using so many words, that I had been hired to teach adults how to dance.

They assumed I meant my students would come to my studio, but I didn't. I always went to Rouge to teach the girls. Unless they were in my area, we never practiced at my place of work.

"Miss?"

I jumped, finding several pairs of eyes staring up at me. "Sorry, girls. I'm distracted. Keep practicing for another ten minutes and then hit the change rooms."

While they went to get changed, I went to my notebook sitting by my bag on the floor.

I flipped through the pages, sighing when I read through my notes. I loved ballet. I lived and breathed it but now that I could only teach it, I had to pick up something else. I had taught myself to learn other genres and dance techniques. Mostly because I had been bored. But none of them called to me like ballet did. I was thankful for Candace and her husband, Ronny, giving me a teaching job at Rouge. My father eventually found out where exactly it was that I was teaching and even though he frowned upon it, he understood my need for more, so he never gave me a hard time over it.

Once class was over, I greeted the parents as they picked up their kids. One by one, I watched them leave. It had been the same routine for the past two years. I loved my job. The business. Everything about it. It had been my calling. But as much as I loved it, something was still missing. I loved teaching but there was something other than dance that I needed. I just couldn't figure out exactly what that was. Maybe in time. But right now, I was in a rut.

Once my last student left, I locked up, shut the blinds, and took a deep breath. Looking out at the large dance floor, I smiled to myself. My body buzzed with anticipation.

Pulling the remote from the pocket in the back of my sweatpants, I pressed play, my smile widening when the sensual beat thumped through the speakers in the corners of the large room. The bass was hard, heavy, and it drummed into my heart. It made every nerve ending inside me, tingle with delight.

Stepping onto the dance floor, I stood in front of the mirror and let the music take me away. It controlled my moves like invisible strings hanging from my limbs. The music was the master, and I was its ever-willing puppet.

Several songs later, I was panting and wiping the sweat off my face when my phone rang. I took a couple of deep breaths to ease my racing heart and went to my phone. My eyes widened when I saw who was calling me.

"Hey," I greeted. "What's up?"

"What's wrong?" Vincent Junior asked me without even giving me a *hi* back.

My stomach tumbled. How he always knew when something was wrong was beyond me. Add to the fact that he always seemed to call me at the most awkward time.

After our one night together before he went off to school, we had been talking non-stop. He got his degree quickly and now that he was home, we hadn't met up yet. Not by ourselves anyway.

Rumors had gone around that when he was done school, he was going to come for me but that hadn't happened, and he had been home for almost a month.

"Gigi?"

"Nothing's wrong." I pulled the cap off a bottle of water and took a long swig.

"You sure?" he gritted out. "You sound like you just had your brains fucked out," he said, his voice a little harsh.

I coughed, choking on the water. "I was practicing, if you must know." Was he jealous? "Not that it's any of your business."

"Oh, but that's where you're wrong. It is my business." He chuckled. "So, you're at the studio?"

"I am." My heart stuttered. Clearing my throat, I sat on the floor, put the phone on speaker and placed it on the ground beside me so I could stretch.

"What are you doing now?"

"Stretching." I smiled, shaking my head.

"Interesting." His voice lowered.

"What do you want, Vince?" Not that I was complaining that he called me when he had been calling me every day for as long as I could remember but something was up with him tonight.

"How was your day?" he asked the same question he always asked every time he called.

"Not too bad. I wrote a new routine." One that I hoped I could share with him eventually. But there was something off between us. A wall of some sort and I had no idea if it was him or me that put it up, but I couldn't seem to crack my way through it.

"What kind of routine?"

I bent forward at the middle, rested my head against my shins, and grabbed on to the bottom of my feet. "A sexy one." I waited for him to comment and when he didn't, I continued. "I have an adult class coming up and wanted something fun for them. The one woman is getting married and her maid of honor said that it would be exciting to dance. And it also gives them a good workout before they spend the night drinking. I'll even have wine for them here."

"That does sound fun, Gigi. You should do that for my sister. If they ever decide to get married that is."

"They will." I laughed. "I think they want to wait for Jaron and Piper to be able to make it." Our two friends had been through hell when Jaron saved Piper from a monster. Jaron ended up in jail and they had been struggling ever since. None of us knew at the time that Piper was actually pregnant either. We were all hoping and praying that he would get out soon so he could be with his family.

"Makes sense."

I thought a moment. "Can I ask you a question?"

"Always, Queenie."

"What are we doing?" I sat upright. "I mean, nothing's happened since your…since we…" I coughed. "And you've been home for a few weeks already. I haven't even seen you, except for at your welcome home party." I cleared my throat. "Anyway. I was just wondering."

"I'm trying to get things in order. Working with my dad has taken up a lot of my time and I also don't want to take you away from your job."

"You wouldn't be," I pointed out. "So is it my fault that we haven't done anything since your birthday?"

He chuckled. "Babe, you're so damn defensive."

I huffed. "Well I need to know—"

"We are doing whatever you want to do, Gigi." His voice took on a tone I had never heard before from him. Not directed at me anyway.

"But I don't know what that is," I blurted.

"You'll figure it out and when you do, I'll be here."

I rolled my eyes. "Fine. Be cryptic."

"Don't roll your eyes at me, Queenie," he warned.

The hairs on the back of my neck tingled. "Vince." I picked up the phone and pushed to my feet before heading to the back where the showers were. "I don't know what we're doing." This was the first time since the night of his eighteenth birthday where we even came close to talking about what happened.

"Are you staying at the studio tonight?" he asked, ignoring my comment.

"I don't know." I usually spent the night in my office when I didn't want to go home. Tonight, was one of those nights but I found that I didn't want to be alone either.

"Go home, Gigi. I'll meet you there." And with that, Vince hung up.

I stopped suddenly, staring at the phone. My stomach tumbled over the fact that Vince was coming over, finally, and that I wouldn't have to be alone tonight.

I wasn't sure what he wanted but I had a feeling I was about to find out.

TWO

Gigi

"WHAT ARE YOU DOING here?" I asked as Vince came up the sidewalk leading to my house.

"You sounded off on the phone. I wanted to make sure that you're okay." He shoved his hands in his pockets. "And you also said that you didn't want to be alone. So, here I am."

I stared up at him as he closed the distance between us. I took him in. I really took him in. His black hair had grown in some. His eyes were as dark as charcoal, maybe darker. It was almost unnatural how dark they were. But what I had noticed first about him was that smirk that always tilted his lips whenever he looked at me. Being half Japanese and half Italian, his skin had a natural tan to it that most would kill for. He was beautiful.

My stomach fluttered, my heart jumping at the mere intensity rolling off of him.

Vince was my muse. Always had been. Whenever I danced, I danced for him. Even though he didn't know it, he had always been my inspiration. Thinking of him when

I danced kept the noise of my failures at bay. It was dumb really, but Vince kept me sane.

"Staring at my pretty face, Queenie?" he teased, pushing a loose strand of hair behind my ear.

A shiver raced down my spine, my stomach fluttering at the soft contact. Even more at the nickname he had given me as a kid. It was short for Dancing Queen. I also remembered the first time another boy tried calling me the nickname. Vince punched him, got suspended, and walked away proud, like he had just won an award. I didn't know it then, but I definitely knew it now.

Vince was impulsive. Especially when it came to me.

"Gigi." Vince licked his bottom lip.

"Sorry." I cleared my throat and headed back into the house. "You didn't have to come over."

"I know I didn't." He shut the door behind him and followed me. "But I am a nice guy and all."

I laughed, heading into the kitchen. "You are but I'm sure you have an ulterior motive." Not that I knew if he did or not, but it didn't mean that I didn't like messing with him a bit.

"Nah, baby." Vince followed me. "I can be a gentleman. It's you who's going to have to learn to control yourself and keep your hands off of me."

I scoffed, rolling my eyes. "Right."

He chuckled. "So, talk to me."

"About what?" I asked, pulling two bottles of water from the fridge.

"How come you didn't want to be alone?" He took a bottle from me.

"This house freaks me out sometimes." I shrugged. "It's lame but ever since…Anyway…it's just overwhelming at times. It's too big." Piper had been attacked when she lived with me and ever since, I had nightmares. But I couldn't afford to move, and I also didn't think it was fair when the house was built specifically for us. Although, now that I was living in it by myself, I *was* lonely at times.

"I get that." Vince headed out to the living room and sat on the couch. "Are you joining me?" he called out.

I took a breath. I could do this. Right? I could keep my hands to myself. I wasn't sure why I was fighting it now, especially when I didn't on his eighteenth birthday. I didn't know anything anymore but craved it just the same. The unknown was terrifying yet exciting.

Joining Vince on the couch, I made sure to sit at the other end. Any closer and I knew where I would end up. Beneath him or on top. Either way sounded delicious.

He chuckled, taking a sip of his water and winking at me over the rim of the bottle.

"What?" I glared at him.

"Nothing at all, Queenie." His laugh deepened. "Nothing at all."

I tossed a throw pillow at him.

Vince raised an eyebrow, the laughter stopping.

I swallowed hard. Just as I was about to jump from the couch, he caught me by the waist and threw me down. His fingers jabbed into my ribs.

I shrieked. "Vince, stop." But I couldn't control the laughter bubbling up from somewhere deep inside of me.

He laughed along with me but wouldn't let up.

"Vince." I couldn't breathe. My sides ached from laughing so damn hard. "I can't…I can't breathe," I said, panting.

He chuckled, no longer tickling me but staring down at me instead.

I realized then that I was beneath him and he was kneeling between my legs. All breath left me at feeling his powerful body above me. My mouth went dry. My hands were on his broad shoulders, his muscles jumping beneath my touch. This wasn't like before. It had been three years. Three long years since I felt him inside of me. Three years since I heard his *filthy* words.

His eyes dropped to my mouth, his tongue licking along his full bottom lip. "I said you wouldn't be able to keep your hands to yourself."

A laugh escaped me. "Ass."

He grinned, giving me a wink.

As much as I didn't want him to, he pulled away and moved to the other end of the couch.

I sighed, sat up, and straightened my shirt.

"Come here."

I caught his gaze.

He patted the spot beside him.

I took a chance and did as I was told and moved beside him.

He wrapped an arm around my shoulders and pulled me into his side. "I promised I would be a gentleman." He kissed my temple. "But I never promised that I wouldn't touch you."

I snorted. "So, this is you being a gentleman then?"

He chuckled. "Yup."

I sighed, snuggling into him. "Well…okay. I can handle this."

"Good." He placed a soft peck on my head. "I won't pressure you into anything you don't want to do, Gigi. But I promise you, I *will* fuck you again."

My core clenched at the promise.

"And when that happens…" His mouth brushed along the shell of my ear. "I'm never letting you go."

(Vince)

As much as I wanted to have sex with her again, I enjoyed spending time with her just as much. Maybe more.

Gigi was my weakness. When I was a kid, while other boys my age played sports, I pined after the one person I couldn't have. If she noticed me then, she never acted like it. She had always been nothing but kind to me but until I started getting older, she never treated me anything more than just a kid.

Well I was going to show her that I was now a man. A man who could make her happy. Sure, I was turning twenty-one and she was older than me, but none of that mattered. Not when I had been in love with her for as long as I could remember. But I hadn't told her that. She had been focused on her dancing career and I didn't want to cause anything to disrupt that. I loved her too much for her to give up her dream for me. Not like that. So I would show her, little bit by little bit that we were meant to be.

While Gigi slept with her head on my lap, I ran my hand up and down her side. She started yawning halfway through the movie and I told her to lay down. She never even argued.

I almost hesitated coming over tonight because I knew that I wouldn't be able to keep my hands to myself. No matter how hard I fought it, my body reacted to her before my brain could catch up.

A low moan escaped Gigi, pulling me from my thoughts.

She sighed, rolling onto her back. She grabbed my hand, holding it tight in hers.

"Gigi?" I had assumed she was awake but when her eyes remained closed and she hadn't stirred, clearly, I was mistaken.

"Vince," she breathed.

My cock jumped. Holy. Shit. Was she dreaming about me?

"More." She moaned, the sound hitting me square in the dick.

I should wake her up. Shouldn't I? Wouldn't that be the polite thing to do? I had meant what I said when I told her that I was going to be a gentleman tonight but when those low moans kept leaving her throat and her hold on my hand tightened, my morals were suddenly sounding really fucking stupid.

As much as I knew I should wake her up, a part of me was curious. I wanted to know what she was dreaming about and what exactly was happening.

Gigi tightened her hold on my hand, placing it on her breast.

My throat dried.

Pushing my hand down the length of her, she guided me to where I wanted to be. Where *she* wanted me to be. "Please."

My dick leaked. Fucking hell.

Still holding my hand, she pushed it to the waist of her leggings. She was a strong little thing because as much as I tried pulling away, her hold only tightened. Her brow creased in the middle, a growl leaving her throat.

I wanted to laugh. I wanted to fuck her. I wanted to wake her up and tell her that this was wrong but right all at the same time. I needed her to be in her right mind before—

Gigi pushed my hand into her leggings, my fingers grazing the soft skin above her pussy.

"Gigi," I barked. "Wake the fuck up."

Her eyes popped open, her cheeks reddening. "I…"

"What were you dreaming about?" I cupped her jaw, towering over her when she didn't answer me. "Tell me. *Now.*"

"You," she whispered, her hold on my hand loosening.

"No." I squeezed her jaw, tilting her head back. "Show me what I was doing in your dream."

She swallowed, her jaw clenching behind my hand. Her eyes locked with mine. They hinted, silently begging for me to take it further. I would but not yet. First, I wanted to tease and play. I wanted to build the anticipation.

"Show me," I repeated, brushing my fingers that were still down her pants, over the soft skin.

Gigi tightened her grip on my hand, pulling it lower to where she wanted it most.

"That's it, baby. Show me what I was doing in your dream." My voice took on a low tone I had never used before. My cock was ready to explode but this was all for her. She was in control. Until the next time we had sex, and there *would* be a next time, this was all Gigi's say.

She bent her knees, letting one fall to the side as her body opened to me. Grabbing hold of my wrist with the other hand, she guided me lower between her legs.

When my fingers grazed her opening, a growl left me at how wet she was. "What was I doing in your dream?"

"Fingering me," she said with no hesitation.

"Like this?" I inserted a finger inside of her, thrusting it slow.

"No," she whispered, her breath wavering.

"How then?" I asked, thrusting the single digit in and out of her.

Her eyes locked with mine. "Rougher."

My lips pulled up into a wicked grin. Pulling my finger from her body, I slid two back inside of her. "Like this?" I asked, pumping my hand against her core.

"Mmm…rough…" She panted. "…er."

That's my girl.

Lifting my knee onto the couch, I kept a firm grip on her jaw while our joined hands were between her legs.

"If I was rougher, show me just how rough I was, Gigi. Take what you want, baby."

"I…" Her cheeks reddened.

"Take it," I demanded, not moving my hand from between her legs but not thrusting either. She needed to know that I wasn't going anywhere. Literally. She could trust me. She could trust that I would make her feel better. I would be there to dry her tears and kick whoever's ass hurt her, please her when she woke up from a sexy dream and so much more. I would always be there.

Gigi pulled her hand from her leggings and pushed them, along with her panties, down her legs to her ankles.

"Show me," I grit out.

She spread her legs, wrapping her hands around my wrist and began fucking herself with my fingers.

(Gigi)

I couldn't believe I was doing this. Not because it was with Vince. But because I had never been open about the things I liked. Not that I was overly experienced when it came to sex. I only had sex once and that had been with Vince. As delicious as that had been, this was different. This was almost…better.

"That's it, Gigi. Take what you want from me."

God, his voice. His deep delicious voice washed over every inch of me, giving me that sense of bravery I needed to take from him exactly what I wanted.

Lifting my hips up and down, I thrust his fingers in and out of me. My thighs trembled; soft whimpers escaped my lips as the unexpected pleasure completely consumed me.

"Chase that orgasm, baby. Chase it. Catch it. And make it fucking yours."

I was vaguely aware of Vince sliding off the couch.

With his fingers still inside of me, my back bowed, tremors wracked through every inch of me.

"Look at me."

Not realizing I had closed them; I opened my eyes. Vince was kneeling between my legs.

"What else did I do in your dream?" he asked, his voice low and guttural.

"You almost made me come but then I woke up." I silently pleaded for him not to stop.

"Maybe I should stop then." He went to pull from my body, but I latched on to his hand.

"No." I shook my head quickly. "Please no."

He chuckled, thrusting his fingers deeper inside of me. "You sure you don't want me to stop?" he asked, running his thumb along my swollen clit.

I moaned, my eyes rolling into the back of my head when the phone rang. I could have cried at the interruption. "You have got to be fucking kidding me."

THREE

VINCE

PULLING MY HAND FROM between Gigi's legs, I stuck my fingers between my lips. A low groan left me as the acidic flavor exploded on my tongue.

I dropped my hand, finding Gigi staring up at me with wide eyes and a flush on her cheeks. She sat there while her phone continued to ring.

"Phone, babe. Now." I lightly tapped her hip.

She gave herself a shake, rose from the couch, and quickly redressed before heading to the kitchen to answer the phone. Who had a house phone anymore? She did. Because her father, a large father, insisted on it. He said what if the cell phone towers went out? What then? He was right but we never told him that. Much like all of our fathers, they didn't need their egos stroked more than they already were.

I stood, adjusted myself, and went to the kitchen.

"Yes, Daddy. I know." Gigi sighed, running a hand over the back of her neck. "I know I can come there. No. I'm not going to stay with Meadow and her husband. As much as I miss my nephew, they need their alone time."

I stepped up to her, running my fingers along the back of her neck.

She sighed again, leaning back against me.

That's it, baby. Lean on me and I'll carry the weight of your world forever.

"I know," she continued. "I don't want to sell the house. I know that too. Okay. I love you. Give Mom a hug for me." She said her goodbyes and hung up the phone. Stepping away from me, she turned around and leaned against the counter. Her caramel eyes met mine. So many questions danced behind them. Questions that I would give the answers to as long as she asked.

"What is it?" I asked, figuring that would be safer than revealing my true feelings to her.

"Tonight." She yawned, a light laugh leaving her.

I smirked, closed the distance between us, and grabbed her hand. "You need sleep."

"Wait." She pulled her hand from mine.

"What?"

"Are you staying?" she asked, hope dancing in her eyes.

I tilted my head, trying not to smile. "Do you want me to?"

"Yes." She snapped her mouth shut. "I mean, if you want to that is."

I chuckled, grabbed her hand again and led her to her bedroom. "I'll stay and don't worry, I'll keep my hands to myself this time."

She snorted which was always cute as hell when she did that. "I think what happened just now was my fault."

"Semantics." I looked down at her over my shoulder. "Was I complaining?"

She laughed. "No. I guess not."

A thought came to me. I stopped suddenly, spinning on her.

She jumped, her wide eyes landing on me.

"Listen to me." I cupped her face, tilting her head back. "I don't give a shit what you do or how you do it. You need me? You fucking call me. You understand?" Rumors had gone around that she was dating some other fucker. I wasn't sure if it were true or not, but it didn't matter. She was mine and I needed her to know that no matter what, she could depend on me.

She searched my face. "Vince."

"I mean it, Queenie. If you wake up horny as fuck because you had a dream about me, you call me. You have a hard day at work and want to take the edge off, you call me. You want to just fuck each other until one of us taps out, you *call me*. You understand?"

"Yes," she whispered. "I understand."

"Good." I placed a soft peck on her forehead and continued walking down the hall with her hand in mine. I wasn't sure where all of that came from, but it needed to be said. I was on edge. On the verge of snapping because I wasn't sure how much longer I could wait. I had gone into this, delaying the inevitable, only because I wanted to grow for her. I wanted to be the man that she deserved and more. I wanted to be her everything. But the longer it took before she was in my arms and for good, the more on edge I felt. I was on the verge of losing that very control I had trained for years to master.

"Vince?" Gigi's soft voice pulled me from my thoughts.

"I promise I'll behave," I told her when she looked between me and the bed. Pulling away from her, I tugged my shirt up and over my head. I pointed to the bed when she didn't move. "Either you get in bed or I'll put you in it. But you need sleep, Queenie."

"Really?" She glanced at the clock sitting on her nightstand. "It's only ten. It's not that late," she mumbled.

I chuckled, unbuckling my belt. I lowered the fly and slid my jeans down my legs, watching her cheeks redden.

Gigi looked away.

"Hey." I closed the distance between us, brushing my fingers down her arm. "We've already fucked, Queenie," I reminded her. "And besides, I'm wearing boxers." As much as I wanted her again, she wasn't ready. Not yet. She would be and whenever that happened, I would be there with open arms.

(Gigi)

I was sleeping with Vince. He was beside me. I was beside him. In my bed. I never shared my bed with someone before, let alone someone like him. For someone who was younger than me, he never acted like it.

But like he promised, he kept his hands to himself. He pulled the comforter that was folded at the base of the bed and used that as a blanket while I slept beneath the others.

When he laid back down, he closed his eyes.

"Vince?"

He looked at me then. "Yeah?"

"Did you like school?" I wasn't sure why I asked him that but as tired as I was, I was also wired. Especially with what happened tonight, add to the fact that I never got my orgasm.

"Yeah, Queenie." He gave me a small smile. "I did. But I'm happier here."

"I'm sure your parents are too." I knew his mom missed him terribly, along with his sister. Even though she never said it. She joked and said he was your typical annoying sibling, but she definitely missed him in her own way. He was a good little big brother.

"No." He turned onto his side, facing me. "I'm happier here. With you."

My heart leapt to my throat. "Vince."

"You can think what you want, Gigi. But we're meant to be and I'm going to prove it to you. I'm even in your dreams. Remember that." He turned away from me, rolling onto his other side.

My hand tingled, itching to reach out to him. Before I could change my mind, I touched his shoulder. "Vince."

His body stiffened. "Go to sleep, Gigi. We can talk in the morning."

My chest tightened. I pulled my hand back and rolled away from him. Turning onto my stomach, I let out a hard sigh.

The bed shifted beside me. A heavy arm wrapped around me. "I'm here," Vince murmured, placing a soft peck on my shoulder. "I'm always here." With his body half on top of mine, he hugged himself around me, holding me tight.

I turned my head, meeting his dark eyes. "Tell me a bedtime story."

"Once upon a time, there was a boy," he started, not even hesitating or finding it weird that I would ask him for a story. "He was twelve years old in fact. He had his whole life ahead of him but in his eyes, he had one mission and one mission only."

"What mission was that?" I asked, hanging on to every word Vince was saying.

"To make the girl of his dreams notice him. You see, she was older than him. Not by a lot but enough that it would be frowned upon for them to be together. Especially at that age." Vince kissed my shoulder again, his eyes not moving from mine. "So he spent the next few years, growing up and being the man for her. But she was hesitant. He wasn't sure why, but he made a promise to her that he would prove just how much they should be together."

"Did they end up together?"

"Not sure." Vince inched closer to me, his gaze falling to my lips. "They're still living their story."

"Is the story about us?" I whispered.

"It could be about many people, Queenie," he murmured.

"I'm not scared," I corrected him. No, in fact, I was excited. I wanted to be with him, but it was new. He never gave me any reason to believe that whatever he wanted with me, would only be casual but I still wanted to take it slow. I had seen our friends go through so much in such a short amount of time. I found myself wanting to take this one day at a time with Vince.

"I never said you were scared, Queenie," Vince pointed out. "You're hesitating but that's fine. I'm still not going anywhere," Vince said, resting his head on my pillow. "Sleep, baby. Everything will happen as it's supposed to."

(Vince)

After Gigi fell asleep, I spent the rest of the night tossing and turning. I eventually went to the couch, tried sleeping there, and when that didn't work, I went back and joined her. She had moved and was sprawled out like a starfish across the bed. I couldn't help but chuckle. So that was what I got to look forward to whenever we ended up together for good.

My little story I told her earlier had been the truth. We were meant to be and she was who I wanted, but my feelings for her still scared me. They scared me because I knew that I would do anything to be with her. I would go through anyone and everyone to have her in my arms for good. I had known for a while that my feelings for Gigi ran deep. They bordered on obsession. I lived and breathed her. I damn near worshipped the very ground she walked on. When she smiled, everything was right in the world. When she laughed, it was like time stopped. I made it my mission to keep her happy. To keep that smile on her face and to make her laugh as much as I could.

A couple of hours later and I was still on the verge of snapping. Giving up on sleep, I left her warmth and got dressed. Making my way out into the hall, I glanced back at Gigi's still form. When she didn't move, I softly closed the door behind me.

Once I stood in front of Piper's old room, I pushed the door open. Nothing was out of the ordinary. The room was filled with boxes but all of Piper's stuff was no longer there.

My thoughts traveled back to that night that felt like it had been so long ago. Gigi's party. A vile monster who didn't get what he wanted but attempted to take it just the same.

Although a friend had gotten shitfaced and I was taking him home, I couldn't help but stay back and watch Gigi. Before everything went down, she laughed and smiled whenever the conversation had called for it, but something was still missing. It had amazed me how no one else saw it. But I could.

Heading to the kitchen, I looked for everything I needed to make Gigi her morning tea. While most of us were coffee drinkers, she liked to be different and enjoyed herbal teas to help start her day.

"Vince?"

I jumped, spun around, and found Gigi standing in the entranceway to the kitchen. "Morning. I was making you tea," I told her, nodding toward the kettle.

"Really?" She came toward me. When she was standing directly beside me, I couldn't help but notice the faint scent of her sweet perfume. It was a mixture of candy and cake. It wasn't too powerful, but it could sure bring me to my knees.

Her shoulder brushed against my arm. "You remembered I drink tea?"

I swallowed hard, my dick jumping at the soft contact. "Yup."

She looked up at me, her perfect brows narrowing in the middle. "Something wrong?"

"Nope. Not at all. Why would you think that?" I said a little too quickly.

She laughed, shaking her head.

The husky sound shot right to the tip of my cock, making it harden even more.

"Well thank you for starting my tea for me." She reached into the cupboard and brought down two mugs but not before I noticed how her t-shirt lifted and showed some of her bare mid-drift.

Before I could stop myself, I brushed my thumb along the soft skin.

She jumped, her breath catching in her throat which sounded sexy as hell. "Vince."

"Three years, Queenie," I said, my voice raspy.

"I know." She placed the mugs on the counter but much to my surprise, never pushed me away.

I took that as my chance and pushed my hand higher under her shirt. My fingers grazed the soft skin just beneath her breast. My bones vibrated beneath my skin over the fact that she wasn't wearing a bra. Her nipples puckered, hardening to the point it made my mouth water.

She chewed her bottom lip.

"I can't stop touching you," I told her, my voice low.

"I know," she whispered. "But you said you were going to be a gentleman."

"Yeah but it doesn't mean I can't touch you," I reminded her. "Do you want me to stop, Gigi?"

"No."

I grinned, cupping her breast. "You fit perfectly in my hand, baby."

"I'm small." She looked at me then, giving me her beautiful caramel eyes.

"Don't care." I smirked. "I'm more of a pussy man anyway."

She laughed, her cheeks reddening.

My grin widened. I leaned down, placing a kiss on her cheek. "And your pussy is the only one I want."

"God, Vince." She shivered.

I moved behind her, slid my other hand beneath her shirt, and pushed my body up against hers.

She gripped the edge of the counter, her head falling back against my shoulder. "Your hands feel so good."

Before I could stop myself, I lowered to my knees behind her. Grabbing a handful of her ass, I sunk my teeth into the flesh.

Gigi yelped, pushing back into my touch. "Vince."

"Shhh…" I hooked my fingers into the waist of her black leggings and lowered them below the seat of her ass. My dick jumped at the sight before me. A red string sat between the cheeks of her ass, the thong barely covering any inch of her. Cupping the flesh, I spread the cheeks and lowered my face to her center.

Her breath caught, her body shaking in my hands.

Brushing my nose along her slit, I inhaled, a low groan leaving me. "You smell so fucking good, Queenie."

She whimpered. "Vince, I…"

"I got you, baby."

Her body relaxed at my words.

Raining kisses and gentle bites along her flesh, I inched a finger into the string of the thong and pulled it to the side. Brushing a knuckle from the tight little spot at her ass to her center, I reveled in the way her body reacted to me. A drop of cream slipped from her core. "Fuck me, Gigi. I could feast on you."

"Do it," she demanded, her voice husky.

Just as I was about to shove my face between her legs, the sound of the front door slamming open, startled us both.

I jumped to my feet, helping Gigi pull her thong and leggings back up.

"I swear having a newborn at home is kicking my ass." Gigi's sister, Meadow, took that moment to come around the corner. She stopped at the entrance to the kitchen, her gaze moving back and forth between us. "Vince, I wasn't expecting you here so early."

Gigi stepped in front of me, her body shielding my erection.

Brushing my hand along the seat of her ass, I gave it a pinch.

Her head whipped around, her brow raising.

"I was in the area and texted Gigi to see if she wanted a ride to the center." The lie slid off my tongue so easily, I was kind of proud of myself.

Meadow also didn't need to know that I had spent the night or that I was just about to eat the fuck out of her sister.

"You still having car trouble?" Meadow asked, grabbing a bottle of water from the fridge.

"Yeah." Gigi met my gaze.

I gave her a wink.

"Well, I guess you don't need me then." Meadow's eyes welled.

"Whoa." I held up my hands. "You can take her. It's not that big of a deal."

Gigi laughed. "Post-pregnancy hormones got you all emotional?"

Meadow scowled, wiping under her eyes. "Yes. I just assumed having Andrew would get rid of them."

"Your body went through a lot, Meadow," I reminded her. "I think being emotional is understandable."

"True." Meadow shook her head. "I just want things back to normal." She sighed, looking between us both. "Did I interrupt something?"

"Nope," both Gigi and I said at the same time.

Meadow laughed. "Right."

I went to finish making my coffee and a tea for Gigi, trying to ignore what I had been about to do before her sister arrived. My tongue tingled, needing to get a taste of her.

"How's Shade doing?" Gigi asked, pulling me from my thoughts.

"He's getting there. We both are." Meadow sighed, rubbing the back of her neck. "We have our good days and bad. Shade's strong."

I felt bad for Meadow. She had been in a polyamorous type relationship with two guys, only to lose one of them after he was shot and killed.

Gigi hugged her. "Well, anything you need, we're here."

"Thank you." Meadow patted her hand. "I'll head to the center. Vince can drive you." She winked and gave her sister a hug.

I chuckled, taking a sip of my coffee.

"You coming to Vince's party?" Gigi asked her.

"Yeah but Shade doesn't want me out too long. So we'll make an appearance and then head home. I hope you have fun though," she told me.

"Thank you." I was turning twenty-one and Gigi was throwing a party for me in a couple of weeks. Or that was the rumor anyway. I didn't care really. I appreciated the gesture but, in all reality, I would rather have her all to myself because I knew that it would be the night that I would finally fuck her again.

"Alright, I'm going to head to the center. Are we still on for a girls' night?" Meadow asked.

"Yes, we are. I'll see you soon," Gigi said, giving her another hug.

We said our goodbyes and once Gigi and I were finally alone again, I went to take a step toward her when she sidestepped around me.

Gigi only smiled and finished making her tea.

Before she could bring the mug up to her lips, I closed the distance between us.

She stared up at me with wide eyes.

I know, beautiful. I have no idea what I'm doing either but I'm glad I'm doing it with you.

I placed my mug on the counter beside hers. Reaching out to her, I pushed a strand of hair behind her ear before cupping the side of her neck.

With my hand wrapped around her throat, I begged for her to open up to me. My thumb brushed back and forth over her jugular, the shiver trembling through her, making my dick twitch.

Gigi tilted her head back, licking her lips. "Vince, I want…God, I need…"

"What?" I leaned down and kissed the corner of her mouth. "What do you want? What do you *need*?"

"You," she breathed.

That single word shot to the tip of my cock. "I don't know what I'm doing," I confessed. "But I know that I want to do it with you."

"This feels…intense."

I leaned my forehead against hers. "It does."

"We were about to do something before my sister showed up and this…what we have…whatever it is we're doing, Vince, it feels…"

"Intense?" I asked again, raising an eyebrow.

A husky laugh left her. "Yeah."

I smirked, placing a soft peck on her forehead. "This *is* intense, but it's also meant to be." I ran my hands through her hair, messing up her ponytail. "I know you feel it. And what I was about to do before Meadow showed up…" I leaned down and pressed my lips against her ear. "I was about to eat your pussy and ass."

"It's fast," she whispered.

"Fast." I laughed. "I've known you my whole life." *And been in love with you just as long.* "This is not fucking fast. You can fight it all you want but I know you want me."

"Last night was amazing, Vince," she told me. "And I love when you touch me. But…"

"What?" I tugged her head back, pushed her up against the counter, and ground into her. "Tell me. I want to know your thoughts. Your feelings. I want to know every single thing."

Her chest rose and fell. She latched on to my hips, pulling me closer.

I smirked, leaned down, and kissed the corner of her mouth. "I know you feel it and I'm not talking about how hard my cock is either."

She panted. "Yes, I feel it. And I feel that too."

"Well it belongs to you, Gigi." I continued grinding into her. "Only you." I trailed my mouth down the length of her jaw. "Every single inch. I know you remember how big it is."

A soft whimper left her. "Yes, I do."

"That was the best birthday present I've ever received." We hadn't talked about that night. Even when we saw each other the handful of times I had been home while in school. But now that I was home for good and I got my degree; she would be mine. No waiting this time. "I can still feel your pussy wrapped snug around me." Pulling one hand from her hair, I cupped the back of her thigh, lifted her leg, and wrapped it around my hip. Pushing into her hard, I savored the way her breath caught and her back arched. "Can you still feel me, Gigi?"

"Yes." Her dark eyes locked on mine. They were wild, hungry and fierce. She wanted more. She would get what she wanted but not yet. I wanted to play. A little teasing wouldn't hurt either of us and it would make the final outcome even hotter.

"Do you wish I was inside you right now?" I circled my hips against her for added effect.

She nodded.

"Words, Queenie. Tell me."

Her pupils dilated. "Yes, I wish you were inside me right now. I wish you were fucking me. I wish you would give me that orgasm I didn't get last night. I wish you never went off to school." She snapped her mouth shut, looking away.

I lifted my head, staring down at her. "What do you mean?"

"I missed you," she whispered.

I pinched her chin, crouching until we were at eye level. "I'm here now."

"I know."

"You know why I had to go to school. I'm trying to work with Ashton and Aiden. You know all of that." Ashton and Aiden were twins and were working toward taking over their father's business. My dad had liked working with him and I enjoyed getting my hands dirty, so I thought why not? I didn't want to join the Navy like all of our fathers had done. Not that there was anything wrong with it, but it wasn't my calling. I also saw firsthand how it messed Aiden up. So much so that he wouldn't talk about it and drowned out his demons with a bottle of anything he could get his hands on.

"I know that. I know all of that." Gigi placed her hands against my chest.

"You were focused on your own career too," I reminded her, a hot shiver rippling down my spine at feeling her hands on me.

"I know." She pushed away from me only because I allowed her. "Will I see you later?"

"You will." I stuffed my hands in my pockets because if I didn't, I would have reached out to her and pulled her into my arms. I would have touched her, caressed her, done things to her that she could only ever fantasize about. Because I knew, deep down I knew, there was a kinky woman inside of her and I wanted to explore every inch of her desires. With her. Only her. It had ever only been her.

"Vince." She chewed her bottom lip. I had come to realize over the years that she did that whenever she was nervous or when there was something on her mind, but she didn't know how to voice it.

"Let's head out, Queenie." When I went to walk away, a gentle hand landed on my upper back.

"Thank you for last night," she said softly. "I mean it."

"You're welcome." As much as I didn't want to, I pulled away from her and headed to the front door. I was a patient person, but little did she know that I was a stubborn fucker. Before my birthday, we would be together again. She would be mine as much as I was already hers.

And more.

FOUR

Gigi

VINCE'S PARTY WAS COMING up and I hadn't seen him since he spent the night at my place. We texted back and forth but that was it. We hadn't talked about what we almost did, but I could still feel his hands on me, his fingers deep inside me, and his teeth on my flesh. I never even saw him in passing when I visited the center.

The Dove Project was created by all of our moms when they brought down a human trafficking ring before any of us were born. It was a safe haven for victims. Both male and female. It helped them start a new life. I knew at first it had been hard for our parents when they didn't have funding for it but as it became more recognized over the years, the government eventually stepped in and helped out. It looked good for them, so it was a win-win all around for everyone involved.

All of us kids worked or volunteered at the center as well. It held a piece of each of us and helping those in need was satisfying in ways I could never explain.

"Have a good night, Clara." I smiled at the blonde standing behind the counter as I was heading to the door to leave.

She looked up from the computer. "You too." She gave me a small wave.

Once I left and started heading to my car, a text came through on my phone.

Meadow: Girls' night at Luna's.

Me: On my way.

I was thankful to hang out with my best friends. It had been awhile and maybe they could reassure me that I wasn't making a stupid decision for wanting to explore this further with Vince.

When I pulled up to Luna's place, I turned off the car and left the vehicle. As soon as I started walking up the steps, the front door opened.

"It's about time you show up," Luna teased.

I laughed, giving her a hug. "How's it going?"

"Good." She grinned. "I have wine. Benjamin's with Zach's parents and Zach's in the city. So, it's just us."

"I've been itching for a girls' night." I closed the door behind me and kicked off my shoes. "Is Piper here?"

Luna's face fell. "No."

"Oh." My stomach sunk. "I hope her and Jaron can work things out," I said, following Luna into the living room.

"I'm sure they will." Luna sat on the couch and poured a glass of wine before handing it to me.

"Hey," Meadow greeted, coming from the hall. "You got here fast."

"I was at the center. I am so glad you girls decided to do this tonight." I took a sip of the wine and let out a soft sigh.

"That bad?" Meadow laughed.

"What's going on?" Luna took a sip of her own wine, staring at me over the rim of her glass.

"I…Alright. I'm just going to come out and say it." I took a deep breath. "I don't know what to do about Vince and it's weird because I want him. God, I want him so much. But what I feel for him is so damn intense, I can't control it. I dream about him constantly. It's like he's taken up residence in my head and it's fucking with me." I was met with two pairs of eyes staring back at me. "What?"

Meadow and Luna looked at each other.

"Girl," Luna laughed lightly. "You're in love with my brother."

"No. I…" Even trying to deny it, left a sour taste in my mouth. Truth was, I had been in love with Vince for as long as I could remember. I wasn't sure if he felt the same way. Sure, he liked me, that much was clear, but I didn't know how deep those feelings went.

"You are." Luna tilted her wine glass toward me. "I've seen the way you two look at each other anyway." She grinned. "And besides, you're way better than those other girls he's dated."

My stomach twisted. I didn't know what Vince's deal was with the other women, but I didn't like it. The thought of him touching someone else forced bile to my throat. Just the idea of him even giving another woman one of his famous smiles, made me want to cut a bitch.

"He never actually dated them," Meadow said, correcting Luna. "They tried. I remember seeing him at the damn grocery store and women went up to him. They were trying to get him to help them buy the right kind of melon." She rolled her eyes. "It was weird."

"Maybe he didn't actually date them, but they still definitely wanted to date him." Luna waved her hand in front of her face. "It doesn't matter. What does matter is I just saw that look on Gigi's face. She's jealous."

"Wouldn't you be jealous if you found out Zach…" Meadow's word trailed off. "Never mind."

Luna scowled. "Yes, I know he's had so many more women before me." She rolled her eyes. "But that's in the past." She looked at me. "Anyway. What I'm trying to say is, Vince didn't date those women. Whatever you've heard, it never happened."

I frowned. "But you just said—"

"Ignore her." Meadow sat forward. "He's never touched anyone besides you."

"How do you know he's touched me?" I asked, taking another sip of wine.

A look passed between Meadow and Luna.

"Your car was pretty fogged up during his eighteenth birthday party." Meadow waggled her eyebrows.

"Oh God." I slapped my forehead, a bubble of laughter leaving me. "You saw us?"

"No but you just confirmed my suspicions." Meadow winked.

I threw a pillow at her.

We all laughed.

"Well, all I know is, I look forward to having you as my sister in-law." Luna's smile widened.

"Now we're talking about marriage?" Just the thought of being married to Vince, did something funny to me but it was a thought I could get used to.

While the girls talked, I continued to drink and stew over their words. Maybe I should just talk to Vince and find out exactly what it was that he wanted with me. Besides sex. He said that we were meant to be together. One thing that I did know, the night of his twenty-first birthday party, he would be mine again.

(Vince)

My party needed to come faster because I was itching for another taste of Gigi. To feel her sweet body rippling over me as I gave us both what we wanted. What we needed. What we craved.

As I was about to turn down my street, my phone rang. I pressed answer on the steering wheel. "Hello?"

"Hey, Vince."

I frowned. "Meadow?"

She laughed lightly. "Yeah…uh…listen. Can you come grab Gigi? We had a girls' night tonight at Luna's and my sister had a little too much wine and can't drive."

"I'm on my way." I disconnected the call and turned the car around without even hesitating.

Twenty minutes later, I was standing at Luna's door. Before I could knock, it swung open.

Gigi had an arm wrapped around Luna's shoulders. "I think I had too much wine," she slurred, pinching the bridge of her nose.

Luna laughed. "Yeah, you did but that's okay."

"I'm going to feel like shit tomorrow." Gigi sighed, swaying on her feet.

"Probably." I chuckled, pulling her from Luna. "Let's get you home."

"Thank you," Luna said, giving her a hug. "Take care of her," she told me.

"Always." With my arm wrapped around Gigi's shoulders, I led her to my car. Or rather, it was more like dragging her. "How much did you drink?"

"Two bottles. I think. I started off with white and then red. The red is kicking my ass. By the time I was done the first bottle, I forgot I drove here." She sighed, leaning into me. "Thank you."

"No need to thank me, Queenie." I kissed her temple. "I'll be sure to get your car home."

Once we reached my car, I opened the passenger side door and helped her into the vehicle. Doing up her seat belt, I tried hard not to think about how close we were again. Or the fact that she was brushing her finger along my jaw. Did she just spread her legs?

My throat went dry. "Gigi."

She giggled. "You're handsome, handsome."

I chuckled. "And *you* are drunk."

"Maybe." She sighed. "Are you taking me home?"

"I am."

"I don't want to go home," she murmured more to herself than to me.

My stomach clenched. As much as I wanted to bring her back to my place, she wasn't ready. Because once I had her there, I wouldn't let her leave. Not in the creepy stalker way. But in the way that I would make her my wife.

FIVE

Gigi

I WOKE WITH A heavy pounding in my head. What the hell did I do last night? Oh yeah. I drank too much wine. It wasn't my fault my friends always bought the good stuff. I was a sucker for a good wine and clearly, this morning was a result of my lack of control.

"Gigi."

My heart jumped at the deep voice coming from somewhere in my room. But as much as I appreciated Vince being there, I didn't want him to see me this way. So instead, I grabbed the blanket, curled it up over my head, and rolled onto my stomach.

He chuckled. "Feeling a little rough?"

I only grunted.

"I have water and some meds for that headache."

I sighed, lifting my head as he sat on the edge of the bed. "I need to brush my teeth." I grimaced, my mouth tasting like something died in it.

His laugh deepened. "Take these first." He handed me the water and two little pills.

I took them, mumbled a thanks, and flopped back onto my stomach. "I'm never drinking again," I grumbled.

"Says everyone when they're hungover." He laughed.

I threw my pillow at him, but I couldn't hold back the smile.

Forcing myself to sit up, I took a deep breath, thankful that my stomach wasn't rolling, and that I was dressed. Even though it was just a tank top and shorts, it was better than being naked. I thought back to the night before, not remembering changing at all. A thought came to me. Maybe Vince changed me himself. A simmer of regret rushed through me that I didn't remember him helping me into sleepwear.

Sliding off the bed, I bit back a sigh and went to the bathroom. I brushed my teeth and made myself look somewhat presentable before joining Vince back on my bed.

"Feel better?" he asked, moving closer and leaning against the headboard.

"I do. Thank you."

His gaze burned into me. "Do you remember anything from last night?"

I thought a moment. "Not much."

"You don't remember anything at all?" he asked me, brushing a finger down my arm.

I shivered at the soft touch. "No. Should I?"

His dark eyes met mine. "Do you remember how you begged me to fuck you?"

"What?" My eyes widened. "No, I didn't do that."

"You did. It was hot as hell, Queenie." He leaned forward, placing a soft peck on my shoulder. "We came in here. I was going to put you to bed, but you started stripping. I went to leave to give you some privacy and you stopped me. You pushed me toward your bed." His mouth brushed back and forth over my shoulder while he linked his fingers between mine. With his eyes locked on mine, he continued. "You got on the bed, spread your legs and said some of the nastiest things to me. You told me to call you a filthy slut and to fuck you like one."

My cheeks burned. "I didn't."

He chuckled, the sound deep. Dark. *Delicious.* "Oh, but you did. You started touching yourself." He brought my hand up to his mouth. "These fingers were all over and inside your pussy."

"Vince." I watched as he stuck my index and middle fingers between his lips.

"I can still taste you." His gaze locked with mine. "Ask me what else happened."

"What else happened?" I whispered.

He grinned. "You told me that if I wasn't going to fuck you, I was going to at least watch you make yourself come."

"Vince, I need you." My hips undulated as I fingered myself. My body was soaked. The hairs on my skin tingled. But he still wouldn't touch me. Was I that drunk? I didn't know. I couldn't be sure but having him watch me fall apart by my own touch, was hot as hell.

The memory slammed into me. I couldn't believe I did that in front of him but at the same time, I could.

His grin widened. "You remember."

I nodded, chewing my bottom lip.

"Do you remember how hard you came for me?" He brought my hand to my lap, inching it up my inner thigh. "Do you remember how soaked you were? I could smell you and I wasn't even touching you."

"I remember it all," I whispered, cupping his face with my free hand. Brushing my thumb along his bottom lip, I let him push my other hand higher up my thigh until we reached that spot that had only ever been his. Spreading my legs, I turned toward him. Hooking my fingers into the crotch of my panties, I kept my eyes locked on his as he slid his middle finger into me.

"You're fucking incredible," he murmured, pushing his finger even deeper inside me.

My core clenched down around him.

He kissed my cheek, trailing his mouth to my ear. "You want me."

"Yes." I trailed my hand down the center of his chest until I reached the bulge in his jeans.

"Good." He slipped a second finger inside of me. "I'm going to make it so the only thing you can think about is fucking me. I'll get you so damn fired up that the only thing you can focus on is having my fat cock back inside this tight little body."

I sighed, my eyes fluttering closed. "Sounds delicious."

His laugh deepened. "I thought so."

"Think you can last that long?" I asked, nodding toward the large lump in his jeans.

He smirked, sliding a third finger into me in a rough move.

I jumped, his fingers stretching me.

"I've waited three years for you, Gigi. What's a little longer?" He brushed his mouth along the shell of my ear. "I want you to come for me."

"I want you to fuck me," I threw back at him.

"Hmm…" His fingers pumped hard and deep inside of me, forcing this newfound awareness throughout me. "I don't think you're ready for my cock yet."

"But I am." I turned toward him and knelt on the bed.

His fingers picked up speed.

I cried out, my eyes rolling into the back of my head. "God, Vince."

"Your pussy's nice and wet, baby." He kissed my cheek. He slammed his hand against me, forcing his fingers deeper and deeper. "You want more?"

"Always," I said on a low moan. Much to my surprise, he pulled his hand from between my legs and slid off the bed. Kneeling in front of me, he gave me a wink.

My belly did a flip and I knew right then that I was done.

(Vince)

I was going to make her wait. I had every intention of having her writhing and begging, pleading for me to give her that orgasm she had been desperately craving since she fell asleep on me last time. The release she gave herself last night was nothing compared to what I was about to give her. Feeling Gigi's soaked pussy sucking my fingers in even deeper, forced that final band to snap. It controlled my actions, making me do something I had never actually done before. Everything with her was new, fresh, and so damn exciting. We would learn together and grow as a couple. Even though she wouldn't reveal all of her feelings at the moment, it wouldn't take long before I was all that she needed.

Whether she cared to admit it or not, Gigi was mine and I was hers.

"Vince." Her breathless voice pulled me from my thoughts. She leaned back on her elbows, watching my every move.

Even though I had never gone down on a woman before, I read, and I read a lot. I knew the basics and I wasn't one of those men who didn't know where the clitoris was. Hell, how could I not know where it was? It was my favorite spot.

"I've never done this before," I murmured, placing a soft peck on Gigi's knee.

Her breath caught in her throat.

"Have you ever had a man go down on you?" I asked, brushing my mouth higher up her inner thigh.

"No," she whispered.

My cock twitched at her confession. "I think I'm going to enjoy this more than you."

She laughed, which came out husky and was music to my fucking ears.

I smirked. "Lay back on your elbows, baby."

Gigi did as she was told, watching me through hooded eyes.

Running a finger over the waist of her red panties, I licked my lips at the wet spot in the crotch of the fabric. Before I could stop myself, I lowered my nose to her center and inhaled.

She sighed.

A low grumble left me as the sweet scent of her wafted into my nose. Keeping my face between her milky thighs, I grazed my teeth over the fabric covering her clit.

She jumped. "God."

I hummed against her center, sucking the fabric covering the swollen nub.

Her breath came out in soft pants.

Holding her thighs, I pushed her legs open even more and continued sucking her clit through the thin fabric of her panties.

"Vince," she whined, bucked her hips, and tried to get me to do what she wanted most.

Well my girl was going to have to be patient because teasing her turned me on more than I ever thought possible. Shoving my mouth against her hard, I bit down gently on the little nub, forcing a cry from her mouth.

The scent of her became more pronounced the longer I teased her.

Her panties were soaked. My cock was hard. It was perfect.

Before she could come like I knew she wanted, I hooked a finger into the crotch of her panties and pulled it to the side. My mouth watered. Her clit was red and swollen, begging for my mouth. A drop of cream slipped from her center, forcing my cock to harden even more against the fly of my jeans.

Swiping a tongue over the tiny bundle, I reveled in the way her hips bucked beneath my face.

I slowly licked at the tiny nub, forcing her hips to move hard against my mouth but the fabric was still in the way. Before she could get that orgasm she craved, I released her, slipped the fabric off of her, and pulled it down her legs.

She stared at me with wide eyes, a beautiful red flush on her cheeks.

I winked, pressed my hands against her thighs, and spread her open before diving back in.

(Gigi)

Vince was brutal as he attacked my center with his mouth. My cries sounded around us.

He growled, shaking his head back and forth. Slipping two fingers back inside of me, he thrust them in and out of me while sucking my clit between his teeth.

Pleasure consumed me. It felt so damn good, I didn't want it to go away but at the same time I did. It was almost too much. It took control of my thoughts and actions. I was on the verge of snapping and throwing him to the ground.

"Please," I heard myself say. I needed more. I needed him.

Vince pulled his fingers from my body and covered my core with his mouth. He thrust his tongue inside of me, forcing my eyes to roll into the back of my head.

My back bowed off the bed.

Holding the backs of my knees, I spread myself even more for him.

He purred against me, the vibrations rippling through every inch of my body. He lifted his head, thrust two fingers into me and removed them. He repeated the movements, his fingers glistening with the juices from my body.

"Vince," I whispered.

His dark eyes caught mine. Giving me a wink, he swiped his tongue from the spot at my ass, back up to my clit.

I shivered, a soft sigh escaping me.

"My dirty girl," he murmured, sinking his teeth into the cheek of my ass.

A breathless laugh left me.

Just when I was about to ask for more, Vince lowered his mouth back to my center. His tongue rubbed and pushed against my clit. A spark of electricity hit me, rushing from my toes all the way to the top of my head.

I was about to demand for him to fuck me when a sudden release slammed into me. His name left my lips on a scream, my body shaking beneath him.

He growled, sucking my clit hard between his lips.

My screams turned into pleas for more, but he never took it further. When I calmed down, I reached for him.

Spreading me apart, he lifted his head, his gaze glancing down at my center.

My cheeks burned under his scrutiny.

"You're beautiful." His eyes popped to mine. "And you taste so fucking good," he said, licking his glossy lips.

"I need you," I whispered, running my thumb along his bottom lip before bringing it to my mouth. I sucked it between my lips, swallowing the essence from my body.

His nostrils flared, his eyes darkening at what I had just done. Lowering his mouth to mine, he swallowed my sigh and ran his hands down the sides of my body.

Wrapping my arms around his shoulders, I breathed him in. Everything that made up Vincent Stone. The man who had consumed every waking thought I ever had. He was a piece of me, and he didn't even know it.

Vince brushed his hand over my head, deepening the kiss. Spreading my legs even more, I invited him in. His jeans rubbed against my naked center, pulling a moan from the back of my throat.

He undulated his hips against me, pushing and thrusting, forcing the pleasure inside of me until it grew and billowed around us. It consumed me, controlled me, and it took everything in me not to shove Vince back and jump into his arms.

He felt so damn good above me. The one time we shared in my car years ago was nothing compared to having him in my bed. But it still wasn't enough.

I broke the kiss, panting for air when he crushed his mouth against mine. He swallowed my gasp of surprise, not letting me up for air unless he gave the go-ahead. Our tongues danced, dueled for that ownership that neither of us had. Truth was, he owned me. Completely and utterly. I was his. I had always been his.

"Vince," I murmured against his mouth.

He lifted his head, brushing my hair off my forehead. He reached between us, the sound of a zipper lowering a moment later sending a flutter of nervousness racing through me. He kissed my forehead and then my nose.

"Please," I whispered, grabbing onto his t-shirt like my life depended on it. I just wanted to feel that connection with him again. To feel him, hard and powerful, moving inside me and taking us both to new heights of pleasure neither of us would ever be ready for.

Vince tapped the head of his cock against my clit, pushing it back and forth over the swollen bundle.

I whimpered, fisting his shirt. "Please, Vince. Please." I couldn't help but beg. I had never wanted something this badly. I was so damn ready for him that it physically hurt not to have him inside of me.

"Gigi."

I met his gaze.

He opened his mouth to say something when the phone rang. "Fucking hell." He pulled away from me.

"No." I latched on to him.

He chuckled. "Baby, it could be important."

"I don't care. This is more important." I lifted my hips, trying to get him to do what both of us wanted but when the phone continued ringing, he pulled away instead.

I could have cried over the phone interrupting our little moment. It had been so long since I felt Vince against me, I got carried away and didn't think about anything else but having him back inside me.

He muttered a curse, pulled away from me, and grabbed my phone that was sitting on my nightstand. "It's your dad."

"Oh, crap." I grabbed the phone, sitting up. "Hey, Daddy."

"Hey, kiddo. You forgot. Didn't you?"

"Uh…" I tried wracking my brain for what I was supposed to be doing this morning.

"We have a breakfast date with your sister and brother," he reminded me.

"Oh right. Yes, I forgot. I'm sorry. She didn't remind me last night."

"Not surprised. I'm just pulling onto your street."

"Okay. I'll quickly get ready. See you in a few." We said our goodbyes and I disconnected the call.

"Everything okay?" Vince asked, moving to the spot beside me.

"Yeah." I looked at him then, getting lost in his dark eyes. He had righted his pants, but his shirt was wrinkly from where I had grabbed onto him. "I have a breakfast date with my brother, sister, and father that I forgot about."

"Oh." His gaze dropped to my mouth. "Would we have had sex if we weren't interrupted, Gigi?"

I quickly looked away, my cheeks burning at what we almost did. At what I was desperate for from him.

"No." He pinched my chin, forcing me to look up at him. "Tell me."

"Yes," I whispered. "I think we would have."

Vince smirked, placing a soft peck on my mouth. "I know we would have, Gigi. We were interrupted now but it'll happen again. Over and over and over. No inch of you will go untouched by me, Queenie." He kissed my shoulder. "Go take a shower. I'll greet your father."

My heart jumped. "Really? Are you sure that's a good idea?"

"Why wouldn't it be?"

"Uh…" I stood. "Cause I remember how your father acted with your sister seeing a guy." And how it almost destroyed Luna and Zach's relationship.

"I can take your dad." Vince rose from the bed and closed the distance between us. "Besides." He kissed the side of my neck. "I haven't fucked half the city which bodes well for me." Before I could respond, Vince left my bedroom, taking all the air in my lungs along with him.

SIX

VINCE

I **NEVER HAD TO** deal with a raging father before. I remembered what my sister and her fiancé went through in the beginning. My father had his reasons for acting the way he had. But there was a big difference between Zach and me. I was not going to give up.

I respected Zach now. In the beginning, he was lucky I didn't kick his ass for the shit he put my sister through. But now I loved him like the brother I never had. And I was even more thankful for my nephew and the future children Zach was helping add to our family. When it came to my feelings for Gigi though, nothing and no one was going to stand in my way of getting what I wanted. That included her father.

When the doorbell rang, I stood up taller and made my way to the front door.

Angel Rodriguez lifted a dark eyebrow when he saw that it was me and not his daughter greeting him.

"Should I ask why you're here, kid?"

I stepped to the side, letting him in. "You can."

He came into the house, stopping directly in front of me. Even though I was now older, he was still a few inches taller than I was and he was definitely wider. But he didn't scare me. And he sure as hell wasn't going to stop me from making his daughter happy.

"Tell me why you're in my daughter's home this early." Before he broke every bone in my body, went unsaid. Or maybe it would have been a different threat. I wasn't sure but I was highly amused just the same.

"She went to my sister's place last night and had a little too much wine, so I picked her up and drove her home. I made sure she was safe and came back this morning to see how she was feeling." I was shocked at myself at how quickly the lie rolled off my tongue.

"Really?" Angel turned toward me. "Her car's in the driveway."

"It is. I took a cab over to my sister's place, picked it up, and drove it back here. Did you want a coffee?" I went to the kitchen, not waiting for him to respond. A part of me wondered if he had met Matt like this. The fucker Gigi apparently dated for who knew how long. I wasn't sure if they ever did anything sexually but when she told me that no man had ever gone down on her before, I wondered if she only dated him to piss me off. Either way, the reason didn't matter, because it worked.

"What do you want with my daughter?"

And there it was.

I poured two cups of coffee before turning around to face Angel.

I want to fuck her. Break her. Make her give me every single inch of her until she's begging and screaming for more.

"We're friends," I said instead.

He grunted, coming toward me and taking the cup of coffee I offered him. "Right. You must think I'm stupid. I've seen the way you look at her. I've heard the rumors."

"Your daughter's walls are hard to crack, so whatever's going on between us, stays right where it is." She had walls up and I needed to figure out why. It probably had something to do with her career and the accident she had but at the same time, it wasn't like I had ever given her any reason to doubt my feelings for her.

"Her mother was the same way." Angel shook his head. "Even after I made her fall in love with me, it still took years for her not to worry every damn day that I'd leave her."

"What did you do?" I had never actually carried on a full conversation with him. But I found that I wanted it. No, I needed it. I needed to prove to Gigi and her father, that I was it for her. That *we* were it.

"It was the small things. I bought her flowers at random. Even though she joked and said she hated them because they always died too quickly, I still bought them anyway because her eyes lit up every time I came home with them." He went to the dining room table and sat, waiting for me to do the same.

I joined him and soaked up the information he was giving me.

"I also made sure to never forget the important dates. Her birthday. Our wedding anniversary. Even the anniversary of when we first kissed." Angel sat forward. "It's the small things, Vince. If you want to prove to my daughter that there is something between you two, first, you need to have patience. Second, don't give up."

"I don't plan on it." I took a sip of my coffee. "But there's no reason for her to be guarded with me."

"Does she know that you're in love with her?"

I choked, coughing when the coffee went down wrong.

Angel stared at me. "She doesn't."

"Uh…we haven't gotten there yet."

He nodded. "Listen, I'm not your dad. I won't give you a hard time like he gave your sister and Zach. But Gigi is my baby girl. She's my first. If I find out that you hurt her, I'll make you disappear."

Somehow, I didn't put it past him. I went to comment when the scent of lavender wafted into my nose. I turned, finding Gigi coming toward us.

All breath left me as I stared at her.

Her hair fell down around her shoulders in waves, a fresh coat of cherry red gloss sat on her lips. She was wearing a white knee length dress that made the caramel in her eyes, pop. Her gaze caught mine. She gave me a small smile before joining us at the table.

"Did I miss something?" she asked softly.

An answer was on the tip of my tongue but all I could do was stare at her. Fuck me, she was beautiful.

Her cheeks reddened.

I sat back, mentally patting my own back at putting that flush on her cheeks.

Angel chuckled, rising from his chair. "No. I'll be in the car." He turned to me. "Thank you for the coffee."

As soon as he left the house, I stood and went up to Gigi.

"Did he say anything?" she asked, staring up at me.

"What would he have to say, Queenie?" I asked, my voice low. I reached out, brushing my thumb along the length of her jaw.

A notable shiver trembled through her. "I don't know. I've never had a guy here before. The twins don't count."

I leaned toward her, running my mouth along the shell of her ear. "He threatened me. Said some things. Gave me some tips." I kissed her cheek. "Same old."

She leaned back. "He threatened you?"

I winked, pulling away from her. "Have a good date with your family, Queenie. I'll see you later."

Before she could respond, I left the house and jogged to my car. I gave Angel a wave and slid into my beater of a vehicle, driving away with a smug smile on my face.

SEVEN

Gigi

AFTER ALMOST HAVING SEX with Vince that morning, I couldn't get him out of my head. Not that I could ever get him out of my head anyway, but now it was worse. There was just something about him that I craved. I often wondered at first if after he went away to school, there had ever been other women. But since talking to Luna and Meadow, a sense of satisfaction slid over me that there hadn't. Even though the rumors said that he had some psycho exes. Now that it wasn't true, it made me realize that I needed to break down my walls and tell him how I felt.

With his party coming up the following weekend, I knew Ashton would be getting him a stripper. It was tradition. But I wasn't sure how I felt about someone else dancing for him. Maybe *I* could be that stripper. Although, I wasn't sure how Vince would react to me dancing in front of our friends.

He had given me a necklace so many years ago as a birthday present. It had been my favorite gift I had ever received. I wanted to return the favor. Fingering the necklace around my neck, I smiled to myself at the memory of Vince giving it to me.

I was leaving the bathroom and about to rejoin everyone out in the backyard to continue my birthday celebrations when I was stopped by Vince. He was coming down the hall, holding a small box in his hand.

"Hi." He smiled.

My heart fluttered. "Hi."

Even though he was so young, he was now the same height as me. I also knew that give him a year and he would be much taller and probably wider. He had that boyish charm to him and even though that were true, he still did something funny to my belly.

"I just wanted to give this to you before everyone stole your attention again." He stopped in front of me and handed me a velvet box.

"This is from you?" I asked in awe, taking the box from him.

He nodded, standing up straighter. "I saved for it."

I opened the box, my eyes widening at the gold necklace with a ballet slippers pendant hanging from the chain. "Oh, Vince. It's beautiful."

"I saw it and instantly thought of you." He took the necklace out of the box and moved behind me.

I lifted my hair off my neck. "Thank you."

When the chain was clasped securely around my neck, the pendant fell between my breasts. Vince's fingers lingered, brushing along the base of my throat.

It had been years since he gave me the necklace and I could still feel his touch on my skin.

I didn't think he even knew what it meant to me. To be that thoughtful at such a young age. His parents raised him well. And whether he ended up with me or not, he would make someone happy.

Me.

He made *me* happy.

I sighed.

Suddenly, I felt eyes on me.

I looked up, finding my dad, sister, and brother all staring back at me.

My cheeks burned, not realizing I had sighed loud enough for them to hear.

"What's going on?" Ryder, my younger brother asked, raising a dark eyebrow. Even though he was a couple of years younger than I was, he was definitely bigger. Almost as tall as our dad with the same scowl on his face that most of our fathers had, he could have been our dad's twin. If Dad were younger anyway.

"Nothing," I murmured, glancing at Dad.

"How are you feeling, Meadow?" Dad asked, thankfully changing the subject. Not that I was ashamed of whatever was going on between Vince and I. The problem was, I didn't know what that was, but I knew that I wanted to take it one day at a time.

"I'm feeling fine." Meadow sat back in the chair.

"Are you sure?" I asked, remembering her telling me she had post-partum depression.

"Yeah. We're dealing with it." She sighed. "Shade has been amazing. Losing Sunny…" She shook her head. "It was rough at first but we're slowly doing better."

I couldn't imagine what she had been through, losing someone I loved like she had.

When I had found out that my sister was dating two guys, I wasn't surprised in the least. Sunny and Shade were older, much older than her, but they were good to her. I loved Shade like a brother and was thankful that he was part of our family. Even our dad liked him. I just wished I could have known Sunny.

While my dad and siblings talked, I discreetly pulled out my phone and sent Vince a text.

Me: Thank you for taking care of me last night.

Vince: You haven't seen anything yet, Queenie.

My cheeks burned when he responded right away.

Me: You're making me blush.

Vince: Good. Shouldn't you be visiting with your family?

Me: I can't concentrate on what they're talking about.

Vince: Oh? And what's making it hard for you to concentrate, baby?

I chewed my bottom lip.

Me: You.

Vince: I know.

I laughed lightly to myself, imagining the smug smile on his face after reading my text.

Me: What are you doing?

Vince: I went home to have a cold shower.

Suddenly a picture came through.

My eyes widened at what I was looking at.

"What's wrong?"

I jumped, finding my sister staring at me. "Nothing. Excuse me. I have to go to the bathroom." I rushed out of the booth, making my way to the bathroom at the back of the restaurant. Once I was in a stall, I leaned against the wall and checked my phone. The image was of Vince's abs but what I noticed most was his hand wrapped around his thick cock. He was standing in the shower with drops of water sliding down his lower body.

Me: God, Vince. You can't send me pictures like that.

Vince: Did you not like it?

Me: Of course I liked it!

Vince: Good. Now send me something.

He wanted me to do what? There was no way.

Vince: I'm waiting, Gigi.

Oh God.

Making sure the stall door was locked, I got an idea. Pressing the video on my phone, I placed it on the back of the toilet and pressed record. Stepping back a couple feet, I turned around. Glancing at the small screen over my shoulder, I made sure you could actually see all of me. Reaching under my dress, I pulled my thong over my hips and down my legs before slipping out of it and stuffing it into my purse.

Vince wanted to play dirty? Well I could do it better.

Facing my phone, I leaned against the door and pulled the hem of my dress to my waist. The camera would get a full shot of my naked waist. Knowing I would be sending this video to Vince gave me the courage to keep going.

Placing my hand against my stomach, I slowly slid it down until it reached the apex of my thighs.

My breath caught in my throat when my fingers came into contact with my clit. Knowing I wouldn't have enough time before Meadow would come looking for me, I started rubbing the swollen bundle.

My thighs trembled, my other hand cupping my breast.

Locking eyes with the camera, I licked my lips and started undulating my hips against my hand. Needing to give myself better access, I lifted my left foot and placed it on the toilet paper dispenser. It opened my body, giving Vince a full view of my core whenever he watched the video.

Reaching around behind me, I slipped two fingers deep into my body and started finger fucking myself.

A hot tingle started in my toes, racing up the length of my body.

With the hand between my legs, I rubbed my clit in hard rough moves. I knew there would be no way that I would last long. Not with how worked up I had been. The orgasm Vince had given me earlier that morning wasn't enough.

As soon as the door to the bathroom sounded, a fast release left me. I gasped, my eyes rolling into the back of my head.

I knew right then that Vince would want to explore this more.

Once I calmed down, I lowered my foot to the floor, pulled my fingers from my body, and grabbed the phone. Before I got caught doing something I shouldn't be doing in a public bathroom, I lifted the phone to my face, blew Vince a kiss and stopped recording. I quickly sent it to him, fixed my dress and made myself look presentable again before joining my family.

As I sat beside Meadow, my phone buzzed.

Vince: You play fucking dirty, baby girl.

Me: Did you like that?

Vince: I had to take another cold shower.

Another image came through of his stomach.

My eyes widened when I realized that drops of his cum coated his abs.

Me: I'm glad I gave you something to jerk off to.

Vince: Next time, I'm going to make you watch.

I only grinned and put my phone away, a hot shiver racing down my spine at thoughts of what he would do to get back at me. And I couldn't wait.

(Vince)

I was not expecting Gigi to send me a damn video. A picture sure, my girl had a freaky side to her. But a video? Seeing her make herself come made me hard as fuck but when she gasped, I was done. It took everything I was made of not to turn around and join her in that bathroom stall. I imagined what her reaction would be. She would probably gasp with her eyes wide, maybe her cheeks would turn pink. She would chew her bottom lip and then I would suck on that same lip and give it a gentle bite.

My dick hardened once again, threatening to burst behind the fly of my jeans.

The orgasm I gave myself didn't do shit.

We were so close to having sex again earlier that morning, but it was like life was playing a cruel joke on us. Although, as much as I wanted her, this teasing going on between us was hot as hell.

I smiled to myself, scratching my jaw as I drove to The Dove Project to help with some more construction that was being done on the place. If Gigi and I kept doing what we were doing, teasing but not actually doing anything about it, I couldn't wait to see how it would be when we finally fucked again. It would be like an explosion as we crashed into each other. And I couldn't wait for that to happen.

EIGHT

Gigi

IT WAS A COUPLE of nights before Vince's birthday party. I hadn't seen him since I sent him the video, so I wasn't sure how it would be to see him again, but I was itching for another taste. I wanted to take it further this time. I needed all of him. Every inch. No more waiting.

I was getting ready to call him when my phone suddenly rang, making me jump. When I picked it up, my stomach did a flip. "Hey," I answered.

"Hey, Queenie," Vince said, his deep voice sending a flush of heat washing over me. "You home?"

"I am."

"Good. I'm just pulling onto your street."

"Oh, okay. I'm in my room, watching a movie." Or I tried to. I had every intention of rubbing one out before I called him up, but this was better.

"Perfect. I'll see you in a few." He hung up and like he said, the sound of the front door opening jarred through me a moment later.

Vince appeared at my doorway. "Hey, you really need to learn how to lock your door," he said, kicking the door closed and coming toward me.

"Hi," I breathed, taking in the sight of him. "I always lock the door before I go to bed."

He scowled. "Not the same."

He was dressed in his work clothes still, but what I noticed most was the bags sitting under his eyes. "Rough day?" I asked, ignoring his comment.

He grunted, sliding onto the bed. He laid down, resting his head on my lap and wrapping his arm around my waist. "It wouldn't have been so bad, but we were dealing with a difficult client."

"Oh. I'm sorry," I said softly, running my fingers through his hair.

He hummed. "That's okay. This helps. But that video you sent me the other day was even better."

I laughed lightly. "I'm glad."

"I wasn't expecting that."

"Well, I wasn't expecting you to send me a picture of your…"

He lifted his head. "What?"

"You know what I mean."

"I do but I want you to actually say it, Gigi."

I searched his face, swallowing hard. "Cock."

He smirked. "Good girl."

My stomach fluttered unexpectedly at the approval I got from him.

"I missed you." He lowered his head, snuggling his face into my lap and taking a deep breath. "You smell good."

"I missed you too and it's just body lotion." My heart jumped over the fact that he was smelling me.

"Nah." He lifted his head and pulled back the covers. "It's something else."

"Oh?" I cupped his jaw. "And what's that?"

He smirked, licking his full mouth. "I can smell your pussy."

My breath caught.

"What were you doing before I got here?" he asked, raising an eyebrow. "Were you playing with this pretty little kitty?"

"Nothing like that." I laughed. "I was watching a movie and trying to read."

He kissed my knee. "A sexy book?"

"Hardly." I rolled my eyes. "It was a Stephen King novel."

"Interesting." He cupped my knee, pushing my legs apart. "I like this. Being here with you."

My heart jumped to my throat. "I like this too." There was still so much we hadn't talked about that we needed to discuss. But right now, I wanted him to use me. I wanted to feel him taking control of my body and using it to make both of us feel good.

"Yeah?"

I nodded, spreading my legs wider for him.

"Hmm." Vince trailed his mouth down my inner thigh. "I've wanted to come over so many fucking times since I spent the night here but after work, I've been exhausted."

"I understand," I said, watching him with his head between my legs.

When he was only a few inches from where I wanted him most, he bit down.

I yelped.

He chuckled, swiping his tongue along the spot he just bit. "Mine," he murmured.

My heart hammered, the blood pounding in my ears.

"Kiss me," he demanded, lifting his head.

He didn't have to ask me twice.

When I lowered my mouth to his, everything around us fell away until it was just him and I.

Vince pushed me back, deepening the kiss.

Snaking my arms around his shoulders, I spread my legs, hoping that he would take the hint.

Much to my dismay, he broke the kiss. "You don't have any unexpected plans tonight that you forgot about, right?"

I laughed breathlessly. "No. I'm all yours."

"Good." In a quick move, he pulled me under him.

I gasped, another laugh escaping me. "Want something, handsome?"

"Yes." He gave me a cheeky grin. "You have no fucking idea how much I want it."

"Then show me." I kissed his chin, trailing my hands down his chest.

"Hmm…" He lowered his mouth to my neck, giving it a gentle bite.

A sigh escaped me, a flood of heat rushing between my legs. "Vince."

A low growl left him.

"Please." I arched beneath him, rubbing myself over the hard length between his legs. "I need you."

Grabbing my hands, he pulled them up and over my head before linking our fingers. His mouth soon found mine. He pushed against me, thrusting back and forth. Even though he wasn't inside me and our clothes were in the way, I could still feel him everywhere. The pleasure was almost too much. I couldn't think of anything else but having him fuck me.

We worked up a rhythm, teasing each other. But as much as I wanted him, I couldn't stop. He pushed into me, rubbing at the perfect spot.

I broke the kiss, gasping for breath as his hips undulated against me.

His dark eyes locked with mine, watching. Waiting for me to fall and crash into that sea of pleasure that only he could ever provide for me.

I whimpered, squeezing my eyes shut but felt his burning into me. My fingers tightened in his, my thighs shaking.

Vince licked up the side of my neck, his hot breath fanning over my ear. "You want to come?"

"Yes," I whined, rubbing myself against him.

He pulled a hand from mine, hooked it under my thigh, and pushed my knee out. "Then give me that orgasm, baby."

We moved. Back and forth. Side to side. The pleasure took control as I chased the orgasm, I was so damn desperate to have.

"Fuck, you're greedy," he murmured against the side of my throat.

It was as if he could hear the thoughts running through my head. Yes, I was greedy. Hungry. I wanted him in ways I never even knew someone could want another person. I read. I watched movies. I heard my friends talk but they never told me it would be like this. Maybe it was something that couldn't be explained.

"Gigi, give me that orgasm," Vince growled, sinking his teeth into the spot at the base of my neck.

Spots danced in my vision, my thighs shook, a hard cry left my lips as the release crashed into me.

"That's it. Keep coming," he demanded, biting me again.

The pain mixed with pleasure slid over me. "God," I cried out.

"So fucking beautiful."

As soon as I came down from the high, I was on Vince. I shoved him back, crushing my mouth to his.

His hands went to my hair, holding me tight against him.

Deepening the kiss, my fingers dug into his shoulders. I wanted to bury myself beneath his skin and bask in the warmth of his passionate embrace. I needed him like I never needed anything else in my entire life.

Pushing him back hard, my legs got tangled in the sheets on the bed and we fell over the side.

I landed on my back with an oomph, a bubble of laughter leaving me.

"Geezus, babe. You okay?"

"Yes." I covered his mouth with mine once again, ripping at his clothes. Too many layers stood between us.

"Fuck," he whispered against my lips.

"Please, Vince." My foot was still on the bed, opening my body to him. It was an odd angle, but I didn't care. I had only been with him once. Hell, I only had sex once, period, and I knew that it would hurt but I needed that ache. I would give him what he wanted at his birthday party as well, but this was for us. I needed him like I needed air to breathe. No more foreplay. I wanted him to fuck me.

"We should wait." And although he said the words, his fingers trailed up my inner thighs.

"No. The anticipation is killing me," I whined.

He chuckled, releasing my mouth with a smack and trailing hot kisses down the length of my jaw. "Is it now?"

"God, yes." I reached for his belt, unbuckling it and ripping down the zipper.

He jumped. "You gotta be careful with that shit, Gigi."

"Oh." My cheeks burned. "Sorry."

He shook his head, his eyes darkening. "You hurt it, you gotta kiss it better."

"Sounds like a delicious plan to me." I licked along his bottom lip, igniting a shiver to tremble through him. When I was about to reach into his pants, he grabbed my hands. "Vince, please. I—"

"I'm not stopping you. Fuck, Gigi. You have no idea how much I want this to happen." His eyes roamed down the length of me. "Especially when you're sitting here half naked and begging me to fuck you. But I need you to know that once this happens, that's it for us."

"What do you mean?" I asked, breathless.

"It means that there's no one else. Just you and me."

"I…" We couldn't talk about that right now. There was no way that either of us were ready to take that next step when we hadn't even made our relationship official.

"Gigi," Vince barked, grabbing hold of my chin. "You want my dick?"

"Yes." I tried pulling my head from his firm grip, but his hold only tightened.

"Do you want my dick?" he repeated, slower that time.

"Yes," I said, glaring at him.

He leaned forward, placing a hard kiss on my mouth. "Then tell me."

"We're really going to talk about this now?"

He gave my bottom lip a gentle bite.

The unexpected pain shot to my clit. "Vince."

"What the fuck did I just ask you?"

"Yes, I want your dick. I want you to fill me up and make me scream your name. I want you…God, I want…I want it all."

"Then say it." His brows narrowed. "Gigi," he said, his voice filling with warning.

"You're it for me. It's just us. No one else. There's never been anyone else," I said all in one breath.

"Good girl." He released my chin and wrapped his hand around my throat, pulling me toward him. "Now do it."

I quickly undid his pants the rest of the way and reached a shaky hand inside. When my fingers came into contact with his cock, I almost whimpered at how hard he was.

His eyes darkened, waiting, watching, never leaving mine.

As much as I wanted to look at his cock, I couldn't help but keep my eyes locked on his.

Pulling him from the confines of his pants, I wrapped my fingers around the thick length. I had forgotten how big he was, my fingers barely closing around his girth.

A groan escaped him, but his fingers never loosened from my throat.

"Do it," he growled, his pupils dilating.

Pulling the crotch of my panties to the side, I ran the head of his cock against my clit.

"Gigi." He leaned his forehead against mine.

Our breath came out in pants.

Moving his hand to the back of my head, he fisted my hair, forcing me to look down. "Watch me enter you."

Before I could brace myself, he thrust into me.

I cried out, unable to look away from our joined bodies.

"You see that?" he asked between thrusts. "My cock remembers your pussy, baby."

"Yes." My thighs shook, burning from the odd angle.

"Fucking hell, I forgot how tight you are." He kissed the side of my neck, keeping a firm grip on my hair.

Leaning back, I lifted the hem of my tank top.

Vince released me so I could take it off and was back on me seconds later.

He cupped my breast, leaning down and taking a nipple between his lips. His thrusts were slow and deliberate, owning me with each pump of his hips.

The pleasure consumed me, traveling from my toes to my head. Every inch of me tingled. Even though it was slow but powerful, I couldn't help but get lost in him. This was what I wanted. All this time.

Wrapping an arm around his shoulders, I held him against me and started moving my hips back and forth.

A rough growl escaped from somewhere deep in his chest. He released my nipple, trailing hot kisses up my chest, to my collarbone, before reaching my mouth.

"Faster," I begged. "Please. I need…"

Vince wrapped himself around me and stood, lifting me into his arms before placing me gently on the bed. Pulling from my body, he undressed, standing naked before me. He was hard. Everywhere.

"Wow," I breathed.

He chuckled, shaking his head. He towered over me, grabbed my hips, and pulled me to the edge of the bed. "You're a dirty girl, Gigi," he said, pulling my panties lower and placing a soft peck on my stomach.

I laughed, cupping his face. "You like it."

"I do." He ripped the panties down my legs, threw them to the floor, and crawled up the length of my body before crushing his mouth to mine.

No more words were said between us as he lifted my legs, placed them on his shoulders and entered me in one smooth thrust.

He swallowed my whimpers, holding me in place and pumping into me hard. His thrusts turned deep, violent. It was like all of our pent-up sexual frustration finally caught up with us.

I couldn't control the thoughts rushing through me at how right this felt. How much I had needed him. How desperate I was. And the fact that I was willing to do anything to have him back inside me, scared the shit out of me.

NINE

Gigi

SITTING ON THE EDGE of the bed, I fixed my hair and piled it on top of my head into a messy bun.

Vince was sitting against the headboard with the white sheets covering him from the waist down. Both of us had planned on waiting to have sex again until his birthday party but something changed where we needed each other. Now, I wasn't sure if it was just me, but it was awkward. I didn't know why. It wasn't like he was a random stranger or anything.

"Queenie," he said, his voice low.

I rose from the bed and went to get dressed when a growl stopped me. I glanced at Vince over my shoulder.

"You have bruises."

I looked down, finding a dark bruise on my hip and what looked like fingerprints on my inner thighs. "Oh. I guess I do."

"Come here," he demanded.

"I should get dressed." I ignored his intense stare and went to my dresser.

"Gigi."

I wasn't sure what was wrong with me. I had gotten what I wanted from him. He felt better than I remembered but being with him didn't make this ache, this need for more, this pain, go away.

"Baby," he said gently.

I was vaguely aware of him coming up behind me.

Vince brushed the loose strands that had fallen from my bun off my nape, and placed a soft peck on my shoulder. "Talk to me."

His touch was so gentle, it forced a lump to my throat.

"I don't know what to say," I confessed.

"Gigi." He wrapped an arm around my middle.

Both of us were naked with the remnants of what we had done written all over our skin but for whatever reason, I couldn't face him. It wasn't like before. Even though we had only been together once, that had been three years ago and in the back seat of my car. But I wouldn't have changed it for anything. So why the hell did I feel like I was about to do the walk of shame?

"Hey." Vince tried turning me, but I wouldn't budge.

I could feel his eyes burning into me, but I couldn't even meet his gaze in the reflection of the mirror.

"Do you regret what we did tonight?"

I looked at him then, my gaze landing on his face.

His dark eyes stared back at me, waiting, hoping for an answer that wouldn't break either of our hearts.

"No," I finally said.

His shoulders slumped like that one word held so much weight all by itself.

"Then talk to me." His thumb brushed along my hip bone. "I feel like you regret something. Was I too rough? Not rough enough? You gotta give me something here, Queenie."

"No." I inhaled a sharp breath and leaned against my dresser. Even though we were both naked, his cock was flaccid and nothing sexual slid between us. This was more than just sex. There had always been an air about Vince that was intense. I had never seen him look at another woman. I had some hot friends, but he only ever looked at me.

"What do you want out of this?" I finally asked him.

He tilted his head, his eyes searching my face. "The same thing you do, baby, but I'm willing to wait until you're ready."

Would I ever be ready?

"Is this the age thing?"

"No." I shook my head for added effect. "Not at all. I just…" Could I tell him that he had broken my heart? It had been lame, and I shouldn't have cared so much but the night we spent together, meant something to me and I thought it meant something to him too.

"You're freaking me out, Gigi." Vince stepped away, running a hand over the back of his neck. "I don't know what I did."

"Please don't." I went to him and before he could protest, I wrapped my arms around his hard middle. "I don't know what's going on but I just…I need this. I need you. I always need you."

"Alright, Queenie." He returned the embrace, wrapping me up in his arms. "I'll be patient and wait for you to tell me when you're ready." He crouched until we were at eye level. "Okay?"

I nodded, cupping his handsome face. "Okay."

"Good." He stepped away from me and held out his hand. "Let's grab a drink and watch a movie."

"Shouldn't we get dressed?"

His eyes roamed down the length of me. "Yeah. As much as I don't want you to, I know people just randomly walk into your house."

"Well…" I went to the dresser, bent over and started rummaging for pajamas from the bottom drawer. "I guess you'll have to bring me to your apartment, and then I can be naked as much as you want."

He groaned. "Fucking hell."

I laughed lightly, thankful that the weight of our conversation had lifted some. I was also thankful that Vince had patience because I wasn't sure if either of us were ready for that conversation. Even though I wasn't exactly sure what all needed to be said or how it would go, I just wanted to enjoy his company. It was why I hadn't said anything for so long. I had hoped that I would just get over it but when you love someone and they hurt you, it's almost impossible.

While Vince got dressed, I did the same. "Vince?"

His head shot up. "Yeah?"

"Thank you," I whispered.

He did up his jeans and came toward me. Pinching my chin, he placed a soft peck on my mouth. "Whatever is going on in that beautiful head of yours, I'm not going anywhere, Queenie. No matter how much you push me away, I'll always be here."

It was the day before Vince's birthday party and as much as I was trying to distract myself from thoughts of him, nothing worked. His words bounced around in my head. How he wasn't going anywhere no matter how much I pushed him away. God, could he be serious? Did he want more out of this than just sex? I wasn't sure but what I did know was that I enjoyed his company. That was nothing new but now that we'd had sex again, things changed. Quickly. He slept over a few nights ago, after finally doing what we both wanted, but we didn't have sex again. He had the patience of a damn saint because I knew that I sure as hell didn't.

Letting out a hard sigh, I pulled into the parking lot of The Dove Project and put my car into park. Hopefully getting some work done would help distract me from thoughts of the man who constantly invaded my dreams and every inch of my body. But I knew no matter what had happened previously between us, it would be nothing like what was coming. I had no idea how I knew, but I could feel it. Vince was intense. I had seen the same thing in his father. Whenever he looked at Vince's mom, Creena, it was like she was all that mattered. While he loved his kids, his wife reached a part of him that no one else ever could and I wanted that.

A gentle tap on the window made me jump.

Ashton Donovan opened the driver door. "You just going to sit there or are you coming in and helping us?"

I scowled and left the vehicle. "It's not my fault you guys are behind because we got some new volunteers that you can't stop drooling over."

He chuckled, wrapping me up in a hug. "How's it going?"

"Not too bad." I squeezed him, my heart warming. Ashton gave perfect hugs. They were firm enough where you felt safe and protected in his arms, but they never became inappropriate. Although, maybe it had just been me. He once had a thing for our friend Luna, and slept with both Piper and my sister for a short time. He got around but I knew there was someone out there for him. He just had to find her.

"Gigi."

I jumped at the deep voice coming from behind me.

Ashton released me, glancing over my head. "Problem?"

"Nope." Vince came up to my side, lightly brushing his fingers over my hip. "You good?" he asked me.

"Yeah." My body heated at the subtle touch coming from him. It wasn't like we had ever announced whatever this was that we were doing. We never made it public or even put a label on it. But I liked that he touched me in public, not caring at all who was around.

Ashton glanced between us. "This is new."

"Nope," Vince repeated. "Not new. Just continuing."

"Really." Ashton scratched his jaw. "Interesting."

"Alright." I rolled my eyes. "If you two are done. I have work to do." I turned on my heel and headed toward the large building that I had been volunteering at for as long as I could remember. The Dove Project had been a part of our families before us kids were ever born. It was a part of us, and I knew even after our parents were gone, the center would continue to grow and expand and be there for people in need.

When I entered the large building that now looked more like a compound than anything, I waved to the receptionist and passed a couple of girls putting up flyers on the activity board. I made my way to the office, put my purse in one of the lockers, and grabbed a bottle of water from the mini fridge we kept stocked.

"Well, I don't know what you want from me, Angel. The center is growing, and I'm needed here."

I stood up straighter at the sound of Mom's voice coming from down the hall.

"I know, baby. Yes, I'll let the girls know." She laughed. "I think they'll be able to handle us going away since we never really got a honeymoon. Yes, we'll do it after Ryder leaves. God, do you not know me at all?" Her laugh deepened. "Fine, fine. Meadow isn't coming in today. The little one had a rough night, so she's tired."

I left the office, finding Mom leaning against the wall.

Her head snapped up, her gaze landing on me. She smiled. "Gigi's here. Yes, I will. Okay, love you too." She said her goodbyes and shoved her cell in her back pocket. "How are you doing?"

"Good." I gave her a hug, reveling in the feel of being in my mom's arms. That single moment relieved some of the stress of not knowing what the hell was going on between Vince and me.

"Your dad said that Vince was at your place the other morning."

My stomach flipped. "Uh…yeah. He came over to make sure I was okay."

Mom leaned back, searching my face. "Your father may believe your lies but I'm not stupid, Gigi. You're more like me than your sister and brother."

I pulled away and tugged at the end of my t-shirt. "It was nothing. I went to Luna's, had a little too much wine and Vince picked me up and drove me home."

"And?"

I sighed, hating at the moment how well Mom knew me. "He spent the night, but nothing happened."

She gave me a small smile. "You don't have to justify your actions to me, sweetheart. It's not like Vince is some random guy."

"I know." I looked down at my feet. "It's just…it's complicated."

"I get that." Mom hooked an arm around my shoulders, kissing the side of my head. "But that boy loves you. You can tell me I'm wrong all you want but I see it. Your dad sees it. Your brother isn't around much and even he sees it."

"Do you guys talk about it or something?" As much as I wanted to be pissed that they discussed my love life or lack thereof, I couldn't. "Do you have any advice?"

She gave me a small smile. "Let the walls down. Rip the Band-Aid off and get to talking, girl. If I had done that sooner with your dad, we would have had a much easier road. But I'm thankful every day that he loved me enough to keep pushing and to not give up on us. Give the kid a break, don't make him have to fight as hard…but don't make it too easy either." She winked.

I laughed. "Thank you."

"Of course. I know it's been hard since your accident. You had other plans for your life, but I know that Vince has always been in those plans as well. Hasn't he?"

I thought a moment, mulling over her words. "He has," I finally said.

Mom smiled and placed a kiss on my head. "I figured. But enough of this." She pulled away, gave me a wide smile, and started listing off things she needed me to work on.

I committed them to memory and went to get started when I remembered the conversation she was having with Dad. "When you and Dad go away, you should choose somewhere warm."

Mom's smile grew. "We were discussing Mexico. I just want to leave the country and go somewhere we've never been. We'll let you know of course."

"I'm glad." I gave her a quick hug. "Thank you."

"Don't need to thank me. I'm your mom. It's what I do. It's kind of my thing."

I laughed, released her, and started backing up. "Well whenever I become a mom, I hope I get at least half of your mom traits."

"You will." She winked. Her phone suddenly rang. Pulling it from her back pocket, she sighed and placed it at her ear. "You know, I love you with every inch of me but you're driving me crazy. Yes, Angel, I just told Gigi. I know you're excited." She shook her head, gave me a wave, and went into the office. "I'm doing everything I can to get things set up so we can leave," she said, shutting the door behind her.

I laughed.

Making my way to the storage closet, I grabbed a ladder to start changing out the lightbulbs in the hall. Our moms wanted the bulbs changed out to eco-friendly ones, to save money. Even though the center was receiving funding from the government and people were constantly donating to help, they still wanted to do everything they could to save money and to help the environment.

Setting up the ladder, I quickly checked my phone to see if I had gotten any new text messages. Truth was, I had hoped Vince was still around. My body burned, remembering the way he had used me the other night. Although, I had used him just the same. He had felt so damn good. Almost too good if you asked me.

When my phone came up empty, I sighed and shoved it back in my pocket.

As soon as I went up the ladder and got to the highest step I needed to change out the lights, it gave out beneath me. I stumbled, lost my grip, and expected to fall to the ground. But instead, when I landed against something hard, it didn't hurt like I thought it would.

"Gigi."

I opened my eyes, not realizing I had closed them and found Vince holding me.

"Are you okay?" he asked, his face pale.

"I…" I looked around me.

The step on the ladder was split in the middle like someone had cut it in half. My stomach twisted, bile rising to my throat.

"Queenie." Vince put me gently on my feet but kept his arms around me. "Hey."

"I'm fine," I finally told him.

He turned me, checking me over to make sure that I was actually fine like I told him. "Are you sure?" he asked, keeping me close.

I nodded but I couldn't help but wonder if the ladder had been tampered with. No. I was being paranoid. There was no way that someone could be that ruthless. Not at the center. Everyone who came into The Dove Project was there to help others, provide for them, care for them. It wasn't possible that someone would want to hurt me.

"Gigi." Vince wrapped an arm around my shoulders, leaning his forehead against the side of my head. "You sure you're good?"

"Yes." I cupped his arm. "Thank you for catching me."

"Always, baby. I'll always catch you."

I shivered, knowing that he wasn't just talking about me falling off the ladder.

"Hey guys."

Both of us turned to my mom coming toward us from down the hall.

"What's going on?" she asked, glancing at the ladder.

"The step broke and Gigi fell," Vince explained, keeping his hand on my hip.

"Oh God. Are you okay?" Mom asked, inspecting the step.

"Yeah." Even though what I had with Vince was new, I liked the fact that he wasn't afraid to touch me in front of people, especially my mom. I stepped back, a soft sigh escaping me at feeling his hard body pressed up against mine.

His eyes burned into my head, his hold tightening on my hip as if to say, *'I got you, babe.'*

"Your dad isn't going to like this," she mumbled, inspecting the ladder. "We got some new volunteers. I'll have to look into things."

"I'm sure it was just an accident." But even though those words left my mouth, I knew they were a lie. Someone did this deliberately. I just didn't know who or why.

"We run background checks on everyone, but I'll see if I can find out if anyone was here who wasn't supposed to be," Mom gritted out, giving me a hug. "I'm glad you're okay."

"Me too." I didn't want to think what damage falling off the ladder could have caused. I had already destroyed my knee by doing a spin and jump wrong. I could still feel the pain as my leg had twisted in a way that hadn't seemed humanly possible.

"Queenie."

I jumped, forgetting Vince was behind me. "I'm fine," I told him when that frown between his eyebrows deepened. "I promise." I stood on tiptoes, placing a soft peck on his cheek.

When I went to pull away, he wrapped himself around me.

"If something happened to you..." His voice trailed off, his face pushing into the crook of my neck.

I was momentarily shocked by the nervous energy coming off of him. "Hey." I returned the embrace. "I promise I'm fine."

He lifted his head. "I need to see for myself."

Before I could ask what he had meant by that, he grabbed my hand and led me to a nearby storage room. No one ever went into this room. Even though it had been packed with stuff, it was like we kept everything just in case we needed it one day.

"Vince." I spun on him when he gently shoved me into the room. "Listen, I promise I'm fine."

He slammed the door shut, clicking the lock into place and closing the distance between us. "You can tell me that all you want but it's still not convincing me otherwise. I need to see."

"You can't expect me to get naked in here." Not that I was opposed to getting naked in public, but I could never do something like that at a place like this.

"As much as I want you naked, we're not doing that here." Vince lowered to his knees. "Hold onto me."

My heart jumped but I did as I was told. Cupping his shoulder, I waited. I wasn't sure what he was going to do but knew that I needed to reassure him.

"Are you sore at all?" he asked, wrapping his hand around my shin.

"I…" I realized then that I was a little stiff. "Not sore exactly."

His dark eyes shot to mine. "Stiff?"

I nodded.

A shadow passed over his face. "Your body must have tensed when you fell." He trailed his fingers down my shin. "You sure you're good?"

"I am. I promise." I ran my hand to the back of his neck. "See?" I kicked off my sandal and wiggled my toes. "All good."

Cupping my foot, he leaned back and brought it up to his mouth. He placed a soft peck on top of it before helping me back into my sandal.

But that small movement did something funny to me. It made me realize that no matter what, he would drop everything and do anything to make sure that I was in fact okay.

"Vince?"

He pushed to his full height.

"Are you convinced now?" I asked, placing a hand on his chest.

He covered my hand. "If something happened to you, I don't know what I would do."

"Nothing happened."

"Not now it didn't," he snapped.

"Hey." I pulled my hand from his and cupped his face.

Vince pushed his cheek into my palm. That single touch alone seemed to calm him. As his shoulders dropped, he let out another slow breath.

"You don't think it was an accident. Do you?"

"No." Vince pulled away and ran a hand through his hair. "But it doesn't matter right now. I'm just glad you're okay."

"Are *you* okay?"

"Yeah." He came back toward me and placed a soft kiss on my mouth. "I'll see you tonight?" he asked, pinching my chin and tilting my head back. "I'd like to ring in my birthday balls deep inside you."

I coughed, my body heating at what he was suggesting. "Well, that's an image."

He smirked, his gaze dropping to my chest. "I can't believe you still wear this," he said, fingering the pendant hanging from the necklace he had bought me so long ago.

"Why wouldn't I?" It had been my favorite present I had ever received. There was no way that I would ever take it off.

His jaw clenched, his thumb moving over the small ballet slippers pendant.

"Are you sure you're okay?" I asked, staring up at him.

"Yeah." He placed a soft peck on my forehead before pulling away. Heading to the door, he unlocked it but turned back to me before he opened it. "What time will you be home tonight?"

"I have to finish up here and then I'll be heading to the studio." I had a routine to work on before teaching my students next week. "But I shouldn't be too late."

"I'll text you when I'm on my way."

"Actually." I went toward him. "Come with me."

Vince didn't ask any questions as we left the storage closet. I led him to the office, needing to give him something that I probably should have given him a while ago.

When we reached the room, I was about to step inside when I almost bumped into Ainsley Cloet. "Oh God. I'm sorry."

She gave me a small smile, shrugging her shoulders in a quick move. I actually wasn't sure if I saw it or not. She quickly rushed off, hugging a book to her chest and disappearing around the corner at the end of the hall.

"I feel bad for her," Vince said, voicing my thoughts.

My heart stuttered. I did too. Not knowing exactly what Ainsley had been through, I just knew that she didn't talk. She could hear perfectly fine but from what I had been told, she hadn't spoken more than a few words in several years due to a past trauma. She knew American Sign Language and used it to communicate. She kept to herself most times but had always been nothing but nice.

"Queenie."

I jumped, finding Vince staring at me. "Oh." I laughed. "Sorry. Distracted."

He chuckled, shaking his head.

Making my way into the office, I went to my bag and started looking through it for a specific item. I smiled when I found it. "The girls have one and so do the twins." I turned, holding a key in my palm. "I want you to have one too."

Vince frowned, his gaze dropping to my hand. "This a key to your house?"

"Yeah. The girls still have theirs even though they moved out. I figured since you're coming over more, it would be easier for you to have one. Then you don't have to wait for me to be home or awake."

Vince took a step toward me, something flashing in his eyes. That familiar tick in his jaw, jumped.

My heart stuttered. Maybe I had read into this wrong. I went to pull my hand back, my cheeks heating over the fact that he clearly didn't want a key to my house, when he grabbed my wrist.

I gasped, the key falling to the ground.

He crouched, picking it up.

"Vince," I whispered, when he rose to his full height. "What is it?"

"The twins have a key to your house?" he asked, his voice rough.

"Oh." Was he jealous? "Yes. There's a bar near my place that they started going to. I figured it was safer that they crash on my couch. You know Aiden has problems." But he wouldn't admit it. "I'm just looking out for them."

"You have a big fucking heart, Queenie." Vince took the key from me and shoved it into his pocket, keeping hold of my wrist with his other hand. "I don't like that they have a key to your house. I don't give a shit that you've known each other forever. What if they come over and you walk out in those sexy as fuck panties and a tank top?"

"Well, if you must know, they always text me when they go out, letting me know that there's a possibility that they could be coming over. So I always make sure to dress properly." I pulled my hand from his grasp. "Not that I have to explain anything to you. They are family."

"Ashton fucked your sister. That's some fucking family."

"Whoa." I pointed at him. "I don't know where this is coming from, but I can promise you that nothing has ever happened between anyone and me. Ever." I should have told him that he had been the only guy that I had ever slept with, but his jealousy pissed me off.

A smug grin spread on Vince's face. In a rough move, he pulled me against him and captured my mouth in a hard, bruising kiss. "Tell me I'm the only one you've let into your bed."

I shivered at his deep voice.

"Tell me that I'm the only one who's seen every inch of you." He nipped my bottom lip.

I yelped, my eyes welling.

He smirked, licking the spot soon after. "Tell me."

"You're an asshole," I muttered, pushing away from him.

He chuckled, tapping my butt lightly. "Thank you for the key, Queenie. I'll stop by later. I have some things to do first."

I nodded. "Okay."

He pulled me back into his arms, placing a soft peck on my cheek. "I'll see you later."

(Vince)

I knew I had no reason to react the way I did but when I had been told, quite often in fact, that Gigi had been dating that Matt fucker, I was on edge. Now knowing that Ashton and Aiden could come and go from her house as they please, didn't sit well with me. I wanted her in a spot that no other guy had been in. I knew that the twins wouldn't touch her. I *did* know that, but it didn't mean that the ugly beast called jealousy, didn't rear his ugly head. She made me possessive to the point all I could think about was taking her from there and tucking her into my arms to keep her safe.

When I saw her fall from the ladder, my world flashed before my eyes. If something happened to her before I could tell her how I truly felt, I would never get over it. But her walls had been built up for a while. It would be hard to get through to her, no matter how hard I tried.

After I left Gigi at the center, I drove to my parents' place. I was supposed to stay and help the twins and the other guys with some work The Dove Project needed, but this was more important.

When I pulled up in front of my parents' home, I killed the engine and ran up the sidewalk just as the door opened.

Both Mom and Dad were coming out of the house.

"Hey," I called after them.

"Vince?" Mom smiled. "What are you doing here?"

"I actually wanted to talk to Dad, but it looks like you're both leaving," I said, coming to a stop at the base of the steps.

"Nope." Dad kissed Mom on the temple. "Your mom's heading to the center. I'm staying here to do fuck all."

Mom laughed. "Right. I'll come home to a completely renovated backyard or something."

Dad chuckled. "You never know." He winked.

She shook her head. "Your dad's been bored since he retired."

"I'm a hands-on kind of man. You know that, baby girl." He waggled his eyebrows.

Mom rolled her eyes, her cheeks reddening. "Yeah, yeah." When she reached me, she cupped my shoulder. "Don't let him convince you to help him renovate anything. Okay?"

"I won't, Mama." I kissed her cheek and followed my dad into the house.

"Something's wrong."

I sighed. "I wouldn't say something's wrong exactly."

"Does it have to do with Gigi?" Dad went into the kitchen, pulling two beers from the fridge. He handed me one and leaned against the counter.

"Uh…I don't turn twenty-one until tomorrow," I reminded him.

"I won't tell your mom, if you don't." He winked, taking a swig of his beer. "Besides. She wouldn't care anyway. You're home. You're safe."

I nodded, slowly taking a sip of the beer. I swallowed the liquid, bubbles popping in my nose. It wasn't overly hoppy. It was light and fresh, good for a warm summer's day.

"Tell me what the problem is."

I didn't meet my dad's gaze and started picking off the label instead. "I've known Gigi my whole life."

"And been in love with her just as long." Dad tipped his beer to me, giving me a wink. "You can tell me I'm wrong. That's fine."

"My feelings don't matter at the moment." If I was going to admit to loving Gigi to anyone, it would be her. She needed to hear those words first. She needed to know that I was willing to do anything to get into her heart and make her mine. "I need advice on how to break down her walls."

A dark shadow passed over Dad's face. He finished off the rest of his beer and tossed it in the recycling bin before turning to me. "When I first met your mom, she had walls up as well. She had a job that her brother, your uncle, didn't let her get out of very easily." Dad paused. "Before you kids…" His jaw clenched. "Well…before you, it was hard. I had your sister, but I went through a period where I was doing everything I could to give her the perfect life. She stayed with your aunt while I did that. I met your mom, and the rest is history."

But I knew it was more than that. They just never told us. I did hear Dad talking to Mom every now and again about Luna's birth mother. She died when my sister was only six months old and it fucked Dad up. More than he wanted to admit.

"You're wanting to make this work with Gigi?"

"Yes." There was no question about it. No room for hesitation because it wasn't needed. Gigi was mine. It had always ever just been her. Only her. I wasn't oblivious to other girls trying to get me to notice them, but it never mattered. Gigi was the only one I wanted noticing me.

"Vince."

My gaze snapped to Dad's.

He smirked. "You remind me so much of me. It's unreal."

"I hope that's a good thing."

"I like to think it is." He chuckled. "But back to your question. The only thing I can suggest is to have patience but still be persistent. Has she hinted at all as to why she has walls up?"

"She doesn't need to. Her accident messed her up pretty badly. But I haven't done anything for her to be so guarded with me." I wanted to be the one to protect her from her emotions. To take care of her. To be with her. To be the man *for* her. It was why I had gone off to school and finished faster than I needed to. I was doing everything I could to be the man she deserved.

"Maybe she's scared to reveal her feelings because it would make her vulnerable. I don't know but I do suggest having as much patience as you can." Dad went to the fridge and pulled out another beer.

Patience.

I had all sorts of patience when it came to her but even I knew that it was wearing thin. I just prayed that both of us were ready for the moment it disappeared.

If the bruises and bite marks on her skin from the other night were any indication, I would say neither of us had the control we liked the other to believe.

TEN

Gigi

"YOU GAVE MY BROTHER a key?" Luna asked from the video on the computer screen and stared at me with wide eyes.

"That's what she said, isn't it?" Meadow snipped from the video in the top right corner.

We had been video chatting for the past hour. I had used the excuse I needed the distraction when really, I just wanted to kill some time while I waited for Vince to come over. I was sore from practicing my routine at the studio and needed to do some stretching but was too wired to focus on anything but the man I was sleeping with.

"All of you still have your keys and the twins have them too, so I just thought it made sense for him to have one as well," I explained, taking a sip of my wine.

"Did you tell him that the twins have keys too?" Piper asked softly. She had initially said that she wouldn't join in on our video chat. She was missing Jaron and wanted to mope around the house but with Meadow's persistence, she finally agreed.

"I did." I looked up when no one said anything. "What?"

"Girl, are you fucking insane?" Luna laughed.

I was momentarily shocked by her outburst. I expected it from my sister but not Luna. "What?"

"Gigi." Luna sat forward. "My brother is obsessed with you. Has been for as long as I can remember. Remember when he bought you that necklace? He was gloating for weeks how he saved the money to buy it for you."

"If he was so proud, then why didn't he make his move before he went off to school?" I fingered the necklace around my neck, my heart stuttering at her words. "And besides, it's just a necklace." But even I knew it wasn't.

The girls laughed.

"I think he was trying to grow up for you," Luna told me. "I'm not sure but I know my brother. You are all that he's wanted. The only thing. But when he heard that you were dating Matt, he asked me to tell you that he was dating someone, but I wouldn't."

"I never even dated Matt. That was a rumor." That I never corrected but that was beside the point. We were friends. That was it. He was too much of a controlling ass for me anyway. But every time Vince saw me with him, jealousy reared its ugly head and as immature as it made me, I enjoyed making him jealous.

"You two need to talk," Luna said, taking a sip of her own wine. "You're worse than the rest of us."

"We're fine," I mumbled.

"Right." Meadow rolled her eyes.

"Oh, girls. I have some crazy news." Luna took a deep breath. "I got some crank calls the other night and I thought Zach was going to lose his shit. He called up his dad and wanted someone to hack into my phone to see who was calling me. It was a bit extreme."

"Wow," both Meadow and Piper said at the same time.

"Did they say anything to you?" I asked, knowing the way Zach reacted was probably not as extreme as Luna let on.

"No but they kept calling over and over. From different phone numbers too." Luna shrugged. "It was weird, and Zach hasn't let me out of his sight since." She sighed. "I love him but he's a little intense at times."

"Our guys would do anything to protect us," Piper pointed out.

"True." Meadow laughed. "I remember a few weeks ago when someone just looked at me weird and Shade went off on them. I have to say, as annoying as the overprotection can be, I like it as well."

Luna and Piper nodded in agreement.

"Now, Gigi, back to you and my brother. Have you talked about things yet?" Luna asked, taking a sip of her wine.

"Not exactly," I mumbled.

Meadow waved a hand in front of her face. "You really don't see it, do you? You don't see any of it."

"Remind you of a conversation we had back when I was trying so hard to deny my feelings for Zach?" Luna raised an eyebrow. "Huh? Does it?"

I laughed then. "Okay, well…I told Vince that the twins have keys so they can crash if they drink too much. There's nothing wrong with that. Is there?"

"There isn't. If you were sleeping with a guy who wasn't my brother." Luna tapped the screen. "Come on, Gigi. I love you. We all do. But you're so damn oblivious. Probably worse than I was."

"It's true," Piper and Meadow said at the same time.

"I have no idea what you're talking about." My face burned.

"Yeah." Piper laughed. "And the father of my unborn baby isn't currently in jail either."

"I bet he's the type that loved the fact that he got you pregnant. It probably turned him on, and I bet money that you're in for it when he gets out of jail." Meadow sighed. "I miss when my husband was like that."

"He liked it." Piper laughed.

"I bet he did." Meadow waggled her eyebrows.

While the girls talked about their guys liking the fact that they got them pregnant, I checked my phone.

Vince: Hey, Queenie. I'm going to be late.

I checked the clock. It was almost ten at night.

Me: Okay.

My phone rang then, Vince's handsome face showing up on the small screen. I quietly excused myself and went into the kitchen to answer the phone. "Hey."

"Hey yourself," came his deep reply. "What's wrong?"

"You know I never dated Matt, right?" I figured there was no point in beating around the bush and just came out with it.

"This is not a conversation I want to be having over the phone," Vince said, his voice curt.

"Your sister said that you wanted her to tell me that you were dating someone too. Listen, Vince—"

"No, Gigi. You listen to *me*," his deep voice sent a shiver down my spine. "I wanted to start that damn rumor because I heard about how that fucker was all over your pretty little body, so yeah, I wanted my sister to lie to you."

"Why?" I whispered, gripping my phone tight in my hand.

"Because I was jealous."

"Oh." I wasn't actually expecting him to answer honestly.

"I'll be right there," he said, his voice muffled.

"Who are you talking to?" I asked, frowning.

"I'm at a friend's place trying to fix their plumbing issue. Because I work in construction and renovations, they get me to do all the nasty shit."

"Oh okay."

"Vin, you coming?" came a female voice.

My body stiffened. A feeling slid up my spine. It was something foreign to me. Something I had never felt before and I wasn't sure if I liked it.

"Yeah, one sec. Gigi, I have to go."

I swallowed hard; my throat suddenly dry. "Oh." I coughed. "Okay."

"What's up?"

"Nothing." But something *was* up, and I couldn't figure out what it was.

"Gigi." His voice took on a warning that told me not to lie to him but how could I tell him the truth when I didn't even know what that truth was?

"I'll let you go and see you when you get here. Or if you want to wait until tomorrow, that's fine too. Either way, I'll see you tomorrow for sure." I disconnected the call before he could question me further. I didn't like this feeling sitting in the pit of my stomach. Whatever it was, it hurt.

I couldn't get the female voice out of my head. And she called him Vin. I rolled my eyes at that.

She could just be a friend. Or a friend's girlfriend. There was no harm in that. I had guy friends. It made sense. And I trusted Vince. But if I trusted him, why the hell did this uneasy feeling start poking at me, putting all these thoughts in my head?

I sighed, grabbed the bottle of wine off the counter, and went back to the living room.

"There she is," Meadow said, a yawn rippling through her. "I have to go. I'm getting knocked on my ass and not in the good way either." She laughed at her joke.

"I should go too. Zach wants some mommy time before Benjamin demands my attention again." Luna waggled her eyebrows.

"That sounds like a whole other kink I've never explored." Meadow laughed. "Yet." She winked.

"You're disgusting." I giggled.

"Night girls." Piper blew us a kiss.

We said our goodbyes and I shut down the laptop. That killed another ten minutes but what would I do while I waited for Vince to show up? If he even decided to come over tonight.

My phone rang again, my stomach twisting when I saw that it was Vince calling me. "Hey."

"What was that about, Gigi? I'm now in my car, on my way to you because I keep thinking my girl is pissed at me for shit I haven't done."

My heart warmed that he called me his girl. "It's stupid."

"Nothing you say, or feel, is stupid. Tell me."

"I had a moment of jealousy," I admitted, waiting for him to laugh at me.

"Jealousy?" He paused. "When?"

"When I heard the girl in the background and I'm also jealous of the women that you apparently didn't date." I braced myself. It was coming. I knew it was. He would laugh and tell me I wasn't making sense.

"Baby, she's a friend's girlfriend. I only know her because of him. Trust me. It's not like that with Tenise. Rory would lose his shit if that were the case. And those other women?" He sighed. "I wanted to start the rumor myself. I was sick of hearing about you dating Matt and how happy as a fucking clam you were. It pissed me off, so I wanted to spread a bunch of lies. I shouldn't have even thought of doing that and I'm sorry. I promise that there are no other women."

My shoulders slumped in relief. "Okay."

"You believe me?"

"I do but I told you it was dumb," I mumbled.

"Listen, I'm about ten minutes from your place and then we can talk. Okay?"

"Okay." We said our goodbyes and I let out a sigh of relief that he never made fun of me. Placing my phone on the coffee table, I turned on the TV and laid down on the couch.

A warm mouth brushed over mine.

I sighed, a soft moan leaving me.

"Wake up, Queenie."

"I'm having a good dream." I rolled onto my stomach, keeping my eyes closed.

"Wake up. I have a present for you."

I lifted my head then, my gaze landing on a box of donuts. "Are those Meadow's?"

"They are." Vince grinned. "I stopped off at the bakery earlier tonight and picked them up. Good thing too, since now you're mad at me."

"I'm not mad at you." I sat up, running a hand through my hair.

"Here." He handed me one of the donuts that Meadow had called a surprise when she first made them. I was so damn proud of my sister and the fact that her baked goods were now being sold in restaurants.

I took the donut from Vince and bit into it. A sigh left me as I chewed, the random fruity flavors bursting on my tongue.

Vince placed the box on the table and knelt between my legs. "I'm sorry you were jealous. But I guess I deserved that when I reacted the way I did with the twins having a key to your place."

"You know they've never tried anything with me, right?" When Vince didn't answer, I cupped his cheek. "I mean it. They had a thing with Piper. Ashton slept with my sister and wanted Luna for half a second. But they never hit on me. Never even hinted at it. It's like they knew."

"Knew what?" Vince asked, his gaze popping to mine.

"That I was taken," I whispered.

"No." He shoved to his feet, towering over me. "You *are* taken. You always have been. Always will be."

I looked away. "Matt never counted."

"Don't say his fucking name." Vince pinched my chin, forcing my head around to meet the hard impact of his mouth. "Ever."

Desire for Vince burned through me, but it still didn't mean that he could tell me what to do. I bit his bottom lip, smiling when he jumped. "I thought you dated girls too, Vince."

In a quick move, he wrapped his hand around my throat, forcing me back against the couch. "Am I with them now? Are you with Matt now?"

"Vince." I tried shoving out of his rough hold.

"The answer you are looking for is, no, Vince, I am not with him." He looked down, his thumb brushing over my jugular. "You're fucking beautiful. You know that? You also drive me absolutely insane."

"You drive me insane too." I pushed him back, finished my donut, and downed the rest of my wine before I took his hand. "It's almost your birthday and you're going to make good on your promise."

Before I could say anything more about it, Vince had me up and over his shoulder and charged for my bedroom.

FINALLY US

(Vince)

Brushing my hand up and down Gigi's side, I smiled when a small shiver trembled through her. Her back was to my front, her naked ass pressing into my crotch. Her soft snores trembled through me, making my heart lighter and fuller. Knowing she could trust me and sleep peacefully, made me happy. She still had walls up, but I was determined to break them down one by one.

Gigi sighed.

I smiled, placing a soft peck on her shoulder.

My hand brushed over her hip, grazing just beneath the cheek of her ass, then delved deep between her thighs.

Her mouth parted, another sigh leaving her, but her eyes remained closed.

That's right, baby. Feel me. Dream of me. Love me.

Gently running my fingers over her swollen center, I rubbed the ache out of her body that she was surely feeling. I hadn't been gentle when I brought her to her bedroom.

"That's it, baby. Fuck, you take my cock like such a good girl."

I grinned at the nasty words that had left my mouth.

"Choke me."

My body stirred at the dark memories. I had heard Gigi being called a prude over the years but if people only knew. I enjoyed that I got a piece of her she never shared with anyone else. She shared her love and desires with me. Her fantasies and kink. It was all mine. It made me stand up taller, knowing I was the only one who knew her delicious and filthy little secret.

When I had wrapped my fingers around her throat, careful not to actually hurt her and to show her that she was the one who was in charge, her pussy had gripped me even tighter.

The orgasm that had slammed into her made me want to explore every fantasy she had even more.

Bruises and bite marks marred her pale skin. My cock twitched, swelling with need for her again but as much as I wanted her, she needed a break. But a little tease wouldn't hurt. She deserved it. She deserved all of it.

When midnight had hit, I had her begging me to fuck her harder. I was quickly learning that my girl liked it not just dark but rough as well.

"Vince," she whispered, pulling me from my thoughts.

"Yeah?" I kissed the spot beneath her ear, still running my fingers back and forth over the hot flesh between her thighs.

"Happy birthday, baby." She grabbed my wrist, pulling my hand closer until my fingers slipped into her.

I smirked, nipping along the length of her throat. "Something you want?"

"God, yes." Her eyes popped open, her gaze meeting mine.

Fisting her hair, I tugged her head back and began thrusting my fingers in and out of her. Her pussy was still soaked from the many times I had come inside her earlier but the alpha in me, didn't care. It had been my way of marking her, claiming her, letting her know that I was the only man who made her feel the way I had. She was mine. I was hers. And I wouldn't have it any other way.

"You sore, baby?" I murmured against her ear.

"Not sore enough." She pushed her ass into my waist, the tip of my cock bumping her center. "I want more."

"You're a greedy little thing, aren't you?" I pulled my hand from between her legs, wrapping it around my cock and brushing the head against her pussy.

"Please, Vince," she whined, her body shaking.

"No." As much as I wanted her, I was in the mood to tease her more.

"God." Her hips moved back and forth, running herself over the tip of my dick. She tried lowering her body down the length of me, but I was having none of it.

In a quick move, I landed a hard swat against her ass. "I said no."

"Vince." Her eyes locked with mine, dark and wild. "But you…you're hard. I know you want me."

I chuckled, rolling her onto her back and moving to the spot between her legs. "Of course, I want you." My dick rested against her mound, a hot shiver racing down my spine. It took every ounce of control I was made of not to thrust inside her. But we had only just started sleeping together again after waiting three years. What was a few more hours?

"Please."

Resting my elbows on either side of her head, I placed a soft peck on her mouth. "As much as I want to fuck you until you can no longer walk, that has to wait." My lips slid down the length of her jaw until they reached her ear. "I'll see you tonight at my party. You're going to come home with me. And I'm going to spend all night doing things to you, you've only ever read about."

She shivered. "Promise?"

"Yeah, Queenie." I kissed the tip of her nose. "I promise."

"Good." She pushed against me. "Then if you're not going to fuck me, you need to get off of me."

I laughed. "Grumpy much?"

She giggled, a flush of red hitting her cheeks. "I need to take a shower. Or we can take one together." She waggled her eyebrows.

"We can but I'm still not fucking you. Not until tonight. Because you know, anticipation and all."

She rolled her eyes.

"Careful," I growled.

"Whatever." Gigi rose from the bed, walking past me in all her beautiful naked glory. "It's not like you're going to do anything about it anyway."

Before she got very far, I was on her.

Her squeals turned into laughter followed by moans shortly after. When I shoved my face between her milky white thighs, all thoughts of waiting to have sex again left her once I had her coming on my tongue in a matter of minutes.

ELEVEN

VINCE

IT HAD BEEN A few hours since I left Gigi's place. I cooked her breakfast and we ate in a comfortable silence. It was now later into the evening and my birthday party she had planned, was in full swing. I never thought her of all people, would plan it at a strip club but I had heard that she taught some of the dancers and became friends with the owners. So it made sense.

I understood why she danced. She was never comfortable with anyone else to show them exactly who she was. So she spoke through the way she moved her body. Even I had issues breaking down her barriers, but I would. If I had to use her body to get her to talk to me, I would. And eventually, I would help her embrace every kinky desire she craved.

I should have told Gigi that I didn't need a party. I would rather spend the day with her. Maybe have dinner at my parents' place. Spend some time with my sister, Zach, and my nephew. Then finish the night off wrapped up in Gigi. But I knew that she had been planning the party for months, so I never said anything.

"Vince."

I lifted the beer to my lips, finding Ashton and Aiden coming toward me. "Hey." I took a sip, letting the carbonated liquid tickle my taste buds before swallowing. As much as I was thankful that I could finally have a drink legally, I didn't really care about it at the same time. I wasn't overly a drinker. My friends were. Hell, they drank enough for all of us.

"This is some party," Ashton said, looking out at the vast room that held our friends and parents. "I'm surprised Gigi was able to rent this place."

"She didn't rent it," Aiden corrected his brother. "She knows the owners and is helping them out, so they're helping her out in return."

"I wish I was friends with strippers," Ashton mumbled.

"No, you don't. You'd just fuck them and treat them like shit," Aiden reminded him.

"I don't treat any woman like shit." Ashton shook his head. "It doesn't matter." He turned to me. "I just wanted to tell you that I got your stripper. She should be on her way soon."

My back stiffened. "I can't have a stripper."

Ashton frowned. "Yeah, you can. It's tradition. All of us had a stripper on our twenty-first birthdays."

"All of you were single on your twenty-first birthday. I'm not having a stripper." I went to walk away, hoping my words were final and left no room for argument when Ashton's next words stopped me.

"Are you dating Gigi?"

I stopped, slowly turning toward him. "Why? You want to try and fuck her too, Ashton? I heard you got around but come on. You hit on my sister, caused shit for her and Zach, and then you fuck Meadow. Oh, and you even fucked Piper too. Are you just wanting to go through all the girls we know?"

Ashton's brows narrowed. "That's not…it doesn't…I don't want Gigi."

I raised an eyebrow. "No? Why not? Something wrong with her?"

Aiden watched the exchange, a small smirk splaying on his face.

Ashton scowled. "Nothing is wrong with her, but I know that she could never belong to me. Not even for a second."

"And why is that?" I asked, crossing my arms under my chest and staring him down. It didn't matter that he was bigger than me. It didn't matter that it revealed feelings I didn't want to think about yet. It didn't matter that I had known the twins my whole life. What *did* matter was the fact that Gigi belonged to *me*.

"Because." Ashton's jaw clenched. "She belongs to you, fucker."

"Exactly." I turned on my heel and walked away. I knew that little conversation wouldn't stop Ashton and that he would still have the stripper for me, but it didn't matter. There was no way I was letting another woman touch me. I had heard the stories after the guys had their own twenty-first birthdays and what went on behind closed doors. It wasn't my thing and the only woman I wanted dancing for me, had suddenly disappeared. I hadn't seen her most of the night and it didn't sit well with me.

"Vince."

I turned at the sound of my sister's voice. "Hey, Luna."

"You good?" she asked, coming toward me with her fiancé hot on her heels.

"Yeah, just looking for Gigi," I told her.

"I haven't seen her," Zach confessed. "Have you?" he asked Luna.

"No." Luna took a sip of her drink. "But I know she gets a little weird during these parties. She's like Monica from *Friends*. Everything has to be perfect."

I scratched my jaw. It made sense but it still didn't mean I had to like it. "You're probably right." I wished I could see her even just for a second. I wanted to thank her for the party. I wanted to hold her, kiss her. I was damn near vibrating out of my skin with need for her. There were several private rooms at this club that I could drag her off to for a little party of our own. But I had a feeling that Gigi wouldn't overly mind if I just slipped my hand between her legs while she carried on a conversation with someone else. I imagined my fingers lightly touching her hot flesh. Her breath would catch, her words would falter, and I would grin like the lovestruck fool that I was. My girl was a freak and I couldn't wait to explore that side of her.

"He has it bad."

I was snapped out of my little fantasy, finding both Luna and Zach staring at me.

She laughed, hooking a hand around Zach's arm. "He does."

Zach grinned.

I huffed. "I'm fine. I just need to see Gigi."

"If I see her, I'll let her know that you're looking for her," Luna told me.

"Thank you," I muttered. "How are you doing? How's Benjamin?"

"He's good. Growing way too quickly." Luna laughed.

Zach looked down at her. "Yeah, everything's good."

The hackles on the back of my neck rose. "Did something happen?"

"It's nothing." Luna shook her head, rolling her eyes. "I got some stupid crank phone calls that are bothering

Zach a bit more than they should." She patted his arm. "But it's fine. Nothing happened."

"No one crank calls people anymore, Moonbeam. You get spam and shit on Facebook." Zach shook his head. "It doesn't matter. It's just fucking with me."

"Don't tell Dad," I warned. "He'd blow up the interwebs before you could even think about getting another phone."

"I know." Luna grabbed Zach's hand. "I'm fine."

"Well I'll leave you two to deal with this." I chuckled, giving my sister a hug. "I need a beer." I didn't but since I couldn't find Gigi, I went to the bar to grab another drink anyway. Might as well enjoy myself.

Several people came up to me for the next half hour or so. They wished me a happy birthday, said how much fun they were having, and how they had never been to a party like this one. Some even said they had never been to a strip club before.

I thanked them and made the appropriate comment, but there was still no sign of Gigi. Anywhere. Did I scare her off? Had I been too rough the night before? Did I read into things wrong and she didn't want to explore this further with me?

I slumped my ass on a nearby stool and downed my beer but even that left a sour taste in my mouth.

"Son."

My head whipped around.

My mom and dad came toward me. The sight of them walking hand in hand made me look away. Their love never used to bother me before but when I had a girl who was closed up tighter than a nun's—

"Vince." Mom's gentle voice pulled me from the stool and right into her arms. "Hey." She hugged me, giving me that special hug that only moms could give. "What's wrong, sweet boy?"

Before I could answer her, something caught my eye.

Gigi was talking to Ashton and Aiden. She laughed every so often, the sound hitting me square in the dick, but as hard as it made me, it pissed me off more that she had been ignoring me all night.

"Vince." Mom leaned back. "You good?"

"I'll be back." I kissed her cheek and pushed away from her. My feet took me out of the large room and toward Gigi.

Ashton looked my way first. He raised an eyebrow, a slow grin spreading on his face.

I stomped toward the woman I had spent the night and morning with, wondering why the hell she had been avoiding me for the past couple of hours.

Gigi's head turned in my direction, her eyes widening.

Yeah, beautiful. I see you. I caught you. And I'm going to make you pay for disappearing on me.

As I was about to catch up to her, my best friends blocked my path.

Rory Jaxon and Mason Houle, guys I had grown up with, were mouthing shit that I couldn't focus on.

"Move," I finally heard myself say.

Rory's girlfriend, Tenise Webber, joined our little huddle.

"Did you see the stripper Ashton got for you?" Mason asked, his brows waggling. "She's hot as fuck."

"Don't care." I went to push between them when Rory stopped me.

"What's your deal, Vince?" He cupped my shoulders, spinning me around. "We need to do a shot."

"No." I tried shoving away from him. I loved him but right now, he was pissing me off. "I need—"

"Vin." Tenise took that moment to step in front of me. "What's wrong? It's your birthday. You're supposed to be having fun and right now, it looks like you're on a rampage." She looked at Mason. "Let him go."

Mason shifted behind me. "But—"

"Seriously." She stomped past me and pushed Mason back. For someone who was tiny, she had some strength behind her.

"Thank you," I told her.

She gave me a small smile, something flashing in her eyes.

My stomach twisted, unsure as to what that was about but at the moment, I didn't care. "Listen, I'll be back later. I just need to go find someone." I hooked an arm around Mason's shoulders and stretched my other arm out.

Rory sighed but came toward us.

Wrapping my arms around both of them, the three of us shared a hug.

"You're doing a shot with us, fucker. And an extra shot for being an ass," Mason mumbled.

"Yeah, yeah." I released them and punched Mason in the shoulder. "I'll see you in a bit. Go mingle. Have fun." I rushed off before they could stop me again but not before I caught that same look in Tenise's eyes. Something was going on, but I had no idea what it was. Either way, I was sure I would find out whether I wanted to or not.

TWELVE

Gigi

I HADN'T SEEN VINCE all evening. Not because I hadn't tried but every time I attempted to go up to him, someone or something called me away. It was getting old and fast.

"Gigi."

I let out a soft sigh when a warm body stepped up behind me.

"You're a hard person to find." Gentle fingers pushed the hair off my nape. "Have you been avoiding me?" A warm mouth pressed against my ear. "I think you have. Maybe I should punish you."

My core clenched at the thought. "I haven't been avoiding you."

Vince fisted my hair, tugging my head back.

My body burned at the rough hold he had on me. Under normal circumstances, I probably should have looked to see if anyone was watching this exchange, but this would never be normal, and I also didn't care who saw. What we had. What we shared. The things we did. The things we craved.

"Are you lying to me?" Vince asked, pushing me into a dark corner. But I knew that even he didn't care if someone saw us. No, because then that meant they would know that I belonged to him.

"I've been busy. You know how I get when I plan parties," I reminded him. It wasn't like this was my first party, but I was a perfectionist. I needed to make sure that everyone was having a good time and taken care of.

Once we reached the darkest corner, he released my hair and turned me around. Pinching my chin, he tilted my head and brushed his mouth over mine.

I sighed, snaking my arms around his neck.

"I just wanted this." His hands trailed down my sides, his fingers hitting the hem of my dress that fell just above my knees. It was classy but tight and red because that had been his favorite color. "You look beautiful tonight." He leaned his forehead against mine.

"Thank you. You look handsome." Hot as hell was more like it. He was wearing a navy-blue dress shirt tucked into black dress pants. The dark colors brought out the natural tan in his skin and made his chocolate brown eyes, pop.

"I have a confession."

Vince leaned back but kept his hand on my hip. I realized then that he always touched me, no matter who was around. Even if it was something small, his hand was still on me.

"I kind of wish I never planned this party," I murmured.

"I figured." His fingers brushed over my knee before sliding up my inner thigh. "I don't want that stripper."

My stomach sunk. I had forgotten about that. "It's tradition," I heard myself say.

He stared at me, his fingers dancing higher along my skin. "You want me to have some other woman dancing all over me, Gigi?"

My stomach twisted at the thought of another woman touching him. "No," I whispered.

Vince's fingers reached the crotch of my panties. "Tell me you want someone else dancing for me."

"The thought of another woman dancing for you, makes me want to commit murder." I hooked a leg around his waist and placed my hands on his chest, letting them roam down the length of his torso. In a quick move, I cupped him over his pants. "This is mine."

He smirked, placing a soft peck on my forehead and slipping a finger into my thong. "You bet your sweet ass it's yours." He slid his finger into me. "And remember who this cunt belongs to."

I grabbed onto his dress shirt, pulling him down to meet the impact of my mouth.

He groaned, sliding his tongue between my lips when he began pumping his hand between my legs. "Fucking hell, baby, you're soaked."

Circling my arms around his shoulders, I deepened the kiss, silencing his dirty words as I rocked my hips against his hand.

Before we could take it any further, our names were being called out.

Vince broke the kiss, giving me a lopsided grin. "We should make an appearance before people come looking for us." He pulled his hand from between my legs and brushed the finger that had just been inside my body, over my upper lip. The heady scent of my arousal made me lightheaded and ache for him more.

He smirked, lowering his mouth to mine and licking along my lip. "Hmm…fucking delicious."

A breathless laugh escaped me. "Such a tease."

"Until later, Queenie." He helped me smooth down my dress, adjusted himself, and held out his hand. "Don't disappear on me again, okay?"

I stood on tiptoes and kissed him softly on the mouth and took his hand. "Let's go mingle together."

"I like that idea."

I gave him a small smile.

"Actually, I want you to do something for me first." His hot breath sent a shiver down my spine. "Take off your panties."

Moving back to the dark corner, I reached under my dress and pulled my thong down my legs. Bunching it in my palm, I sidled up to Vince. "A present. For you," I said, stuffing the thin fabric into his pocket and making sure my fingers brushed along the length of his cock for added effect.

"Fuck me," he groaned.

I laughed, stepped away from him, and blew him a kiss.

"You're going to pay for that, babe."

"I look forward to it." I walked away from him, sashaying my hips. A newfound awareness rushed over me now that I wasn't wearing any panties.

As much as I enjoyed this little game Vince and I were playing, I really needed to talk to Ashton and cancel that stripper.

"Gigi." A warm mouth kissed the side of my neck.

I smiled up at Vince, wishing that we were alone. "I need to talk to Ashton."

Vince opened his mouth to argue when his friends came up to us. The guys had gone to a few of my parties with Vince. But I never met the woman who was currently eye-fucking the man who only just a minute ago, had his finger deep inside me.

The hackles on the back of my neck tingled as her eyes roamed down the length of him.

"Vin, are you having a good time?" she asked, her voice dripping with sweetness. She stepped up to him but still kept her hand locked in her boyfriend's grip. While he talked to another guy, this woman was staring at Vince like he was a piece of meat.

"I am," he told her. "Thank you for coming."

"Of course." She licked her full mouth, not giving a shit that it was *my* hand he was holding. "I wouldn't have missed this for the world."

I rolled my eyes. I needed to go find Ashton and cancel that stripper and also get away from this chick before I caused a scene and punched the shit out of her.

I went to pull away from Vince when his grip tightened. I caught his gaze.

"Where are you going?" he asked, his thumb brushing along the edge of my hand.

"I'm going to grab us drinks." The lie slipped from my lips before I could stop myself. Truth was, I wanted to go to Ashton, cancel the stripper and surprise Vince with a little dance of my own. I knew it wouldn't get very far but it didn't matter.

Vince raised an eyebrow, but he didn't argue with me. He only nodded and let me go.

As I searched the main part of the club, I half expected Ashton to be holed up in some corner with a woman. The guy liked to get around. I couldn't wait for the day that a woman told him no, just to see what his reaction would be.

After about fifteen minutes of looking for him, I finally saw him coming from the hallway. He was adjusting his shirt. He looked up, his eyes landing on me. He gave me a small wave when a woman came up from behind him. She gave him a wink and disappeared into the crowd of people.

"Really? You couldn't have waited?" I asked him.

He only smirked, popping the collar of his dress shirt. "Jealous?"

I snorted. "Ew."

Ashton stopped suddenly, the smile falling from his face. "Ew?"

I laughed, patting his chest. "I'm sure you're amazing but you don't do it for me. And you're like a brother to me."

"Trust me, babe. I do it for everyone. Just ask your sister." When he went to walk past me, I grabbed his arm.

"Don't be a dick." I released his arm, dropping my hand to my side. "I need you to cancel the stripper."

"That's a good one," Ashton said while checking his phone.

"I'm not kidding," I told him.

His head snapped up, his sapphire eyes landing on mine. "You're serious, aren't you?"

"Of course, I'm serious. Why wouldn't I be?" I lifted my chin, not backing down.

"Why?"

"Why what?" I scowled. "Just cancel her. Please."

"And why the hell would I do that? That shit cost me a lot of cake, Gigi. I'm not canceling her." He went to walk away when I grabbed his arm again.

"How much?" I was desperate and was willing to pay anything.

"Gigi." He shook me off and took another step away when I rushed in front of him. "What gives, woman? You know Vince gets a stripper for his twenty-first birthday. It's tradition. We all got one and he's the last one of us guys to turn twenty-one."

"Yeah, I know. And he *will* have a stripper. But not the one you ordered for him."

Ashton frowned. "I don't know what you mean. Who's going to strip for him then if I cancel the stripper?"

"Me." I crossed my arms under my chest. "I'm going to strip for him."

Ashton laughed, bending over at the waist, his laughter booming through him the longer time wore on. When he calmed down, he wiped under his eyes. "You can't be serious."

"What if I am?" I huffed. "You know I can dance."

"You do ballet," he pointed out. "That's far from stripping, Gigi."

"No, I *did* ballet. But now I actually dance everything. And all of these girls who work here? Who do you think taught them to move like they do?" I hadn't danced ballet since my accident, but no one knew that. Not even my parents. "Please, Ashton. I don't ask you for much. Do this for me and I'll owe you."

"Gigi." He shook his head. "One, I can't get over the fact you just told me you teach strippers how to dance and two, Vince will cut off my balls if I make this happen."

"He won't know anything. It'll all be me." He could punish me all he wanted. My body burned at the idea of him fucking me while he was angry.

"Whatever you two have…" Something flashed in Ashton's deep blue eyes. "Anyway, it doesn't matter. I love you both, but I can't do that."

"Yes, you can. I don't want another woman dancing for him." The mere idea of another female touching Vince made me want to throw up. "It can't happen."

Ashton searched my face.

"Please," I pleaded, needing him to see that I meant what I said.

"I still can't cancel her." He paused, scratching the scruff on his jaw. "She cost five hundred. That's a lot of money wasted if I cancel her. There's no refunds, babe."

I reached into my purse and pulled out my wallet. Counting the bills, I grabbed five of them and shoved them against Ashton's chest. "Five hundred. Take it." I didn't normally carry that kind of money around in my purse, but I had just been paid by Candace, so I didn't mind giving it to Ashton. Especially if it prevented the stripper from getting anywhere near Vince.

"What?" Ashton's eyes widened. "I can't take this shit," he said, trying to hand me back the money.

"Yes." I swatted his hand away. "You can. Keep the stripper and do whatever you want with her but she's not dancing for Vince. I am. And I don't care what you do with the money. But she better not get anywhere near him."

"What's in this for you?" Ashton asked, hesitating, but eventually taking the money and shoving it into his pocket.

"Everything." I spun on my heel and rushed down the hall that led to the large room where the girls got ready.

"Gigi."

I stopped suddenly, spinning on my heel and found my best friends coming toward me.

"We saw you head this way," Luna said. "Is everything okay?"

"Yes. Actually, it's better now. You girls can help me." I stopped in front of the dressing room just as the door opened.

Corbin Wane jumped, his chocolate brown eyes moving back and forth. "Gigi, sweetheart. Just making sure the room is good to go for you."

"Thank you but how did you know I was ready to use it?" I asked him, my heart warming at the thoughtful gesture.

He smiled and tapped his temple. "I know everything that goes on in this club before and after it happens." He winked. "Don't ever forget that."

I laughed, standing on tiptoes and kissing his cheek. "Thank you."

"Always." He stepped to the side so we could enter the large room. "I'll go keep your man occupied." And with that, he headed out into the hall and closed the door behind him.

"Who was that?" Meadow asked, sitting in a nearby plush chair.

"Corbin Wane. He's been a bouncer here for as long as the club has been opened," I explained, stepping in front of a floor-length mirror.

"He's handsome," Luna added, running her hand down a purple feather boa.

"He is but unfortunately, no one here would ever do it for him." I laughed.

"What do you mean?" Piper asked softly.

"Uh…apparently he has a sexual appetite that goes beyond these walls." I shrugged. "I don't know. That's the rumor and that's what he's told me time and time again. But he sure does love hitting on the men." I laughed to myself, remembering when Corbin hit on one of the Hell's Harlem club members when they had stopped by.

"Interesting." Meadow tapped her chin.

"You're married," I reminded her.

She huffed. "I know that, but a girl can imagine things."

We all laughed.

"Listen, I need help with what I should wear. I got Ashton to cancel the stripper for Vince," I explained like it was no big deal, when really, it was a very big deal.

"Are you two finally getting your heads out of your asses?" Luna asked, holding up a G-String. She raised an eyebrow, shook her head, and dropped it back on a nearby table.

"What we're doing is fun. He's fun. I just…" I didn't want to have this conversation with them. Even though they were my best friends, Vince deserved to hear how I felt first and foremost.

"You want to talk to him first," Piper finished for me, handing me a short black skirt.

"Is it bad that I just want us to keep having fun and not actually talk about our feelings?" Now I was starting to sound like Ashton.

"Now you sound like Ashton," Meadow said, taking the thought right out of my head.

Piper nodded. "It's true."

"You can have all the fun you want," Luna told me. "But just make sure that you're only having fun with him."

"Trust me, there's no one else in the picture." The thought never even crossed my mind. "I know about Vince and his possessive ways."

"I don't think you do." Luna looked between all of us. "What? I'm serious. Gigi may have never seen it in action but I sure as hell have. How many guys have you heard ask us if she's single only for them to disappear?"

My eyes widened.

"She's being dramatic." Piper came up to my side. "What your future sister in-law is trying to say is that Vince has overheard guys asking us if you were single and he stopped it from going further than that."

"That's not much better than what Luna just said." I wasn't sure if I should be pissed or flattered.

"Yes, it is." Meadow winked. "Besides, it's hot as hell."

"You'd probably think fucking a pineapple would be hot." I turned away from them and started rummaging through a pile of clothes that I could possibly wear for my little dance.

"Probably," she said just as the door opened.

All of our heads whipped around, finding Vince leaning against the doorframe. “You know the party’s not in here, right?”

“Did you see Corbin?” I asked, ignoring his question.

“I did. First time meeting the guy and he told me that we’re now best friends.” Vince chuckled, shaking his head.

“What’s this I hear that you stopped guys from asking me out?” I asked, casually picking up ripped fishnet stockings.

“On that note, we should go.” Piper rounded up the girls, heading to the door.

“Careful with her,” Meadow murmured, patting his arm. “She’s a firecracker.”

He didn’t say anything but came farther into the room before kicking the door closed. “I happen to agree with your sister.”

“What do you want? Shouldn’t you be mingling?” I turned away from him and reached for the pile of clothes when a dark shadow loomed over me.

“What’s going on?” Vince asked gently, covering my hand and slipping his fingers between mine.

“You stopped guys from asking me out.” I met his intense stare. “Didn’t you?”

“Not exactly.”

Crossing my arms under my chest, I leaned against the table and stared up at him. “Then tell me what happened.” I had always wondered why guys flirted but it had never amounted to anything more than that.

“I overheard the girls talking about some guys wanting to ask you out. Random fuckers who went to your parties and shit.” Vince pinched my chin, brushing his thumb over my bottom lip. “The thought of another man taking you out, wining and dining you, possibly even kissing you or more, made me want to burn the mother fucking world down. But I never stopped it. I just spread some rumors."

"What kind of rumors?" I ran my hand down his dress shirt, remembering that I had stuffed my panties into his pocket.

"I had it spread that you had a boyfriend who had family in the yakuza."

I opened my mouth to say something but thought better of it. "Oh."

Vince gave me a small smile. "I like you, Gigi. I've always liked you. I wasn't going to let someone else ruin you before I got a chance to."

"So romantic." I tried pushing him back when he grabbed my hips in a rough move.

"It is romantic." He leaned down to my ear, giving it a gentle nip. "Can I ask what you're doing in here?"

A breathless laugh escaped me. "I was waiting for you."

His head snapped up. "Really?"

"No." I patted his chest. "I was getting changed."

"For what?"

I turned around. "You'll see."

"Queenie." He cupped my nape, pulling me back against him. "Fuck, I just want to take you out of here."

"And do what?" My skin burned at the rough hold he had on me.

"Every nasty dirty thing imaginable."

My stomach tumbled. "Well…" I pushed out of his hold, grabbed the clothes I would wear for the dance, and stepped away from him before he could grab me again. "I guess you'll have to show me later what you're wanting to do."

"Gigi," he groaned, his dark eyes roaming down the length of me.

"Trust me, baby. I think you'll like my present." Or punish me for it. Either way, one of us was going to enjoy it at the very least.

"Oh?" Vince raised an eyebrow. "Can I have a hint?"

"Nope." I rushed into one of the dressing rooms and locked the door before Vince could do what we both wanted him to do.

"Gigi, you're being a damn tease," he said, wiggling the doorknob.

"You really don't like surprises. Do you?" He needed to leave or else we would never get on with our night.

"Let me see what you're changing into at least."

"Ha. No. Go have fun. I'll be out soon." As soon as those words left my mouth, a voice called out. I couldn't hear what they were saying but the voice sounded high. For whatever reason, the hairs on the back of my neck tingled, along with my stomach clenching with unease. I didn't like this feeling. This jealousy. This need to keep Vince close by and not let anyone else near him. It was possessive and unnecessary.

"Fine, but Gigi?"

I shivered at the deep baritone of Vince's voice. "Yes?"

"I'll make you regret not letting me in there."

Before I could think on it, I unlocked the door and opened it.

Vince grinned, coming into the dressing room. "You didn't want to see what my threat consisted of?" Instead of waiting for me to answer, he crushed his mouth to mine.

Ten minutes later, he had me screaming his name.

He chuckled, sinking his teeth into the side of my throat. "Good thing there's music playing."

"God." I shivered. "I don't even care."

A wicked grin spread on his face. "We'll see about that."

Almost a half hour later and Vince was doing up his pants, while I was slipping back into my dress. His cum dripped out of me, causing a shiver to ripple down my spine.

"Thank you for the birthday present." He winked.

I laughed, shaking my head. "Now you have to leave, so I can get ready."

He smirked. Coming toward me, he pinched my chin and placed a soft peck on my forehead. "Don't clean yourself up," he murmured, brushing his nose over the tip of mine.

The move had been so gentle, it caused an ache in my chest. "I won't."

"Good girl." He kissed me one last time and left the dressing room.

"Vince, where the hell have you been?" I heard his friend ask.

"I was opening my birthday present," Vince told him.

I smiled, my cheeks heating.

I knew that the stripper would come out as soon as our parents left. Good thing too because I didn't want my father seeing me grinding against Vince. God, I couldn't believe I was going to do this. I was going to dance for him. It reiterated the fact that no one else should be touching him. It wasn't like he hadn't felt the same way when it came to guys and me. Hell, he stopped them from asking me out. Even if it was indirectly, he still stopped it.

My feelings for him scared me. But tonight, all I wanted was sex. Nothing more. Nothing less. After the last couple of weeks together and then waking up next to him this morning, it was almost like it was meant to be. No, it *was* meant to be. Maybe everyone was right, and we did have our heads up our asses. Or it was me who did anyway. Vince seemed to know what he wanted even though he never came out and said it.

By the time I finished getting ready, even though I had no help from the girls like I had hoped, I gave myself a once-over in the mirror. It would have to do. It wasn't like the outfit was going to stay on long anyway.

I adjusted the red bra beneath the white ripped tank top and made sure the plaid short skirt was centered before I slipped into the sky-high heels.

Remembering the rough way Vince had taken what he wanted from me not too long ago, I couldn't help but smile. I was thankful that he didn't care where we were. As long as he could get what he wanted and give me the same in return, he was happy.

The outfit left little to the imagination and I knew that Vince wasn't going to like that part. Not unless he had something do with it. I learned rather quickly that he liked being in control. But tonight, it was my turn. At least for a little bit. Maybe a few minutes. Probably even shorter than that. Even though I was going to be wearing a mask, as soon as he saw the pendant between my breasts, he would know.

Giving myself a final once-over in the mirror, I took a deep breath and headed to the door just as it slammed open with a bang.

I jumped back.

Corbin appeared in the doorway, his eyes raking over me. "Good, you're ready. Your man is ready to lose his shit that his friends are blocking him from getting back to you."

My eyes widened. "I just saw him a few minutes ago."

"Sweetheart." Corbin smiled. "It's been a half hour."

"Oh." A nervous laugh left me. "I must have been stuck in my head."

"No." He cupped my shoulders, guiding me out of the room. "You're in love. Big difference. Now go get him. I'll leave this room unlocked for…" He waggled his eyebrows. "You know."

I giggled, slipping the mask down onto my face. "Thank you."

"For you?" His grin grew. "Anything." He started backing up. "We still have that date?"

"Yes. Next Friday, I am all yours."

He beamed. "Good. Have fun," he sang and disappeared down the hallway.

Thankful for Corbin's gentle but sassy personality, it helped ease some of the nerves racing around in my stomach.

Once I reached the end of the hallway, the music switched to something slower. It was sensual but held a beat that I felt down to the marrow of my bones.

From where I was standing, I could see out onto the dance floor.

Vince was sitting on a chair with his arms crossed under his chest. A deep scowl was set on his face. Oh God, did he think he was getting the stripper? Maybe that was why he looked pissed. I wasn't sure. Looked like I needed to move this along and fast.

I took a step forward just as Vince stood.

His friends rushed to him and pushed him back on the chair.

I could tell even from where I was standing that Vince was enraged. He looked around him and went to stand when Luna came out onto the dance floor and stopped him. Whatever she told him, relaxed him a bit. Thank goodness for that. I didn't want my surprise to piss him off, but I knew that Ashton wouldn't have gone without him having a stripper tonight. This was the only way for it to happen because I refused to watch another woman dance all over him.

Stepping out onto the dance floor, I adjusted the red mask that completely covered my face. I knew that once Vince found out it was me; he was going to lose his shit. I didn't have a lot to take off. I was also ready to go all the way, but I knew it wouldn't happen. He would find out it was me before I even got a chance to take off my top. Especially when he saw my necklace.

When the music switched to a different song, I made my way out onto the dance floor. I stopped in Vince's direct line of sight. His head lifted, his brows narrowing in the middle. Our eyes locked. His jaw ticked but then, much to my surprise, he grinned.

Sitting back in the chair, he scratched his jaw and waited.

My stomach tumbled. He knew. How the hell did he know that it was me already?

Giving myself a shake, I ignored the question and did what I did best.

I had never been an overly confident person. I was skinny. Too skinny at times. But when the music played and my hips moved, it was like the beat took over and my body became possessed.

Stalking toward Vince, I stepped between his spread knees and turned, bent over, and gave him a full view of my ass. I wasn't wearing anything beneath my skirt, but the move had been so quick, I knew that he would be the only one who saw that part of me. Not that it mattered. Anyone could see me, and he wouldn't care. No, because he knew it would be him I would be spending the night with.

Straddling his lap, I grinded against him, and felt every inch of him harden beneath me.

Vince dropped his hands to the sides of the chair, gripping the edges like it took everything in him not to grab me and drag me out of there.

He would.

I was counting on it.

Whistles and hollers sounded around us but I ignored them and focused solely on the man beneath me.

THIRTEEN

VINCE

I KNEW THE STRIPPER was Gigi. I wasn't sure if she knew that or not but it didn't matter. Every male instinct in me wanted to make her pay for dancing the way she was, in front of our friends. But then the other part of me, the dominant part, the part that enjoyed voyeurism, didn't care. Because I knew that I was the one she was going to go home with. I was the one who had fucked her good and hard in the change room not too long ago. And I was the one whose bite marks were currently spread out on her inner thighs. So I played it cool. For the moment anyway.

While she grinded against me and started unbuttoning her shirt, that was when I'd had enough. I grabbed the necklace that was around her throat, *my* necklace, and pulled her toward me.

She gasped, the dancing stopped.

"I will give you two seconds to get your ass to that change room, Gigi," I said loud enough in her ear so that she could hear me over the music, but not too loud that people nearby could listen in. "I know you want to be watched but I don't think you want our friends seeing you getting violently fucked."

Her throat worked over a hard swallow. "I have no idea what you're talking about." She went to struggle against me when I fisted the chain and gripped it tight.

"One second," I growled in her ear.

Gigi jumped off of my lap and rushed toward the hall that led to the change room.

When the music switched to another song, I took a deep breath and stood from the chair.

"Vince."

I looked at Ashton over my shoulder. "Keep the party going," I told him, stalking toward my prey.

He nodded once. "On it."

Sauntering to the hall, I took my time knowing it would build up the anticipation of what was to come. I enjoyed making Gigi wait. I also loved it even more when she couldn't control herself and ended up begging for it. For *me*.

As soon as I rounded the corner, I saw Gigi heading down the hall to the change room. She stopped suddenly, looking at me over her shoulder. "Miss me?"

I grinned, catching up to her. Before she could get away, I caught her around the waist and crushed her against me. "You have no idea, baby. No idea at fucking all."

When her breath caught in her throat, my grin grew. I ripped the mask off her head and cupped her jaw. The mask slipped from my fingers, dropping to the floor at our feet.

Gigi grabbed onto the waist of my pants, pulling me closer.

I was vaguely aware of the sounds going on around us. Music continued from the party and people milled about, but all I could focus on was the woman in my arms.

Pushing her back until she hit the wall, I closed the distance between us and pressed my pelvis into hers.

She sighed, tilting her head back.

With a firm grip on her jaw, I pulled her toward me until our mouths met in the middle.

My cock was hard between us. Knowing how much I wanted her. How much I craved every inch of her. I couldn't help but tease us both. It took everything in me not to shove her up against the wall and dive into her wet heat. I would, but not yet. I wanted to play. I wanted to see just how far she was willing to go before she embraced that kinky side of her. I didn't know all of her desires, but I made a vow to myself that I would. Eventually. We would learn together. What we liked. What we didn't like. And I would take full advantage of the fact that my girl liked to fuck dirty.

Much to my surprise, Gigi started unbuckling my belt.

Digging my fingers into her jaw, I deepened the kiss.

In a quick move, I had her shoved up against the wall and my pants undone. Cupping the back of her thigh, I wrapped her leg around my waist and ground into her. I swallowed her moans and cries of pleasure.

Reaching between us, I pulled my aching cock out and thrust into her.

Gigi gasped, arching against me.

A deep chuckle sounded from somewhere. Maybe from the end of the hall. Maybe it was someone we knew, but it didn't matter because all I could focus on was how Gigi's pussy gushed when we were caught.

"Vince," she whined, rocking her hips against me. "We have an audience."

"Don't care," I growled, deepening the kiss and pumping into her in rough smooth moves. Reaching behind her, I fumbled for the doorknob but finally pushed it open. We stumbled into the change room.

"God." She broke the kiss. "There are cameras in here."

"Don't care about that either." I bit the side of her throat, thrusting into her hard and deep.

"I…" She shook against me, trembling with the need to come.

Fisting her hair, I stared down into her eyes and slowed my hips. "This is yours. All of me. And you are mine. My cock owns your cunt. Don't ever fucking forget it."

Gigi grabbed onto my shirt. "Never."

(Gigi)

"Are you mad that I stripped for you?"

Vince pinched my chin, tilting my head back. "No. Because you didn't actually strip. Not completely anyway."

I stared up at him. "I'm surprised you let it get as far as you did."

He smirked. "I know you like being watched but I can only assume that you would prefer for it to be in front of strangers and not our friends."

My cheeks heated. Looking away, I continued getting dressed. "I don't know what you're talking about."

"No?" He cupped my shoulders, placing a soft peck on the side of my neck. "Then tell me why your pussy became soaked when we were caught."

"It's weird. I shouldn't like it," I confessed, slipping the dress up and over my head.

Vince helped me lower it down my body. "Why does it matter what you like?"

"Because…" I huffed. "It's weird."

"No. It's not." He turned me toward him. "Look at me."

But I wouldn't meet his gaze.

"Gigi."

"What?" I went to pull away from him when he enveloped me in his arms. "Vince."

"What you like, your kinks, your desires, it's all natural." He cupped my chin, kissing me softly on the mouth. "It's not like you're into some sick shit anyway. So, you like being watched. Who gives a fuck?"

"You don't judge me?"

"Nah, baby." He kissed my nose. "I'm sure lots of guys don't want to show off that part of their woman but that's not me because I know that while I'm fucking you, while I'm balls deep inside of you, it's only us. Doesn't matter if other people are watching because it's just you and me, babe. No one else can touch you. No one else can touch me. It's *just us*."

A shuddered breath left me. His words helped but I wasn't sure if they were enough. "My sister calls me a prude."

"You are *not* a prude." Vince brushed his thumb over my bottom lip. "You just never had anyone to explore your desires with. Until me."

"Thank you." I stood on tiptoes and kissed him softly. "We should go back out and enjoy the rest of your party."

"We should but I'm rather enjoying this."

I laughed, stepping out of his embrace and leaving the change room. "We can continue later."

"Get ready, Queenie." He came up behind me and wrapped his arms around my middle. "We're going to go all night. I hope you're prepared to fucking hurt tomorrow."

I shivered at the thought. "I look forward to it."

Once we left the change room, we were met with his friends.

"We never officially met. I'm Mason." Vince's friend stuck his hand out, giving me a wide toothy smile.

"You've been to a few of my parties but it's nice to officially meet you." I returned the handshake. "I'm Gigi."

"It's nice to meet you too." He brought my hand up to his mouth, placing a soft peck on the back of it. "I don't remember much of those parties, but I do remember always waking up with a hangover the next day."

I laughed. "Yeah, they were fun."

Mason winked, keeping my hand in his.

"Alright, that's enough." Vince gently shoved him away.

Mason chuckled.

"Ignore him. We've met before but in case you forgot, I'm Rory, and this is my girlfriend, Tenise." Rory smiled down at me. His girlfriend latched on to Vince, pulling him away.

"Let's go do a shot," she said, giving him a wide smile.

Vince looked back at me as he was being dragged away and only shrugged.

Rory laughed and went to join them while Mason stood back with me.

"You want to join us?" he asked me.

"No. Thank you. I should go." And do what, I wasn't sure. It wasn't like I had to make sure people were having a good time or anything. The party was at a strip club and the drinks were cheap. You couldn't get much better than that. "I need to make a phone call." Before Mason could question me, I went back down the hall Vince and I had just come from, and checked my phone. I had a few text messages from clients, a couple of emails from my students' parents but nothing that was out of the ordinary. Truth was, I didn't like the fact that Tenise stole Vince from me. It was innocent. I knew that but something about the situation didn't sit well with me.

While Vince mingled with friends, I spent the rest of the night making sure no one trashed the place. I appreciated the owners letting me rent out the club and that they never charged me for it, but it didn't mean I wanted to leave them with a mess of any kind.

"Do you ever stop working?"

I turned, finding two women coming toward me.

Shawnee Drake and Emma Morin both grinned wide smiles at me.

I laughed, holding my arms out. "It's good to see you girls."

"Good to see you too." Shawnee reached me first, giving me a hug. She pulled away just as Emma pulled me into her arms.

She sighed, petting my head. "If only you liked pussy."

I laughed harder. "You'd be the first I'd call."

She pulled away from me, keeping her hands on my shoulders. "Something's wrong."

I hesitated, looking between her and Shawnee. "No. Why would you say that?"

Shawnee placed her elbow on Emma's shoulder. "She's been playing with her tarot deck again."

"Did they tell you anything decent?" I asked Emma. Not that I believed in that sort of thing, but I still found I was curious just the same.

"They said that I'll find happiness." Her smile widened. "And I have. With my girls." She hooked her arm around Shawnee's shoulders, pulling her closer and kissing her cheek.

All of us laughed.

The hairs on the back of my neck suddenly tingled. I looked over my shoulder, finding Vince standing at the bar, looking my way. He tipped his beer toward me, giving me a nod.

My stomach fluttered. I blew him a kiss.

He grinned.

"Oh is that him?" Emma asked. "He's cute. Not that men do it for me, but he really is."

"He's sweet and nice too," I told her. "Which helps."

Shawnee scoffed. "No fucking kidding. Men these days want one thing and one thing only. Just because I dance and take off my clothes for a living, doesn't mean shit. It does not mean that I'm easy."

"Alright, sweetheart." Emma grabbed her hand, patting the top of it. "Take a deep breath."

Shawnee inhaled, letting it out slowly.

"Better?" Emma raised an eyebrow.

"Yeah." Shawnee scowled. "Just annoying."

"I get that," I told them. Just then, I saw Vince approaching us. The closer he got, the harder my heart raced.

"Hello, ladies." He smiled as he neared us.

"Hello there, handsome." Shawnee waggled her eyebrows.

Vince chuckled, coming to my side and sliding his fingers in mine, then kissed my cheek. "Hi," he whispered.

"Hi." I stepped into his side, a sense of relief washing over me just from his mere touch.

Shawnee pulled a lipstick tube from her back pocket. It was a deep blood red. The only makeup she ever wore outside of when she performed. With her face bare, her dark freckles showed. The men loved them, so she always used it to her advantage. When she finished applying her lipstick, she stuck out her hand. "Shawnee but the boys call me Amethyst."

"And I'm Emma." Emma gave me a wink. "Men don't call me, but the ladies do, and they call me over and over and over and over—"

Shawnee gently shoved her.

"And over," Emma added.

"We get it." I laughed.

"Nice to meet you." Vince chuckled, returning Shawnee's handshake. "And I'm Vince."

"Oh, we know." Shawnee grinned. "Your girl has told us all about you."

"She has, has she?" He looked down at me, smirking.

I rolled my eyes. "She's lying. She's bored, so she likes to make up stuff."

Shawnee pouted. "I do not. Maybe I can go play with that slut of a friend you've told me about."

Vince frowned. "Ashton?"

I coughed. "Uh…I never called him a slut but yeah, that's who she's talking about."

Vince chuckled. "He gets around. Hasn't found his person I guess."

I snorted. "I don't think he'll ever find his person."

"Fine with me." Shawnee pulled the elastic from her long blonde hair and shook out the tresses until they fell in waves around her shoulders. "I don't want a relationship anyway. Which one is he again?"

"He's probably standing with another guy who looks like him," I told her as she walked away. "They're twins."

Shawnee grinned, giving us a wink. "Even better."

Emma shook her head. "I'm going to go call Amber and Penelope. See if they want to get together for drinks. Apparently Amber is having some problems with some biker. Who knows? You guys want to join us?"

I looked up at Vince.

"I'll do whatever." He leaned down to my ear. "But I'd rather do you, Queenie."

I shivered, my cheeks heating. "I think we'll pass," I told her.

She laughed. "Sure. Choose cock over your friends. I get it." She closed the distance between us and pulled me into her arms. "He breaks your heart; I'll chop off his dick and feed it to my cat. You hear me?"

"I hear you." I returned the embrace. "Thank you."

"Any time." She released me, gave Vince a look, and headed down the hall toward the bar.

"You have some interesting friends," he said with a grin.

"You mean besides your sister, my sister, and Piper?" I laughed.

"Yeah." He kissed my temple. "They good to you?"

"They are. I'm actually teaching them a routine." I was proud of that little fact.

"Really? And how are you doing that?" Vince asked, his voice coming out rougher than I had ever heard before. Especially with me.

I crossed my arms under my chest, staring up at him. "Problem?"

"I…" He pulled me closer. "No. No problem. As long as you keep your clothes on."

"Don't worry, baby." I stood on tiptoes and kissed his cheek. "You are the only one I take my clothes off for."

(Vince)

I didn't see Gigi for the rest of the night. I did catch her cleaning every so often or picking up after people. She would sometimes throw her head back and laugh at whatever was said to her when she stopped to speak with someone. But other than that, she kept her distance. I was sure it was so I could mingle, hang with my friends and so on, but as much as I loved them, I needed Gigi more.

She would look my way every now and again. I would stand up taller and she would wave. Every time a guy stopped to talk to her, it took everything I was made of not to storm over and punch the shit out of him.

"Vin, you look sad." Tenise came up to me and sat on the barstool beside me. She turned toward me, her knee brushing against mine.

I adjusted myself on the stool, trying to move away as best I could without having to sit on another stool but that only seemed to make her inch closer. "I'm fine," I told her.

"Are you enjoying yourself?"

"I am." I finished off my beer and signaled the waiter. "Can I just get a water please?"

He nodded and came back with a bottle of water.

"Thank you." I twisted off the cap and finished off half the bottle before placing it on the bar top.

"Water?" Tenise raised an eyebrow. "Really?"

"Why not?"

"It's your twenty-first birthday, Vin." She took a sip of her red drink. I assumed it was some fruity concoction. Maybe cranberry juice and vodka. I had seen her drink that a time or two at the parties Rory threw every now and again.

"So? I don't want to be hungover tomorrow," I explained, which I wasn't sure why I had to. I had always liked Tenise for Rory but lately, she was getting too close. It was just little things and I was sure it was innocent, but he was my best friend and that came first.

"We need to make a promise to each other," Mason said, taking a sip of his beer.

"What's that?" I moved to the empty spot beside him on the couch.

"We need to promise that we won't let a girl get in the way of our friendship," he said as Rory came into the living room.

"I agree." Rory slumped onto the chair beside the couch. "Unless it's your mom though."

My head whipped around. "Dude, that's my fucking mom."

"Yeah and she's hot as hell." Rory shrugged. "You know it's true," he said, looking at Mason.

"I'm not saying shit." Mason went back to drinking his beer.

"Leave my mom out of this but yes, I agree. No woman can come between us. Ever." I shook my head, still not impressed that Rory thought my mom was hot.

"Deal." Rory clinked his beer bottle against mine. "What about your sister?"

"Fuck off, asshat," I snapped but I couldn't help but laugh.

That conversation had been so long ago, I'd almost forgotten about it. But I definitely hadn't forgotten about our pact.

"So you and that girl."

My eyes flicked to Tenise. I had forgotten she was still sitting beside me after being stuck in my own head.

"I—" Something out of the corner of my eye caught my attention. A man was hugging Gigi. Before I knew what I was doing, I was off the stool and stomping toward her.

My name was called but I couldn't focus on anything other than finding out who the fuck was hugging my girl.

As I zeroed in on them, Gigi shoved the man back, a deep frown set between her brows. A breath of relief left me, but it still didn't mean that I didn't want his blood.

She stiffened, slowly turning my way. Something flashed behind her eyes when she saw me heading toward her.

The man looked my way, his gaze burning into me, but I kept my sight on Gigi.

"Hey, what are you doing?" he demanded but I walked right past him.

Closing the distance between Gigi and I, I cupped her cheek and crushed my mouth to hers.

She gasped, melting into me.

Slipping my tongue between her lips, the kiss went past being considered appropriate. Especially in public. But I knew that she liked being watched, so I was willing to give her that excitement and also fulfill every single fantasy she ever had.

I was vaguely aware of the cheers and hollers going on around us.

"Vince," she whispered, breaking the kiss.

"Remember who you belong to," I told her, brushing my thumb along her swollen mouth. Releasing her, I didn't wait for a response and walked away with a smug smile on my face.

FOURTEEN

Gigi

After Vince claimed me in front of everyone with a mere kiss, I didn't see him for the rest of the party. When I was cleaning up and most of the people who had attended started to leave, I got a text.

Vince: I'm home.

When I went to respond, another text came through showing an image of him wearing gray sweatpants and nothing else. It left little to the imagination as I saw the outline of his very thick cock behind the fabric.

I shivered, my center clenching with anticipation.

Me: I'm on my way.

I could almost hear him chuckle. He could probably sense the desperation even though we were no longer at the same location. I had no idea that he had left already but I wasn't surprised either. He didn't like parties. The only reason I had thrown him one was to be fair, since everyone else had one for their twenty-first.

"Gigi, thank you for the party."

"It was fucking epic."

"Want to plan mine?"

I smiled, laughed and waved but didn't stop for anyone. Even when my name was called. Even when my phone buzzed and rang. I had one mission and that was to go to Vince's apartment and spend the night with him. It was the only thing that mattered at the moment.

When I pulled up in front of Vince's place, I realized then that I had never been there before. He had moved in before he left for school and his friends stayed in it while he was away. Now that he was home, they no longer lived with him.

Taking a deep breath, I put my car in park, killed the engine, and left the vehicle before I could change my mind.

I shouldn't be here.

We should talk.

It can't be all about sex.

I knew that but I couldn't help myself. Sex with Vince was nothing like I ever thought it would be. It only got better and better. We learned things about each other. Took each other past that brink of sanity and jumped into a pool of madness just to get that ecstasy we craved.

When I reached his apartment, I knocked on the door.

It opened a second later, revealing Vince.

My breath caught.

He was shirtless, his muscles jumping under my scrutiny. I had seen him naked before but every time I did, it still took my breath away. He still had on those delicious gray sweatpants, his cock jumping behind the fabric at my perusal. His hair was a shaggy mess on his head. It glistened in the lighting of the room, like he had just finished having a shower.

Before I had a chance to respond, he grabbed my hand and pulled me against him.

I gasped, slapping my hands against his chest.

"Are you spending the night?" he asked, kissing the corner of my mouth.

"I'm here, aren't I?"

"That doesn't answer my question, Gigi." He wrapped his fingers around my throat. "I'll ask you again. Are you spending the night?" he repeated, slower that time.

Running my hand down his chest, I dipped it into his pants. When my fingers came into contact with his cock, a low hiss left him. The sound was so damn sexy, it shot right to my clit.

"Tell me," he bit out through clenched teeth.

I kicked the door closed before lowering to my knees. "Yes. I'm spending the night."

A wicked grin spread on his face. "Good girl."

Pulling his cock free from his pants, I licked my lips. In all the times we had been together, I had never gone down on him. Now was my chance and although I had no idea what I was doing, the dark lust in his eyes gave me all the courage I needed to give him what he wanted. He looked at me like I was all that mattered in his world. I was his Queen and even though we had things to discuss, this moment was ours.

Pushing his cock against his stomach, I licked up the length of him.

He groaned, cupping the sides of my head and slipping his fingers into my hair.

My pussy burned at the hold he had on me. How he controlled and dominated me. He took what he wanted and made sure I was just as satisfied, if not more so.

Taking a breath, I licked along the slit in the tip of his cock before lowering my mouth onto him. My cheeks hollowed out as I sucked and pulled.

The scent of him was powerful. It was spice mixed with a hint of leather. It was sex. Pure hard delicious sex.

His nostrils flared. Something flashed in his dark eyes before he took a step forward, cupped my head, and began thrusting his cock between my lips. The tip of him bumped the back of my throat, making me gag, but the sound only seemed to turn him on and pump harder.

Opening my mouth wider, I took him farther down the back of my tongue.

Vince pushed into me, going as deep as my mouth would let him and stopped. "You feel that?"

I moaned around him.

"That's all yours. Next time I see you hugging some bastard, I'll force you to your knees and make him watch as I fuck your face."

My core clenched at the image he put in my head.

A sly grin spread on his face. "You like that idea, don't you?" He pulled roughly from between my lips.

"Yes," I croaked, my voice hoarse.

Vince wrapped a hand around himself, brushing the tip of his cock over my lips, up the side of my cheek, back down, and across my mouth. "You look so damn beautiful when you're on your knees." Holding my head with one hand, he tilted it back, forcing my mouth open. "Deep breaths, baby."

As soon as I inhaled, he slowly slipped back down the length of my tongue. I gagged around him, spittle dripping from the corners of my mouth.

"Fuck." He groaned, his deep voice straining. "Take it, baby. Take it all."

I panted, breathing through my nose. Reaching around him, I hooked my hands into his pants and pulled them down his legs.

Vince stepped out of them and pushed me back, pumping his hips harder and faster.

The rough use he made of my throat only turned us both on even more.

He was hard. I was wet. It was damn near perfect.

"Is that pussy soaked for me?" he growled, fucking my throat.

I moaned around him, nodding.

"Finger yourself, Gigi," he demanded, his fingers latching on to my hair.

Spreading my legs, I slipped my hand between my thighs. Not even giving myself the chance to get used to the pleasure rushing through me, I slid two fingers into my body.

"Fuck, yeah that's it, baby." Vince powered into my mouth, not giving me a chance to get used to the brutal way he made use of my throat.

I whimpered, my hand picking up speed. Rocking my hips back and forth, I rubbed my palm against my throbbing clit.

My breathing picked up, my thighs trembling. Before I could come, Vince pulled from my lips and shoved me to the ground onto my stomach. He pulled me to all fours and slammed into me.

I screamed, a violent orgasm piercing through me.

Vince pushed his arm against the back of my neck, holding me down and slamming his pelvis against the seat of my ass.

Spreading my legs even wider, I tilted my hips, trying to take him even deeper.

"My girl likes that," he whispered, nipping the side of my neck. "She likes being used up like a filthy little slut."

"Yes," I panted.

Vince reached between us, pulled out of my body, and lined the tip of him up with the tight rim at my ass.

My eyes widened. "What are you doing?"

"Shhh…" He pushed against me, rubbing the tip of him over a spot I never imagined could bring me pleasure.

"Vince," I whined. "You're too big."

He chuckled, biting the spot at the base of my neck. "Trust me. You're fucking soaked. You'll be fine. Just breathe and let me in."

I took a deep breath.

"That's it. Let your man use every inch of you, baby." Before I knew what was happening, Vince pushed past the barrier and slid into a part that now also belonged to him. He groaned.

I whimpered, the tiny hairs on my body tingling at the unexpected pleasure rushing through me. It burned but at the same time, felt so damn good, I hadn't been expecting how good it would feel. "Please move."

He pushed me onto my stomach, slid his hands beneath my dress and pushed the fabric up and over my head. He tossed it to the side and covered me with his heavy body, pumping his cock into me. Grabbing a fistful of my hair, he kissed the corner of my mouth, licking up the drool that I hadn't wiped from my mouth. "So fucking good."

"Vince." I cried out at the burn. "God, it feels…"

"What?" he bit out.

"Good. It feels so good." My body shook. I could feel him through every inch of me. He was so deep, I could feel him in my chest.

He sunk his teeth into the side of my throat. "You're fucking incredible."

"Vince," I whined.

"Tell me you don't like this. Tell me you don't like my cock in your ass. Tell me that kinky little slut inside of you doesn't enjoy being dominated by her man."

Before I could get any sort of answer out, his name left my lips as a release slammed into me.

He grunted, taking the very control from my body like it had been his. This whole time. I realized then that it had been.

I was vaguely aware of Vince picking me up and carrying me to the second floor of his loft. I wasn't sure how long I had already been at his apartment. An hour. More. Less. Time was lost to me as he fucked me like a savage beast on the floor.

He placed me in his bed and covered my mouth with his before I ever had a chance to catch my breath. My body was stiff like I had just spent hours dancing. Instead of one of my routines, Vince and I had danced together, our bodies moving and molding as one.

He brought things out of me I never knew were there. He made me realize that I didn't need to be ashamed of the kink I was into as long as we were safe.

With his mouth firmly on mine, he took it slow and devoured my body once again. Something switched in that moment between us. Although he had been rough earlier that evening, right now, it was like he was making love to my body in a way that neither of us were prepared for. Our feelings for each other spoke through our bodies alone. While for whatever reason we couldn't voice those feelings, I tried with everything in me to let him know how I felt every time I kissed him. Every time I ran my hands over his body. Every time I said his name.

We still needed to talk. I knew that. But I would take this moment and cherish it.

FIFTEEN

Gigi

I WOKE UP THE next morning not remembering where I was. I lifted my head, looking around me, when it suddenly all came back to me.

Sex.

Passion.

Hunger.

Ecstasy.

My muscles burned, aching at the remnants of what happened the night before and well into the morning.

I couldn't believe I spent the night with Vince and then on the other hand, I could. It was almost like, even though we had spent the past few weeks together at my place, now that I had spent the night with *him*, it became more real.

Slipping out of the bed, I started getting dressed when memories of what we had done came rushing back.

"Harder."

Vince chuckled, biting the back of my neck.

"Please," I whined, lifting my hips even more to take him deeper into a part of my body that had never been used for pleasure before.

I shivered, giving myself a shake. I liked him. God, I liked him so damn much, but this was fast. Too fast. Wasn't it? No, it couldn't be. Not when I had known him my whole life.

"Oh, you're awake."

I jumped, spun around, and saw Vince coming up the stairs.

"I put tea on for you."

I backed up, smoothing my hands down my front. "I need to go."

"What?" He frowned, halting in his steps. "Why?"

"I just…I have things to do. I need…" I needed space and I didn't know why. My heart started racing, my hands became clammy.

"What the hell's going on?" Vince demanded, closing the distance between us.

"I have to go to the studio," I told him.

"Right now? It's only nine." He paused. "Did I do something? I know I was rough, but you seemed to like it. If you didn't, you should have said something."

"No." My cheeks heated. "You were fine. What we did, was fine."

"Fine?" Vince chuckled. "Wow, Queenie. That's not the word I would use to describe what we did last night."

I looked at him then. "What do you want from me?"

"What the hell do you want from *me*? I know your accident messed you up. I get that but you have no reason not to trust me. I've done nothing to make you second-guess my feelings for you." He took a step closer, so close that I could smell the faint body wash lingering on his skin. "I will break down these walls you have up." He spun around and began walking away when he stopped. "You know." He turned to me. "I've been patient. Maybe too patient." He muttered a curse and went down to the main floor, leaving me alone.

My throat burned. I didn't know why I had these walls up. He was right though. He hadn't done a thing for me to push him away. Nothing major anyway. Nothing that I was sure couldn't be explained.

He was good to me. He had always been good to me. He was the best thing I could have ever asked for.

Before I could think twice about it, I rushed after him. When I made it to the bottom floor, I found him in the kitchen, dumping a mug of liquid into the sink.

"Vince."

He stiffened, dropping the mug on the counter roughly.

My heart jumped but I took a chance and went up to him. I needed to tell him how he hurt me so many years ago. Maybe he didn't even realize he had.

"I'm sorry." I stepped up behind him, placing my hands on his strong back and leaning the side of my head against him.

"You need to talk to me." His deep voice vibrated into my ear.

"I don't like talking." I pushed away from him. "I never have. You'd think I was a guy or something." I looked down at my feet. "I hate talking about my feelings."

"And I hate making you talk about your feelings." A firm finger pushed under my chin, tilting my head back. "But we can't move forward if I don't know what's bothering you. I feel like I've done something." He searched my face, waiting for an answer but when I didn't give him any, he huffed, releasing me. "Tell me one thing."

My stomach twisted.

"These past few weeks and last night. Tell me you didn't enjoy yourself."

"Of course, I enjoyed myself," I told him. "You think I didn't?"

He leaned against the counter, crossing his arms under his broad chest. The veins in his forearms popped at the movement. The white t-shirt he was wearing was loosely tucked into gray sweatpants and although he was dressed casually, it still sent this flutter of desire rushing through me. "I'm not sure. One moment I think you want more and then you do this."

"Do what?" But I knew. I fell into myself and I didn't know how to get out.

"You run." He pushed away from the counter and came toward me. "You want to run, you run toward me. You understand?"

"Vince," I whispered.

"I asked you a question, Queenie. Do you understand?"

"Yes," I snapped. "I understand. Of course, I understand. But maybe instead of you just fucking standing there, you should run *with* me." I knew we weren't talking about exercise but a metaphor instead, and if that was the only way I could tell him my feelings, then it was how it had to be.

In a quick move, Vince stood right in front of me. "You have no reason, no reason at all to push me away."

My jaw clenched, my teeth grinding down hard. "I know that." I had to take a step back to look up at him without craning my neck, but I had nowhere to go. I was caged in between him and the wall.

He bent at the waist, meeting me at eye level. "I will spend the rest of my life running with you but if you need some time alone, I'm asking you to make sure that I'm the only thing you're running toward."

My heart stuttered. Reaching out a hand, I brushed my fingers along the dark scruff on his jaw.

"Promise me, Gigi." He kissed my fingers as they passed along his mouth.

"I promise."

(Vince)

I looked for a sign that she was lying but when I didn't see any indication that she didn't mean her promise, I let out a sigh of relief. I could do as she asked and take this slow as long as she never doubted my feelings for her.

I kissed Gigi one last time before pulling away and making her another tea. I had dumped out the original because the walls she had built up, pissed me off. It had taken everything in me not to throw the mug against the wall but then rationale hit me, and I thought better of it.

When I finished making her tea, I handed it to her.

She whispered a thanks and started sipping from the hot liquid. That single word had been so soft, I wasn't even sure I heard her correctly. But it didn't matter. She could try and keep me at a safe distance all she wanted. Little did she know that I would do anything to make her see that we were meant to be together. But I had a feeling that it would be when neither of us could take it anymore and we just…

Snapped.

SIXTEEN

Gigi

AFTER I DRANK THE tea that Vince had made me, I ended up coming up with an excuse to leave. It was immature and lame, but I needed to get out of there and think for a moment. I was stuck in my career and hadn't moved as forward as I would have liked. I had amazing clients and a stable job, but it wasn't enough. Vince was everything I wanted and everything I hoped for when it came to being with him.

"Give the kid a break."

My mom's words bounced around in my head.

Vince never gave me any reason to doubt his feelings for me, but I still didn't want to reveal all only to get hurt in the process. Not that I thought it would happen, but it was okay to be cautious. Wasn't it?

As soon as I pulled into my driveway, I killed the engine and sat there. What the hell was I doing?

Reaching for my bag, I pulled out my phone and sent Vince a text. Knowing it was going to come back to bite me in the ass, I hit send before I could even think about it. I didn't even read the text over before sending it. I didn't even think. I just hit that little button and decided to let fate take its course.

A part of me wondered if maybe I was testing him. If he really wanted me, he would come over after reading the text. He would *find me.* He would demand to know what my problem was and wouldn't stop until I revealed all. My body burned at the mere idea of him showing up filled with rage. I was baiting him, and I couldn't wait to watch him explode.

When my phone started ringing, my head whipped around. Oh God. He read the text.

Leaving the car, I ran up to the front door of my house. I hesitated, looking over my shoulder. I half expected Vince to jump out of the bushes and demand to know why the hell I would send that text but when he didn't, I unlocked the front door and went inside.

Kicking it closed, I let out a sigh of relief that I was finally alone. Even if it was just for a little bit, I needed time to gather my thoughts and feelings before Vince came barreling into my house. He would. I expected it.

My mind traveled back to the night before. I couldn't help but think how close Vince and I had become over the past few weeks. How he touched me, kissed me, made me smile and laugh. I wanted that. Constantly.

Taking a long hot shower, I washed the night before off of my aching bones. I had to give it to Vince. He left me wanting more and made good on his promise. I was sore. I never even hurt this much after working out or going for a long run. It was like he made me use different muscles in my body I never even knew existed.

Suddenly, the bathroom door banged open.

I screamed.

The shower curtain ripped open.

Vince stood there, red faced and breathing heavily. "You're fucking done? That's it?" he seethed. "You're just giving up? What about the fucking promise you made me?"

"I lied," I blurted, shocked that he was there, but excited that he was at the same time.

His face darkened, the muscle in his jaw ticked even more the longer we just stood there, staring at each other. He spun away from me and pulled open the bathroom door so damn hard, I was surprised it didn't come off its hinges. "Get out of the fucking shower. *Now.*"

"No." I wasn't sure why I was defying him, but I wanted to test him. I wanted him to snap. I wanted him to prove to me that this was it. That *we* were it. That I was worth it.

When he looked at me over his shoulder, my throat went dry.

"I've waited my whole life for you." Venom dripped from his voice. "I'm not about to let some damn text stop me from taking what's mine."

"Oh? And what's that, Vince? Me? Am I yours?" I laughed when he didn't say anything. "I thought so." I closed the curtain and finished my shower. When I was done, I turned off the water when arms wrapped around me and pulled me off my feet. "Vince," I cried out. "What the hell are you doing?"

He didn't say anything and only dragged me out of the bathroom as my body heated. I shouldn't like this side of him, but I did. I couldn't help it.

Before I knew what was happening, I was dropped on my bed. "You can't get me to talk by fucking me, Vince."

He chuckled, the sound cold and dangerous. "Try me."

My core clenched. I pushed him back and jumped off the bed. The cool air wafted around my still wet body, sending a shiver down my spine.

"Gigi." He grabbed my hand, spinning me around. "Tell me you don't want this. Tell me you didn't enjoy what we did last night."

I pushed against him, trying to get out of his arms but his hold was too strong.

"Gigi," he growled. "Stop fucking fighting me."

"I'm not fighting you."

"Yes, you are." In a quick move, he had his hand around my throat and my body up against the wall.

"What do you want me to say?" I glared up at him.

"We work well together, Gigi. I don't give a flying fuck what you think. We are good. Together."

"Doesn't matter." I shoved out of his grip.

"What the hell are you scared of? If you didn't want this to continue, you wouldn't have stripped for me last night. How the hell did you get that to happen anyway?"

"I paid Ashton," I told him, shrugging.

Vince only stared at me. "Are you serious?" he asked, shaking his head. "How much?"

"Five."

His eyes widened. "Hundred?"

I nodded.

"So, you paid five hundred dollars so another woman wouldn't dance for me, but you don't want this to continue? If you didn't care, you would have let the actual stripper do her thing." Vince pinched my chin, tilting my head back. "Isn't that right?"

My jaw clenched. "I wasn't letting another woman grind her ass against you or touch you with any other part of her body."

Vince smirked. "So what the hell is your problem then?"

I placed my hands against his chest, pushing him away.

He took a step back. "I'll give you one more chance to tell me what's going on."

"Or else what?" I shivered at the threat hidden in his deep voice.

A dark shadow passed over his face. "You really want me to answer that question, Queenie?"

"Whatever." I went to walk past him when he grabbed me and shoved me up against the wall. "Vince," I gasped.

"Shut the fuck up." He cupped the back of my neck, pushing me face first against the wall. "Last chance, Gigi."

"I have no idea what you're talking about," I whispered.

"I was hoping you would defy me," he murmured in my ear, kicking my legs apart. His fingers slid down the length of my spine, dipping lower and lower until they brushed between my legs.

A breathless gasp escaped me.

"Fuck, baby. You're so damn wet already." He fisted my hair, sliding his fingers deep into my body as he bit my shoulder.

I whimpered.

His hand picked up speed, his fingers roughly fucking me.

I squeezed my eyes shut, rocking against him. I hinted, silently begged, and damn near pleaded for him to take it further. "God, Vince."

His hand slammed against my center, his teeth raining bites along my shoulder to the side of my throat. "You want that orgasm?"

"Yes," I whined, pushing back against his hand.

"Do you think you deserve it? After telling me you don't want to continue this? After lying to me when your body clearly loves what I do to it." He pushed his fingers into me as deep as my body would allow.

My knees buckled, my eyes rolling into the back of my head.

"Answer my fucking question." His hand stopped but I could still feel his fingers moving inside of me.

"Yes, please. I'm sorry. God. Just let me come." The words tumbled from my mouth. It didn't take much. I would have done anything for that orgasm. Especially when he was the one giving it to me.

Vince ripped his hand from my body and shoved his fingers back inside of me.

"Oh." My eyes popped open. "God."

He repeated the movements. It was rough, bordered on violent and everything I wanted from him. Even though it was just his fingers, I loved it. I loved all of it. And I loved him even more for giving me what I needed. Even though I didn't tell him so, it was like he could read my mind.

"Come for me." He pulled his fingers from my body once again and started rubbing his palm over my clit.

I cried out, shaking against him.

"That's it. Come hard. Come all over my hand." His hand picked up speed. It rubbed back and forth, moving over my clit quickly.

"Vince," I panted. "I need you."

"You need me to what, Gigi?" He pulled his hand from between my legs and reached around me. He wrapped his other hand around my throat, pulling my head back against him. "You need me to fuck you?"

"Yes." I cupped his hand that was between my legs, helping him give me what I needed even though he never needed my help. He knew my body like it was made for him. And maybe it was.

He pushed my hand away. "Keep your hands against the fucking wall until I say so," he growled, slapping my pussy.

I gasped, arching against him.

Vince sunk his teeth into the side of my throat and slapped my clit again.

My legs spread even more of their own accord.

"That's my girl." His fingers tightened around my throat. "If you want me to fuck you, you know what to do."

Taking the hint, I reached behind me and grabbed onto the waist of his sweatpants. Slipping my hand into the material, I pulled out his cock in a rough move.

Vince groaned, pushing me against the wall. "Put me inside you."

Turning my head, I met his gaze at the same time he thrust into me. Chewing my bottom lip, I bit back a hard groan, taking him to the hilt.

His fingers released my throat, moving to my hair and holding my head in place as he slammed his hips against the seat of my ass. "Tell me."

"Harder."

Cupping the back of my thigh, he lifted my knee and picked up speed with his hips.

From this angle, I could feel every inch of him. Every vein. He reached a part of me that I never knew existed before him.

Tilting my hips, I took him even deeper. "Vince."

He pulled almost all the way out and slammed back into me in a quick rough move.

I cried out.

He kept up the movement until I was shattering against him.

A scream left my lips, his name falling from my tongue.

Vince let go of my knee, pulling free from my body and wrapping his fingers around his cock. He stroked hard and fast, his breathing coming out ragged.

I watched in awe as he fucked his own hand.

A muttered curse left him as hot jets of his release landed against my ass and lower back. He reached out, brushing his thumb through some of the liquid and rubbing it into my skin on the cheek of my rear. It was almost like he was staking his claim.

"Vince," I whispered.

He stuffed his cock back into his pants. "Don't move."

Much to my surprise, he pulled his phone out of the pocket of his pants. He took a step back, holding the phone out in front of him and snapped a picture.

"What are you doing?" I asked, a flush of heat spreading over my skin.

His dark eyes met mine that time. "I took a picture." He turned his phone around, showing me the image.

My cheeks heated at seeing me naked with his cum on my ass.

"Yeah, I see that." I turned toward him. "But why?"

"It'll give me something to jerk off to whenever we aren't together." He shoved his phone back into his pocket.

My stomach tumbled. "Oh, is that all?" Instead of waiting for him to answer, I went to the bathroom and grabbed a towel. Wiping him off of me, I let out a soft sigh.

"Gigi." Vince came up behind me. He pulled another towel off the rack and started running it through my hair. "You have to know that I'm not giving up."

"I'm sorry for the text. I didn't want to send it."

"Then why did you?" He spun me around. "I've spent years trying to get you to notice me. And then these past few weeks together." His shoulders bunched, the muscles rippling over his bones to the point they were on the verge of snapping. "I'm not having this argument again."

"Why can't we just have sex and that be it?" God, I needed to stop hanging out with Ashton.

"Sorry, babe. It doesn't work that way with me. You're either in completely or…"

I looked up at Vince when his words trailed off. "Or that's it?"

He left the bathroom and threw the towel in the laundry hamper. "I don't know what I've done for you to have these walls up. I get your accident has messed things up for you but there's no reason that you can't trust me."

I looked away.

"There is something. Isn't there? What the hell did I do?"

"I didn't think it was a big deal at first but clearly it is." I huffed. "It's stupid."

His face softened. "Nothing you say, or feel is stupid. Tell me what's bothering you."

"You broke my heart," I murmured. "You went to school and I know you had to. Like I said, it's stupid. But that's not what bothers me most. You didn't talk to me. You didn't come see me when you were home."

His brows narrowed. "What are you talking about?"

"The first years you were gone, we saw each other at every opportunity. It may have been with our friends and family, but we were constantly in touch. Then your last year, when you came home for Thanksgiving, you didn't talk to me. I expected it to be weird after what we did on your eighteenth birthday, but I still thought you would have at least said hi. But you didn't. You didn't do shit. So I thought maybe you were busy. You wanted to see your friends or something. But you didn't talk to me at Christmas either."

"I didn't talk to you at Christmas because I thought you were mad at me. You were cold. You shoved me away." He reached out, tucking a strand of hair behind my ear.

"I *was* mad at you," I mumbled, shivering at the gentle contact coming from him when he had been rough a moment before.

"Then why the hell have we started fucking again?" His eyes searched my face, looking for some form of answer. "Clearly you're not that mad at me or you just really love my cock."

"Don't be an asshole." I glared at him.

"Then you need to give me something here. Not talking to you at Thanksgiving was a misunderstanding." Vince ran a hand through his hair. "You have to know that I would never intentionally do anything to break your heart."

"Well whatever the reason, you still hurt me."

"Why the hell haven't you said anything about this before? We've spent the past few weeks together, Queenie. Why the fuck am I only hearing how I hurt you now?"

"Because I thought my feelings were stupid. I thought I was being unreasonable," I mumbled, turning back to my dresser.

"You're not being unreasonable. I just wish you would have told me this right away." He cupped my shoulders, spinning me around to face him. "We can't move forward if I do something wrong and you won't talk to me about it. Even if it's just a misunderstanding." He closed the distance between us, pushing his hips into me and pressing me up against the edge of my dresser. "You feel that?"

I swallowed hard, my body heating as his thick length twitched against my lower belly.

"That's yours, Gigi." He cupped the back of my head, sliding his fingers into my hair and holding me in place. "I'm sorry I never saw you that weekend. I wanted to. I was fucking desperate for you. We texted often but it wasn't enough. That night of my birthday wasn't enough." He tugged my head back. "I wanted you again."

"I wanted you too," I whispered, remembering the many lonely nights where I would touch myself to thoughts of him.

"I hardly saw my family that weekend too. Rory's mom had died, so I spent the weekend with him. I'm sorry I never told you. I should have told you. But I was drunk for most of the weekend. That's no excuse but it's the truth."

"I'm sorry for his loss." I stared up at him, my chest tightening for his friend. "Now I feel even more stupid for getting upset."

"Don't." Vince kissed my forehead. "I would have been upset too. I should have told you and I'm sorry that I'm only just telling you now."

"I'm sorry I never mentioned it." I ran my hands down his chest, feeling the flutter of his heart beneath my palm.

"You don't like talking about your feelings."

I shrugged. It wasn't like I ever had any reason to. But people judged when they knew how you felt. It made you a target.

"Hey." Vince grabbed my hand, leading me to the edge of my bed. He sat, pulling me between his knees. "However you feel, I will not judge you. You hear me?"

I traced the lines of his face with my fingers. "Vince."

"I asked you a question." His voice came out rough, his brows narrowing even more in the center.

I sighed. "Yeah, I hear you."

"Good." He wrapped his arms around my middle, pulling me onto his lap. "Now that we sorted that shit out, I'm going to fuck you again, then we're going to take a shower and after that, I'm taking you on a date."

My stomach tumbled. "Really?"

"Yes, really." He kissed my chin. "I don't want this to end."

"Neither do I." A sense of relief washed over me. "I shouldn't have sent that text."

"Doesn't matter." His lips pulled up into a grin. "I'm just glad that we're finally talking."

My stomach rumbled.

He chuckled. "I guess we'll have to make this quick so I can feed you." He stood, spinning us around and dropping me on the bed.

A bubble of laughter escaped me.

Vince grinned, crawling onto the bed toward me. When he knelt between my legs, he towered over me and snarled into the crook of my neck.

I giggled, wrapping my arms around him.

He lifted his head. "We good?"

"Yeah." I sighed, brushing my fingers along his strong jaw. "We are."

(Vince)

After I finally got Gigi to open up to me, I made good on my promise and quickly used her body to make both of us feel better. By the time I was done, her taste was on my tongue and my name was on her lips. I had taken another picture of my cock deep inside her. When she noticed what I was doing, her cheeks reddened, and her pupils dilated. My girl liked being on display as long as I was the only spectator. For now, anyway. I knew there was a voyeuristic side to her, and I couldn't wait to explore that little fantasy that she tried to keep hidden.

By the time I was done, I was going to have quite the collection of pictures. They would be our own private stash. We could look at them together, make more, and come up with new ways to just feel good. She was beautiful and I wanted her to see what I did.

"You've been quiet," Gigi murmured, running her finger along the edge of her wine glass.

I sat back, staring at her from across the table. We had driven to a restaurant that wasn't too fancy and served delicious food. The theme was rustic and most of the dishes served were Italian. The portions were big, and you never left hungry.

"I've been thinking of the images of you I have on my phone," I told her.

A small smile splayed on her face, her cheeks turning a beautiful shade of pink. "I can't believe you took pictures of me and us while we were…"

"While we were what, Gigi?" I asked, sitting forward.

"Having sex," she whispered.

I chuckled, shaking my head. "You act all damn shy in public but get you in bed and you're a fucking porn star."

She laughed lightly, shrugging her shoulders. "That's because I trust you. I can be myself with you and no one knows me like you do."

I stared at her. That had been the most honest thing she had ever said to me outside of us fucking. I reached across the table before she could shut down again and grabbed hold of her hand. "Thank you."

She nodded, chewing her bottom lip. "Thank you for today and I'm sorry again about this morning."

"Don't worry about it. It's over." I wasn't going to dwell on it. I had learned quickly that when it came to Gigi, if she said something, she meant it. I believed her apology and I also knew that she sent me that text because she was scared. But now that it was out of the way, we could move forward.

Holding her hand on the table, I ran my thumb back and forth over the side of her palm. I watched her. Really watched her. She continued to sip from her red wine, her golden eyes moving over to the other couples sitting at random tables in the large space of the restaurant.

When we had arrived, I wanted to sit in the booth beside her, but I also didn't want to overwhelm her. We had spent the rest of the morning and most of the early afternoon, wrapped in each other's arms. I had made her a sandwich and salad from items I found in her fridge. When I was satisfied that she was no longer hungry, I fucked her. Again. It was like something had switched between us this morning and I couldn't get enough of her. Even right now as I watched her drink her wine. She was none the wiser over what I wanted to do to her. Or how I wanted to take her to the bathroom and rip into her body before I found out if she was wet enough for me. I wanted to use her up and have my cum dripping from every damn hole in her body.

My thoughts traveled back to this afternoon when we were changing and getting ready for our date. As Gigi shimmied into her black dress, I was on her before she could get the fabric over her ass. I felt like a damn horny teenager.

"Are you hungry?" I heard myself ask. *Of course she was hungry. She wouldn't have agreed to go out for dinner with you if she wasn't.* I mentally scolded myself.

Her eyes flicked to mine. "I am. You helped me work up an appetite."

I coughed. "Yeah, sorry about that. I don't know what's come over me."

She smiled, pulling her hand from mine and leaning against the seatback of the booth. "Was I complaining?"

"No, but—" I jumped when I felt something pushing against my crotch. I looked down, finding Gigi's foot rubbing my dick.

"You're patient with me." Gigi picked up a breadstick and bit off the end. "I don't know how to ever repay you."

I chuckled, cupping her heel. "I think you've had too much wine."

"Nah." She winked.

My dick twitched beneath her foot. This was what I liked. Flirting with her. Teasing each other in public when we had to wait until we were in a more private location to take care of that need.

"Did you do as I asked?" I grabbed her foot, pulling it harder against me.

"You'll have to wait and see." She finished off her breadstick before picking up her glass of wine again. "I could take a picture though."

My cock hardened even more at what she was suggesting. "Do it."

She laughed, pulling her foot from my lap. She reached into her bag and rummaged through it until she found her phone. She brought it under the table.

I licked my lips, my dick jumping with anticipation.

Gigi grinned. "Check your phone."

My cell buzzed as soon as those words left her mouth. When the image of her came through, my cock leaked. Her bare pussy was on full display for my feasting eyes. My mouth watered, my tongue tingling with the need to lick between her thighs.

"Oh, is that all?" I coughed, clearing my throat and putting my phone away.

Her body shook with laughter. "Thank you for this."

"You're welcome, Queenie." But she never had to thank me. Not for anything. I would spend the rest of my days, until my dying breath, making her happy. If it was the last thing I did, putting a smile on her face was all I cared about.

SEVENTEEN

Gigi

I **DIDN'T KNOW WHERE** the bravery had come from to send that picture to Vince but the huge grin it put on his face, made it all worthwhile. I appreciated that he got me to talk earlier. Even if it resulted in yelling. But the angry sex was worth it. I shivered, remembering how he had come on my ass and taken a picture of it.

"Hey." Vince kissed the side of my head, pulling me from my thoughts. "I'm not going anywhere."

"I know." I snuggled into his side as we walked down the sidewalk. "I was thinking though."

"Oh?" He raised an eyebrow. "And what were you thinking about?"

"How you came on my ass." I pulled away from him and started walking backwards. "It was hot."

A sly grin spread on his face. "Don't worry, babe. I'll make sure you never forget how that feels either." He charged for me.

I squealed, getting caught up in his arms before I had a chance to run away.

He snarled into the crook of my neck.

A giggle escaped me at his scruff tickling me.

Vince wrapped his arm around my shoulders, pulling me tighter into his side.

I sighed. He told me he wasn't going anywhere. Well neither was I but even though I never voiced those words, I hoped he knew how I felt.

"Did you want to grab some ice cream?" Vince asked, nodding toward a small ice cream parlor that had some of the best ice cream I'd ever had.

"Sure."

He stepped in front of me and cupped my face, placing a hard peck on my mouth. "I'll go grab us something." He kissed me one last time before running off toward the ice cream parlor.

I grinned, shook my head, and sat on a nearby park bench. It was later in the evening. The sun was setting over the buildings of the city, giving it an otherworldly glow.

The hairs on the back of my neck suddenly tingled. I looked around me, expecting to find someone watching me or even someone I knew approaching, but when I didn't, I gave myself a shake. Turning back around, I tried ignoring the feeling that I was being watched but it was still there.

Even after about ten minutes, when Vince came back to join me, that feeling hadn't gone away. He came back with two bowls of ice cream, a wide smile on his face.

My stomach fluttered at the sight of him.

He had chocolate while I had strawberry. He sat beside me and kissed my temple before he started eating his ice cream.

My heart stuttered at the soft public display of affection coming from him. I realized then that he always kissed me whenever he could. Even if it was just a peck on the cheek or head, he always showed me his feelings even if he never told me. Maybe I could start doing the same.

I took that as my chance and moved closer to him.

His eyes whipped to mine, a twinkle flashing behind them. He gave me a small smile.

"Thank you," I murmured and went back to eating my ice cream.

When we finished, he grabbed our bowls and threw them in a nearby garbage can.

He came back toward me and held out his hand.

I slipped my fingers in his, letting him pull me from the park bench. Looking around me, I still didn't see anyone watching us but felt uneasy nonetheless.

"You good?" Vince asked, bringing our joined hands up to his mouth.

I nodded, watching as his lips brushed over my knuckles.

"You sure?"

"I am. Just a weird feeling. That's all." I pulled my hand from his and wrapped myself around his middle, needing his strength. I thought back to a time when we were kids and he would give me a hug. He would give all of us girls hugs, but saved me for last. When he had wrapped himself around me, his body would relax. I remembered once where his mouth had brushed ever so slightly against the side of my neck. I never thought anything of it and took it as just an accident, but I realize now that when it came to Vince and me, nothing was an accident.

"What kind of weird feeling?" he asked, leaning back and staring down at me.

I laughed at the deep frown etched between his brows. "Nothing bad. Just weird." But even I couldn't be sure if that was the case or not. I needed to reassure him that everything was in fact fine because it wasn't like I could do anything about it anyway.

Vince searched my face but when I just stood there, he finally let out a huff and grabbed my hand. Even though I had attempted to reassure him that this feeling wasn't a big deal, he kept my hand tight in his. We walked until a café came into view.

My stomach twisted, remembering Meadow telling me what had happened outside of it. We stopped in front of a cross that was directly across from the café.

"I haven't been here in a while," I told Vince, staring down at the shrine made for Sunny.

"Do your sister and Shade come here often?"

"I don't know." Getting an idea, I looked across the street. "I'll be back." Making sure no cars were coming, I ran across the street to one of the stores. When I found what I was looking for, I purchased it and joined Vince back at the shrine. "Meadow told me that she comes and collects the stuff once a month. People are good about not stealing anything. For the most part anyway." I placed the small teddy bear at the base of the cross that someone had made for Sunny. It hurt my heart that I never had a chance to get to know him but knew just from what Meadow and Shade had told me, that he loved them with every inch of him.

"I never met him," Vince finally said, pulling me from my thoughts. "I saw him in passing but it was only the once. At your party."

That had been when Piper had gotten attacked. A tremor of unease rushed through me. "I try not to think about that night but every time I'm home alone and walk by her old room, I can't help but remember what happened."

Vince grabbed my hand, giving it a gentle squeeze. "I know. Jaron saved her."

I nodded.

"I would have done the same."

I looked up at Vince then. "Really?"

"Yes." His jaw was hard. "I think Jaron let him off easy."

I hooked my arm in Vince's, leaning my head against his shoulder. "Maybe. He's paying for it though. He won't even see his baby being born."

"Hey." Vince kissed the top of my head. "They'll work it out. If they are meant to be, they'll get through this."

"Do you honestly believe that?" I asked, looking up at him.

"You don't?" Vince searched my face, looking for a sign. Looking for something that I wasn't sure I was ready to give him.

"I don't know." My chest suddenly felt tight. "Can we go? This is…this is starting to feel heavy." And damn near suffocating.

"Fine." Vince grabbed my hand and led me to the parking lot where he parked his car. The air between us became cold and unwanted. Something switched. Something that wasn't for the better. I wasn't sure why but maybe because I hadn't outright agreed with him, it pissed him off.

"Vince?"

"What?"

I stopped, stepping in front of him and placing my hands on his chest. "What we're doing, whatever this is, I like it. I want to continue it."

Vince sighed, cupping the back of my neck. "You have walls up, baby, but I promise you that I will do everything in my fucking power to break them down. Whether you want me to or not." He crouched so he could be at eye level with me. "You hear me?"

"If you hurt me again, whether it's intentional or not, I'll kick your ass. You hear *me*?"

A laugh boomed through him. "Alright, Queenie. Fair enough." He stuck out his hand. "It's a deal."

I smiled, returning the handshake. "Good. Now take me home."

He pulled me against him.

I gasped, slapping my hand against his chest.

His eyes darkened, a hint of lust flashing behind them. It was intense, the air crackling between us like it was only us who existed in each other's worlds. And maybe we were. He was all I needed and all I craved.

Vince cupped my cheek, placing a soft peck on my mouth. The kiss had been so gentle. It was nothing like the man I had spent the day with.

Even though we were still in public, that little fact only seemed to heighten the passion between us. We were in the parking lot, standing by his car but at the same time, I felt as though we were in the middle of nowhere.

Vince deepened the kiss, pushing me back against the side of his car. He cupped my ass, sliding his hand lower until he came into contact with my bare thigh and pushed his fingers beneath the fabric.

My heart jumped.

Snaking my arms around his shoulders, I pulled him against me.

His erection pressed into my lower belly.

Much to my dismay, he lifted his head, licking his swollen mouth. He gave me a small smirk.

My chest rose and fell with ragged breath. "Take me home?"

"I have an early day tomorrow."

"So do I. I live closer to the center and my studio. Spend the night with me." My body tingled with need for him. "Please."

"You want me again, baby?" Vince kissed my jaw, digging his fingers into the spot beneath my ass cheek.

"God, yes."

He chuckled, releasing me completely and handing me the keys to his car. "Then lead the way."

EIGHTEEN

Gigi

IT WAS THE FOLLOWING Friday and I was sitting at a table in a small café, waiting for Corbin. My body burned with memories of telling Vince earlier that morning about meeting up with another guy and how he staked his claim on my body.

I tried my hardest to convince Vince that I wasn't Corbin's type but when Vince mumbled *Mine* against my pussy, I had forgotten what I was supposed to tell him in the first place.

"What would you do if he was interested in me?" I asked Vince, brushing my thumb along his nipple. I knew it was a dangerous question, especially when it came to the man I was sleeping with, but curiosity got the better of me and I needed to know.

"You really want me to answer that question?"

My eyes locked with his. My stomach did a somersault at the rough vibrato of his voice. "Yes."

"First." Vince pushed me onto my back and knelt between my legs. "I'd beat the shit out of him." He lowered his mouth to mine, giving my bottom lip a gentle bite.

I whimpered at the sharp slice of pain.

"Then." He wrapped his lips around my nipple, closing his teeth around the budding peak.

I yelped, arching beneath him.

"I would fuck you in his blood and make him watch."

Somehow, I knew it wasn't Corbin he was referring to. I had heard quite often how he didn't like Matt. Not that I had actually ever dated him. I only let Vince believe I did. Matt had moved anyway, so it wasn't like I would ever see him again.

"You know Matt and I were never a thing, right?" I straddled Vince's lap, pushing him onto his back.

Vince lifted me to my knees and dropped me onto him. "Say that again."

I sighed, shaking my head as the memories burned through me.

"Someone's in love."

My head popped up.

Corbin came toward me, a wide smile on his face.

I stood from the table and stretched out my arms. "Someone needs to mind his own business," I threw back at him, but I couldn't help the smile pulling at my lips.

He chuckled, wrapping me up in a hug. "How's my girl?"

"Good. You?" When he didn't answer, I leaned back. "What's wrong?"

The smile fell from his face. "It's nothing, baby girl. Just work crap. Don't worry about it."

"Uh, I have to worry about it." Corbin was the type of guy who worried about everyone else but not himself. "Talk to me." I sat in the chair, my stomach clenching at the worry evident on his face.

"It's not important." He gave me a small smile, sitting back in his chair and picking up the menu. "Now, should I get one of these new fancy cakes or try a salad?"

"Corbin, maybe I can help with whatever issue is going on," I said gently.

"I've heard some things." He placed the menu on the table between us. "I don't like gossiping. In fact, I hate it. It makes me feel low, but it's hard not to hear what's being said when people aren't discreet about their conversations."

I sat forward. "Okay, now you got me really interested."

He chuckled, rubbing a hand over his bald head. "Your friend Piper is famous."

"What?" My eyes widened. "How? And how do you even know Piper?"

"I don't know her exactly. I just know *who* she is. I've seen her pick up Cyrus and Sammy from time to time whenever they drink too much."

"Oh." I didn't even realize he knew the twins. I had only met them a few times but being in the Hell's Harlem MC alongside Jaron and Shade, I knew they would do anything to keep their own safe. Including Piper.

"She's Jaron's girl and she's the only one who has ever been able to capture his heart," Corbin continued. "That says a lot about her."

I stared at him. "Really?"

He nodded. "Jaron had a thing with Candace. Not saying they were serious. Especially when she was married to Ronny through all of it but…there was definitely something there."

My stomach twisted. Piper and Jaron had enough problems. They didn't need a jealous husband, or a crazy ex added to that list. "Does Ronny know?"

"He does. Whatever Candace and he have, it's toxic but it works for them, I guess. I don't know. But I overheard a couple of the girls talking about it. Bottom line is, Piper needs to be careful."

"Do you think something's going to happen?" I asked, my heart jumping.

"No but that doesn't mean anything."

"I'll warn her." I gave him a small smile of reassurance and made a mental note to text Piper later.

"Good." Corbin clapped his hands together. "Now, enough of the heavy crap. Tell me, how did Vince take you going out with another man?"

I coughed, my cheeks heating. "He was fine with it."

Corbin laughed. "Right," he said slowly.

"He *was* fine with it," I insisted. "After I convinced him anyway." I winked.

Corbin chuckled.

We spent the rest of the afternoon talking about nothing and everything at the same time. I had known Corbin for the better part of a year but never actually hung out with him outside of the club. I learned that his family was from a tiny village in Northern Africa and that he had moved to the USA when he was two. He had been moving around the country ever since and finally settled on our little city that was growing with each passing year. He had also been working for Candace and Ronny for quite some time and enjoyed being a bouncer. We never talked again about what he had overheard when it came to Piper.

After our visit, we went our separate ways but made plans to meet up again and for me to bring Vince next time.

When I pulled into my driveway, I reached for my bag and retrieved my phone. Sending Piper a quick text, I let her know what Corbin told me. All she said was a thanks and that was it. It made me wonder if she didn't already know or had problems already. I wanted to reach out to her and pay her a visit, but I also didn't want to overstep. I knew that she would come around whenever she was able.

As I left my car, my phone dinged again.

Vince: Did you enjoy your date?

Me: I enjoyed convincing you that it wasn't a date, more.

Vince: I bet you did, dirty girl.

I grinned.

Me: I have no idea what you're talking about.

Vince: Sure, Queenie.

I laughed, shaking my head, then went up the sidewalk to my house. It was mid-afternoon but a storm seemed to be rolling in, so it was darker out. Another text came in from Ashton this time, letting me know that both he and Aiden were going to the nearby bar and would probably be by later.

I reminded him not to forget his key, just in case I was sleeping or not home.

Spending the rest of the evening cleaning, I grabbed a glass of wine when I was finally done. It was pushing nine and I hadn't heard from Vince since earlier that evening.

As if on cue, my phone rang, an image of Vince's handsome face flashing across the screen.

"Hey," I answered.

"Hey, yourself."

My stomach did a flip at the sound of his deep voice.

"I just wanted to let you know that I'm going to be late. If you want me to just go home after I'm done helping Rory, I can."

"No." I stood from the couch and went to the kitchen to refill my glass. "Come over whenever you can. The twins will be here."

"Alright, if I can get out of here earlier, I'll let you know."

We said our goodbyes and as soon as I placed the phone on the counter, it rang again. I smiled, picking it up.

"Miss my voice already?" I laughed.

When no answer came, I checked the screen of my phone and saw that it wasn't actually Vince like I thought and an unknown number instead.

"Hello?"

Still no answer.

The dead silence was unnerving, but I just shrugged and disconnected the call. Pouring my glass of wine, I put the bottle away when my phone rang again.

This time a phone number appeared on the screen, but I still didn't recognize it. "Hello?"

Again, pure silence.

An icy cold shiver of unease rippled down my spine.

"Hello?" I demanded.

When there was no answer again, I huffed and disconnected the call. Placing the phone on the counter, I took a sip of my wine but couldn't look away. I wasn't sure what staring at my cell would do but it was the only thing I could think of at the moment.

I wasn't surprised the next time it rang.

Taking a step toward it, I saw a different number flashing across the screen. Even though it wasn't the same as the one that called a moment ago, it still didn't make me feel any better.

Pressing the speaker button, I waited.

Heavy breathing sounded from the other end of the phone this time, followed by mumbled words.

I frowned, trying to hear what they were saying but I couldn't make it out. The words sounded jumbled, like they had something shoved in their mouth.

The mumbled words continued, followed by heavy breathing.

I took a step closer, straining to hear. Lowering my ear to the phone, I tried to understand them. Maybe they needed help. "Hello?"

The mumbled words became louder and louder, forcing me back a step. I still couldn't make out what they were saying but the words turned to screams and then they just all of a sudden stopped.

My stomach fell to the ground beneath me, my skin prickling with goosebumps.

"I'm going to fucking kill you!"

The glass of wine fell from my fingers, shattering to the ground at my feet.

Rushing to the phone, I disconnected the call and tossed it on the counter. My heart was racing, my palms sweaty.

Suddenly, the front door banged open.

A scream ripped free from my throat, reminding me that I should always lock the damn door like Vince told me to.

(Vince)

"I really have much better things to be doing on a Friday night than sitting here and watching you guys work." Tenise was playing on her phone but she never looked up as she spoke.

Rory and Mason passed a glance before they charged for her. Rory was on her first, poking his fingers into her ribs.

She gasped, a scream breaking free. "Stop. That tickles!"

Mason helped and pulled her away from Rory. His hand reached beneath her shirt, digging into her ribs harder.

I tilted my head, watching the exchange before me.

They laughed, finally giving Tenise a moment of reprieve.

I wasn't sure what was going on there, but something told me that it was more than they were letting on.

My phone rang at that moment. When I saw Gigi's beautiful face flashing across the screen, I breathed a sigh of relief, thankful for the interruption from the odd moment happening with my friends.

"Hey, Queenie," I said, answering the phone.

"Vince," she whispered.

My back stiffened. "What's wrong?"

"Are you still busy?" she asked, her voice soft and shaking.

Every nerve in my body tingled over the fact that something wasn't right. "I'm on my way." I disconnected the call before she had a chance to respond.

"Vince."

I turned, finding all three of my friends staring back at me. "Listen, I don't know what's going on here but Mason, you need to be careful."

Rory frowned. "What about me?"

"She's your girlfriend," I reminded him.

Tenise only giggled, kissing Rory's cheek.

He turned, smiling at her.

Mason pushed away from them and walked toward me. "That was weird."

"Is this a regular thing for you?" Not that it was any of my business, but he was my friend first. I liked Tenise for Rory but what they had was not something that Mason should get himself caught up in.

"What?" Mason's eyes widened before he scowled, shaking his head. "No, that…we haven't done anything. I flirt a bit and Tenise has hinted but it's not my thing. Not with them anyway."

"Does Rory know?" I asked low enough for only Mason to hear.

Mason clapped my shoulder, pushing me down the hall toward the door. "He does but he's not always around when she offers. It's weird. I know it is. But she's not my type. And Rory loves her. I wouldn't do that." He looked back at them; a longing was in his gaze. For Rory? Or for what they had? I didn't know.

"Well, whatever you need I'm here, but just be careful." I cupped his shoulder. "You and Rory come first. Before any woman. Remember that."

Mason looked back at me, giving me a small smile. "I know."

"Rory will lose his shit though if he finds out…"

"I'll deal with it." Mason nodded toward the door. "You need to go. Something's wrong."

"How do you know that?"

"Just a feeling." He released me and went back to join Rory and Tenise.

Whatever was going on with my friends, I would deal with later. I needed to help Gigi.

Leaving Rory's house, I quickly made my way to the car and drove across town to Gigi's place. When I pulled into her driveway, nothing seemed out of the ordinary. The street was quiet. Too quiet if you asked me.

Slipping from my car, I jogged up the sidewalk to the front door and pushed it open. My stomach twisted over it being unlocked. I would have to teach Gigi to lock the door at all times.

"Queenie?" I called out, stepping into the house. "Babe?" I closed the door behind me and clicked the lock into place when my gaze landed on a couple dark red spots on the tiled floor. I followed the drops to the kitchen.

Gigi was sitting on the countertop with her ankle crossed over her opposite knee. Her brow was furrowed in the middle. Her head snapped up. "Oh thank god."

"What happened?" There was broken glass mixed with red liquid on the kitchen floor.

"We accidentally scared her." Ashton walked past me with a broom and dustpan in hand. He went to the sink and grabbed a cloth, leaning the broom against the counter. He crouched and started picking up the bigger pieces of glass.

"No." Gigi chewed her bottom lip. "I was already scared. That wasn't your fault."

"What do you mean?" The hackles on the back of my neck tingled. "Who the fuck scared you?"

She waved a hand in front of her. "It was a stupid phone call. They kept calling over and over but wouldn't say anything. Then, when they did, they started screaming and told me they were going to kill me." Her chin wobbled.

I rushed to her, careful not to step in the glass as Ashton cleaned it up. "You're okay." I cupped her nape, placing a soft peck on her forehead.

"I'm okay," she repeated.

"What happened here?" I asked, nodding toward the mess Ashton was currently cleaning up.

He stopped, resting his hands on top of the broom handle. "Aiden and I went to the bar and he got drunk. Fast. We showed up here because he was being a dick." He shook his head. "Anyway, I was having trouble helping Aiden into the house and the door banged open, scaring Gigi."

"I dropped the glass and then I stepped in it." Gigi glanced down at the bottom of her foot. "I think I got all the pieces."

"I'll double-check." I grabbed the first aid kit and started rummaging through it. "Where's Aiden now?"

"He's sleeping. He got in a fight with dad and it all went to shit after that." Ashton sighed and went back to sweeping. "I know I've caused problems and have done shit that I'm not proud of, but disrespecting our parents is not one of them. I don't know what my brother's deal is."

"I don't think anyone does," Gigi murmured. "I hope he figures out whatever it is that he's going through and gets some help."

"It would help if he talked about it, but he won't talk to anyone. Not even a professional. All I know is he was discharged from the navy and that it's. Nothing more." Ashton sighed. "Sorry again for scaring you."

Gigi shrugged. "It's fine. I'm good."

"Well I'll leave you two alone and go see how my brother is." Without another word, he left the kitchen.

"That's odd." I stared after him.

"What?"

"He didn't comment on us or make a joke or anything." I looked back at Gigi. "I'm not sure how I feel about that."

Her shoulders slumped. "I know. I feel bad for Aiden and Ashton too. His brother's problem is hurting him." She pulled the first aid kit closer. "At least I don't need stitches."

I never commented on what she said about the twins because what could I say? Aiden was a borderline alcoholic and was causing shit for those he loved. He needed help before it became worse.

I helped Gigi clean up her feet. Luckily not much damage was done. She had a few scrapes from the broken shards of glass but after years of dancing, her feet were tough which worked in her favor.

"Thank you," she said when we were done.

I stepped between her knees, pushing them open even more. "I'm sorry I wasn't here when you got the phone calls." I brushed my thumb along the length of her jaw. "I should have been."

"You can't be here every time something happens."

It was the on the tip of my tongue to ask her to move in with me so I could be there every time, but I didn't. I knew that we weren't at that point yet, no matter how much I wanted us to be. As much as I didn't want to think it, a part of me wondered if we ever would be.

NINETEEN

Gigi

ATTACHING MY PHONE TO the speaker, I pressed play on Spotify and let the music sink beneath my skin and slide over every inch of me.

The song had been my warm-up song for as long as I could remember. Even when I was doing ballet and not a broken mess because of a stupid mistake. One wrong move and my career was over.

But was it really? That annoying little voice in my head constantly threw it in my face that I had a good life. I had my own business. I taught, which had been what I wanted to do ever since I slipped my feet into a pair of ballet slippers for the very first time. But how come it wasn't enough? It had never been enough.

Moving out to the middle of the dance floor, I was vaguely aware of the door to the studio opening. The tiny hairs on my body tingled, knowing it was Vince who had joined me unexpectedly. He stood off to the side, watching and waiting like he always did. We had done this routine so many times now over the past few weeks, I had it memorized. I danced. He massaged out the kinks and aches after. I hadn't been feeling well the past couple of days, but I needed this. He knew as well that I needed these moments, so he never told me to take it easy.

The bachelorette party I had been planning, had been a hit. The bride loved the surprise and I couldn't have been more honored that they had chosen me to help them celebrate. I suggested doing the same for Luna and she loved the idea. I started keeping notes and writing down ideas for whenever she was ready to start planning. With Jaron still being in jail, I knew it would be awhile before any wedding was taking place but no matter when it happened, I would be ready and would help where I could.

I continued teaching the girls from Rouge their routine for Candace. But with the way I had been feeling lately, I couldn't get into it as much as I liked.

"What's wrong with you?" Emma asked. I had learned quickly that she had always been straight to the point. While she came off curt most times, she meant well.

"Leave her alone," Shawnee scolded her friend.

"Listen." Amber Bishop pulled her long red hair up into a ponytail. "Just tell us what to do. You're amazing at what you do, girl. You instruct. We'll listen."

And they had. I thought I would have to dance alongside them for them to get it, but I underestimated them.

It had been almost a month since I got those creepy phone calls. Every time my phone rang, it still set me on edge. Vince made me promise not to answer my phone if the number wasn't in my contacts list. I listened and that fear slowly dwindled away.

Vince and I spent as much time together as possible and when we weren't together, we were constantly texting or talking on the phone. Sometimes I would send him a sexy picture only to get a video in response or it would be the other way around. We liked teasing each other. It was fun and flirty and everything I could ever hope for when it came to being with him.

Stretching my arms up and over my head, I bent my body in ways most could only ever dream of. Lowering to the ground into wide splits, I bent my upper half forward, reveling in the way my muscles stretched and twitched between the added strain.

Once the song ended, I slowly rose to my feet and stared at my reflection in the mirror.

We got this, girl. We always got this.

When the song switched to something faster and more upbeat, I let my body move to the rhythm. Hip hop had been my calling after my accident. I watched video after video and eventually found myself doing my own routines. The movie *Honey* with Jessica Alba had been a favorite. I studied like I never studied before, but I found the only way to actually learn how to dance was by letting the music take me away.

I was vaguely aware of Vince holding out his phone like he had done quite often. I wasn't sure if he was taking pictures or a video. I never asked. I knew he would tell me when he was ready.

When the song switched to something sexy, I turned to Vince and crooked my finger, indicating for him to come toward me.

He grinned, that single move sending a flutter through my lower belly.

He shoved his phone in his back pocket and stalked toward me. Once he joined me on the dance floor, I grabbed his hands, spun around and ground my ass into him.

By the time the song ended, every inch of me tingled.

Before he had a chance to comment, I cupped his face and brought his mouth down hard on mine.

He slapped his hands against my ass, lifted me in his arms, and slammed me up against the wall.

The next thing I knew, he was inside me, taking my very breath away.

Vince broke the kiss, lowering his mouth to my neck. *"Mine."*

Every time he muttered that single word, a sense of relief washed over me.

My eyes were met with our reflection in the walled mirror across the room. His back muscles bunched, his ass flexing with each powerful thrust of his hips.

That single view shoved me over the edge and seconds later, he was jumping right along with me.

"What is it?" Vince asked, fingering the pendant hanging from the gold chain around my neck.

I watched as his strong fingers moved over the pink slippers. "Why do you keep touching the pendant?"

"Because." His eyes shot to mine. "It reminds me that you belong to me."

My stomach flipped. "You don't need a reminder, Vince. I've always been yours."

He smirked. "Stop trying to distract me. Tell me what's wrong."

After he fucked me against the mirror, he brought me back to my office so I could get some more work done.

"Baby." Vince kissed my temple. "Talk to me."

My body ached. My center throbbed with the need to have him back inside me. We had been going at it non-stop for weeks but no matter how many times we had sex, I constantly wanted him.

"We have three years to make up for, Queenie."

It was true. And while I was sore, I needed more of him.

"Your body has a story to tell and I'm going to be the only one reading it."

I smiled at the memory of his sweet words, but it still didn't mean that I wasn't scared.

"Hey." He cupped my cheek, forcing me to look up at him. "Tell me what's wrong."

"I'm scared," I finally said, not liking how weak I sounded. I looked down at my hands on his lap. We were now sitting on the couch in my office, holding, kissing, touching. Doing everything a couple did.

"Gigi." His fingers brushed down my jaw before pinching my chin. He tilted my head back, staring at me with those beautiful black eyes of his.

My heart picked up speed the longer nothing was said.

Vince continued running his thumb and forefinger over the pendant.

I wasn't sure why but that small touch alone, sent shivers racing down my spine.

"Tell me what's on your mind, beautiful." He kissed my temple. "I want to know your thoughts."

A breath left me. Every damn time. Vince was wise beyond his years. I had no idea how he did it but when he started talking, I was lost to him. Was this love? Was this how it should be?

"I feel consumed," I confessed.

"What do you mean?" he asked, his mouth brushing down the side of my face.

My eyes fluttered closed. "When you touch the pendant. When you hold the necklace while you're inside me." I shivered again. "I can't help but feel…"

"What?" he asked, his voice low.

"Owned."

A soft growl left him. "You are. You're owned by me, baby."

I looked up at him then. "I am?"

He hooked his fingers in the gold chain and pulled me closer until our mouths touched. The kiss was soft but passionate. It demanded my attention and I gave it to him. All of it.

"You're mine, Queenie," he murmured against my lips.

I broke the kiss, running my hands through his jet-black hair and stared intently into his dark eyes. "Are you mine?"

He nipped my chin. "Do you want me to be?"

"More than I can ever explain."

His lips twitched into that sexy smirk I had always adored. "Good."

I laughed lightly. "Yeah?"

"Yeah. But I have a confession."

"What's that?" I asked, brushing my fingers over the smooth lines of his handsome face. He still had a boyish charm to him but at the same time, was becoming the very man I needed.

"I've always been yours."

My fingers paused in their path. "Really? This whole time?"

He nodded slowly. "When I gave you this necklace, it was a silent promise to you. I wish I would have told you sooner how I felt but I didn't. I guess I was scared too."

"How come?" My thumb brushed over a faint scar beneath his bottom lip. I remembered when he got it. He had fallen off his bike and landed face first onto the ground. His teeth had punctured his lip. He thought it was cool. His mom, not so much.

"I was scared that my feelings for you would push you away."

"What?" I met his gaze. "That could never happen."

He shrugged. "They're intense, baby. I've only ever been with you. It's like because of that, it makes these feelings so much worse."

I shook my head. "Wait…what? You've only ever been with me? What does that mean?"

"What do you think it means?" He pulled me into his arms, keeping a hold of the necklace around my throat.

"I think it means that you've only ever slept with one person. Is that right?" I leaned back. "Have you only ever slept with me?"

Vince kissed my forehead and then my nose. "Yes."

(Vince)

Gigi gasped, her eyes widening. "Are you serious?"

"Of course." I stared at her. "I wouldn't lie about this shit."

"Vince." She shook her head. "But you went to school. You would have gone to parties, drank, met tons of girls."

"I only wanted you, Queenie." I tugged on the chain, pulling her closer.

She tried fighting me, no doubt having questions in that beautiful head of hers, but it didn't mean that she had to be so damn far away from me to ask them.

"Ask me," I demanded.

"You…I…really?" She chewed her bottom lip. "Just me?"

I chuckled. "Why are you so surprised?"

"Because you're twenty-one. We had sex on your eighteenth birthday and then didn't start sleeping together again until closer to your twenty-first birthday. But that's almost three years of no sex in between that."

"Exactly." I tapped her nose.

"But…"

"What?" I tilted my head when she didn't continue. "Say it. You can talk to me."

"I know." She huffed. "I'm just shocked."

"How come?"

"Because…you're a guy." She shook her head. "I'm sorry. That's rude. I shouldn't…God, you get me all flustered."

My laugh deepened. I turned her around and pulled her back against me. "I know most guys would have sowed their oats and shit while in college but that wasn't me. I did my schoolwork as quickly as I could so I could get back to you. Being with you is all I've ever wanted."

She sat forward, looking at me over her shoulder. Her eyes searched my face. "What does that mean?"

"Whatever you want it to mean." I cupped her face. "I've only ever been yours, Gigi. And I plan on only being yours forever. Or for as long as you can put up with my brooding ass anyway."

Her breath caught, her teeth munching on her bottom lip.

"Hey." I pulled her lip from her teeth before covering her mouth with my own. "I mean it, sweet girl."

"I've only been with you too." She broke the kiss, looking down at our joined hands on my lap. "I was a virgin on your eighteenth birthday. I wanted to tell you but thought it would scare you away. And then you acted like you knew what you were doing, so I never said anything."

I was taken aback by her words. "Are you serious?"

She nodded, her cheeks turning redder.

"Look at me."

Her beautiful eyes flicked up to mine. "Vince."

"I was a virgin too, Gigi." This whole time, I thought she was the one who acted experienced, but little did I know, neither of us where.

"You were?" She laughed, shaking her head. "Wow. You sure as hell didn't act like it."

I mentally patted myself on the back. "I knew what I wanted and that was you. I also read a lot."

"What do you mean?" Gigi picked at a fuzz on my shirt. "Vince?"

"I did my research. I wanted to know as much as I could before we had sex. And then after that night, I continued to read. Sure, I did my schoolwork and got that shit done but most of my time was spent learning how to please you."

"Uh…I think you did a good job pleasing me on your birthday. And this time together has been amazing." A notable shiver trembled through her.

I chuckled. "Well, thank you, baby, but I'm not done yet. I'm going to continue learning."

"Really?" she asked, chewing her bottom lip.

"Really." I paused. "It has been pretty amazing, hasn't it?"

She nodded. "It really has."

I kissed her cheek.

She sighed, wrapping her arms around me.

My mouth found her throat, a low growl rumbling through me. "Spend the night with me."

"Do you really have to ask?"

I took advantage of that and had her riding me shortly after. It was fast and hard, but needed.

A couple of hours later, she was passed out beside me in her bed. I knew I should have been sleeping as well but I couldn't help but watch her.

"I love you, Gigi," I whispered. That had been the first time I ever said those words out loud, even though they were whispered, and she wasn't awake to hear me. It didn't matter. Just saying them, tasting them on my tongue, gave me the strength to keep going and break down her walls until they were crumbled at our feet.

For good.

TWENTY

Gigi

I WOKE ONE MORNING, rolled over onto my back when a sharp pain erupted through my lower abdomen. I gasped, curling into a fetal position.

Taking a few deep breaths, the pain eventually went away.

Rising from the bed, I went to take a step when another slice of pain slammed into me.

I cried out, dropping to my knees.

"Gigi? You awake?" came a muffled voice from the other side of the door.

"Meadow." We were supposed to meet for breakfast this morning.

"Gigi?" Meadow pushed open the door.

"It hurts." I clutched my stomach, gasping through the pain.

"Oh God, what's going on?" She rushed to me.

"I don't know. But I can't…it hurts so much." Tears started streaming down my cheeks.

Was this it? Was I dying?

I almost wished I had.

Miscarriage.

That single word screamed through my head like a thousand broken promises. Why give me a gift only to take it away from me? I had no idea I was even pregnant. I didn't get a chance to fall in love with my baby. With Vince's baby. I didn't get a chance to feel it kick. To hear its heartbeat. I didn't even get to tell Vince. But now I had to tell him that I lost his baby. How could he forgive me? I had danced this whole time, drank some wine, got drunk once or twice. It was my fault.

My *fault.*

My fault.

I was vaguely aware of my phone ringing and chiming. I could hear Meadow and Shade's voices on the other side of the door while I was currently locked away in my room.

"If you need anything, I'm here. Both Shade and I are." Meadow pulled me into a firm hug. But I was like a statue. I didn't cry. I didn't say anything. I didn't show any emotion. I kept them bottled up because what was the point?

"Don't tell Vince," I heard myself say.

Meadow released me, frowning. "He needs to know."

"I know. I'll tell him…I..." I turned away from her and started walking down the hall to my bedroom. "I'll tell him when I'm ready."

That had been almost three days ago.

When Meadow had helped me to my feet that cold dreaded morning, I could feel the liquid rushing from my body.

Blood.

So much damn blood.

At that point, even before going to the hospital, I knew. It wasn't like Vince and I had ever used protection. We tested fate only for it to laugh and throw our mistake back in our faces.

FINALLY US

(Vince)

Gigi and I had made plans to meet up. I texted her when I left her place the morning after our moment at the studio and let her know that I was at work. By lunch, I checked my phone and never got a response from her but saw that she had read the message. After I was done work, I called her but again, no response.

I had gone over to her place, but her car wasn't in the driveway. I left and drove to my apartment but still wondered what the hell was going on.

Driving by her studio, I saw that the lights were off and continued making my way home instead.

When I arrived at my apartment, I still hadn't received a text or a phone call from her. That had been three days ago.

Something was wrong.

Rory and Mason called me, but I ignored them.

Tenise showed up one afternoon with baked goods she had made for the guys. I let her in, but she wasn't who I wanted to see. I called Gigi for what felt like the thousandth time only to get her voicemail. I kept calling just to get that greeting so I could hear her voice.

"What's going on? Rory said you couldn't get ahold of Jenny."

My back stiffened, my head whipping around. "Her name is Gigi." She knew that. It wasn't like I had been quiet in my feelings for my girl.

"Right." Tenise giggled, slapping her forehead. "Silly me. But here, I brought you some yummy treats."

I had been spoiled by Meadow's baking over the years so nothing could ever compare, but I was polite and took the plastic container from Tenise anyway. "Thank you," I mumbled, placing it on the kitchen island.

"You're welcome." Tenise went to the couch and turned on the TV, making herself right at home.

I stared after her, wondering what the hell was going on? It wasn't like I was up for company. I needed to figure out what I had done and why Gigi was suddenly ignoring me.

Had I said something wrong? We had talked a little more about our feelings. Was that it? Did I scare her away? Did I push too hard? Was she upset that I hadn't told her I loved her yet? There was no reason why I was waiting but it hadn't felt like the right time.

"Come." Tenise patted the empty spot beside her. "You need to get your mind off whatever is going on anyway. Rory is working and Mason went out of town to see his parents. So it looks like it's just you and me."

I didn't want to be rude and kick her out. It wasn't like I could get ahold of Gigi anyway and everyone I called and asked, told me shit all.

Heading to the living room, I sat on the chaise beside the couch Tenise was sitting on.

"Why are you so far away? I don't bite." Something flashed behind Tenise's dark eyes. Something I didn't like but couldn't quite figure out what it was.

Tenise stood and came toward me. "You know, I've always wished I would have met you first."

"Alright." I jumped to my feet and put some distance between us. "That's it. I'm not interested."

"What are you talking about?" Tenise laughed. "It's not like there's anything stopping us."

"Are you kidding me right now? You're dating my best friend and I have a girlfriend." Even though we had never put a label on what we had, Gigi and I both knew that we belonged to each other. And whatever was going on right at the moment was a roadblock in our path to be together. We would get through this. I would make sure of it.

"Come on, Vin." Tenise came toward me but I took a step back.

"I can't do this. You need to leave." I grabbed my wallet and keys off the table by the entrance to my apartment and shoved them in my pockets.

"Do what? We haven't done anything." Tenise closed the final few steps between us, blocking me from getting to the door. "But I want to. We could be good together."

"No." I gently pushed passed her and opened the door. "Out. Now." I thrust my arm out. "*Now!*"

Tenise started laughing. "Alright, alright. Geeze, Vin. Take a joke. Rory put me up to it. He said you would be all weird if I came on to you." She shook her head. "Take care and I'll see you soon I'm sure. I hope Jenny is okay." And just like that, she left the apartment.

Slamming the door shut behind her, I leaned against it and let out a slow breath. I wasn't sure how I would tell Rory about what just happened, but I couldn't dwell on that at the moment. I needed to see Gigi. I needed to figure out what was going on and how to fix it.

Leaving my apartment, I locked up and decided to take the stairs so I wouldn't see Tenise again. I wasn't even aware of getting to my car or driving to Gigi's. I was stuck in my head. I needed to make things right. I thought back over the past couple of months, but I couldn't figure out what I had done. We had talked about the misunderstanding when Rory's mom died, and how I never went to see her. She was good after that. She felt it was stupid that she had been upset but I understood. I would have reacted the same way if it had been the other way around. I finally got her talking and then all of a sudden, something happened where she was ignoring me again.

When I pulled up in front of Gigi's place, I let out a sigh of relief at seeing her vehicle in the driveway. I parked the car and bounded up the steps. Once I reached the door, I slowly pushed it open before I stepped inside only to find Meadow and Shade in the living room.

"Vince." Meadow stood, coming toward me. "You can't be here."

"Why the hell not?" I was thrown off by her words, knowing she had always been rooting for Gigi and I. "Where is she?"

Meadow looked away.

Shade stepped between me and Meadow. He was bigger than me. Much bigger. And older. But it didn't stop me. I refused to back down where Gigi was concerned.

"Tell me where she is. Please. I've called her, texted her. I don't know what I did wrong. It's been three days. I need to know what happened." I didn't give a shit how desperate I sounded. Something happened and Gigi was pushing me away again, but I knew that she needed me just the same. Did I say something wrong? Did I do something? I tried thinking back over the weeks we had been together, but nothing came to mind. It had been perfect. Or so I thought.

"Vince," Meadow said gently. "She doesn't want to see you."

My chest tightened. It felt like someone took a knife and stabbed me repeatedly.

"She…why not? What did I do?" I took a step toward the hall that led to Gigi's bedroom when Shade stepped in front of me.

"Not a good idea, kid," he murmured.

"I need to know what I did wrong so I can make up for it. Wouldn't you do anything for Meadow? Wouldn't you do whatever you could to show her how much you love her?"

Meadow's breath caught.

"Yes," he said without even hesitating. "I would."

"Then please, I need to see her. I need to show her…I need to tell her that I'm sorry. I'm sorry for whatever it is that I did." My heart was beating rapidly, threatening to explode from my chest the longer Gigi wasn't in my arms.

"Vince."

My head snapped around.

Gigi stood at her doorway.

"Baby, please." I took a step toward her, but Shade cupped my shoulder, stopping me.

Her eyes were red, her cheeks mottled with pink like she had been crying.

"What's wrong, Queenie? Tell me what I did. Please tell me what I did," I pleaded, silently begging for her to tell me to go to her.

"Come here," she finally said.

Shade stepped out of the way.

I ran past him and down the hall before barreling into Gigi.

She fell back but not before I caught her around the waist and shoved my face into the crook of her neck.

"I'm sorry." I picked her up and carried her into her room before kicking the door closed behind me. "I don't know what I did but I'm sorry, Gigi."

"No." A sob left her. "*I'm* sorry, Vince. I should have called you. I shouldn't have pushed you away again. That's not fair of me. I'm so sorry."

"Hey." I gently placed her on the edge of her bed and knelt at her feet. "Talk to me."

She covered her face, sobs wracking through her.

"Queenie." I stood, pulling her hands away and covering her face in soft pecks. "Talk to me." I kissed her tears away, tasting the saltiness on my tongue. "Please. Tell me so I can fix it."

She shook her head. "You can't fix it."

"Then tell me what happened so I can help make you feel better. Please." I pulled her into my arms, needing to wrap myself around her.

She continued crying against me, words leaving her lips, but they were muffled by her cries.

"Gigi." I held her against me, running my hand in circles along her back. "Talk to me, please." It couldn't have been a problem with her parents or brother. Meadow wasn't crying, so they must have been fine. It was something else. Something that hurt just as much.

"I…" She lifted her head, wiping under her eyes. "I had a miscarriage." She sniffled, looking at me with red-rimmed eyes. "I'm sorry."

"Wait." I cupped her cheek, my throat closing up. "Why the hell are you sorry?"

"B-Because I lost the baby," she said, her chin wobbling. "Your baby." Her breath hitched. "Our baby."

"It's not your fault." I kissed her softly. My chest tightened. "It's not your fault at all. I'm sorry." I leaned my forehead against hers. "I'm so sorry."

Tears streamed down her cheeks, her body shuddering with each sob she made. "I shouldn't have pushed you away, but I was scared. I needed you but I still didn't call you. You must think I'm a horrible person."

"Never." I lifted my head. "You hear me? We'll get through this. Together."

She nodded.

"Tell me what happened." Not that I wanted her to relive it but I needed to know as much as she was willing to give me so I could help her heal. I was still trying to wrap my head around the fact that I had gotten her pregnant but now was not the time to dwell on that. I could worry about it later. I just wanted her better. I wanted her healthy and to help her through this.

"I…" She pulled away from me and moved to the head of the bed.

I joined her, taking her hands in mine.

"I woke up in excruciating pain. Meadow and I were supposed to go to breakfast. She came in and saw me on the floor. I was bleeding." Gigi looked down at our hands. "I didn't even know I was pregnant, but it still hurts."

I kissed the side of her head, holding her. Letting her know that she was not alone in this. "I'm glad Meadow was here for you."

"Me too." Gigi pulled my hand into her lap. "I'm sorry for ignoring you. I didn't even realize that a couple of days had passed already until this morning." She turned her full body toward me. "I'm sorry for shutting you out. I shouldn't have done that. Can you forgive me?"

I cupped the back of her head and crushed my mouth to hers. "No forgiving needed. I'm not upset with you." I kissed her nose. "How are you feeling? Besides mentally and emotionally I mean."

"I'm fine physically. I wasn't far along at all and was able to pass it naturally and it went…fine." She swallowed hard.

"Shit, Gigi. I wish I would have been there." She needed me and I couldn't go back in time to be there for her. But I could be there for her now.

"I know." Her eyes shone. "I'm sorry I never told you until now."

"No. Don't. I just…" I scrubbed a hand down my face. "We'll move past this. Maybe not forget but in time, you'll heal. We'll both heal."

She nodded. "The doctor said I can't have sex for at least a few weeks. They told me to wait until after my next cycle but I don't know if I'll be ready."

"Geeze, babe." I pulled her into my arms until she was straddling my lap. "I'm not even hinting for sex. This is all on your time. You tell me when you're ready. Do you understand me?"

"I just don't want you thinking that I don't want you."

"Listen to me." I pinched her chin, held her head in place, and stared into her eyes. "What we have goes far beyond just being physical. I'm not like most guys. I'd rather go without sex, as long as it meant keeping you in my arms and at my side."

Her eyes welled. "Why are you so amazing?"

"I have good parents." I gave her a small smile. "My dad was persistent and broke down my mom's walls. I'm just as persistent, Gigi. And I promise, I'm not giving up on us. This is just a little roadblock and together, we will get through it. I'll help you."

"Thank you, Vince." She curled herself around me. "Thank you."

(Gigi)

When Vince reacted to the news better than I expected, I felt a weight lift off of my shoulders. But when the words that I had lost his baby, left my mouth, I could see the pain behind his eyes. He was right though; it wasn't my fault and it wasn't his. It just…happened.

"Does anyone else know besides Meadow and Shade?" Vince asked while we were curled up in my bed.

"No." I cupped his face, brushing my thumb along his bottom lip. "I'll tell people eventually but right now; I just want to heal as best I can first."

He kissed the pad of my thumb. "I get that. Anything you need, you just let me know. I'm here."

"Thank you," I whispered.

"I do have something to tell you though." He rolled over onto his back, staring up at the ceiling. "Tenise came on to me today. It was weird. She came over and brought some baked goods. Rory was working and Mason is out of town. She said it was a joke and that Rory put her up to it. I need to talk to Rory, but I wanted to let you know as well."

"Wow." A tremor of unease rushed through me. "That's…odd."

"Yeah, it was. Very odd." Vince turned his head toward me. "I'm sorry."

"Why are you sorry?"

"Because I don't want you thinking that I asked for it. I didn't." He pushed onto his elbow. "I promise I didn't."

"I know." I cupped his shoulders, pulling him down to meet my mouth. "I know," I murmured against his lips. I knew from the beginning that there was something about Tenise that I didn't like. "I know you're not that kind of guy," I said, looking up at him.

"I'm not."

I smiled. "I know."

Vince laid down beside me, wrapping his arms around me and pulling me close. "You're fucking incredible." He kissed the side of my neck, snuggling his face into me.

I sighed, realizing then that this was it. He was who I wanted to spend the rest of my life with. I just had no idea how to tell him that.

TWENTY-ONE

Gigi

VINCE HADN'T LEFT MY side since finding out I lost his baby. Our baby. Since I lost something I never officially had. Even though I didn't know I had been pregnant, it still hurt. It was like a piece of my soul was taken from me without me even realizing it. I couldn't help but blame myself but every time I felt low, Vince picked me back up and put a smile on my face. He had been my rock over these past few weeks, and I could never repay him for helping me through the agony. He put on a brave face when I needed it most, but I still knew that he was hurting as well. I would catch him brushing his hand over my stomach when he thought I was sleeping. Or hear a shaky sigh leave him whenever he thought I wasn't paying attention. It hurt. But I knew that together, we could get through it.

I ended up throwing myself into dancing. I didn't have alcohol again though. The guilt messed with my head. Drinking while pregnant and not even knowing it. I still blamed myself but every time I saw Vince, he told me without so much as uttering a single word that it wasn't my fault. That none of it was my fault.

Ryder was shipping out on Monday and we were heading to my parents' place tonight for a going away dinner. Everyone would be there. Including Vince. I hadn't seen him in a couple of days because he had been helping Rory with renovations and he was also working at the center, so he was exhausted by the time the day was over. I invited him to spend the night with me but a part of me wondered if he just went home, so he wouldn't be tempted to take it further. But I knew. Tonight, was the night that I wanted us to reconnect. He hadn't hinted in the least to have sex again, which I appreciated but I needed him. I couldn't wait anymore.

After getting ready, I took a cab to my parents' house. My nerves were all over the place, so I planned on having a couple glasses of wine. My stomach felt off. But I just took that as a sign of excitement that I would see Vince and also because my brother was leaving for who knew how long.

When I pulled up in front of my childhood home, the street was already lined with cars. Looked like they weren't the only ones having company over this evening.

As I left the taxi, the twins took that moment to pull up behind me.

"Hey," I said as both Ashton and Aiden came toward me. "How are you guys doing?"

"Not too bad." Ashton pulled me into a hug.

"You sort things out with your dad?" I asked Aiden, returning Ashton's hug.

Aiden rubbed the back of his neck. "Sort of. We both promised to keep it civil at least for tonight or else Mom is going to kick both of our asses."

"Sounds like something my mom would do." I left the warmth of Ashton's arms and gave Aiden a hug. "You good?"

He returned the hug, smiling down at me. "Don't worry about me."

But I did. We all did. Before I could respond, he pulled away from me and walked up the sidewalk to the house.

"I don't know how to tell him that he has a problem," Ashton said, coming up beside me.

"You can't tell him." I crossed my arms under my chest. "You can only be there for him, but he has to come to terms with his issue himself."

"How do you know that?"

I looked up at Ashton then. "I just do. I think Aiden will have to hit rock bottom before he asks for help or even realizes that he has a problem." My stomach clenched, hoping it didn't come to that, but something told me that it would.

Ashton cleared his throat. "Where's your man?"

"He should be here soon if he's not here already."

"You didn't see him today?" Ashton raised an eyebrow.

"No. He's been helping his friend with some renovations besides working with you guys." I frowned. "Why?"

"No reason." Ashton shrugged. "Just wondering if there's trouble in paradise already."

I rolled my eyes. "You may not have a drinking problem like your brother does but you're still a dick." I walked away, not liking whatever accusation Ashton was implying.

"Gigi." Ashton rushed to my side. "I'm sorry. I'm deflecting."

I looked up at him, a laugh escaping me. "Look at you using the big boy words."

It was Ashton's turn to roll his eyes. "Whatever. I just wanted to apologize. You and Vince are good together."

"You haven't seen us together, so how would you know that?"

"I saw you together at his party. But that doesn't matter. I *have* seen the way he looks at you. He's looked at you a certain way for years. Maybe forever."

I stopped, staring up at Ashton. "I have no idea what you're talking about."

Ashton grunted. "Right," he said slowly and walked the rest of the way to my parents' front door, leaving me to stew over whatever it was he meant.

I let out a heavy sigh and followed him. As soon as I entered the house, I was hit by a scent of something delicious. Whatever it was my mom had been cooking, smelled wonderful.

The hairs on the back of my neck suddenly tingled. I looked around me. Vince was nowhere to be found.

When I took a step forward, a heavy arm wrapped around my middle, pulling me back against a hard body. I let out a squeal.

Vince chuckled. "Miss me?" He continued pulling me into a nearby room.

"Vince," I gasped as he shut the door. "What are you—"

He pulled me against him, crushing his mouth to mine.

I sighed, snaking my arms around his neck and pulled him even closer.

A growl left him but before the kiss could become anything more, he pulled away from me.

"What was that for?" I asked, panting.

"I missed you." He kissed my cheek. "I also wanted to mess up your lipstick a bit."

"And for people to notice and say that it's about damn time?" I laughed, wiping my mouth and making sure that my lipstick wasn't messed up too much.

He chuckled. "Yeah." His eyes locked with mine. "So how have you been?"

"Good. How's my lipstick now?"

He winked. "Perfect."

I laughed, closing the distance between us and cupping him over his pants. "I missed you though and I think tonight, you should show me how much you missed me." I gave him a squeeze and kissed his chin before releasing him.

"Fucking hell," he groaned.

I giggled, leaving the room he had pushed me into only to be met by my father. "Daddy."

"Having a good time?" he asked, looking over my head.

I coughed. "I just got here but yes."

Vince came up behind me, placing his hands on my shoulders. "I was just saying hi to Gigi. I haven't seen her in a few days. Wanted to talk to her first without getting interrupted."

Dad looked between us both. "Fine. Gigi, your mom wants to see you in the kitchen."

I nodded, pulled from Vince's grasp, and headed down the hall. I stopped and looked at him over my shoulder. I assumed he would have been talking to my father but when I caught him looking back at me, my breath caught.

Blowing him a kiss, I headed to the kitchen to see what my mom wanted and hoped at the same time that my dad wouldn't kill Vince.

(Vince)

Just when I thought Angel was going to rip my face off, he pulled me in for a hard hug instead. My body stiffened, my eyes widening at the unexpected gesture coming from him. "Uh…Angel?"

He coughed, cleared his throat, and released me. "Listen, I like you for my daughter. She comes around more because of you."

"She does?" She never mentioned that she wasn't visiting her parents. Maybe her accident affected her more than I thought.

Angel nodded. "Maybe I'm just emotional because my son…" He cleared his throat again. "It doesn't matter. Just be good to Gigi. That's all I ask." And with that, he walked away and headed out into the backyard.

Gigi took that moment to step back out into the hall. "Everything okay?"

"Yeah."

She smiled. "Good. Supper's ready. Save me a seat at the table?"

I only nodded and joined everyone else in the backyard. I was greeted by people I had known my whole life, but I couldn't concentrate on anything other than Angel's words. I had pulled Gigi into the room off the hall because I wanted to kiss her without being seen but in all reality, I wanted to stake my claim in front of everyone. I wanted the world to know that she was mine and that I was hers. I wanted her to know the same.

Sitting at the table, I waited for her to come out. Once the last bit of food was on the table, I stood and waited for her to come back outside.

Her laughter rang out at whatever she heard or saw that was funny. That sound did something funny to me. It forced a ripple of pleasure down my spine. I wondered what she would sound like if I forced that laugh to turn into a scream.

When she came back outside, I stood.

All eyes turned my way, but I didn't care.

Gigi caught my gaze. A slight tinge of pink hit her cheeks. It was like she knew.

I left the table and went up to her.

She backed up a step, staring up at me. "Vince," she whispered.

Closing the distance between us, I captured her hair in my hand and crushed my mouth to hers.

(Gigi)

A collective gasp sounded around the group of people we had known our whole lives.

I knew what Vince and I had was serious when he claimed my mouth and made it his own in front of our friends and family. I had been feeling lost for so long and it took him finding me to make it better. He made everything better.

Before the kiss could turn into something that would be deemed inappropriate in front of our families, Vince broke the kiss. He smiled down at me. "I meant what I said. It's just you and me, babe. Always and forever."

My throat burned. All I could do was nod at the sincerity coming from him.

"Well, that was interesting," someone said but all I could focus on, was the man who made me feel…safe.

"What was that for?" I whispered.

Vince winked, pulling away from me and heading into the house. I was left standing there, staring after him.

My dad took that moment to come out of the house. "What's going on?"

My cheeks burned.

A round of laughter erupted.

"Your daughter just got kissed in front of all of us," Mom explained, patting her husband's chest.

"Kissed?" Dad raised an eyebrow. "It better have been by Vince and no one else."

My jaw dropped.

Mom grinned, coming up to me. "I think he likes your boyfriend."

"We…he's not…we haven't…" I chewed my bottom lip.

The patio door opened. Vince popped his head out, looking squarely at me. "I like the sound of that."

"What?" I squeaked, unable to believe that we were doing this. In front of everyone and in front of my dad no less.

"What do you say, Queenie?" Vince asked, still standing at the door. "Want to make it official?"

I could feel all eyes burning into me. "Okay," I finally said. "Boyfriend."

Vince grinned, winking and stepping back into the house.

A breath left me on a whoosh.

"I really have no idea what's going on or maybe I'm just super emotional, but that kiss was hot as hell," my sister said, fanning herself.

Shade chuckled, placing a kiss on her cheek.

Ignoring her and the stares from everyone else, I headed into the house. "Vince?" I called out.

"Fuck you, man."

My back stiffened.

Vince was coming down the hall with Piper's dad following behind him.

"What's going on?" I asked Vince.

He spun on Dale. "Just because you were a pussy who had to screw a bunch of whores to learn how to use the thing between your legs, doesn't mean shit. Not all of us need to be coddled and trained by a woman to know how to be a real man. Don't come at me with that shit ever again."

I gasped, never hearing him talk like that to anyone before. Especially not to the father of one of our friends.

Vince stomped toward me, cupped my face, and kissed me hard.

"What was that about?" I asked, staring up at Vince.

"He was giving me a hard time about kissing you in front of everyone." Vince kissed me one last time before heading into the kitchen.

"What's going on?" Stone asked, entering the house.

"Your son gave me shit." Dale scowled. "Looks like he's more of a man than I ever was at his age."

"I am so proud of my son right now." Stone stood up taller.

"Vince," I called out, heading in the direction he had gone.

He came out of the kitchen, holding a tray of veggies. "What's up?"

"What was that?" My stomach fluttered at the sight of him.

"What was what?" He came up to me and placed a soft peck on my forehead. "Do you not want to be my girlfriend?"

"It's not that. I'm just surprised you would ask in front of everyone. Especially my father."

Vince tilted his head. "You should know by now that I'm not scared of him, babe." He kissed my cheek. "Save me a seat, girlfriend."

I shivered, watching him head out into the backyard.

"Stop staring at my ass," he called out.

I laughed, shaking my head.

"Gigi."

I jumped, spinning around as Ryder came up beside me. "Hey."

"What was that show about?" He nodded toward the way that Vince went. "Do I need to threaten him?"

"Hardly." I rolled my eyes, patting my brother's arm. "So, how was your date?"

Ryder grinned, gave me a wink, and headed to the patio doors.

"Ryder, you gotta tell me something." I rushed after him. "Did she like her surprise?"

"Oh yeah." Ryder chuckled and went out into the backyard.

He had called Meadow and I the day before, asking for our help when it came to a date he was going on. Apparently, our brother was rusty. I wished I could have seen Clara Blanco's face when Ryder opened up the bed of his truck and revealed the picnic basket, feather mattress, and twinkling lights. I sighed. So romantic.

As much as I wanted to know more, I was stopped short by Vince's deep laugh. It did something funny to my belly and reminded me that it had been quite some time since we'd had sex. He had been a gentleman and left me alone since the miscarriage. He never even hinted. He often asked me how I was doing. He would flirt just the same but never pushed.

Vince chuckled again, his gaze locking with mine that time. He looked down, a sly grin spreading on his face.

My phone vibrated.

Fishing it out of my pocket, my eyes widened when I saw the text staring up at me.

Vince: You're more addictive than any drug. I'm craving your pussy more than anything. The more I get it, the more I want it. Who needs cocaine when there's you?

I looked up.

Vince was no longer looking at me but at Ashton who was now sitting beside him.

Me: I miss you and I'm ready.

I hit send and joined Vince and everyone else at the large table.

When I sat down at the empty seat beside him, he leaned over. "I miss you too, baby."

"I meant what I said in the text," I murmured low enough for only him to hear.

"I meant what I said too." Vince rested his arm across my lap. "I'll be here for whenever you are in fact ready." He brushed his mouth along the shell of my ear. "I promise."

I shivered. "Good. Because I can't wait anymore." Linking our fingers, I held his hand on my lap.

He looked down at me, something flashing behind his eyes.

"I'm ready," was all I said, not caring if anyone heard. Truth was, although it meant that I was ready to have sex again, it also meant that I was ready for more. No more pushing him away. No more keeping my feelings locked inside. I needed him. I had always needed him, but I also realized that I needed to let him in or else I was going to lose him forever.

He squeezed my hand, letting me know that he understood.

I was thankful for that.

TWENTY-TWO

VINCE

IT WASN'T MY INTENTION to kiss Gigi like that. Especially not in front of our friends and family. After dinner, I got told quite a few times that it was about time Gigi and I were making things official. If they only knew.

We helped Jay clean up. Gigi went off to do the dishes and I followed. I wasn't letting her out of my sight. Especially when she told me that she was ready for me again. Not that it mattered. I would have waited the rest of our lives to have her again.

Every so often, she would look my way. A small smile would splay on her beautiful face. Her cheeks would flush. Her eyes would darken. She would sigh and I would grin.

It made my cock motherfucking hard that I caused her to react that way without even trying.

"Thank you both for helping me," Jay said, emptying the sink. "Dessert is in the fridge, but I don't think anyone's ready for it yet."

Gigi paled. "I…" She swallowed, giving herself a shake.

"You good?" I asked her, the hackles on the back of my neck raising.

She nodded. "I haven't been feeling well. Maybe it's just stress from making sure this routine is perfect for the girls." She shrugged, hanging the dish towel over the edge of the sink. "I'm fine."

But I wasn't reassured.

"Did you go to the doctor's?" her mom asked, a deep frown settling between her brows.

"Who's sick?" Angel asked, his deep voice booming from the dining room.

"No one." Gigi huffed. "I'm fine." She looked up at me. "I'm fine. I promise that I am."

She could tell me over and over, but I still didn't believe her. We hadn't told anyone about the miscarriage. I wasn't sure if her feeling ill had anything to do with that. They never taught us that part in sex-ed.

"You not feeling well, sweetheart?" Angel asked his oldest daughter.

"I haven't been, no, but it's probably just a bug." She sighed heavily when no one budged. "Seriously." She went to walk away when I caught her hand. Her eyes met mine. "I promise, I'm fine."

I linked our fingers, holding her hand tightly in mine. I needed reassurance that she *was* fine, but I needed to touch her, more. I looked forward to spending the night inside of her but if she wasn't feeling well, just holding her would be good enough for me. Truth was, I just wanted her at my side. Constantly. I wanted her stuff in my home. I wanted to see her random hairs in the sink or shower. I wanted her scent on my pillowcase. I wanted *her.*

"Vince," she whispered.

I gave her hand a gentle tug, pulling her closer.

She stepped toward me, her shoulder brushing my chest.

I let out a slow breath.

"Do you remember when we were like this?" Angel asked.

I looked up then.

Angel's arms were crossed under his chest.

Jay laughed lightly.

"We're still like this." She kissed his cheek and left the kitchen but not before giving us a small smile.

"Thank you for dinner," Gigi told her father. "We should go," she told me.

My body stirred at what was to come. I only nodded because I knew if I had voiced my thoughts, Angel wouldn't have let his daughter go anywhere with me.

Gigi's lips twitched, pulling up into a slow smile.

I couldn't help but chuckle. Looked like she knew me better than I thought.

While Angel's gaze burned into the side of my head, I kept my hand in Gigi's.

"You sure you're feeling alright?" Angel asked, pulling us both from our staring contest.

"Yes. I probably just ate something that's not sitting right with me." Gigi shrugged, pulling from my grasp and leaving the kitchen. "I'll go say bye."

I watched Gigi head outside to the backyard and laugh at something Ashton had said to her. Her arm was around Piper's shoulders. My stomach did a flip at the mere sight of Gigi interacting with her friends. Could she ever be close to Rory and Mason because of me? I never expected her to be close with Tenise. Something weird was going on there but I loved the guys like brothers, and I knew that they would protect what was mine.

"I'm finally starting to break down her walls." I blurted, meeting Angel's gaze.

He nodded. "I knew you would. Just continue being patient with her."

I would. If it was the last thing I did.

(Gigi)

As soon as Vince started driving us back to my place, I leaned across the console between us and cupped him over his pants.

He jumped, his head whipping around.

I laughed, licking my lips. "I missed you."

"Fuck." He stepped harder on the gas. "I missed you too, but we don't have to do anything if you're not feeling well."

Unbuckling his belt, I pulled his length from his pants and began stroking him. "I appreciate that but I'm fine now. I had some Gatorade which helped."

"Thank fuck." The car swerved causing a bubble of laughter to leave me.

"Like that?" I kissed his cheek, stroking him from base to tip.

Vince shivered, keeping one hand on the wheel and wrapping his other around mine. "You have no idea how much I like it. Get me hard for you, Queenie."

"I think you need to pull over somewhere," I purred in his ear. My body ached for him. I could no longer wait for us to make it to my place. I needed him fast and hard, something to please this need and then we could take our time later.

"You can't wait for me?" he asked, his voice coming out rough.

"No." As soon as the word left my lips, Vince turned down a side street that was vacant of houses. It was an industrial area with abandoned buildings. It was early in the night, but the sun had finally set, so as long as we were quiet, we wouldn't get caught. But just the idea of a cop finding us, set my blood on fire.

He pulled us into a parking lot by a random building and as soon as he killed the engine, I was on his lap.

Crushing my mouth to his, I ripped open his dress shirt and scratched my nails into his chest.

He growled, gripping my waist and rocking me against him.

I deepened the kiss, needing him more than I needed anything in my whole entire life. He was the sustenance I needed to survive. The very air in my lungs. The blood rushing through my veins. He was my *life*.

Vince trailed his hands up my hips beneath the hem of my dress. "Tell me what you want," he murmured against my mouth.

"Your cock," I breathed, giving his bottom lip a gentle bite. "Inside me. Right now." I rose to my knees, reached between my legs, and pulled the crotch of my thong to the side.

"Do it. Now," he demanded. He was damn near vibrating out of his skin.

I lowered onto him in a smooth move, a cry leaving my lips at how good he felt inside of me.

"Fucking hell," he groaned, nipping the side of my throat.

We stayed like that. Unmoving and just holding each other.

"You feel that, babe?" he whispered, licking up the side of my throat to my jaw. "My cock owns you. Every inch of it."

"Belongs to me," I added, undulating my hips against him.

"Fucking right it does." He wrapped his arms around me, tightening his hold and picking up speed with his hips.

I whimpered, lowering my mouth to his.

Vince cupped the back of my head, slipping his tongue between my lips. "You're fucking incredible," he whispered.

I grinned, lifting my hips up and down. I took him deeper and deeper until he bottomed out inside of me. I moaned, throwing my head back. "God you feel good."

"Did you miss me?" he asked, reached between us, and started thrumming his thumb against my clit.

I jumped, cupping his shoulders and slamming my hips against his. "Yes, God yes. I missed you so fucking much."

"Prove it," he demanded. "Show me how much you missed me."

My eyes flicked to outside.

Vince followed my line of sight, a wicked grin spreading on his face. "Get up." He gently pushed me to the passenger seat before opening the door. "I suggest coming with me."

I shivered at the threat hidden in his voice.

Slipping out of the vehicle, I stood there.

Vince came up to me, his one hand wrapped around himself. "You want me?" he asked, cupping my cheek.

"Of course." I nodded.

"Good." In a quick move, he bent me over the hood of his car. With rough hands, he shoved my dress up to my hips and tore the thong from my body. "You won't be needing this."

He shoved two fingers deep inside of me before swiping them over the tight spot at my rear.

Before I could beg for more, he thrust into me.

I screamed, the burn making every tiny hair on my skin tingle.

"Come on, baby. I've been prepping your body for this. I know you can take me."

Although he had taken my ass several times already, it was almost like I could never get used to it but each and every time, the tingle, the fucking burn, felt so damn good. I couldn't get enough. And he knew it. Which made him fuck my ass every chance he could.

"Vince," I whined, trying to lift my upper body off the hood of the car but he was too strong for me.

He fisted my hair, his hot breath scorching the side of my neck. "Every inch, baby."

"Please," I whined, needing more. Even though it hurt, the pain enveloped me in a blanket of bliss. I could feel him. Everywhere. All throughout my body and it only made me crave everything he had to offer.

"You like that?" Vince grabbed hold of my hair and pulled my upper half off the hood. His hips slammed against my ass, his cock thrusting in and out of me in rough moves. He reached a spot somewhere inside of me that he had never hit before. It was like he was grabbing it with his fist and keeping it safe in his hand until he was ready to let it go.

Please let it go.

"You're beautiful with your ass wrapped around my cock," he said, pressing his lips to my ear.

Please.

"You want to come?" he asked, brushing his mouth along the base of my neck.

"Y-Yes," I panted.

Vince reached around me. When his fingers came into contact with my clit, I jumped, bucking against him. The pleasure was almost too much. I could feel the orgasm starting from my toes and slowly sliding up my body.

"You sure?" he murmured, moving his fingers lower and inserting them inside me.

"Oh." Stars danced in my vision at the sudden fullness I felt.

"Gigi." He pulled his hand from my body and pressed my upper half back onto the hood of the car. "If you want to come, then be a good little girl and do it. *Now.*" He landed a hand against the flesh of my ass. "*Now*, Gigi."

Vince pushed into me as deep as my body would allow.

My eyes widened.

A sudden scream fell from my lips as the release rocked me to the very core.

After our unexpected moment in the parking lot, Vince drove us back to my place as fast as he could. Truth was, when I came for him, he didn't last much longer than I had.

Every inch of me burned. I couldn't sit still. Every time I moved; I could feel him.

When he caught me squirming, he would smirk and scratch the scruff on his jaw, all proud of himself.

Now we were in my bed, wrapped up in each other again.

I almost forgot that I hadn't been feeling well but when Vince knelt between my legs, my stomach rolled. I shook it off and kissed him, trying to ignore the fact that my belly was feeling off.

As soon as Vince thrust into me, my stomach churned. "Oh."

He lowered his mouth to my neck, sinking his teeth into the skin. "Fuck, baby. I've missed you. The parking lot wasn't enough. Once a day is never enough. Not with you."

"I…" Bile rose to my throat. "Wait." I pushed him.

"What's wrong?" He lifted his head, staring down at me.

"I can't." My stomach churned again. "I'm going to be sick." I shoved him back and slid off the bed before rushing to the bathroom. I fell to my knees by the toilet and threw up my mom's wonderful dinner. My stomach heaved. It was so damn hard, it felt like my body was trying to puke up everything inside of it.

"Gigi?"

"I'm sorry." I hung my head in the toilet, hugging the bowl and waiting for the nausea to stop.

"Don't be sorry." Vince knelt beside me, pressing something cold to the back of my neck.

I didn't have enough energy to ask what it was but appreciated the gentle gesture just the same.

"How are you doing?"

I took a deep breath, lifting my head. When my stomach seemed to settle, I moved away from the toilet and gave him a small smile.

He chuckled, wiping a cloth along my mouth. "You good?"

My heart warmed. "I am. Thank you for taking care of me."

"That's my job." He kissed my forehead.

"I'm sorry for ruining the mood." I had been aching for him all night and even after the parking lot and then my stomach ruined it.

"Did you want me to make you some tea?"

My stomach churned at the thought. "Oh God." I threw up again. "I think I'm just going to stay here for the night."

"Maybe you ate something bad like you said earlier," he offered. "I'll make a call and see if anyone else is sick." He pushed away from me.

I gave him a wave. I didn't care anymore. I just wanted my stomach to stop clenching.

I hoped no one else was sick. Everything tasted wonderful. I wasn't sure what my issue was but when I thought of the delicious meal I had earlier, my stomach erupted again.

A thought came to me. No. There was no way. We hadn't had sex since the miscarriage. Not until tonight.

"So, no one else is sick." Vince came into the bathroom and knelt beside me. "Maybe we should take you to the hospital. It could be something else."

"Maybe." I let him pull me to my feet. I flushed the toilet and brushed my teeth. Looking at my reflection, I wondered if it was possible. I tried thinking back to sex-ed and all the things I had learned over the years, but I couldn't figure it out. I didn't tell Vince my thoughts because I didn't want him to worry about my sanity.

"Hey." He cupped my face, staring down at me. "You good?"

"I don't want to go to the hospital. I'm fine. I'm sure it's just a bug." I pushed past him and crawled onto the bed.

Vince joined me, pulling me into his arms. "If you're still not feeling well tomorrow, I'm taking you to the hospital."

I turned toward him. "I'm fine, Vince."

He kissed my nose. "You may be fine now, but it could be something…"

When his voice trailed off, I lifted onto my elbow. "What?"

"It could be something worse." He sat up. "If I don't take care of you and it's something bad, I would never forgive myself. And your dad would kick my ass."

"I promise that I'm fine," I said, trying to reassure him. It was just a bug. It was the only thing that made sense.

"You better be, Gigi." Vince laid back down, pulling me into his arms. "I can't have it any other way."

I spent the next couple hours staring at the ceiling. Vince's words kept bouncing around in my head. I didn't know what he meant by them but if I could take a guess, he clearly wanted more out of this than us just being girlfriend and boyfriend.

"Gigi," a deep voice murmured in my ear. "Wake up."

I stirred, not realizing I had fallen asleep. "What's wrong?" I asked, hearing the panic in Vince's voice.

His eyes were wide. He looked down, back up at my face and then down again.

"What is it?" I asked, my heart thumping hard.

He met my gaze that time. "You're bleeding."

TWENTY-THREE

VINCE

As Gigi cleaned herself up, I put the linen in the laundry hamper but while I did that, I couldn't get the blood stain out of my mind's eye. I didn't know what was going on and I didn't like it. I asked her if I had been too rough, but she reassured me that it wasn't because I had a thing for her ass. Her words.

She was trying to lighten the mood, but it didn't make me feel any better.

I was rattled, on the verge of snapping all because I didn't know what was going on with her health. It wasn't her period. It wasn't because I had hurt her. But it was something. We just didn't know what.

Once I got the laundry in the hamper, I stomped to the bathroom door and gave it a hard knock. "Babe, we have to go." *Or else I'll break this door down and drag you to the hospital.*

"I'm almost done," she called from the other side of the door.

I took a breath and then another. I understood. I got it. I did. She didn't want to go to the hospital. Who did? But we needed to find out what was going on with her.

The door finally opened. Gigi was wearing gray sweatpants, a white long-sleeved shirt that had three buttons undone at the collar. Her hair was piled on top of her head, loose strands falling free around her beautiful face. Even though she was dressed comfortably, she was hot as hell. My dick stirred, agreeing with me.

"We need to go," I grumbled.

"Why are you so grumpy?" she asked, grabbing her phone, wallet, and keys.

"Because I need to know what's going on and I don't know what's going on and I don't like it," I said all in one breath.

Gigi stared at me. "It's probably just my cycle being weird. It happens."

"I don't care. I'd rather err on the side of caution."

"Why?"

"What the fuck do you mean, why?" I demanded, my voice coming out harsher than I intended it to.

She raised an eyebrow. "I'm fine, Vince. You're worrying way too damn much."

I grunted. If I didn't worry, her father would cut me up into little pieces and spread me out across the fucking earth. "Don't care." I grabbed her hand, kissed her hard on the mouth, and led her from her house.

She huffed and mumbled complaints as I dragged her to my car but again, I didn't care. Her health and safety came first and foremost.

(Gigi)

When we got to the hospital, much to my dismay of course, I checked in and told them what the issue was. Surprisingly, I was put in a room right away. My vitals were checked, and blood work was drawn. Now I was sitting on the edge of the hospital bed, waiting.

Vince was pacing. With every step he took, the anxiety increased.

"You need to come here," I told Vince, staring down at my hands that were resting on my lap.

"I'm always here," he murmured, stepping up beside me.

He was losing it. I knew because I could sense it. I looked up then, being met by stormy dark eyes. Eyes that I could get lost in.

Vince slid the back of his hand down the length of my arm before slipping his fingers between mine. "I haven't called your parents. I figured we would wait until we got answers before we worried them."

I nodded, thankful that he was there with me and that I wasn't alone. "Thank you for being here," I said, voicing my thoughts.

"You never have to be without me again." His eyes locked with mine. "It's just us. You and me against the world, Queenie."

I smiled, my heart stuttering at the passion in his eyes. But there was something else. There had always been something else.

He tilted his head. "What?"

I shook myself, not realizing I was staring at him. "Nothing," I said as the doctor came into the room.

"Miss Rodriguez?"

"Yes, doctor?"

"We got the test results back." She smiled at me. "You're pregnant."

My eyes widened.

"What did you just say?" Vince demanded, squeezing my hand.

"I'm sorry, Doctor. Not to be rude but that's impossible. I had a miscarriage and we haven't…" I looked at Vince.

"We haven't had sex since," he finished for me. "Not until last night. I'm no expert but even I know that symptoms don't usually happen that fast."

"Interesting." The doctor frowned, looking at her chart again. "Your hCG level is high enough for an active pregnancy and not a lost one. I'll order an ultrasound and we'll get to the bottom of this for you." The doctor took that moment to leave.

A nurse came in a moment later, took more blood and left.

"I can't be pregnant, Vince," I told him.

"It doesn't make sense." He kissed the top of my head. "But whatever it is, we'll deal with it. Together. Okay?"

I nodded. "God, I'm so glad I have you."

"Always and forever, baby," he whispered in my ear. "Always and forever," he repeated.

"What if I *am* pregnant? How is that possible?" I asked as the doctor came back into the room after what felt like years.

"The blood work states that you are in fact pregnant." She flipped through the pages on her clipboard. "So, lets get that ultrasound set up and see what's going on."

"I…" I paused when a technician wheeled in a machine and stopped it beside the head of my bed. "I can't be pregnant." Not that I would complain if I was, since I lost the first baby, but this didn't make sense.

The technician instructed me to lay back. She lifted the gown to my knees and gently pushed a wand inside of me.

Both Vince and I waited with bated breath.

A moment later, she smiled and turned the screen toward us. "There's your baby," she said, pointing at the screen.

My eyes welled, my throat burning at the hard lump suddenly lodged in it. "But how?"

The doctor took that moment to enter the room. "Do twins run in your family?"

I looked up at Vince before glancing back at the doctor. "Yes. My mom's a twin."

"Well it looks like you were pregnant with twins but as you already know, you lost one baby. But this one survived." The doctor went on to talk about some medical things that I didn't quite understand. All I could focus on were her words, *this one survived.*

"How far along is she?" Vince asked, pulling me from my thoughts.

"About eight weeks." The doctor smiled at both of us. "I know that this has come as quite a shock."

"That's an understatement," I mumbled.

"Did you want to hear the heartbeat?" the technician asked.

I gasped, nodding quickly.

Vince sat on the stool beside me, pulling it closer to the bed I was lying on, and gripping my hand tightly in his.

Suddenly a woosh sound filled the room. It was the most beautiful sound I had ever heard. Tears streamed down my cheeks.

"Your baby is healthy." The technician pointed at a small spot on the black and white screen. "And your baby is strong."

"I understand that you were bleeding tonight," the doctor added. "So as a precaution, please try and take it easy. Eat as best you can. Take pre-natal vitamins. Get lots of rest. And this baby and you will be just fine."

"Our baby," I whispered.

The technician removed the wand from my body, pulling the gown back over my knees to cover me. She handed us a small picture of the ultrasound. "We'll give you two a moment." She left the room with the doctor following behind her.

I quickly got dressed before sitting back on the edge of the bed. Vince took the hint and stepped between my knees. He held me against him, wrapping his arms around my shoulders. I breathed him in, taking all the strength I could muster. "Vince, can we do this?"

He leaned back, pinching my chin and tilting my head. "We can and we will." Brushing the back of his hand over my stomach, he let out a shaky breath. "I wasn't sure if I ever wanted kids. But after our first time together, I realized that I did. It wasn't like we've ever been safe anyway. I know we've only been together for technically a few months, but I feel like we've been together for years." Vince brushed his mouth along mine. "We can take this one day at a time, but I just want you to know that I'm not going anywhere. You and our baby have nothing to worry about. I am yours. I am both of yours."

"Really?" My breath hitched. "You mean that?"

He gave me a small smile, cupping my cheek. "Gigi, I'm in—"

"Sorry to interrupt."

I jumped, my head whipping around.

The doctor laughed. "Didn't mean to startle you."

Vince pulled away from me. "I'll be outside." And with that, he left the room.

The air around me suddenly grew cold. I wasn't sure what that was about.

"I just wanted to prescribe you something to settle your stomach. This isn't harmful to the baby but please only take it if you can't keep anything down for more than twenty-four hours. That includes water."

I nodded, taking the prescription from her. "Thank you, Doctor."

"You're welcome." She walked me out. "Anything you need, please don't hesitate to call." She handed me a business card. "But I have a feeling that it'll work out fine for both of you." She turned on her heel and headed down the hall, barking orders at her staff.

"Queenie."

I spun around, finding Vince coming toward me holding a yellow Teddy Bear.

"I got yellow just in case we wait to find out the sex. Although, even if it's a boy, he can like pink all he wants, and our little girl can like blue." Vince shrugged. "They can like whatever color they want."

I took a breath and then another. Yes, the doctor was right. We could do this. And Vince was the only one I wanted to do this with.

(Vince)

Gigi was pregnant. With my baby.

I meant what I'd told her. I was in this. For the long run. For however long she could put up with my brooding and possessive ass anyway.

"Vince?" Gigi hugged the Teddy Bear against her chest, looking up at me with those big beautiful eyes of hers. "Thank you."

Pinching her chin, I placed a soft peck on her mouth. "You don't need to thank me. Ever." I stepped back, holding out my hand. "Come home with me."

Something flashed behind her eyes. "Okay. Can we stop off at my place first?"

"We can do whatever you want." I still couldn't wrap my head around the fact that she was pregnant. Every male instinct in me wanted to shout it from the fucking rooftops that my baby was in her tight little body. But I wouldn't. I would in time but not until Gigi gave me the go-ahead.

When we reached my car, she went to pull her hand from mine, but I refused and tugged her back against me.

She gasped, slapping her hands against my chest. "Vince?"

"Listen." I cupped the side of her neck, wanting to tell her that I was in love with her. No, that I was fucking obsessed. With her. I almost did earlier and then the doctor interrupted us. "Whatever you need, I am here. I already told you before. If you need something to take the edge off, you fucking call me. Alright?"

Gigi frowned, her eyes darting back and forth over my face. "I'm not sure the sex you like would be good for the baby."

I grinned, leaning down to her ear. "You mean, the sex we both like, Gigi. My girl has a dark side to her. Isn't that right?" I kissed her cheek, mentally patting myself on the back at the shiver that trembled through her.

"I have no idea what you're talking about." She pulled away from me, only because I let her, and went to open the passenger side door. I stopped her instead, slapping my hand against the top of it and stepping up behind her.

"I'll remember that the next time I'm balls deep inside your ass." I pressed my lips to her ear. "When you're begging me to go harder, faster, *rougher*." I growled the last word, pushing my hips into her.

"God, Vince." She shook herself.

I chuckled, stepping away from her and going around to the driver's side of the car. "Just remember, Gigi. I've been in every inch of you. I know what you like and what you don't like. Which doesn't seem to be much."

She stared at me from the other side of the car. "I'm sure we could come up with something that neither of us like."

I raised an eyebrow. "Is that a challenge?"

Gigi grinned, giving me a wink. "No, Vince. It's a damn promise."

My cock twitched at her words.

Even better.

TWENTY-FOUR

VINCE

IT HAD BEEN A few days since we found out Gigi was still pregnant. We kept it a secret, basking in the glow that we still had the life we unexpectedly created, when we thought we had lost that chance for at least a little while.

Gigi's morning sickness started up again, coming at any time of the day but she never took the medication she was given. Luckily, she was able to keep crackers down for the most part, so it helped settle her stomach.

One night she was sleeping beside me, but I was restless. The fact that she was pregnant with my baby, stirred the beast within. I became more protective.

She would laugh.

I would kiss the hell out of her.

She would blush.

I couldn't control it. This need. This want. This feral obligation to make sure she was in fact safe. If I could have baby-proofed my apartment and her house without her questioning my mental health, I would have. I didn't understand it. Was it always like this? Did other guys go through this when the love of their life was growing their child?

Moving farther down the length of the bed, I leaned on my elbow and cupped her stomach. Gigi wasn't showing yet, but I couldn't wait for her to grow and become swollen with our baby.

"I don't know you," I told her stomach, careful to keep my voice low so I didn't wake her. "But I'm already in love with you." I brushed my thumb back and forth over her still flat belly. "I'm sorry we couldn't keep your sibling but, God wanted them to come home and stay with Him." I wasn't overly religious. I believed in a higher power and that everything happened for a reason, but it wasn't something I practiced daily. I just tried to be a good person and wanted to raise this baby and my future children, to be the same. "You're strong, little one. We'll keep you safe and protect you from the terrors of the world as best we can. I can't wait to meet you and fall in love with you even more. You stay safe and warm in there, okay? And be gentle to your mama." I kissed Gigi's stomach and went to lay back down beside her when I caught her smiling at me. I chuckled. "I couldn't sleep."

"Did you have a good chat?" she asked softly.

I nodded, wrapped her in my arms, and cupped her stomach. "You weren't supposed to be listening. We were having a private conversation."

She laughed.

Pushing my face into the crook of her neck, I breathed her in.

"Vince?"

"Mmmhmm?"

"Thank you."

I lifted my head, staring down at her. "For what?"

Gigi rolled over onto her back. "I know you're young. We're both still young. I'm sure you weren't expecting to have a baby at twenty-one."

"I don't give a shit about my age. We could have gotten pregnant the night of my eighteenth birthday, and I would be here." I cupped her cheek. "I will always be here. I'm not leaving you and I'm definitely not leaving our baby." And future babies, but I kept that little thought to myself.

Gigi's eyes welled.

"Why the tears, baby?"

"You're just…I can't…" She sighed. "Thank you."

I chuckled, laying back down beside her. "You never need to thank me, Queenie."

She rolled over onto her side, facing me and cupping my cheek. Her thumb brushed along my mouth, sparking a hint of need somewhere deep inside of me. My cock twitched, jumping against the fly of my pajama pants. It begged for her but as much as I always wanted her, we hadn't had sex since finding out she was pregnant a few days ago.

"Vince?" Her eyes darkened, her voice dripping with lust. "Can we…"

Slipping a hand beneath the covers, I brushed the back of my knuckles over her stomach and delved lower until I reached the apex between her thighs.

"Please," she whispered.

"Shhh…I'll take care of you." I kissed her forehead, slipping my fingers into her panties. I wouldn't have sex with her. Not yet. I feared that I would hurt the baby. Add to the fact that she wasn't out of the first trimester yet, it increased the anxiety rushing through me.

"I want you." She licked her lips.

"And I want *you*. I always want you, but we can't."

She pouted. "But—" My finger slowly slid inside of her. "God."

"I want to make sure the baby is safe first."

"It is." She panted.

I chuckled. "I'll take care of you, Queenie."

And I did.

It was the following weekend and I was stuck helping Rory with the renovations he was doing on the house he had purchased. I hadn't seen him in what felt like forever and even longer since I'd talked to him.

When I showed up at his house, my stomach twisted as he bounded out of it, down the steps, and stomped toward me. Guess we were doing this now.

"What the fuck is this I hear that you hit on my girlfriend?" he demanded, closing the distance between us and pushing me.

"Excuse me?" I shoved him back. "That's not what happened."

"That's not what she said." His face was red, his eyes dark with fury.

"What the hell? I tried calling you, fucker. I wanted to tell you what happened, so we wouldn't be where we are now, but you've been ignoring my calls and texts." I took a step to the left when he went to shove me again. "Listen to me. She came over and hit on me. She said that it was a joke and that you put her up to it."

Rory's brows dropped in the center. "Why the hell would I do that?"

"How the fuck am I supposed to know?" I sidestepped away from him when he went to push me again. "Listen, something is going on with her, but I don't know what it is. It's none of my business but—"

"You're right. It's not your fucking business." He walked past me, shouldering me in the process.

"That's how it's going to be? We made a fucking promise that we wouldn't let a woman come between us,"

I reminded him, unsure what the hell this was about. "We've known each other way too damn long for our friendship to end because you believe your girlfriend over me."

Rory stopped, looking at me over his shoulder. "She's always had a crush on you."

My eyes widened, my stomach clenching. "What?"

"She hinted at a threesome one night when she was drunk." Rory looked away, his shoulders slumping.

"Listen, I love you and Mason like brothers. I would never do that."

"I know." Rory sighed, meeting my gaze that time. "I told her that you were in love with Gigi and that there was no way you would ever consider doing that shit with us. Even if you were single. It's not even my thing but I wanted to make her happy. So I suggested we ask Mason." He shrugged. "But nothing happened. Just some flirting. I wouldn't put him in that position anyway, but she's been…"

"Weird?" I offered.

Rory nodded.

I took a step toward him. "I *am* sorry. I never wanted anything to happen. I kicked her out after she hinted for more."

"Did you tell Gigi?"

"I did. She took it better than I thought she would."

"Better than I did?" Rory stared up at the house we were renovating together.

"Yeah." I cupped his shoulder. "But I would have reacted the same way."

"This is fucked up." Rory sighed. "I'll talk to her, but I swear that I never put her up to it."

"I didn't think you would." I gave his shoulder a squeeze. "Lets get these renovations done and over with."

"Sounds like a plan." He shoved his hands in his pockets. "I only put my name on everything."

My head whipped around. "Really?"

"Yeah." He shrugged. "Something told me to. Tenise never even questioned it, which I guess should have been a red flag." He shrugged again.

"Listen, whatever happens, both Mason and I are here for you."

"Thank you." He huffed. "Is it too early for a beer?"

I chuckled. "It's five o'clock somewhere."

A couple of hours later, another car pulled up into the parking lot. My body stirred when I realized that it was Gigi. As if on cue, Tenise came out into the kitchen that we were working on. She showed up after Rory and I had finally talked.

I left the house as Gigi slipped out of the vehicle. Picking up speed, I closed the distance between us and wrapped her up in a hug.

"Hi." She returned the embrace, holding me tight.

Reaching a hand between us, I brushed my fingers over her lower stomach. "How are my girls?"

She laughed. "You don't know it's a girl, baby."

I kissed her forehead, then her nose, and finally placed a soft peck on her full mouth. "I do. I can feel it." I had told her this morning that we were having a girl. I wasn't sure why I felt that we were, but I could feel it in my blood. Add to the fact that I kept dreaming about it.

"As long as they're healthy, I don't care what the sex is." Gigi cupped the back of my neck, her eyes dancing along my face.

I grinned, slipping my hand around to her ass and pulling her flush against me.

She shivered. "God, Vince."

I chuckled, kissing her neck. "I missed you."

"You saw me this morning when you left my bed," she murmured.

"And when I left your shower."

She leaned back. "And my kitchen." She winked.

I laughed. "I'm enjoying savoring your body."

"As much as I appreciate the attention, I miss *you*."

I cupped her face. "I know." As much as I missed her just the same, I was having fun taking care of her pleasure and getting nothing in return. It wasn't like she hadn't hinted for it, but I wanted to take care of her instead. It was also refreshing.

"I'll be three months soon." Gigi cupped me over my pants, making me jump. "And then this is mine."

"Yes, ma'am." I growled into the crook of her neck.

She giggled, giving me a squeeze.

I shivered. "Fucking hell." I pulled her hand away before I forced her to her knees and fucked her face in public. "Not the time, babe."

"Fine. Tonight then. I get waiting to have sex, Vince, but I need something. At least a little thing."

A sly grin spread on my face. "Trust me, Queenie, you of all people should know that it's not a little thing."

"I don't know, Vince." She walked past me. "I seem to have forgotten the size of it. I guess you'll just have to remind me." She sauntered her hips, giving me a wink over her shoulder.

Catching up with her, I caught her around the waist. "You'll remember the size when you're gagging on it." I gave her ass a smack and walked away, a smug smile forming on my face at the flush I left on her cheeks.

(Gigi)

I found as much as I missed Vince, I enjoyed the tension brewing between us. Especially the flirting. The constant touching. The dirty and vulgar words. My body burned for him, my mouth watering at what he threatened.

When I woke up that morning, his face had been between my legs. I begged, pleaded for him to fuck me, but he refused. It was sweet in a way but also frustrating at the same time.

As he walked toward Rory's house, Tenise had greeted him at the front door.

My stomach twisted at the sight of her. Even though I wasn't her biggest fan, I could still admit that she was beautiful. She was shorter than I was but not by much. She had curves that I was sure made most men drop to their knees. Her tits were also bigger than mine but luckily, Vince wasn't a boob man. That little fact made me feel somewhat better at least.

He walked around her and disappeared into his best friend's new home while Tenise stayed back and stared my way.

I swallowed hard, my heart jumping to my throat. I never had to deal with a jealous woman before. Even though she was dating Rory, I could still see the longing stares she had for Vince. I wondered if Rory knew about her feelings for his best friend.

"You and Vin seem to be happy," she said as I neared her.

"We are." But it still pissed me off that she called him Vin. I wasn't exactly sure why, but it annoyed the hell out of me that she had her own little nickname for him.

Her brows narrowed, her eyes roaming down the length of me. Her lip curled up in disgust as she crossed her arms under her chest. "You guys serious now or what?"

A tremor of unease rippled down my spine. I was thankful at that moment that I was wearing a loose-fitting sweater. Not that my bump was showing yet, but something told me, that teeny tiny little voice warned me against letting her know that I was pregnant with Vince's baby.

"We are." I went to walk by Tenise when her next words stopped me.

"He'll leave you."

I looked back at her. "And you know that how?"

"Because he's young. He's only twenty-one. You're holding him back." She leaned against the banister of the porch. "He probably fucked around when he went to school too. Rory, Mason, and I went up to see him. You should have seen the women hanging off of him. I'm not a lesbian but even I would have given them a shot."

My jaw clenched, my teeth grinding against each other.

The door opened then, revealing Vince. "Queenie?" He stepped up behind me. "What's going on?"

I stared at Tenise, his friend's so-called girlfriend. "Apparently you fucked around when you went to school and had women hanging off of you," I told him.

Tenise's eyes widened.

"What the fuck?" Vince grabbed my hand, spinning me around. "You know that's not true. Tenise, did you tell her that?"

"Women were constantly hitting on you," she reminded him, crossing her arms under her chest.

"That doesn't matter. I didn't do shit with them." Vince's eyes darted back and forth. "You have to believe me." He pulled me against him. "Please, Gigi."

"What's going on?" Rory asked, joining us on the porch.

"Your girlfriend is trying to cause shit," Vince told him. "I never fucked those women." He looked down at me. "I swear I didn't."

"I know." I wrapped my arm around his waist. "I believe you."

"Tenise," Rory barked. "I think we need to talk."

"Of course, baby." Tenise came toward us and stopped directly beside me. She leaned down toward my ear. "I hope he thinks of me the next time he's inside you."

My mouth fell open.

She stood up straight, walking into the house.

"I'm sorry," Rory mumbled, following his girlfriend.

"What the hell was that about?" Mason asked, coming outside.

"What did she just say to you?" Vince asked me, ignoring his friend.

"Nothing important," I told him.

"Gigi, tell me," he demanded.

"It doesn't matter because I know it won't happen." I clutched his shirt in my hand, pulling him down to meet my mouth. "Kiss me."

Vince huffed but placed a hard peck on my mouth. "I don't like that she's saying shit to you."

"I don't believe her but the actual reason I'm here is because I wanted to see if you were done and wanted to go out for a late lunch."

"Yes." Vince pulled a screwdriver from his back pocket, grabbed Mason's hand, and slapped it in his palm. "Here, have fucking fun." He came back toward me, grabbed my hand, and led me from the house. "Weird, that was so damn weird."

I rushed to keep up with him. "Vince, it's not a big deal."

He stopped, spinning on me. "It is a big deal. She's fucking crazy."

"Hey." I stepped up against him, wrapping my arms around his middle and linking my fingers behind his back. "I'm not worried."

Vince cupped the side of my neck. "You better not be fucking worried. I want you and only you."

I grabbed the collar of his t-shirt and pulled him down to meet my mouth. "I think you should reassure me," I whispered against his lips.

"You want her to see you claim me, baby?" He cupped my ass, pulling me against him.

My breath caught. "Yes," I heard myself say. I ran my hands up his strong back, slipping my fingers into his hair. "Kiss me. Hard."

"Fuck," he muttered, pressing his lips against mine.

Shoving my tongue into his mouth, I deepened the kiss. It turned frantic, hot, desperate. It had felt like so long since we had sex even though it hadn't been. Add to the fact that another woman wanted him, and I was ready to combust. If it wasn't frowned upon, I would have shoved him to the ground just to show Tenise that he was in fact very much mine.

Vince groaned but broke the kiss. "Claim me later."

"I plan on it," I whispered, running my fingers over his mouth.

"How?" he asked, leaning his forehead against mine.

"I miss your taste."

He muttered a curse, his cock twitching between us.

I laughed. "Take me out for lunch. Your baby is hungry."

Vince kissed me one last time, reminding me that I had nothing to worry about. I knew that. I trusted him but I didn't trust Tenise.

Not one bit.

My phone suddenly rang, startling me. I pulled it from my bag, seeing that it was my mom calling. "Hey, Mom. How's it going?"

"Your dad," her voice trailed off.

"What's wrong?" I asked, my stomach sinking.

Vince's brows narrowed in the middle.

Her breath caught. "Gigi." She paused. "Your dad had an accident."

TWENTY-FIVE

Gigi

WHEN WE ARRIVED AT the hospital, I felt like I was watching myself from afar. Vince had called Meadow for me and left a message on Ryder's phone. I wasn't even sure if Ryder would get the message or when he would be able to get back to us. But at least he would know that he was thought of and would check in when he could.

Mom didn't give me a lot of information over the phone. Just that Dad was working at a job site and fell off a ladder, but that was it.

Suddenly the passenger side door opened, revealing Vince.

I looked around us, not even realizing we had parked. I left the car, grabbed Vince's hand for strength I wasn't sure I would ever feel, and let him lead me into the big building.

When we reached the floor my dad was on, I found my mom standing with Meadow and Shade. I let go of Vince's hand and rushed toward them. "Mom."

She turned, facing me and opening her arms.

"I'm going to kill your father, that's what's going to happen."

I leaned back. "What are you talking about?" I asked as Vince joined us.

"Dad was a bad boy," Meadow mumbled.

"I've been on him to get glasses," Mom explained. "He can't see worth shit but he refuses because it makes him feel old." She scowled. "Anyway, he went up a ladder and lost his footing and slipped. He fell and landed hard. Knocked himself out. There was a lot of blood and the guys freaked. Turns out he has a concussion."

"But he's fine? Besides that, and you wanting to kill him?" I asked, needing to know that the first man I ever loved, would be okay.

"Yeah." Mom gave me a small smile. "He's fine. He has to take a few days off. If he expects me to take care of him and wait on him hand and foot…"

"You'll do it," Meadow finished for her.

Mom sighed. "Yeah, I will. Listen, don't either of you do that shit, you hear me?" she told Shade and Vince.

They chuckled.

"I'm serious." Mom glared at them.

"Yes ma'am." Vince linked his fingers with mine. "I'll be a good boy."

"Same here." Shade wrapped his arm around Meadow's shoulders. "I'm sure Meadow will punish me if I don't anyway."

Meadow only grinned. "I have no idea what you're talking about."

We all laughed that time.

"Can we see him?" Meadow asked. "So *I* can kick his ass?"

Shade grunted. "No ass kicking, baby."

Vince gave my hand a gentle squeeze.

We followed Mom into the room that Dad was staying in.

He was sitting up, a deep scowl on his face. "It's about time you came back in here, woman."

Mom stopped in her steps. "Seriously, Angel? You are in no position to throw any of that shit at me."

Dad huffed. "Come here," he demanded. "Please," he added gently when she wouldn't budge. "Princess."

"Men," she mumbled under her breath and went to her husband. "You scared the shit out of me, asshole." She sat on the edge of the bed, grabbing hold of his hand.

"I know. I'm sorry." He looked at the rest of us. "I am sorry."

"We heard you need glasses," I said, going up to Dad. "You should probably listen to your wife." I gave him a hug. "Right?"

"Have you told Vince you love him yet?" Dad whispered in my ear.

My eyes widened. "No." I coughed, releasing him so Meadow could give him a hug as well.

"We were worried," she said.

"I know." Dad sat up straighter. "I'll get glasses." He scowled again. "But I'm going to complain about it."

"I don't care about that." Mom placed a kiss on his cheek. "I just want you to be safe." She looked back at me. "That reminds me. Gigi fell off a ladder a few months ago."

"What?" Dad's head whipped around. "And you're just telling me now?"

Mom rolled her eyes. "She's fine." She waved a hand toward me. "Clearly, she's fine. And Vince saved her anyway."

Vince shifted beside me.

My cheeks heated as all eyes landed on us. "I am fine," I reassured Dad. "I was at the center, putting in a new lightbulb but I promise, I'm fine. I'm not the one who needs glasses though."

"What happened?" he demanded.

"The step gave out and she fell but I caught her," Vince explained.

"Wow. Talk about being in the right place at the right time," Meadow said, shaking her head.

"And who the fuck am I killing for leaving a faulty ladder at the center?" Dad growled.

"I'm just glad you're okay," I said, needing to take the conversation away from us when I could see the pink in Vince's cheeks. Looked like he didn't enjoy being the center of attention. Neither did I, unless I was dancing.

"Me too." Dad looked between us, something flashing behind his dark eyes.

While Mom and Meadow carried on a conversation, Dad only stared at me.

I shifted from foot to foot, my hand dropping to my stomach. I winked, wondering if he would get the hint.

He caught the movement, raising an eyebrow. "Yes?"

I glanced up at Vince.

He chuckled. "Yes."

I grinned, looking back at Dad and found everyone else staring our way. "Yes," I whispered.

"Yes, what?" Meadow asked.

"Really?" Mom pushed off the bed and came toward me. "Really?" she repeated, excitement dancing in her eyes.

Vince placed his hand on my stomach. "Really."

Meadow gasped.

Mom pulled me in for a hug, wrapping her other arm around Vince. "I knew you would find your way to each other," she whispered.

I hugged her back, my eyes locking with Vince's.

"Your daughter is a tough one to crack but I was determined," Vince said, winking at me.

"How far along are you?" Mom asked, placing her hands on my stomach.

"Almost three months," I answered. "I'm sorry we didn't tell you." I looked at Meadow. "It was a twin."

Her eyes widened. "Oh God."

"What do you mean?" Dad asked.

I explained the miscarriage and what the doctor had said when we found out that we were still pregnant.

"I'm so sorry." Mom hugged me again.

"Thank you. I'm fine. We're fine." I absentmindedly reached out for Vince. When his fingers came into contact with mine, I let out a breath and let my worries get shared between us.

"Now that we know your dad's okay, we should go," Vince whispered in my ear. "I'm throbbing for that hot little mouth of yours."

My core clenched at the thought. "We're going to go," I told my family. "I'm hungry."

"Fuck, baby." Vince groaned, digging his fingers into the sides of my head. "Take it. Take it all."

I was but I still enjoyed hearing him telling me what to do. His cock was thrusting back and forth down the length of my tongue. My wrists were tied behind my back by one of his belts. He didn't want me touching myself before he had a chance to.

Vince thrust between my lips, pushing his cock into my mouth as deep as it would go. "Fucking hell, Gigi. I love how you suck cock like a damn porn star."

A muffled laugh left me.

Opening my mouth wider, I breathed through my nose and took him even deeper.

His eyes landed on me. They were dark, so damn dark I couldn't see the pupils. He pushed into me, leaning me against the edge of the bed. "You know I respect the hell out of you right?"

I nodded, running my tongue back and forth along a vein.

He shivered. "You want rougher?"

I moaned, nodding.

A wicked grin spread on his face. "Brace yourself, baby. I've been saving my cum for that little belly of yours."

His words were vulgar but made me wet just the same.

I enjoyed this side of him, and it only seemed to get worse the longer we went without having sex. While we had foreplay, it wasn't the same and definitely not enough to curb that craving we had for each other.

Vince thrust his cock between my lips. It was hard, rough, fast. My lips burned at being open for so long. Spittle dripped out of the corners of my mouth but that only made him fuck my face faster. His breathing picked up, his chest rising and falling when he threw his head back. He ripped his cock from my mouth and wrapped a hand around the base, pumping hard and fast. Hot jets of his cum splashed against my face.

I stuck my tongue out, a couple of drops landing on it.

Vince's dark eyes met mine, his grin widening. "I'm yours."

"You're mine." I licked my lips, the saltiness of him making my taste buds tingle.

When he calmed down, he petted a hand over my head. "Stay there."

Not like I could go anywhere anyway.

He went to his pants that had somehow landed on my dresser and pulled his phone from the pocket. He came back toward me and held the phone out.

"Are you taking a picture right now?" I asked, a nervous laugh leaving me.

Vince winked. "Oh yeah."

I shook my head, but I couldn't help the smile forming on my face.

"We have quite the collection," he told me, snapping a picture and placing his phone on my nightstand.

I couldn't wait to see them but right now, I really needed him inside me. Even if we went slow, I didn't care. I needed to feel him. I needed more than just foreplay.

Vince went to the laundry hamper and grabbed a towel before coming back and kneeling in front of me. He wiped my face, giving me a small smile. "Thank you."

I only nodded. My bones were practically vibrating out of my skin.

When he was done cleaning me, he removed the belt from around my wrists.

As soon as they were free, I jumped into his arms and crushed my mouth to his.

"Gigi," he murmured against my lips.

"Please make love to me," I whispered. "We can go slow."

"You know neither of us like slow," Vince reminded me, placing a soft peck on my jaw.

"I don't care. I need you inside me."

Vince wrapped his arms around me and lifted me. Placing me on the bed, he lowered his mouth to my nipple. "Slow?" he asked, sinking his teeth into the budding peak.

"Slow," I whimpered, pushing my fingers through his hair. "Please. I need you, Vince."

His dark eyes met mine. Crawling between my knees, he crushed his mouth to mine and took things as slow as we could handle. Although we liked it rough and fast, hard and intense, the sweet slow movements of his lovemaking forced these newfound feelings deep inside of me. It was nothing like I expected coming from him. He was dirty, vulgar, giving me every amount of pleasure I could ever hope for and more. He took me away, forced me over the edge of ecstasy and jumped right along beside me until the only thing we could focus on was each other.

TWENTY-SIX

VINCE

IN THE WEEKS FOLLOWING, we soaked up as much time together as we could, despite our busy schedules. We told the rest of our friends and family about the baby. I had actually wanted to keep it to myself and not tell Tenise but being Rory's girlfriend, she found out rather quickly.

Gigi was now in her second trimester. We still hadn't had sex like we used to. That could wait. It was now sweet and slow but as gentle as I tried to be, it was still intense.

As I was driving to Gigi's place after picking us up dinner, my cell rang. Pressing the button on the steering wheel so I could talk to the person through the car speakers, I noticed then that it was Rory calling.

"Hey. What's up?"

"Tenise and I broke up," he said, his voice low.

"Shit, man. I'm sorry." I paused. "Are you okay?"

"I don't know. I'm sitting here staring at a bottle of Jack, wondering if I should drown myself in it or not. Mason's on his way to help me decide." He sighed. "You busy tonight?"

"Yeah, I'm heading to Gigi's with dinner. The baby is craving pizza with salt and pickles on it. Not anchovies. Just salt." I grimaced at the thought but was happy to make my girl's craving disappear. Until the next time anyway.

"And pickles?" Rory chuckled. "I like salt but not on pizza and definitely not with pickles."

"Same." I gripped the steering wheel. "Listen, I'm sorry about what happened."

"Don't be. It's not your fault. Before we even started dating, she asked me if you were single. I should have taken the hint then, but I was blind I guess."

"No, you were in love," I corrected him. "I get it."

"I just wanted to tell you that there are no hard feelings or any of that shit and if you and Gigi need anything, I'm here. Both Mason and I are here."

"Thank you." A thought came to me. "Actually, I'm going to hold you to that offer." I explained what I needed and how it would have to be done before the baby was born. It would be my little surprise for Gigi, and I knew that with the way things were going between us, she wouldn't complain.

Rory agreed and I knew that Mason would as well.

When I arrived at Gigi's house, it was pushing nine at night. I had spent the day with my dad, helping him fix up the center. It was constantly being worked on. Our moms were wanting to expand it some more. The place had become so big that large corporations were donating as much money as they could to help with the upkeep of the place. I wasn't sure our moms ever thought it would become as big as it had.

Parking the car in the long driveway, I grabbed the pizza box and garlic bread sticks and left the vehicle.

When I entered the house, there was no sound of anyone moving about. "Babe?"

Closing the door, I locked it and kicked off my shoes before heading down the hall. I was stopped short by Gigi sleeping on the couch with her hand on her stomach. She was sporting a small bump now and she looked absolutely beautiful carrying my baby.

My heart swelled at seeing her and my dick stirred, clearly happy to see her as well.

Placing the pizza box on the coffee table, I pulled the blanket off the back of the couch and spread it over Gigi.

She stirred, her eyes fluttering open. "Hi."

"Hi." I leaned over and gave her a soft kiss on the mouth. "I have food for you."

"Oh." She sat up, rubbing her eyes. "I was going to watch TV but must have fallen asleep instead."

I sat beside her and opened the box. "You need as much as rest as you can get." I handed her a piece of pizza.

"Thank you." She took the slice from me.

By the time I was done my first slice, she was already on her third. "Hungry?"

She laughed. "Apparently."

I chuckled.

"How was your day?"

"Good." I finished my slice before continuing. "Rory and Tenise broke up."

"Oh." Gigi's shoulders slumped. "That's sad." She pouted.

"Hey." I pulled her into my arms, kissing the side of her head. "If they are meant to be, they'll work through this. And if it's not, they'll find someone who's meant to be their person."

Gigi looked up at me then. "Like us?"

"Am I your person, Queenie?" I asked, cupping her face.

"Well I am having your baby." She waggled her eyebrows.

"You are and you look so damn good doing it too." I kissed her hard on the mouth.

"Vince." Gigi moved to my lap, straddling me.

"What are you doing?" I gripped her hips, pulling her down hard against me.

She sighed, her dark hair falling around her face. "I like this. Sitting here. Eating pizza. Cuddling."

"Being happy," I added, lifting her shirt to reveal her stomach.

"Exactly." She cupped her swollen abdomen.

"How are you feeling?"

"Good. She's being nice to me. The morning sickness isn't as bad as it was."

My heart jumped that she had referred to our baby as a her. I couldn't explain it, but I kept having dreams that we were having a baby girl. Not that it mattered to me either way, but I could feel it down to the marrow of my bones that we were having a daughter.

"Maybe she'll be a dancer like her mama." I reached for the oil that Gigi kept on the small table beside the couch and squeezed some into my palm. Rubbing it onto her stomach, I massaged the oil into her skin. Apparently, it helped prevent stretch marks. I just liked rubbing it on her, so I had another excuse to touch her.

"That feels good," she said softly.

I grinned, inching my hands higher beneath her shirt until I reached her breasts. "How does *that* feel?"

She laughed, pulling the shirt up and over her head. "How does that *look*?"

Pushing her tits together, I took a budding nipple between my lips.

Gigi moaned, her fingers latching on to my hair. "God, I've been aching for you."

"Really?" I bit down when she didn't answer.

She yelped. "Yes."

"Tell me more." I swiped my tongue back and forth over the sharp peak. She had become more sensitive since getting pregnant and I enjoyed seeing just how far I could take it before she exploded for me.

"It hurts." She pulled me against her and started rocking her hips over my crotch.

My dick lengthened, begging to get back inside her. "Gigi." I licked and kissed to her collarbone. "Get up and sit on the couch."

Without me having to ask twice, she did as I said and spread her knees.

I knelt on the floor in front of her and pulled her to the edge of the couch. "Place your feet on the edge, baby."

She chewed her bottom lip and did as she was told.

Lowering my mouth to her center, I inhaled and blew against her.

She sighed, spreading her legs even more.

I latched on to her fabric covered clit.

"Vince," she whined.

"My girl's greedy for me."

Her eyes were dark as they landed on me. "God, baby, you have no idea."

Hooking a finger beneath the crotch of her panties, I pulled it to the side and covered her with my mouth.

(Gigi)

I woke to Vince sleeping soundlessly beside me. His long eyelashes were fanned out on top of his cheeks. His hair was messy thanks to my fingers constantly running through them when he went down on me earlier that night.

My body still burned from his mouth. When he had finally given me the release I craved, he continued taking everything he had wanted from me.

In a rough move, Vince pulled me from the couch and spun me around before thrusting into me.

I gasped, arching against him.

"I'm sorry." He bit my shoulder. "Fuck, I didn't mean to be rough."

"I'm fine." I trembled against him. "I'm good. Just please don't ever stop."

And he hadn't for at least an hour.

Now we were in bed and I was supposed to be sleeping, but something had woken me up and I couldn't fall back asleep. I wasn't sure what it was. I laid there for what felt like forever when suddenly, the sound of the smoke detector went off. I shot upright.

"What the hell?" Vince grumbled, sitting up and rubbing his eyes.

"Vince."

He looked at me.

I nodded toward the door. There was smoke coming into the room from under it. I quickly got dressed and handed him his clothes.

"Shit, the light's not working," Vince grumbled, trying to turn on the lamp on my nightstand.

I went to the end table on the other side of the bed. "Where's my phone?" My charger was still plugged into the wall, but my phone wasn't attached to it like it was when I had gone to bed.

"I can't find mine either." Vince got dressed and went to the door. He tapped the doorknob. "Fucking hell. Gigi." He looked my way.

Even though it was dark, the moonlight had cast an eerie glow into the room, so I could still see the fear in his eyes.

"Vince," I whispered. "What is it?"

"I think your..." His voice shook. "I think your house is on fire."

TWENTY-SEVEN

Gigi

I HAD NEVER FELT fear like I did tonight. The fact that the fire had happened while we were sleeping, set me on edge.

Vince rushed to the window, trying to pry it open. "Fuck, I can't open it."

I went to his side and tried helping him but even with both of us trying, it wouldn't budge. "Do you think something's blocking it? I open this window all the time. There's no reason for it not to open now." I tried again but as strong as I was, I couldn't get it to budge.

"Hold on." Vince went around the room, searching for something in the dark that he could use to break the window glass.

There was more smoke coming into the room when suddenly, the door went up in flames.

"Vince." I gasped, grabbing whatever I could to help him break the window.

My lungs felt like they were on fire.

Vince ripped off his shirt and ran to the en suite bathroom before coming back. He tied a wet piece of fabric around my head, covering my nose and mouth.

"What about you?" I demanded when I saw that he hadn't done the same for himself.

"I don't give a shit about me." He gently pushed me out of the way and smashed whatever was in his hand against the window glass.

"But I do." I pulled the fabric from around my face and covered his mouth and nose with it.

"Gigi." He tried pulling it from his face.

"Fight me later but right now, you need it too."

"You're fucking pregnant." He ripped my hand from his face and tied the fabric back around my head. "*You* can fight *me* later." His eyes were dark with fury. Not at me but at the situation itself, and I knew when to back down.

Vince smashed the object that he was holding against the glass until it finally broke. When he reached for me, I stepped back.

"What are you doing?"

"I'm going to help you out." He grabbed a blanket off the bed and threw it over the windowsill. He grabbed my arm and lifted me.

"What about you?" My heart was pounding in my ears, the smoke making me cough.

"I'm right behind you." He cupped my face, kissing me hard on the mouth. "I promise."

The blanket made it easier so we wouldn't get cut by the broken glass. Once I was out the window, I landed on the ground with an oomph. My house was only one floor and the window wasn't too high but it had still been quite a drop. I turned back for Vince to help him.

"Go get help."

"What?" I tried reaching for him. "No. I can help *you*. The window is big enough. You can get out and we can get help together."

"I'm too heavy, baby. Go get help," he said, his voice firm but hoarse from the smoke. "I'm right behind you."

"No, I'm not leaving you." I tried tugging him closer, but I wasn't strong enough. "Please."

"Gigi, go." He pulled my hands from around his neck and kissed my forehead. "Go get help. *Now*."

I huffed and rushed off, running through my backyard to the other side of the house. Unlocking the fence door, I continued running to the nearest neighbor. When I arrived, I bounded up the front porch and started banging on the door. "Help me! Please help me! My house is on fire. Please, someone!"

I didn't know what time it was. It was the middle of the night. That was all I knew. But at that point I didn't care. I looked behind me, my stomach sinking that Vince was nowhere in sight.

A light turned on inside the house, followed by the porch light.

"Please!" I continued banging on the door.

The door opened, revealing an older man. "What's going on?"

"My house is on fire and my boyfriend told me to go get help, but I think something happened. He didn't follow me. Please, call 911." I was frantic with worry, my heart pounded hard against the walls of my rib cage but all I could think about was losing Vince when I had only just finally found him.

"Marge!" The older man called out. "Call 911. There's a fire." He looked back at me. "Show me where your boyfriend is."

I ran back down the porch.

"I'm going to help the kids next door," he called out to who I could only assume was his wife.

"I called 911!" she yelled back. "Firemen are on their way!"

"Alright, sweetheart, show me where he is." The older man continued following me. I realized then that he was holding an ax. "What happened?" he asked me.

"We were sleeping, and the smoke detectors went off. We saw smoke and then the door caught on fire and…and…" I stopped suddenly. The house, my house, was fully ablaze. "Vince." A sob left me.

"Show me!" the man demanded, running up the side of the house.

"In the back." I followed him, leading him to my bedroom window. "I was able to get out and he should have been right behind me. The window isn't too small but something—" I stopped by the patio door as the man ran past me.

"Where?" I heard him ask.

I pointed, unable to take my eyes off the scene going on inside my house. The living room was fully engulfed. Nothing would be salvageable. Not that it mattered. They were only material items and they could be replaced, but watching your house along with everything you own go up in flames, was like losing a piece of yourself.

"I got him."

I snapped out of my trance at those words.

The man came toward me with his arm around Vince. "He must have passed out from the smoke. That's why he didn't follow you."

"Oh God." I rushed to them, hooking Vince's other arm around my shoulders.

"I'm fine," Vince coughed.

We walked back up the side of the house to the older man's yard. Sirens sounded, the fire trucks barreling down the streets as we walked to safety.

An ambulance parked in front of the neighbor's house and the paramedics rushed toward us with a stretcher between them. They pulled Vince from the man who helped us and laid him on it, placing an oxygen mask on his face.

"No." He sat up, handing me the mask. "She needs it more."

"Vince." I went to his side, trying to calm him. "They're going to help you."

"You need this more than I do." He tried handing me the mask again.

"Stop." I placed the mask back on his face and kissed his forehead. "You were in the smoke longer than I was."

"She's pregnant," he told the nearest EMT, ignoring me. "She needs it more."

"I'm fine, Vince." But my words didn't stop the other EMT from guiding me to the ambulance and giving me my own oxygen. "Wait." I pushed away from her and went back to the man who helped Vince.

He was talking to a police officer. They both turned toward me.

"Sorry for interrupting. I just needed to thank you." Before he could respond, I hugged him around the middle.

"You don't need to thank me at all," he told me, stiffening.

"You went into a burning house and got my boyfriend." I squeezed him. "Thank you. Thank you for bringing him back to me."

The man relaxed and hugged me back. "You're welcome."

I released him and went to head back to the ambulance when another officer came toward us.

"We just have some questions," he said. "You're the homeowner?"

"Yes I am."

He nodded. "We'll meet you at the hospital. Go get checked out."

"Thank you." I went to the ambulance and stepped up into the back.

"What's going on?" Vince asked, pulling the mask off his face.

"I thanked my neighbor for saving you and the police are going to meet us at the hospital to question us." I wasn't sure why, but I imagined they needed to rule out arson. It was probably faulty wiring. No. My dad wouldn't have let that happen when he and the guys built the house for us girls.

"I need to check you out," the female EMT told me.

"Put your mask back on," I told Vince.

Something flashed behind his eyes.

I grabbed his hand, holding onto it for dear life, thankful that I didn't lose him.

The EMT checked my vitals, put an oxygen mask on my face, and did what they could before we got to the hospital.

When she was done, I moved closer to Vince and leaned my forehead against his. "We're fine, baby."

He nodded, his eyes fluttering closed. He squeezed my hand.

I kissed his knuckles, trying to give him all of the strength I could even though I didn't feel strong.

At all.

"What the fuck happened?"

"How the hell did this happen?"

"Where is she?"

"Don't tell me to calm down. Where's my daughter?"

I sighed, swinging my legs over the edge of the bed just as my mom and dad came into the room.

"Baby." Mom rushed to me, pulling me into her arms. "You okay?"

I nodded, returning the embrace. I waved my dad over, needing his big teddy bear hug that always made me feel like I could get through anything just by having his arms around me.

"What happened?" he asked gently.

"We woke up to the smoke detectors going off and the house on fire." I swallowed hard. "The police are investigating." After Vince and I had shown up at the hospital, they arrived shortly after and asked me a bunch of questions. Vince needed extensive care since his lungs were damaged from the smoke more than mine were. But once the doctor gave the go-ahead, the police asked him questions as well. When it was determined that neither of us had anything to do with starting the fire, the officers left. But I still hadn't seen Vince since we were separated from the start.

"Have you seen Vince?" I asked my parents.

"Not yet. Creena and Stone are here though," Mom told me, petting a hand over my head. "You sure you're good?"

"Yes." I gave her a smile for reassurance. "Just a little freaked out."

"That's understandable." Mom looked up at Dad. "Angel, stop."

He huffed. "I'm not fucking doing anything."

"You're plotting." She wrapped her arm around his middle. "Let the police do their job."

"Someone set my baby girl's house on fire while she was in bed. Add to the fact that she's pregnant with our grandbaby. We've been through a lot, princess. But this…" Dad pulled away from Mom and started pacing. "I just need a moment."

"I'm fine, Daddy. I promise." I cupped my stomach. "We're both fine. The doctor gave us a clean bill of health."

Dad rubbed the back of his neck, his shoulders tense. "I know you're fine. I see that you're fine but it's not making me feel any better."

"How are you feeling?" I asked, remembering the accident he had a few weeks ago that freaked us all out.

"I'm fine." Dad dropped his arm to the side. "Your mother has been my rock and I've even started wearing glasses while working." But he wasn't wearing them at that moment. He scowled. "I'll start wearing them regularly. I swear you two have the same brain."

Mom and I laughed.

A knock suddenly sounded at the door.

Stone peeked his head inside the room. "Can we interrupt?"

"Of course," Mom told him.

"Someone was ready to kick some ass to get to you," he said, giving me a smile and coming farther into the room.

Creena pushed Vince into the room in a wheelchair.

Before I could say anything, he was up and out of the chair and in my arms like I needed. He sat beside me, pushing his face into the crook of my neck. "You good?" he asked, cupping my stomach.

"Yes," I whispered. "We're good. Are you?"

His dark eyes met mine. "The doctor said that I'm good to go. My lungs will be tender for a few days though."

"But are you *good*?" I asked, turning toward him.

"She knows him well," Creena pointed out.

"Vince." I grabbed his hand. "Answer me."

He leaned toward me, his mouth brushing over the shell of my ear. "I want to skin the person alive who set your house on fire and risked your life and our baby's life. Does that answer your question, Queenie?"

I shivered at the image he put in my head. "You don't think it was an accident?"

"Nope." He kissed my cheek. "Not at all, babe."

"But they would have seen our cars. Do you think they wanted us to be home?" I swallowed hard at the thought that someone would deliberately set my house on fire, hoping we would be home at the same time.

"I…" Vince hesitated. "I don't think it was an accident," he said again.

While our parents talked, I couldn't help but wonder if maybe Vince was right and that someone *did* set the house on fire. But I wasn't sure why they would do that. What could they possibly get out of burning my house down? Was it a random person or someone we actually knew? Either way, it didn't make sense but if I knew our dads, they were already trying to figure out a way to get the answers I was looking for without me even having to ask them.

I looked at my dad.

His gaze locked with mine.

He nodded once.

I swallowed hard.

I almost felt sorry for the person who tried to hurt Vince and I but then again, maybe they deserved whatever was coming to them.

TWENTY-EIGHT

VINCE

AFTER LEAVING THE HOSPITAL, we headed back to Gigi's parents' place. My mom and dad offered to take me back to theirs and as much as I appreciated that, I wasn't leaving Gigi. Ever. Luckily, I had to just say no once, and they understood. Dad shot me a look that meant he knew exactly how I felt. I didn't want to know how he understood, knowing him and my mom had it hard in the beginning.

When I made sure that Gigi was safely tucked away in her bed, I left her childhood bedroom and stepped out into the hall. Once I shut the door behind me, it was like the weight of the night had come crashing down onto my shoulders. I rubbed my chest, my lungs still aching from the smoke damage. The doctor said it would be a few days before they were back to normal. No marathons for me anytime soon.

I took one step before I fell to my knees.

My heart started racing, my breathing becoming uneven. Spots danced in my vision.

I could have lost Gigi. I could have lost our unborn baby. I could have lost them both. If that had happened,

I wouldn't know how to live without them. They were fine. They were okay. But it didn't make it any easier. The fact that they were almost taken from me, forced this newfound rage from the very depth of my soul. It was an anger I had never felt before. It scared me because I knew that I would go to the ends of the earth to get the person who did this and make sure they never hurt us, or anyone, ever again.

"Breathe it out, son." A heavy hand landed on my shoulder. "You got this."

I took a deep breath and then another. I didn't know what happened or who had set Gigi's house on fire, but I had a feeling. And it was a feeling that I didn't like. I wanted to be wrong and I prayed that I was.

When my heart calmed down, I sat back on my ass and leaned against the wall.

Angel sat beside me, stretching out his long legs in front of him. "You good?"

"Nope," I bit out. "Not one bit."

He stared straight ahead. "What about Gigi?"

"She didn't want to rest. She told me that I needed it more than she did." I scrubbed a hand down my face. "But she finally listened and fell asleep."

She had tried fighting the exhaustion but eventually, fell asleep in my arms. It was where I always wanted her. Tucked in my hold, safe in my touch and at peace in my heart.

"She's like her mother that way. Meadow and Ryder are more me. But Gigi?" Angel shook his head. "Jay will always be walking this earth as long as Gigi's around."

"I could have lost her and our baby tonight and it's messing with me," I blurted, leaning my head back against the wall. "I don't know what I would have done if I'd lost them."

"You saved her," Angel pointed out. "And you saved your unborn child."

"I'd die first before I let anything happen to them."

"You were raised well, Vince." He paused. "I remember the first night we brought her home with us. I put her in her crib while Jay took a shower. I wanted to give her a little bit of time alone. Pregnancies and births aren't easy. Even the quickest deliveries can still be stressful, so I was trying to give Jay a moment of reprieve. Anyway." Angel cleared his throat. "I never really prayed before that night. Not outside of the missions I'd been on. It's hard to have faith with the shit I've seen. But that night I did. I prayed hard, Vince. I prayed for a man like you to come into my baby girl's life and take care of her like I do. To love her even more than I can and ever will. Thank you for answering my prayer."

A lump formed in my throat. "Thank you for giving your daughter to me."

"You have my blessing. I know you haven't asked for it, but you don't need to. I've seen the way you are with her." Angel looked at me then. "I always said that I would threaten any of the guys my girls ended up with but you and Shade? I haven't had to threaten either of you."

"Meadow and Shade have been through a lot." I crossed my arms under my chest, looking at the man I hoped would one day be my father-in-law.

"They have. I didn't know Sunny for long. I had a hard time wrapping my head around the fact that my youngest kid was dating two men who were closer to my age than her own." Angel sighed. "But when it comes to Meadow, she does what she wants and doesn't care what anyone else thinks. She has a good head on her shoulders. They all do but Gigi was the one I was worried about the most. Until you broke down her walls."

"I'm in love with her," I finally confessed to him.

Angel smiled. "Oh I know and I'm happy you are."

"You're in love with me?"

My head whipped around.

Gigi stood outside her bedroom door, staring down at me with wide eyes.

"You should be sleeping," I said, rising to my feet and going up to her.

"Vince." She grabbed the hoodie I was wearing, thanks to Angel letting me borrow one of his, and pulled me closer. "Tell me that again."

I looked over my shoulder.

Angel nodded. "I'll be downstairs. I'll try and calm your dad down. He's more furious than I am." He shook his head and went back down the hall, leaving Gigi and me alone.

"Vince."

I turned around and grabbed Gigi's hand, pulling her back into her bedroom.

"Vince," she repeated, her voice firmer. "I need to know. Did you mean what you said?"

"I wouldn't have said it if I didn't mean it." I cupped her shoulders. "I'm in love with you, Gigi." It felt so damn good to finally get those words off my chest. Words that I had been wanting to say ever since I gave her the necklace so many years ago.

"You love me?" she asked through unshed tears.

"Yeah, Queenie." I kissed her forehead, brushing my nose against hers. "I've always loved you. From the first moment I met you."

"I've known you since you were born," she whispered.

"Exactly." I pinched her chin, tilting her head back to meet the soft impact of my mouth. "I loved you then. I love you now. And I'll spend the rest of my days, continuing to love you."

A lone tear rolled down her cheek.

"Don't cry, Gigi." My tongue peeked out, licking up the drop. "I've been in love with you for so long." I fingered the necklace wrapped around her throat. "Probably since before I gave you this necklace so many years ago."

"God, Vince." Her chin wobbled. "I'm in love with you, too."

I cupped the back of her head and crushed my mouth to hers. "I know."

A shaky laugh left her. "How?"

"Just do, babe." I kissed her nose. "I have to tell you that it feels so much better getting that out. I've been wanting to tell you for years that I'm in love with you, but I was scared that you would reject me."

"Never. I would never reject you, but I was scared about that too. I wish you would have told me sooner and I wish that I would have told you too." Gigi stepped out of my embrace and went up to her dresser. Opening a drawer, she reached inside and pulled out a small box. Her gaze met mine in the mirror. "Come here."

I did as I was told and stepped up behind her, leaning my chin on her shoulder and wrapping my arms around her middle.

"Do you remember when we took this?" She lifted a picture of her and I. We were smiling for the camera. It had been the night of my eighteenth birthday. She had a glow on her cheeks since it was right after I fucked her in her car. Looked like we started taking sexy pictures long before I even realized it.

"I forgot we took this." I cupped her stomach. "We looked good together."

"We still look good together." Gigi ran her hand up and down my arm that was holding her tight. "I love you."

I kissed the side of her neck. "I love you, Queenie. More than I could ever tell you but promise to show you just the same."

Gigi placed her hand on her stomach. "We're good."

"No." I turned her in my arms and cupped her face. "We're fucking perfect."

(Gigi)

Vince and I sat at my parents' dining room table. Much to Vince's dismay of course. After we confessed our love for each other, finally, he insisted that I go back to bed. I refused. I could sleep later. It was after eight in the morning and everyone looked exhausted, but our dads were determined to figure out what had happened.

The landline rang off in the distance, but we were too tired to bother.

Vince took care of it for us and came back a few minutes later. "They got the fire out but…" His voice trailed off.

"What?" My heart jumped to my throat.

"It's bad, Queenie," he said gently. "They also determined that the window was glued shut along with a few nails hammered into the windowsill."

Curses muttered around the room but all I could do was stare at Vince over what he was telling me.

I exhaled a shaky breath, looking down at my hands on my lap. I had known all along that the fire wasn't an accident, but it didn't mean I wanted to be right.

"Gigi."

I looked up at the sound of my dad's deep voice. "I'm sorry."

"Why are *you* sorry?" Dad scowled. "You didn't start the fire. Whoever this asshole is that tried hurting my baby..."

Mom went up to him, placing her hand on his chest.

He sighed, wrapping his arm around her shoulders.

"The police are investigating," Vince added.

"Maybe the window became stuck. It is old." I was grasping. "Maybe someone from one of my parties messed with it or the wires or…" I didn't want to believe that someone would intentionally hurt Vince and I.

"Baby, the house isn't that old, and you know that's not what happened," Vince told me gently. "The police are still doing their search but it's not an accident. I wish it was. I'm sorry that it wasn't."

"But why? Why would someone go through all that trouble? Why would they try and hurt us?" A lump formed in my throat. "Why would they take our phones and burn down my house?"

"I'll get us new phones." Vince wrapped an arm around my shoulders, leaning his forehead against the side of my head. "I don't know any more than that, but I promise we will find out."

"When we're given the go-ahead, we'll check out the house," Dad said, looking at Stone.

"Fucking hell." Stone ran a hand over his head.

Creena started pacing. "I've been retired for years but I'll come back. I'll find this fucker who hurt you kids. I'll…"

Stone went up to his wife and pulled her into his arms, mumbling something low to her.

Her shoulders slumped.

A look passed between Vince and I. I didn't know what Creena meant by her coming out of retirement but I was sure that I didn't want to know.

"Maybe one of the houses nearby has security cameras that picked up something," Stone suggested. "I'll mention it to the police if they haven't tried that already."

While my dad and Stone continued talking about their plans to try and figure out what had happened, my energy level dwindled. I just wanted to go home and curl up in my bed but now I couldn't do that.

"Come home with me," Vince suggested.

"I don't have anything. I have…" I swallowed hard. "I have nothing."

All eyes turned to me that time.

"Take whatever you need from your room here," Mom offered. "But I do suggest getting some rest before you go through your things."

I only nodded. I was too tired to argue.

"Come." Vince stood. "I'll tuck you in."

I gave my parents both a hug, along with Vince's mom and dad.

"I like you for him," Creena murmured in my ear as she squeezed me tight. "I wouldn't want him with anyone else." She cupped my stomach. "Thank you."

My eyes welled. I could only nod for fear that I would be a blubbering mess if I tried to voice my thoughts.

"Sleep well, kiddo," Stone said, giving me a small smile.

I thanked him and let Vince walk me to my bedroom. "I want to go home," I told Vince once we were in my room.

He closed the door behind him and came toward me, wrapping me up in his strong arms. "Move in with me."

"What?" I wasn't sure why I was surprised. I was having his baby and all. It only made sense that moving in together would be the next step.

"I have room for a nursery." Vince kissed my forehead. "And I want you in my bed. I want you in my home. I want your things in my bathroom and dresser. I want your touch. Everywhere."

I cupped his nape and gripped his shirt with my other hand. "I want that too."

"Really?" he asked, lifting his head.

"Yes." I stood on tiptoes and kissed him softly on the mouth. "I love you."

Vince slid his hands down my back to my ass, pulling me flush against him. “Say that again.”

A breathless laugh escaped me at the deep vibrato of his voice. “I love you, baby.”

“Fuck.” He dug his fingers into the flesh of my rear, lifting me into his arms. “I need you, but we shouldn’t. Not here.”

“Why not?” I licked up the length of his throat. “Make us feel better.”

He shivered, placing me gently on my bed. “No. Get some sleep and then you can come home with me later. I’ll take care of your sweet pussy then.”

I sighed, brushing my fingers along his mouth. “Lay with me then? Until I fall asleep?”

Vince nodded, lying down beside me and pulling me against him. “I love you, Queenie.” He kissed the side of my neck. “I love you so fucking much.”

I woke with a start.

“Gigi?”

I jumped, my head whipping around. Vince was sitting up, a deep frown settling between his brows.

I scrubbed a hand down my face, not realizing I had fallen asleep and so quickly. The remnants from the nightmare sat deep inside me. Although I couldn’t remember what the dream was about, I could still feel the fear crawling along my skin like tiny spiders.

“You’re fine.” He kissed my shoulder. “I promise you’re fine.”

I nodded, blowing out a slow breath. “Take me home. Please, Vince. I just need to move on.”

“Did you want to grab stuff from here?” he asked, leaving my bed. “And then we’ll go get new phones before we head home.”

“Okay.” I went to my closet to grab a bag and started packing a few things. I would have to buy more but this would do for now. When I was done, Vince and I left my room.

Our parents were still sitting around the dining room table. They looked up when we approached.

"Did you get some rest?" Mom asked me.

"A little. I'm going to go home with Vince," I said as he came up behind me. "Actually, I'm going to move in with him."

"Good." She hugged me tight. "It's about time."

I laughed lightly. "I love you."

She leaned back, cupping my cheek. "I love you too, sweetheart."

"If you find anything at the house that's worth saving, can you set it aside for me please?" I asked Dad and Stone. "I don't know if I can go over there right now."

Dad nodded. "Of course."

"We'll get to the bottom of this," Stone said, rising from the chair. "We should go too," he told his wife.

After another round of hugs, Vince's parents drove us to get new cell phones before we headed to the apartment building that would now be my new home as well.

"We got this, Queenie," Vince murmured in my ear as I gripped my bag tight in my arms. "Here."

I looked down, seeing a key in his open palm.

"I have a spare key since Rory and Mason moved out." He placed it in my hand, curling my fingers around it before bringing our hands up to his mouth. He kissed my knuckles, that soft touch sending a flutter of desire unfurling deep in my belly.

I chewed my bottom lip, unable to respond. What could I even say? Someone burnt down my house with Vince and I inside it. The only good thing that came out of this was that it gave us a shove to confess our feelings for each other. Finally. After all this time. And now we were moving in together.

I believed that everything happened for a reason but my house burning down, was a bit extreme.

After his parents dropped us off, Vince and I walked hand in hand down the hall leading to his apartment.

"I haven't been here since the night of your birthday," I told him.

"That was a good night." Vince waggled his eyebrows.

My heart stuttered. "It really was. That was when I realized how controlling you are in bed and I liked it. I liked it a lot."

Vince kissed my cheek. "I know." He unlocked the door to his apartment. "I have a surprise for you." He pushed open the door and stepped aside, letting me enter first.

"A surprise? You didn't have to do that." I went into his home and placed my bag on the floor by the door.

"Look." Vince shut the door behind him and clicked the lock into place. He pointed to the spot above his TV.

I looked in the direction he was pointing, my eyes widening. I walked closer to the picture hanging from the wall. "That's me." It was an image of me changing out of my shoes and into my ballet slippers. On one foot I was wearing my Converse and the other foot was in a ballet slipper. The image was in black and white with a hint of pink in it. You couldn't see my face, but the picture was stunning.

"I took it one night when you were practicing. You put on your slippers but never danced and took them off shortly after."

My throat went dry. "I know. It's been hard for me to pick up ballet again."

"I know that, baby. You won't get any pressure from me, but I know you'll pick it up again whenever you're ready." He walked past me and headed into the kitchen. "I have another surprise for you, but you'll see it when you go up to the loft." He came back a moment later with a bottle of water in hand. He handed it to me, giving me a small smile.

"Thank you." I took it from him. "I never thought this day would come."

"What? Moving in together?"

I nodded, looking out at the vast room before me. "Something told me that we would end up together, but I just wasn't expecting everything that's happened to…well…happen."

"I know." He held out his hand. "Come. Let's get you settled."

I took his hand, letting him lead me up the stairs to his room.

(Vince)

"I like you in my space," I told Gigi later that night while we were sitting in bed.

"Me too." She rolled onto her side, placing her hand on my chest. "Thank you. For everything."

I kissed her forehead. "You don't have to thank me for anything, Queenie. It's my job."

Gigi gave me a small smile, a flush hitting her cheeks. She sat up, pulling the photo album that was resting on the bed, onto her lap. "I can't believe you've taken all of these pictures. I don't even remember half of them."

"I wanted it to be a surprise for you." I pulled her back into my arms, watching her flip through the pages.

Each image was black and white. It was of her and I or just her. Some were sexual. Some were downright filthy. Others were sweet. It showcased our time together and I would keep adding images to it throughout the rest of our lives. I found that my favorite picture I had taken of her was when she was wearing a red bra and panty set under one of my white dress shirts. The buttons weren't done up so you could see her swollen stomach. It was erotic in the way she looked sexy as hell but at the same time, it was sweet with the way she was cupping her stomach and looked down at our little bundle she was growing.

"I like this one." Gigi brushed her finger over an image of us. She was smiling. My hand was fisted in her hair and my mouth was against her ear. I had been muttering dirty words to her and took a picture as soon as I thrust into her body.

"I like it too."

She looked up at me then. "You're talented, Vince. I'm surprised you didn't go to school for this."

"Nah. You're my muse, babe, and you're the only one I want to take pictures of." I cupped her stomach. "Until our baby is born anyway."

Gigi closed the album and placed it on the end table. "Tell me a bedtime story."

I pulled her into my arms, her back to my front. "Once upon a time, a boy fell in love with a girl. They had some hard times, but their love conquered all. They created a new life together and lived happily ever after."

"And had tons of sex," Gigi added. "The end."

I chuckled, pushing her onto her back. "Is that so?"

"Yes." She giggled, cupping my face. "Now make love to me."

She didn't have to tell me twice.

TWENTY-NINE

Gigi

I WAS ALMOST IN my eighth month of pregnancy and huge as a whale but at the same time, loved the added weight just the same. Especially when Vince couldn't keep his hands off of me.

We had been living together for a while but you would think we had been living together for longer. We easily fell into a routine. We each had our quirks but nothing that was super annoying like I had heard about with some couples. Fact was, I loved living with him, and I knew that he loved even more that I was constantly around. It was like the further along in my pregnancy I became, the more we had sex.

"I never thought that you being pregnant would turn me on." Vince nipped the side of my breast. "But the fact that you're carrying my child makes me want to rip you open and fuck more babies into you."

I smiled to myself at the memory of his dirty words. His need to claim me even though there was no reason for him to be worried. It wasn't like I was going anywhere.

My house hadn't been salvageable. The burnt debris was torn down and the land was cleaned up. Another family bought the property and began building their own house. It was surreal how one bad thing led to Vince and I finally confessing our love for each other.

The police weren't any closer to finding out who had set my house on fire, but they did determine that it had been arson. We already knew that, but it still didn't make me feel any better to have that little fact confirmed.

I couldn't work as much as I used to. I would teach as often as I could but found that I couldn't stand on my feet for long once my ankles started swelling, but I tried not to complain. I eventually hired another teacher to take my place while I was off on maternity leave and so I wouldn't have to shut the business down during that time.

I was able to teach the girls from Rouge their routine and even though I couldn't dance with them like they had wanted, they pulled it off and left Candace in tears at the thoughtful gift. It was amazing to see my routine up on stage like that and I promised the girls that once the baby was born and the doctor gave me the go-ahead, I would do a routine with them. I just wouldn't tell Vince until it actually happened.

One evening after I had cleaned up the apartment, I was cooking dinner for Vince and I. The baby was craving pasta, so I made us one of my dad's famous dishes that he used to cook for us as kids.

Vince had spent the past few weeks with the guys fixing up the center, so we hadn't been able to spend much time alone. A bad storm had rolled in that knocked down a tree and blew off a few shingles. No one had been hurt thankfully. But tonight, he would be home, and we had the whole evening together.

My phone suddenly rang, startling me. Vince's handsome face flashed across the screen. "Hi," I answered.

"Hey, Queenie. How's my girl?"

"Good. I'm cooking for you."

"Naked?"

I laughed, looking down at myself. "No. But I am wearing just a tank top and little shorts."

"Good enough for me." He chuckled.

"Supper's almost done."

"I'm on my way home. I was going to stop by the bakery and pick up dessert."

"Oh wonderful." I gave him a list of pastries that I wanted.

"Okay, I'll stop there, grab what you want, and then be on my way home."

"Thank you." We said our goodbyes and disconnected the call. About ten minutes later, the door to the apartment opened. "You got here fast," I called out, dishing the pasta. It was perfect timing actually. He must have hit every green light. "Did you grab the donuts Meadow had set aside for me?" I placed the plates on the table when the hairs on the back of my neck tingled.

I glanced up, a gasp escaping me. I backed up a step. "Tenise."

She was holding a pistol, aiming it directly at me.

"What are you doing here?" I continued until I hit the bookshelf behind me. "How did you get in?"

Her eyes were wild as they moved back and forth over my face. They dropped to my stomach, something flashing behind them. "How far along are you?"

I swallowed hard. I didn't want to answer but at the same time, I didn't want to do anything that would cause her to pull the trigger. "Almost eight months."

She nodded, looking around her. "You live here now."

"I do," I said, even though it hadn't been a question.

She nodded again. "Rory broke up with me."

"I-I heard that but that was months ago." What did she want?

Her dark eyes landed on me. "Did you fuck him too? You probably fucked all of them."

"Excuse me?" I was taken aback by her question. "I didn't sleep with Rory or Mason if that's who you mean."

"No. I asked if you fucked him. Not if you slept with him." Tenise moved to the dining room table and sat.

"What do you want, Tenise? We haven't seen or even heard from you in months. What's going on? Why now? Why not before?" I tried controlling the fear trembling in my voice, but truth was, I was terrified. Especially for my baby.

The way Tenise kept glancing at my stomach made me realize that she was jealous. She longed for something she couldn't have and a part of me felt sorry for her because of that.

"I want Vince." She looked at me then. "You willing to give him to me?"

"What?" My eyes widened. "You can't be serious."

"I am serious. You asked me why it took so long for me to come around. For me to do this." She waved a hand between us. "Truth is, I knew you were pregnant. That last time I saw you at Rory's place. You tried hiding your bump but you didn't do a good job of it." She sat forward, her brows narrowing in the center. "I want Vince to suffer. He took Rory from me. So I'm going to take you and your baby from him."

"Vince had nothing to do with Rory breaking up with you."

"No?" She laughed. "Doesn't matter. What does matter is now that your baby is big enough, you could give birth now and probably be fine. But that's not going to happen. Vince is going to suffer. He's spent these months getting used to the idea of having a baby coming. So have you. I wonder what would happen if I popped his little dream."

I swallowed hard.

She sat back, placing the pistol on the table beside the plate of food in front of her. "You should sit and eat. Gotta feed that baby of yours. Is it Vince's? I heard you were a slut and fucked around with half the guys in the city. You probably fucked Rory and Mason too. Maybe all three of them at the same time, like some sick gangbang."

I wasn't sure why she kept bringing up Rory and Mason. I had only met them a handful of times since making things official with Vince. But we never actually hung out. In time I knew we would because they were Vince's best friends, but they had been busy with work. "I have no idea what you're talking about."

"No?" She laughed. "You're a slut."

I had no idea where she could hear that from. It wasn't like we hung out with the same people.

"Sit," she said, nodding to the empty chair across from her. "Eat. *Now!*" She landed a fist on top of the table.

I jumped, did as I was told, and sat in the chair opposite her. "What do you want?"

"Right now, I want you to eat." She placed her hand on the pistol, waiting.

When she didn't say anything and only watched me, I picked up the fork and began eating, but I couldn't enjoy the food. Not with her watching me. Not with the pistol beneath her hand.

Once I finished, I went to stand when she lifted the pistol.

"Where do you think you're going?"

"I was going to put my dishes in the sink," I told her, my eyes flicking to the gun.

"But you're not done." She pushed the second plate of food toward me. "Eat up."

I slowly lowered back to the chair. I could have said that I wasn't hungry, but truth was, the pregnancy had upped my appetite. A lot.

"Babe, you should really be nicer."

My back stiffened at the deep voice coming from the hallway. With my fork halfway to my mouth, I watched as Mason came farther into the apartment.

Tenise only grinned.

"Surprised?" He chuckled, stepping up behind her and cupping her shoulders.

"W-What's going on?" I whispered, unable to believe what I was seeing. Mason and Tenise, together, working as one. The pieces suddenly started falling into place.

The crank phone calls. The fire. There was no way that Tenise could have done it alone. She was probably the one who called Luna too just to throw us off her trail.

"How did you get in?" I asked, taking another mouthful of pasta.

"Rory had a key from when he stayed here a while ago. I was never given one, so I stole it and had a copy cut for me. I had Rory's key back on his set of keys before he even noticed it was gone." She laughed. "He was so oblivious." The way she spoke, it was like she was talking about the weather and not the fact that both her and Mason came into the apartment unannounced.

"What do you want?" Maybe if I could get them talking, she would forget about the gun and doing whatever it was she had intended to do with it.

"What do I want?" Tenise sat back in the chair, watching me. "What do I want, Mason?"

He moved to the end of the table between us, picking up a dinner roll off a plate, and began breaking off pieces. He popped one into his mouth before looking at me. "Did you know that we had a pact that we wouldn't let a woman come between us?"

"Looks like you broke that pact," I mumbled.

Mason's grin grew. "I guess I did." He leaned over Tenise, cupping her cheek and placing a hard peck on her mouth. "But honestly, it's been worth it."

She giggled.

"I thought you were with Rory," I said. "And I thought you wanted Vince."

"I was with Rory, but he was only a ruse to get me closer to Vince and yes, I wanted Vince. Still do."

"And you're fine with this?" I asked Mason.

He shrugged. "As long as I get her, I don't give a shit."

Tenise sat forward. "I want them both. I want them all."

"Vince will never go for that. He doesn't share," I told her, still unable to believe what I was hearing.

A dark shadow passed over Tenise's face. "You see, that's where you're wrong. Vince will want me when he has nothing left. When you die, he'll be all alone and I'll be there to pick up the pieces."

"Why?" None of this made sense. "What's in this for you?"

"Something was taken from me. Because of his family, I lost everything. I tried getting through to his sister, but her boyfriend is too damn protective." Tenise looked up at Mason. "You should have broken into their home like I suggested."

"I tried." Mason huffed. "But they were always together. I couldn't get Luna alone."

Tenise scowled. "No matter. This is actually better."

"I don't understand what's going on. Why are you doing this?" I wanted answers but at the same time, I feared what they would be and how this would play out.

"Vince's parents took something from me and now I'm going to take something from them." Tenise lifted her arm. "Oh look at the time, Vince should be home soon."

I swallowed hard when I realized that she wasn't actually wearing a watch. She was unstable. "What did his parents do?" I needed to keep her talking, hoping that Vince would come home soon before she did anything else.

Tenise's brows narrowed in the center. "They took my father from me."

My stomach sunk. Shit. "How?" I was vaguely aware of Mason pulling up a chair.

"My father was Vince's Uncle," Tenise said, waiting. For what I wasn't sure but when she didn't get the reaction she wanted from me, she continued. "His mother had him killed. I was just a baby but because I never got to know him, my life was hell."

"So, now you're avenging him?" I asked, trying to process the information she was giving me. "That would make you and Vince cousins."

"No." She shook her head. "My father and Vince's mom weren't blood related. Her family took mine. Her father had my grandparents killed and raised my father as his own. He was supposed to be heir to everything, but Vince's bitch of a mother was a greedy whore and took that from him."

"Why are you in on this?" I asked Mason.

"Because I'm in love with Tenise," he said like I should have known. Like it was the most obvious answer.

"Now what?" I whispered, wishing I could go back in time. Wishing that none of this had happened. Wishing that Vince and I had moved and not told anyone. But with the way things were going, Tenise and Mason probably would have found us no matter where we were. This was going to destroy both him and Rory. Just when you thought you truly knew someone and find out they are not as they seem. My heart ached for Vince. For both of them.

A knowing look passed between Mason and Tenise.

"I want to know why you took Vince from me." Tenise placed her hand on the gun. "I want to know why you messed everything up."

"I didn't know he was yours. You were with Rory." I took a chance and glanced at Mason. His face was impassive, almost like he was waiting for Tenise's next instructions.

She scoffed, waving her hand in front of her face. "Please. Rory was just a reason for me to get closer to Vince. That's the only reason I stayed with him. It was all a ruse anyway. I never loved Rory."

"You want Rory and Mason? As well as Vince?" I asked, looking between them both.

"I haven't decided yet." She looked up at Mason. "What do you think?"

Mason smiled. "Whatever you want, baby."

I gaped at him. He was seriously delusional. They both were but to stand there and listen to her wanting to be with Vince when he was clearly in love with her, didn't make sense to me.

"I wanted a threesome with him and Rory, but Rory was all about his friendship and shit." She scowled. "What guy turns down a chance to have a threesome?" She grabbed the gun and brought it under the table.

My heart started racing. I didn't know if she was aiming it at me, but I could only assume that she was. "Please, Tenise. I don't know what you want but you don't have to do this."

"I told you what I want." She sat forward, the sound of a click erupting through the quiet of the room. "I want Vince. I want to avenge my father. I can't take out Vince's parents. I could try but this is actually better. I already tried getting rid of you, but you're determined to make things difficult for me. So now, this is the only way."

"What do you mean?" I asked, my voice shaking.

"How's that house of yours?" She laughed. "I also heard you fell off a ladder. That must have been scary."

My eyes widened. "That was you? But how?"

"The ladder was all Mason." She sat up straighter.

Mason only grinned.

"But it was simple really. I stole your phones when you were sleeping and Googled how to make a Molotov cocktail, threw one down the hall so you couldn't escape your room the easy way and then threw one in your living room." She shrugged. "And you know the rest."

"Why would you set my house on fire and risk killing Vince when you clearly want him?"

She tilted her head, a slow grin spreading on her face. "Because, silly. If I can't have him. No one can. And that means you."

My throat went dry. "Please, you don't want to do this."

"Yes, I do. Rory didn't want me." The smile fell from her face. "And Vince doesn't want me, but he will. I'll make him see that we are meant to be together. I'll give him proper babies. Not that diseased thing you're carrying. And if he refuses, then I'll take him out. I have Mason to spend the rest of my life with anyway. So either way, I'll be happy but Vince's parents won't be. They'll be sad that they lost their little boy because his mom took out someone who didn't deserve it."

I didn't know much about Vince's uncle, but I had heard that he wasn't exactly stable. Obviously that trait was passed down to his damn kid.

"What are you going to do to me?" I whispered.

Tenise's gaze dropped to the plate in front of me. "I want you to finish eating the fucking food."

Mason chuckled.

I lifted the fork and went to grab another forkful of food when a loud pop sounded. It made my ears ring. It had been so damn loud; I wasn't expecting it.

I could see Tenise's lips moving but was unable to make out what she was saying.

My head suddenly felt light, a sharp pain hitting my abdomen. "I…I need to lay down," I heard myself say. I went to stand but fell to my knees. The pain became worse. I clutched my stomach, the agony enveloping me in a blanket of fear that something was wrong.

A dark shadow loomed over me.

When I pulled my hand back, it was coated in a red liquid. My eyes widened even more. "Help me."

Tenise's shoes stepped into my line of sight.

I fell to my side, holding my stomach and begging with everything in me that my baby was unharmed.

"You should have eaten faster." Tenise looked down at me, a wicked grin spreading on her face. Mason stepped up beside her, wrapping his arm around her shoulders. He grabbed the gun from her and aimed it directly at me when footsteps sounded in the apartment.

He jerked his arm back, another pop sounding at the sudden movement.

Their heads whipped around but I couldn't follow their line of sight. Everything was heavy. I couldn't move, even though I wanted to.

I tried pushing onto shaky arms to get away from them, but I wasn't strong enough. The agony ripping through my lower stomach forced all of the breath from my lungs.

The last thing I saw was Tenise blowing me a kiss before everything went dark.

THIRTY

VINCE

WHEN I HAD FINALLY reached my apartment building, my body stirred, knowing I would see Gigi in a matter of minutes. I had been working so much and so often over the past few weeks that I only got to see her later into the evening. But she never complained. She greeted me with open arms, sometimes it turning into unexpected sex. Truth was, I always wanted her. Every inch. Every breath. Every moan.

I was running late this evening thanks to a pipe bursting at the center. It just went downhill from there, but I finally got out of there and home to my girl. Rory and Mason were still helping me with my surprise for Gigi and I couldn't wait to reveal it to her, but I still had a few weeks left before I could do that. I just hoped the baby wouldn't come first.

When I reached our floor, I moved the bouquet of flowers and box of donuts to my other hand and fished for the keys in my pocket. I had taken Angel's advice to heart and picked flowers up for Gigi as often as I could.

It was the little things he had said, and I would spend the rest of my life doing just that.

Once I neared the door leading to the home I was now sharing with the woman I loved, my heart suddenly jumped to my throat.

The door was ajar.

Slowly opening it, I stepped inside and shut it behind me. "Babe?"

No response.

"Queenie?" I called out, the scent of pasta hitting me.

When I rounded the corner, I was stopped short by the bundled heap on the floor by the dining room table. The flowers and box of donuts fell from my fingertips. The very reason I lived was unmoving.

It was like I was having an out-of-body experience as I rushed to Gigi's side. Dropping to my knees, I checked her over. A red splotch was seeping through her white shirt in the side of her stomach while another sat on her upper thigh.

"Gigi!" I yelled, lightly tapping her cheeks. "Please wake up, baby. Wake up."

But her eyes remained closed.

"No." A sob broke free, agony hitting me somewhere deep in the chest. "Please, Gigi. I can't lose you." Fishing out my cell, I called 911. Police were on their way and that was all I heard as I threw the phone on the floor. "Please, Gigi." I kissed her mouth. Turning my head, I listened for a sign that she was breathing. Checking her pulse, I felt a faint heartbeat. I wasn't a medical professional but even I knew that it wasn't strong enough.

I rained kisses on her face, cupped the wound in her lower abdomen to try and stop the bleeding, and just held her.

"I got you, baby. I'm here. I'm always here. Don't give up. Please keep fighting. For our daughter and for me. I can't live without you."

Tears rolled down my cheeks, sobs breaking through me.

I was vaguely aware that we were no longer alone.

EMTs came in with a stretcher, lifting Gigi onto it. One was asking me questions, but I couldn't focus on anything other than seeing them work on my girlfriend.

I was suddenly surrounded by police officers, each of them trying to ask me questions, but I couldn't hear them. "Gigi," I finally got out. I took a step toward her as she was wheeled out of our apartment.

"Sir."

My head whipped around, finding a woman in a suit looking at me with sympathy. I didn't need fucking sympathy. I needed to find out who shot my girl. "I need to go with her."

"I'm Detective Baldwin." She stuck her hand out. "But you can call me Jessica."

"Vince." I returned the handshake because my parents raised me to be polite but as soon as I pulled my hand back, I turned and headed in the direction that the EMS workers took Gigi.

"I'm sorry, Vince. But you can't go with them."

"Why the fuck not?" I demanded, my voice raising.

"I need to ask you some questions, but I promise you that a police officer is going with your girlfriend and will be in the back of the ambulance with her for her protection." Jessica gave me a small smile. "Let's sit and get this done and over with so you can go to her."

I looked between her and the door and back to her. "Fine."

"Now." Jessica pulled a notepad and a small stick out of the inside of her suit jacket. "I'm going to write down everything you say but also record it just in case I miss something."

I nodded, slumping onto the couch and dropped my head in my hands.

"Now, Vince."

I looked up then.

Jessica's gaze was hard and determined. "Start from the beginning and tell me everything."

I was pacing back and forth waiting for my parents and Gigi's parents. I had called them once the detective let me leave after I answered all of her questions. She didn't know anything more than what I told her. Or she didn't act like she did. But something wasn't right. Besides the fact that my girlfriend and baby were fighting for their lives, there was something else. Something that I couldn't put my finger on.

Detective Baldwin was a hardhead, but reasonable, and finally let me go once she was satisfied I didn't try to kill my girlfriend and unborn child.

An hour after she started questioning me, she finally got everything she needed. At that point in time, she told me to go to my girlfriend and baby.

I rushed over to the hospital and called both Gigi's and my parents on the way. It was the hardest phone call I ever had to make and one that I didn't want to make again. Ever.

"Vince."

I stopped suddenly, spinning around and seeing my mom and dad rushing toward me. I ran up to them, throwing myself around my mother and right into her arms.

"God, my sweet boy." She held me as I shook against her.

"Vince." Dad cupped my nape, wrapping his big body around us both. "I'm so fucking sorry."

"Vince?"

I lifted my head, seeing Gigi's mom and dad coming down the hall.

Mom cupped my cheek, giving me a small smile.

I squeezed her hand before releasing her and went up to Jay but stopped in front of her.

She held her arms out, her eyes welling.

Stepping into her embrace, I hugged her.

"How's my girl?" she asked, her voice trembling.

"I don't know anything yet," I told her, my voice thick. "But it doesn't look…it doesn't…" My throat burned. I couldn't even get the words out.

"Gigi's strong," Angel said, his voice morose.

She was but she was shot twice. I wasn't sure if her or our baby would make it out of this. A fresh set of tears filled my eyes.

Pulling away from Jay, I wiped my face as Meadow and Shade came down the hall. I looked between my parents and Gigi's.

"Gigi and your baby need all the love, support and prayers they can get right now." Jay went up to her husband's side. "We called everyone."

Angel kissed the top of her head.

"Have you heard anything?" Meadow asked, giving me a hug.

"Not yet," I murmured, returning the embrace.

Shade cupped my shoulder, giving it a squeeze. "Whatever you need, we're here."

I nodded; my tongue thick.

More people came down the hall. Practically everyone I had grown up with, joined us.

Luna and Zach were first. She rushed toward me, throwing herself around my middle. "God, Vince," she cried against my chest.

Zach gave a small nod of his head, gently prying his fiancé from me and pulling her into his arms. "My parents wanted to come but both Benjamin and my dad have colds, so Mom's staying home with them. She didn't want to pass on any germs. But they send their love."

A lump formed in my throat.

You feel that, Gigi? Do you feel all of the love surrounding you and our baby?

Ashton and Aiden, along with their parents, Meeka and Asher, came toward us with Piper and her parents following behind. I had never felt this overwhelmed by love and support before. I just prayed that Gigi could feel it.

"Vince."

I looked up as Dale approached me.

"Listen, I never got a chance to apologize," I told him before he could say anything to me.

"No need." He stepped in front of me. "I'm a shithead and shouldn't have said anything anyway, so I apologize for that. But you're right. You are more of a man than I ever was and ever will be, but I'll keep proving to my wife over and over that I am enough." He cupped my shoulder. "You need anything at all, you don't hesitate to call. I'd also like to take you out for a beer sometime." He gave my shoulder a squeeze and joined everyone else in the waiting room.

I watched him walk away just as the doctor came down the hall. My back stiffened.

"Mr. Stone?"

"Yes?" I pushed away from the wall and went up to him. "I'm Vince Stone."

The doctor nodded. "Angelica is out of surgery and is stable."

My knees shook. "Oh thank God."

The doctor smiled. "I agree. It's still touch and go for the next little while but she's resting. You should be able to see her in a bit but first, did you want to meet your daughter?"

"What did you just ask me?" I leaned a hand on the wall for support. "My daughter." I was right. I was fucking right that we were having a girl.

"Yes. She's in the NICU but she's a strong little thing." The doctor spun on his heel. "I'm sure she wants to meet her father."

My heart pounded against the walls of my rib cage. "I just have…let me tell everyone." I went to the waiting room and updated them on Gigi. "I'm going to go meet my daughter."

Mom sniffed, giving me a hug. "You tell your baby girl that we're all here. She has a big family and we can't wait to meet her."

I swallowed hard, pulling free from my mother. "Thank you. For everything." I kissed her cheek and joined the doctor as he led me to my baby.

While we walked to where my daughter was, the doctor was filling me in on how her lungs weren't fully developed and how she needed some help to breathe. I was just thankful she was alive.

We rounded a corner and walked through a double set of doors. He swiped his card along a black box sitting on a wall and pushed open the door for me. "You need to wash your hands and gown up but she's just right in there."

I did as I was told, waiting with bated breath for the chance to meet my daughter. Gigi's and my baby girl.

A nurse guided me into the room with beeping machines and monitors. She stopped in front of a small glass box that had tubes coming out of it and gave me a small smile. "Here she is."

That time, my knees gave out beneath me and I fell.

(Gigi)

Every inch of me hurt. I didn't want to open my eyes for fear that they would hurt too but I felt a sense of loss. Something was missing and I couldn't figure out what it was exactly.

I shifted, a sharp pain shooting through my abdomen.

I tried thinking back to the past twenty-four hours, but I couldn't remember much.

The scent of pasta hit my nose.

I was cooking for Vince. Yes, I remembered that now. I had been making supper for us while I waited for him to come home and greet me with his passion and kisses like he always had. But something was different this time. He didn't come home. Not at first. No. Someone else came home instead.

Tenise.

Mason.

Secrets and betrayal were revealed.

Pain. So much damn pain.

My eyes shot open.

White lights blinded me.

I blinked a few times, the room finally becoming clearer. I was in what looked like a hospital room.

"Vince," I mumbled, my throat dry.

"Gigi."

I turned my head, my gaze landing on Vince's handsome face.

"Baby." He closed the distance between us, wrapping himself around me as best he could without hurting me. "I thought I lost you."

"Never," I said, my throat hoarse.

He kissed me softly on my mouth, my nose, my forehead, and my mouth again. "I love you."

"I love *you*." I wanted to touch him, but my arm was heavy. "What happened?"

"You were shot twice." He ran the back of his knuckles along my cheek. "The police are here and will want to ask you questions when they find out you're awake."

"It was Tenise and…and M-Mason," I told him.

Vince lifted his head, staring down at me. "What?"

"Tenise." I cleared my throat. "Mason. They shot me."

THIRTY-ONE

Gigi

WHILE VINCE AND I filled each other in on everything, I watched his face morph from shock, to sadness, to outright rage.

"I can't believe Mason was in on this," Vince murmured, staring down at our joined hands.

"I know. I'm so sorry. I was shocked to see him and then with everything Tenise told me." I shook my head. "I didn't know."

Vince's shoulders slumped. "I had no idea that she's technically my cousin. My mom has even met her and never said anything. She obviously never made herself known." He went to pull away, no doubt wanting to drive through town to confront Mason, but he couldn't. I wouldn't let him. Not yet. I needed him there with me and our baby.

I told the police the conversation I had with both Tenise and Mason. I found out that I had been shot twice. Once in the stomach by Tenise and once in the upper thigh by Mason because he had been spooked by a noise.

I needed surgery after the bullet hit some vital organs. I was also made aware that I had an emergency C-section and gave birth to a baby girl. No wonder I felt…empty. I still couldn't believe that Vince had been right when it came to the sex of our baby. I had only said that she was a girl because that's what he believed. But I never expected him to actually be right about it.

We couldn't go back to our apartment just in case Tenise and Mason showed up. But now that the police had their names, they would search for them.

I met Detective Baldwin and gave her all of the information I could. I had a feeling from the beginning that there was something more to Tenise than her just being friends with Vince, but I could never figure out what it was. She made me uneasy and now I understood why. A part of me felt sorry for her. I just hoped the police could find her before she hurt herself, or someone else, and she got the help she needed.

Then there was Mason. I never knew and neither did Vince. He was as shocked as I was, but I felt even worse for him. He lost a best friend. Both him and Rory did. Someone they had considered a brother.

"What are you thinking about?" Vince asked, helping me into a wheelchair.

"Tenise and her desperation and…and…Mason and Rory." I sighed, my stomach twisting. "I'm sorry. I'm sorry for both of you."

"Why are you sorry?" Vince knelt in front of me and took my hands in his. "I should be apologizing to you. I brought them both into your life."

"That's not your fault at all but I know you were friends with them. Even if it was just because Tenise was Rory's girlfriend." I linked our fingers, taking all the strength I could from him. "That doesn't matter. But I'm really sorry about Mason."

"I'm sorry too," Vince's voice came out rough. Something dark flashed in his eyes and I knew that if I let him, if I only said the word, he would go hunt him down. He probably would once he was satisfied that I was safe. Couldn't say I blamed him any. Whatever happened, I would be there to help him pick up the pieces.

"Yeah but I only knew her because of him. So I wouldn't have been friends with her if she wasn't his girlfriend. And Mason..." Vince's voice trailed off.

"It's not your fault either," I reminded him.

Vince kissed my knuckles. "The police probably contacted Rory already," he said, changing the subject. "I just hope they find both of them."

"Me too." I thought a moment. "You should probably call Rory yourself and fill him in on everything too. I'm sure he'd rather hear it from you."

"I already did. While I was waiting for you to wake up, I called Rory. I even called Mason but of course there was no answer. I was going to play dumb. But I'll call Rory again and tell him about…" A shaky breath left him. "Everything. I hope I never run into her again because…" A dark shadow passed over his face.

"Hey." I cupped his cheek. I was going to tell him that everything was alright, but I got it. I understood exactly what he was going through. He wanted revenge.

"I need to talk to my parents but first, let's introduce you to our daughter." He wheeled me to the NICU so I could meet our baby girl. He parked the chair in front of the small glass box and pulled up a chair beside me. "I haven't named her yet."

I stuck my hand in the hole in the box, so I could touch her. "That's fine," I whispered. "She's so perfect." My eyes welled.

Vince grabbed my free hand, bringing it up to his mouth. "Both of my girls are."

I smiled at him before looking back at our baby. She was so tiny, but she was strong. "What about Hannah?"

"I love it."

My heart warmed. "Yeah?"

Vince leaned his forehead against the side of my head. "Yes. It's absolutely perfect for her."

"Hi, Hannah," I whispered, tears rolling down my cheeks. "I'm your mommy and this is your daddy. We love you so much and we can't wait to bring you home."

"I know we set up a room for her in the apartment but with everything that's happened, I'm not sure I want to go back there. Ever." Vince cupped my shoulder, brushing his thumb back and forth along the base of my neck.

"Where would we go?" I asked, staring at the little life we created.

"I have a surprise for you. I was going to wait but I guess I can reveal it early."

I frowned. "What surprise?"

He smirked, winking. "I'll bring you there when you're stronger."

"I'm strong now," I reassured him.

He chuckled. "Patience, baby." He kissed my temple. "It's not going anywhere."

I cupped his jaw, staring at him. "Thank you."

"For what?" he asked, kissing my palm.

"For not giving up on me when I pushed you away. For just being patient and for giving me her." I nodded toward Hannah. "And for loving me."

"You have no idea how much I love you, Queenie."

I looked back at him, seeing the worry etched in the lines on his face. "Hey, what happened is not your fault."

His jaw clenched. "It still shouldn't have happened."

"No, it shouldn't have but Tenise is sick and Mason is in love with her. Love makes you do stupid stuff sometimes. She needs help. They both need help."

"Do not make excuses for them," he ground out through clenched teeth. A buzzing suddenly sounded, pulling us from our conversation.

Vince reached into his pocket. "It's Detective Baldwin." He kissed my head and left the room, only to come back a minute later. "She's here and wants to talk to us."

"Okay." I ran a finger down the bridge of Hannah's nose. "We'll be back, baby girl." I didn't want to leave her, but I also knew that if the detective needed to talk to us, it must have been important.

"I'm happy to see that you're doing well," Detective Baldwin said, smiling down at me as Vince wheeled me closer.

"Me too," I said as my dad came down the hall toward us. "Daddy, what are you doing here?"

"I came to see how you're doing, and I actually wanted to talk to Vince for a moment. Your mom was going to join me, but she caught a cold from Brogan and Benjamin. She wanted me to tell you that she loves you and she'll see you soon." Dad turned to Detective Baldwin. "I didn't mean to interrupt. I'm Angel, Gigi's father."

"Detective Jessica Baldwin," she replied, returning the handshake.

"Do you have any news?" I grabbed Vince's hand, keeping his fingers in mine for fear that I would freak out with whatever she had to tell us.

"I do." Detective Baldwin paused. "We found Tenise."

My eyes widened. "Really? Already?"

"How?" Vince asked.

"Where is she now?" I asked, hope dancing in me that we would never have to see her again but wondering where Mason was at the same time.

"Right now, she's been arrested but she'll probably plead insanity. Tenise is a very sick woman but her working with Mason, made her think that she's invincible. She was telling us how it was all his idea. This isn't the first time she's done something like this either. Her ultimate goal has always been Vince, but her other victims were practice runs," Detective Baldwin explained. "She did this with her previous boyfriend before Rory. We've been looking for her for a while, but she moved across States. She's been hard to track down until now. We're still looking for Mason, but I promise you, we will find him."

Vince pushed a hand through his hair. "Have you told Rory this?"

"I've talked to him." Detective Baldwin gave us a small smile. "He's going to need his friends right now. Tenise also won't bother you again. I'm just glad you survived her wrath because the previous girlfriend didn't."

My stomach twisted at the thought.

"Thank you, Detective." Vince squeezed my hand.

"Of course." She handed us a business card. "If you need anything ever, please don't hesitate to call. If you want to speak to a professional, I can refer you to someone."

"A psychiatrist?" I asked softly.

Detective Baldwin winked. "Something like that."

THIRTY-TWO

VINCE

"I NEED TO TALK to your father," I told Gigi, kneeling in front of her.

She grabbed my hands with one of hers, and cupped my face with the other. "I love you. I hope you know that what happened is not your fault. I'm fine and so is Hannah."

I rose to my feet and towered over her, placing a soft peck on her forehead. She could tell me she was fine all she wanted but it didn't mean that I wasn't going to have a little chat with Mason myself.

I wheeled Gigi back into the room to see our daughter. Even though she couldn't hold her at the moment, Hannah needed to feel the love surrounding her. She was already a little fighter, but I knew that having her mother in the same room as her, would help.

"Where are you going?" Gigi asked when I placed a peck on her head.

"I'm just going to talk to your dad. I'll be out in the hall." There was no way that I was going to leave the hospital anytime soon to search Mason out. As much as I needed to confront him, that could wait. I had to stay with Gigi and Hannah. Until they both became stronger and I could bring them home, the shit I had to say to Mason could wait.

"Vince?"

I stopped at the door, turning back to the woman who was my one and only. She was everything I ever needed. Over the years, I saw what my parents had, and I strived for the same. I knew I would have it with Gigi because I could never consider anything less and that was what anyone else would be. Less because she was everything.

As if she knew what I was thinking, a blush hit Gigi's cheeks.

"I love you, Queenie."

Her eyes shone. "I love you, Vince."

When I left the room, I was met with Angel walking down the hall toward me.

"She know anything?" he asked, nodding toward the room that Gigi was in.

"Nope. Not yet anyway." I pulled off the gown and mask and threw them in the trash before following Angel down the hall to a more enclosed area.

"You sure you want to do this?" he asked, pulling his cell phone out of his back pocket. "You know that this can mess you up right?"

I crossed my arms under my chest, leaning against the wall. A smirk splayed on my face. "It won't but thank you for your concern."

Angel raised an eyebrow. "Now's not the time to be cocky, Vince."

"Oh, I'm not cocky." I scratched my jaw. "I'm confident. Mason messed with what's mine. Since I can't confront Tenise about it…" I let my voice trail off, knowing Angel would get the hint. Bottom line, Mason was going to get my full wrath. Tenise was a woman. A very sick woman. But I couldn't touch her. Society frowned on that sort of thing. Mason, on the other hand, was a different story.

"Fine." Angel handed me his phone. "I called in a favor. Mason was found lurking around the center. I've been told that he looked out of it. Maybe drunk. That was last night. I don't know where he is now."

"I'll find him." And I would. I had known Mason since I was a kid, I knew all of his favorite hangout spots.

"Does your other friend know about this?"

I handed Angel back his phone, thinking a moment before I outright told him the conversation I had with Rory. "He knows enough," I finally said.

"Let me go with you," Rory said, cracking his knuckles for added effect.

"No." I turned and headed to the door. "I already told you too much. The less you know, the better."

"Vince, he was my best friend too."

I spun on him. "Yeah, and he tried to kill my girlfriend and unborn baby." Rory didn't deserve my wrath but unfortunately for him, he was in the direct path of my rage.

"I can help you," Rory offered, running a shaky hand through his hair.

"No." He was upset and unstable. I wouldn't put him through that. He lost a girlfriend and a best friend. This was now all on me.

"Vince." Angel came toward me and cupped my shoulders. "You call me if you need anything. You hear me?"

"I will." I nodded. "Thank you."

Since I refused to take Gigi back to our apartment after everything went down, I brought her to her parents' place once she was discharged from the hospital. Both Angel and Jay promised to take her to see Hannah whenever Gigi requested it, but we all knew that it wouldn't do Hannah any good if Gigi didn't get any rest. So, much to her dismay, of course, her parents brought her home and I tucked her safely in her bed.

She had fallen asleep as soon as her head hit the pillow. With my kiss on her lips and my whispered *I love you* in her ears, I left her bedroom.

Angel had promised to make sure to distract his wife, so I wouldn't be questioned as to why I was suddenly leaving. But knowing that both Gigi and Hannah were safe, I needed to get this done and over with so we could all move on.

Once I was seated in my car, I took a deep breath and then another. I lifted my hands, checking to see if they were shaking and when they weren't, a wicked grin spread on my face. I remembered back to a time where I overheard my parents talking. They were reminiscing about the past. My uncle Kenny had been mentioned and I heard something about dogs. I was maybe sixteen at the time, I couldn't recall, but what I *did* remember and promised to take to my grave were a few key words.

Hitman.

Lethal.

Powerful.

Blood money.

I never brought it up to my parents until a few days ago when I revealed everything that had happened and how Mason and Tenise were working together. But what bothered my parents most was who Tenise actually was.

"I had no idea that my brother had a kid." Mom shook her head while Dad paced behind her.

"Tenise did all of this because we…" Dad muttered a curse.

"She's sick," was all I said.

"What about Mason?" Mom asked.

"I'll take care of it." I stood at the same time Dad stopped. Our eyes locked. He knew because he would do the same thing.

Instead of saying anything like most parents would, all he did was nod once.

It was the only indication I needed that I was doing the right thing. The only thing. Not that I was waiting for his permission but the fact I got it, was all that mattered.

Driving across town, I approached the outskirts and pressed my foot harder on the gas. When I left the city limits, my eyes flicked to the mirror, the *See you soon* sign becoming smaller and smaller off in the distance.

Half an hour later, I was pulling down a long gravel road. I stopped the car, killed the engine and left the vehicle. My bones vibrated beneath my skin, my hands clenching into fists, knowing what was to come.

I walked for another thirty minutes before I got to the spot I hadn't been at since we were kids. Mason and Rory brought girls there to have sex with, while I only went for the scenery. I hadn't been to the ravine in so long, I had forgotten about it.

When Mason had problems with his parents because he was your typical shithead teen, he would disappear and come to this place whenever he needed to get away.

Making my way to a clearing, my gaze landed on Mason. He was standing in the middle of a bridge that overlooked a lake and a small waterfall. The water was shallow, so if anyone fell over the bridge, they would break something before actually drowning.

"I've been waiting for you," was all he said as I approached him.

When I was a foot away, I placed my hands on the railing. "Why?"

His breath caught, knowing I wasn't asking about how he waited for me. "I was in love with her. I am, in love with her. You have to understand—"

My head whipped around, locking eyes with one of my best and oldest friends. "I don't have to understand shit."

He looked away, his jaw clenching.

"Tell me one thing." I waited for him to look at me and when he didn't, my hands tightened on the railing. "Did you shoot her?" I knew he did but I wanted to hear him say it. I wanted to hear him admit how he had a hand in almost killing my future wife and my daughter.

Mason's eyes flicked to mine. "Tenise shot her in the stomach."

"I know." I still couldn't get the image of Gigi's blood on my hands out of my mind. "But Gigi was shot twice. Did you shoot her in the thigh?"

He looked away that time. "I heard a noise and missed. I thought it was you. It wasn't but we left anyway."

My heart jumped. "You had the kill shot."

"Yes."

That single word weighed heavily on my soul because I knew that this was it. Our friendship was officially over. Although it had been after I found out that he was involved with Tenise, that single word meant a finality that neither of us were prepared for.

"What are you going to do?" His voice shook a bit like he knew. He messed with something that belonged to me.

"Nothing." I crossed my arms under my chest, looking out at the vast scenery before us.

"What do you mean?" His words took on a tremor that I felt down to the marrow of my bones.

I wanted him to be scared. I wanted him to shake and tremble in fear as he wondered what I was going to do to him. I wanted him to pay for the shit he had done and the pain he caused. The fear he put in me all for the name of love. Love. Fucking please. He didn't love

Tenise. He said he did. But he didn't. If he did in fact love her, he would have gotten her the help she needed long ago. Not play into her little games and destroy innocent lives.

I turned my body toward Mason, meeting him square in the eye. "I want you to suffer and think about what you've done. Taking you out would be too easy." I took a step closer. "Although, I *could* take you out. I have learned from the best after all."

His eyes widened a bit, something flashing behind his green eyes.

Tilting my head, I sucked in a deep breath, channeling the strength I knew I needed to get these next few words out. "I loved you like a brother. You were my family, but you broke a pact," my voice cracked at that single word.

"I fell in love," was all he said.

I bit back a scoff, my jaw clenching. Taking that final step between us, I cupped his nape and leaned my forehead against his. "I loved you. I still love you, but both of you almost killed my girlfriend and unborn child. For that, I'll never be able to forgive you." My hand squeezed his neck. "But you're going to do something for me."

"What's that?" he murmured.

"You're going to jump."

He stiffened, trying to pull away from me but my grip only tightened. "What the hell, Vince? You want me to kill myself?"

I leaned back, looking over the edge of the bridge we were standing on. "You won't kill yourself. Not if you land the right way."

"And what way is that?" Mason pulled out of my clutches only because I let him.

"I'll guess you'll figure that out when you land." I turned to walk away. "I suggest doing it quickly because trust me, you don't want me to be the one who pushes you."

"Vince."

I stopped.

"I *am* sorry."

My stomach twisted at his pathetic apology. "Jump, Mason. It's the only way you'll get out of me killing you."

When I was a few feet away from the bridge, I heard a yell. Pulling my phone out of my back pocket, I dialed a number and brought it up to my ear. "Yeah, I'd like to report an accident." I gave the 911 operator all of the details and hung up before they could ask me for my name. Taking a step toward the bridge, my eyes scanned the ground beneath it.

Mason was lying there, clutching his knee.

Even from where I was standing, I could see that it had bent the wrong way when he landed. Blood seeped from a spot at his head. A bone protruded from his jeans just under his knee. His cheeks were coated in tears. It wasn't enough. It would never be enough, but it would have to do.

"Help me," I heard him say.

My stomach tightened. A part of me wanted to go to him. To help him. To get him to safety but I couldn't. He needed to know and understand.

Others would have used brute force but not me. Not when I had a family of my own that I had to get home to. I couldn't jeopardize that happiness just for revenge.

Mason should have gone somewhere else. Somewhere that had enough water beneath the bridge, that when he jumped, the only thing he would have to worry about was drowning. Instead, he had to worry about bleeding out. He was lucky that making him jump was the only thing I did to him, but I had Gigi and Hannah to get home to. I refused to go to them with that darkness tainting my soul.

He just better pray that I never saw him again because making him jump off a bridge would be the last thing he would have to worry about.

EPILOGUE

Gigi

IT HAD BEEN A few weeks since I was shot. I was healing nicely, and we were finally bringing Hannah home from the hospital.

Ever since he had found out what Mason and Tenise had done, there was an edge to Vince. Something happened but he never told me what. I didn't press and knew that if he needed me, I would be there. Until then, I left it alone.

Vince pulled us up in front of a house sitting on a large property. It was surrounded by trees. The house was just outside the city. It was close enough that it wouldn't take long to get back into town but far enough that the road wasn't overrun with traffic.

"Whose house is this?" I asked, looking back at Vince.

He winked, killing the engine and leaving the car.

I opened the passenger door as he came around to my side of the vehicle and held out his hand. I slipped my fingers between his, letting him help me out of the car. "Vince."

"So impatient." He chuckled, placing a soft peck on my forehead before going to the back of the car and pulling the car seat out of it. Hannah was sound asleep. She looked so peaceful. Not like she had almost lost her life. "Come." Vince kicked the door closed and came up to me, wrapping his arm around my shoulders and leading me up the sidewalk to the front porch.

"I'm not impatient you know. I just have no idea what we're doing here."

"I'll tell you in a moment." He went up the steps and unlocked the front door. "Ready?" He pushed it open and stepped to the side. "After you, Gigi."

I had no idea what was going on but went into the house anyway. My eyes widened at what laid before me. To the right was a large living room. To the left, a set of stairs went up to a second floor. Straight ahead of me, was a hall that I could only assume led into the kitchen. "Vince, who lives here?"

"We do, baby."

I spun around. "What?"

Vince placed the car seat on the floor, lowering to one knee. He pulled a small box out of his pocket and opened it, revealing a diamond ring.

I gasped, covering my mouth. "Vince."

"From the first moment I remember meeting you, I've been in love with you. I made it my mission to crack down your walls and show you that even though you no longer had the career you wanted in dancing, that you could still be happy."

I lowered to my knees, covering his hands with mine.

He leaned forward, pressing his forehead to mine. "I want to spend the rest of my life with you, Gigi. Will you marry me?"

"Yes." I threw my arms around his neck and crushed my mouth to his, knocking him back onto his ass.

He chuckled, hooking an arm around my middle. "You've made me the happiest man in existence." He slipped the ring onto my finger. It had a gold band with a single solitaire diamond. It was perfect. "You hear that, baby girl?" he asked Hannah. "Your mama is going to finally make an honest man out of me."

I laughed, kissing him fully on the mouth. "I love you." I kissed him again. "I love you so damn much," I said between pecks.

"And I love you." His hands cupped my ass, pulling me flush against him. "Let me give my girls a tour and then later…" His thumb brushed along my bottom lip.

A sly grin spread on my face. "You want to christen the house?" I asked, waggling my eyebrows.

"I want to give you a special tour. Later."

"I like that idea." I sealed it with a kiss, a silent promise that I refused to break.

Later that evening, we were lying in bed. Holding, touching, just being together in a way that we almost lost.

Because of Tenise and Mason, everything could have turned out much worse. Vince never told me what happened with Mason, but I knew he had confronted him. How could he not? All he told me was that Mason ended up in jail with a few bumps and bruises and maybe a broken bone or two.

I shivered at the thought of Vince losing his temper like that.

It had been a few hours since Vince proposed. He promised over and over again how he would take care of me. Take care of us. He truly showed me that he was determined to break down my walls.

An impromptu one-night stand so many years ago started our obsession.

And now we were together.

As a couple.

As a family.

Finally, after all of this time, we were one.

BONUS SCENE #1

VINCE

I SLIPPED MY FINGERS between Gigi's, glancing at our wedding rings. All this time after so many years of doing what I could to make her mine, she was finally, in fact, officially mine. In every sense of the word.

I ran my free hand along the scar on her lower abdomen, grazing it lower until my thumb brushed over the scar in her upper thigh. It had been over a year since she was shot by both Tenise and Mason. She still had nightmares, but they were getting few and far between as the days went by.

"Vince," Gigi breathed, throwing her head back and rolling her hips against mine.

I was deep inside her body and as much as I wanted to control the movements, I was enjoying watching her take her pleasure from me. Her husband.

After everything that had happened, I never thought we would get to this point. We didn't talk about how she almost died. And because of that, I never took her, or her feelings for me, for granted.

"Vince." Gigi kissed me softly. "Stop thinking, baby. It's just us. We're fine. I'm fine. I promise you."

She knew me too damn well.

I cupped her nape, deepened the kiss, and took over.

"Tell me a bedtime story," Gigi murmured later that night.

My body stirred as she pushed her ass into me.

"Once upon a time, a boy loved a girl with everything he was made of. He finally got her to fall in love with him just the same and they started a new life together. After some minor setbacks, everything was perfect in their little world." I kissed the side of her neck. "They had a baby girl who was the most perfect little baby." I cupped Gigi's chin, turning her head to face me. "And their love, it went deep. Deeper than anything either of them had ever felt before. The boy couldn't wait to create more lives between them and spend the rest of his life with the girl. His love. His person."

"The end," Gigi whispered, her eyes welling.

"No, Queenie." I kissed her nose. "This is only the beginning."

(Gigi)

We had only been married for a few months before I found out I was pregnant with our second child.

I stared down at the test in my hand, hoping, no, praying that Vince wouldn't be upset that we were having another baby and so soon. Especially when Hannah was still so young.

A warm body came up behind me. "Is that what I think it is?" Vince asked, slipping his arms around my middle.

"It is." I turned in his arms. "Are you upset?"

He lowered his mouth to mine, taking my very breath away. "Never," he murmured, giving my lip a gentle bite.

I shivered. "God." I pushed him back, shaking myself.

Vince chuckled. "You thought I'd be mad?"

"Well…Hannah is still a baby herself." I shrugged, realizing how silly I sounded.

Vince smiled. "I love you, Gigi. I love Hannah and I'll love this baby you're currently carrying in your tight little body." He brushed the back of his hand over my lower stomach.

I threw my arms around his neck. "Thank you."

He smirked, crushing his lips to mine. "No, thank *you*, Queenie. Thank you for giving your heart to me and thank you for being mine."

After all this time. Through the heartbreak, pain, and fear, we were happy.

Finally.

BONUS SCENE #2

Gigi

"I CAN'T BELIEVE WE'RE here."

Vince looked down at me, keeping his hand firmly in mine. "We can go somewhere else. Or just go home."

"No." I smiled up at him. "I just…I've told you my fantasy, but I never thought we'd actually be doing it."

"Why not?" He stopped me before we could enter the large building. "We've been married for over a year. Gotta keep things fresh, Queenie."

"Things are always fresh," I reminded him. "But it's just a fantasy. I don't think they come true for a lot of people."

Vince pinched my chin, tilted my head back, and placed a soft peck on my lips. "You're my wife. That means your fantasies are mine to fulfill."

"Just like yours are mine to fulfill?" I asked, breathless.

He smirked against my mouth. "You fulfilled my fantasy the moment we fucked for the first time."

I laughed, punching him lightly in the stomach and pushing out of his hold. I took a few steps away from him, staring up at the building that, if you hadn't done your research ahead of time, you would never know was an actual BDSM club.

Bondage. Domination. Sadism. Masochism.

God, even those words sounded delicious. The acronym stood for several different things, but the domination and submission were my favorite parts of it.

Vince's fingers lightly brushed over my bare shoulder, his other hand held mine tightly. "We don't have to do anything tonight that you don't want to do."

"I know." I looked around the room. Nothing was out of the ordinary. It looked like a bar with people sitting at tables, talking and having drinks and food.

"There are more private areas here, so we don't have to do anything in public. No one has to watch even though I know you want people to."

My cheeks burned, that familiar ache between my thighs, becoming more pronounced. "Is that wrong?"

"You're with me, Queenie." Vince squeezed my hand. "No one else is going to be touching you. Just me. Your husband."

We had talked early on about our fantasies. I was down for anything really as long as no one else was involved. Just the thought of another woman touching Vince, made me want to commit murder.

Vince smirked, as if he could hear my thoughts.

I turned around, looked back out into the main area of the bar, and just watched.

Vince leaned closer, his hot breath tickling my ear. "You look beautiful tonight."

"Thank you." I cupped his knee. "You look handsome." It was one thing I loved about him. He gave me compliments often. Not that I needed them but even after being with him for a while, it was nice to know that my husband still found me attractive. Especially since I gained weight from having our children.

"Gigi." He placed his hand on my knee and slid it up my leg to my thigh, pushing it beneath my dress.

My breath caught.

"We can't do anything out here. We have to go to another room." His hand stopped mid-thigh, his thumb brushing back and forth. "But it's been awhile."

Meaning, it had been a while since we actually played.

I turned toward him, lifting my knee onto the bench beneath us. Even though there were rules and we couldn't do anything sexually in this room, I could still tease him a bit.

His dark eyes fell to my lap. His nostrils flaring.

I grinned.

Vince pinched my chin. "You teasing me, little girl?"

"Yes," I whispered.

A wicked grin spread on his face. "Good."

People were discreet in their exploits. Most couples fell into the shadows of the large room. I almost expected to walk in on some big orgy when we left the main bar but when we didn't, I was thankful.

Vince held my hand firmly in his and brought me to a vacant corner of the big room. We sat on a plush red couch. A long table sat in front of us with two water bottles, and a board with fruit, buns, crackers, and various types of cheese.

My stomach clenched at the sight, but I was too nervous to eat anything. The music pumping through the speakers was low and deep. While there were no words and it was strictly instrumental, it was like I could feel what the artist was trying to tell us.

"You're nervous." Vince brushed his finger down the length of my bare arm.

I nodded. There was no point denying it when he knew me so well.

"Don't be." He cupped my knee, pushing his hand higher until it slid beneath my dress. "It's just you and me here, baby."

When his fingers reached the spot between my thighs, I spread my legs even more for him.

"That's my girl." His hot breath fanned the side of my face. "We don't even have to fuck, Gigi. We can always come back and keep doing whatever you want until you're ready for more."

I looked out at the vast room before us. Everyone was doing their own thing. People were none the wiser when it came to what Vince and I were doing in the dark corner.

"We can take it slow," Vince reassured me.

"Are you okay with that?" I asked him, leaning back against the couch.

"Of course. Turn toward me."

I did as I was told, facing him and lifting my knee onto the seat of the couch.

His finger slipped beneath the crotch of my panties. "Next time, I don't want you wearing these."

I nodded, chewing my bottom lip.

Vince leaned down to my ear. "I'm going to make you come. Hard. I want you to scream for everyone to hear."

Before I had a chance to respond, he inserted two fingers inside me and began pumping his hand against my center.

I whimpered, my eyes fluttering closed.

"How does it feel, Gigi, knowing that at any time, someone could see you break?" Vince pressed his lips against my ear. "Think they'll be jealous? Think you coming for your husband will get them off?"

"Oh, God." I shook against him, wishing it was his cock deep inside me but appreciating at the same time, that Vince took it slow.

"Nah, baby." He cupped the back of my head, fisting my hair and holding me in place. "Scream out *my* name."

And I did.

*****THE END*****

The Next Generation Series:

#1 – Control Us –
https://www.aboutjmwalker.com/control-us
#2 – With Us –
https://www.aboutjmwalker.com/with-us
#3 – Before Us –
https://www.aboutjmwalker.com/before-us
#4 – Being Us –
https://www.aboutjmwalker.com/being-us
#5 – Finally Us -
https://www.aboutjmwalker.com/finally-us

Add After Us (Next Generation Novel, #6) to your TBR list!

https://www.goodreads.com/book/show/54823668-after-us

ACKNOWLEDGEMENTS

I can't believe that we are halfway into The Next Generation Series already! It feels like just yesterday that I was sending bits of Grit to my Alpha reader, only to scrap it all and start over. Next thing I know, 7 books and another MC series later, and I'm already working on the kids' books!

This series is life. It holds everything we love as romance readers. It has so many tropes, it's unreal! I'd say that I knew about said tropes, but I didn't! That's one thing I love about not being a plotter. The characters lead the story and I'm always left finding out what's going to happen as I write it.

If you've read this far, THANK YOU so much for reading and being part of the TNGS crew! I really can't tell you how much I appreciate each and every one of you.

Angie: I feel like we've both grown. Me as an author and you as my Alpha reader. Your support and help go such a long way with me, I can't even begin to tell you how much I appreciate your assistance with my books. I love your face and miss you so much! #FSForLife

Jennifer and Christina: Jennifer, I know we're still trying to figure out this PA/Author thing but even if you think you aren't helping me much, you really are. Just by you being there, holding my hand, being my sounding board, that's really all the help I truly need. AND thank you for also beta reading for me! Can you believe that your hatred over one of my characters turned this into a wonderful friendship? It's funny how things work out. Christina! I feel like I've known you for forever, but I just want to thank you for beta reading for me. For always being there even if we don't talk every single day. I love you girls so much!

Joanne: Look how far we've come!! Going from beta reading for me to now editing for me, you are a Queen! Thank you so so much for all of your help. I really can't thank you enough. I keep saying this, but I truly mean it. I love your beautiful face!

Authors and bloggers: This was more of a sudden release for me. Even though I had about a month to prepare for it, I didn't book any tours or cover reveals or anything like that. So thank you for sharing, reading and just being there! I appreciate each and every one of you more than I could ever tell you.

J.M.'s Jems: Gosh, where do I even begin??? You put up with my incessant teasing. My random posts. My "I'm not feeling it today" posts and more. "Thank you" doesn't seem big enough. "I appreciate" you doesn't seem big enough either. I wish I could pay you back for all the things you have done for me. Whether it be sending me little gifts in the mail, shooting me a message just to say hi or posting funny memes in my group. Nothing I do will be enough. You are my life. You are the reason I write. You are the reason I'm here, breaking your hearts and putting them back together again one word at a time. I love you all. So so much.

Thank you everyone for reading my words when there are SO many books out there to choose from. The fact that you want to spend a few hours with my characters…I really have no words.

I love you all!

JM
XX

ABOUT

J.M. Walker is an Amazon bestselling author who also hit USA Today with Wanted: An Outlaw Anthology. She loves all things books, pigs and lip gloss. She is happily married to the man who inspires all of her Heroes and continues to make her weak in the knees every single day.

"Above all, be the HEROINE of your own life..." ~ Nora Ephron

Find me!

https://linktr.ee/authorjmwalker

www.ingramcontent.com/pod-product-compliance
Lightning Source LLC
Chambersburg PA
CBHW070624260626
47161CB00007B/2573
9781989782163